Two best friends, trying to e:
follow two very differer

the wedding drums

Marilyn Rodwell

Published by Goldcrest Books International Ltd
www.goldcrestbooks.com
publish@goldcrestbooks.com

ISBN: 978-1-911505-53-2
eISBN: 978-1-911505-54-9

Dedicated to my direct descendants – my children and grandchildren.

Charmaine, James, Rebecca, Beatrix, Elowen, Jameson, Viola. Never forget where you came from. It is part of who you are. Always make peace with your past, so you understand how to move forward towards the future.

To my mother, Clara Johnatty, whose direct ancestors gave me the inspiration to write the novel.

I hope you all find something of value between the pages.

MAP OF TRINIDAD

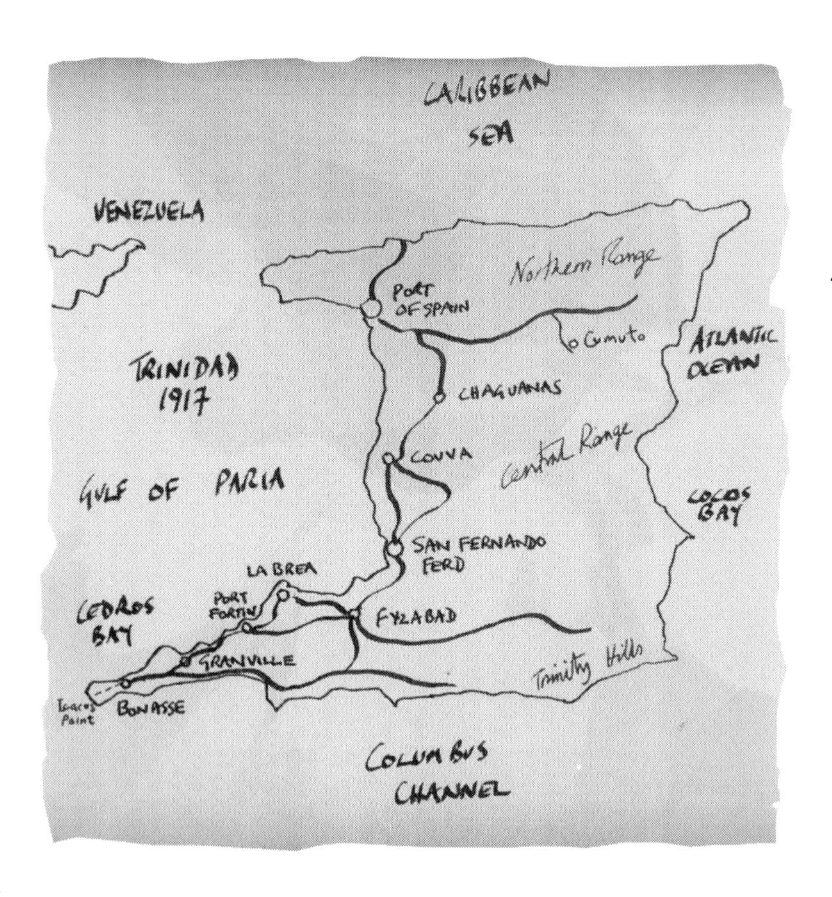

MAP OF GRANVILLE

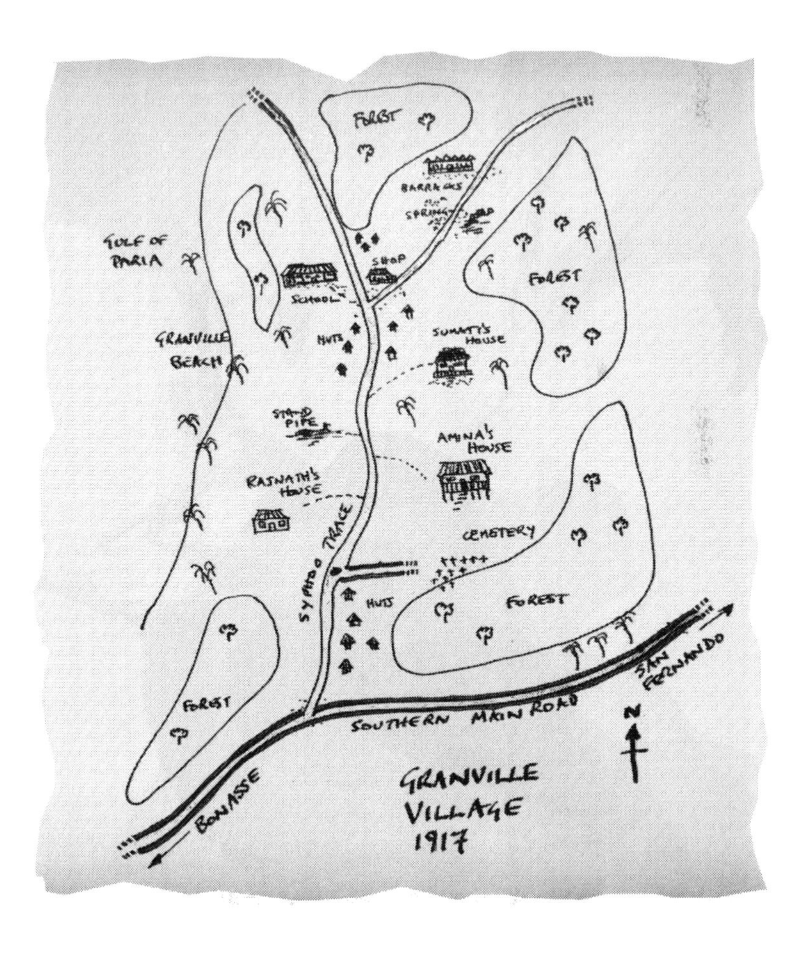

GLOSSARY

Baba – father, term of respect
beti – girl child, daughter, term of endearment.
Bhagavad gita – 700 verse Hindu scripture in Sanscrit
bhajans – spiritual Indian songs
bhajee/bhaji– a kind of spinach
Bhojpuri – a Hindi dialect
biagan – aubergine, melongine, egg plant
bindi/bindiya – small red dot that married women wear on their forehead
carailie/karailie – bitter fruit used as a vegetable
champals – sandals
chokha – cooked or raw seasoned vegetable dish (see page 415 for recipe)
choli – tight bodice to be worn under a sari
Coolie – derogaratory word for people of Indian descent
Country bookie – a derogatory word for someone living in the countryside
cujart – the state of being an outcast from the community
dahee/dahi – curds, homemade yoghurt
datwan – rough toothbrush made from a twig from the hibiscus bush or the soap vine
dhal – made with yellow split peas
dhal puri – a roti filled with seasoned dhal, for special occasions
dharma - duty
diablesse/la diablesse (pronounced, jabless - French Caribbean folklore) – an evil spirit, dressed as a beautiful

woman, who comes out at night to allure unsuspecting men. But she has one foot hidden under her dress, which is a cow hoof.
doolaha – bridegroom
doolahin – bride
haldi/hardi – bridal body art; turmeric
jagabat – whore, promiscuous female
jumbie – evil roaming souls of the dead
kala pani – black water
lotah – brass cup
loyah – balls of flour for making roti
mandap – the tent where a bride and groom sit where the Hindu marriage takes place
mehendi – bridal body art
Obeah – practicing a form of black magic
ohrini – female head covering, veil
panch – village elders
peerha – a wooden bench or stool
Ramayana – the story of Lord Rama rescuing his wife Sita from the demon king Ravana
Sadhu – holy man
sappat – rough footwear made with a thick wooden sole with inverted bicycle tyre rubber
soucouyant – folklore woman who flies at night and sucks blood – mainly of drunken men
saphee – dishcloth/tea towel
saptapadi – the 7 steps of the wedding ceremony before legally becoming husband and wife
sirbandhi – a piece of bridal hair jewellery
Tackoori – Land owning caste
Tackorine – belonging to the Tackoori caste
talkarie – a dish of well seasoned fried vegetables, to accompany rice or roti (see page 317 for recipe)
tawa – a flat iron used for making roti and other flatbreads
tullom – round ball sweet made from grated coconut and molasses

ONE

Trinidad, West Indies. 1917

Amina was so excited, she could barely wait till lunchtime to tell the headmaster that she would be returning to school in September. But by lunchtime, she had developed a terrible headache and went home, intending to return later. Her headache had become so bad that she didn't return to school that day or the next. By the third day, she was suffering such terrible stomach pains and became so ill, that her eyes sank into dark circles and her skin looked the colour of an unripe banana.

News spread in the village that week that children were dying, and because Amina's parents could afford it, they paid for a doctor to visit the house, fearing for her life. Dr Boyle attended and suspected it was typhoid, the same disease that had killed the other children. He gave her parents strict instructions to be followed: no solid food, just rice water, and watered down boiled milk. Amina's mother, Devinia, obeyed the doctor's orders, but also worried about evil spirits and bad karma, so she called

Pundit Lall to perform Hindu prayers. Then something seemed to work. A few days later, the day of her twelfth birthday, Amina begged for something to eat.

'I feel better, Ma. Really I do. I'm so hungry.'

Devinia was alarmed at this request and worried that it was too soon. 'Don't you want the necklace your father promised to make for you instead?' she asked.

'No, just food,' Amina whispered hoarsely, with a pleading look in her eyes. Her mother felt pity, and thought a little mouthful of food could do no harm – not if it was kept a secret.

Devinia eventually gave in. 'I will bring you your favourites,' she whispered, as she often did, so that the gods wouldn't hear. Amina half-smiled, and Devinia smiled back, pleased to see her daughter happy. 'I told your father the prayers were worth it,' she said almost in triumph, as she left to prepare the food.

ᘓ

It was difficult for Amina to be patient after two weeks of starvation, but she waited quietly on her bed, feeling hopeful about her ambition to become a teacher. She reminisced on their conversations. Her father hadn't wholeheartedly approved, but he hadn't disapproved either. He had made noises about it being a far-fetched idea for Indians to believe they could be anything important in the white people's world. Most of her friends' parents had already arranged marriages for them, or sent them out to work in the sugar plantations. But Amina's mother was in favour of her daughter's ambition, because she herself would have liked to have had such a wonderful opportunity.

Amina picked up the blue book Mr Clifford had sent her, and opened it. It was her favourite, *Silas Marner*, and the familiarity seemed to calm her weakened nerves. She began to feel hopeful about her dream of studying and becoming a teacher, and dozed off until the aromas from the kitchen outside drifted up through her bedroom window. She woke to the smell of the starchy-sweet cassava frying in hot coconut oil which made her mouth water. Ravenous with hunger, she felt that every scrape of the metal spoon against the iron pot sounded soothing.

When the food finally arrived, Amina bit into it like a starving dog. But when she tried to swallow, an excruciating pain clamped her chest, her eyes rolled in her head and her whole body convulsed – and it all happened right in front of her mother, who observed frozen in horror.

Time stood still as Amina's body finally jerked and went limp and still. Screams reverberated through the wooden house, high off the ground on stilts, and flew out through its Victorian, lacy latticework, and up the sandy path, travelling on the hot, heavy air through the village of Granville. Gossip passed quickly from mouth to mouth down the gravel road and soft, grassy tracks, from thatched roofs and mud walls, up steps of wooden dwellings, through wide windows and open doorways, and over smooth-sanded floors . . . until the whole village believed that Amina Banderjee was yet another child to die from typhoid that same month. Heavy clouds opened in tropical rage, and the rain pounded like showers of gravel on the corrugated iron roof. Then it stopped as abruptly as it started.

Screams from the house brought villagers running. But Amina had already begun a swift crossing towards a meteoric blizzard, and was being catapulted towards the sky and beyond.

'Amina!' her mother called. 'Come back, come back!'

But Amina was disappearing into the darkness, dizzy and light as a feather, distancing herself from illness and starvation.

People gathered, huddled around her bed, all crying out, 'Don't cross the water! Come back! Don't cross the river!'

English words jumbled with Hindi screams resonated in her head, but Amina was in her own floating world, and she was heading towards a bright light, in a state of bliss.

'Keep calling!' someone yelled. 'Let her hear your voice.'

Devinia swallowed the lump in her throat, and leaned over the bed. 'Come back, *beti*,' she wept. 'Come home to us! You can have anything you want. I promise. Take how much education you want. Please, *beti*, please – just come back!' But Amina didn't move. Devinia shook the girl's body harder, but there was no reaction. In despair, the woman pulled the book from her daughter's hand and flung it at the wall, cursing.

'Damn book! Blasted headmaster! Damn the school!'

Everyone stood shocked, wiping their eyes. Then another woman's voice rang out, breaking the silence. 'She should have been married already! I was nine years old when they married me.'

Then chattering began. 'No sense encouraging children to follow white people and their schooling. It's how girl-children get wild and bring shame on us.'

Heavy footsteps came from the doorway. It was Pundit Lall. 'I came as soon as I heard,' he said, staring at the emaciated figure under the white sheet.

'My daughter is dead,' Devinia sobbed, looking at him reproachfully.

'We didn't do puja for nothing,' he said. 'Prayers are never wasted. The girl is not dead. She will come back – maybe as a butterfly . . . pretty little thing she was.'

Another shuffle came from the open door. Someone was shouting and pushing through. 'Let me in!' It was Sumati, Amina's best friend. 'No! Come back!' she wailed. 'I need you. If you go, I'm coming too!' She stood over Amina's bed, sobbing inconsolably.

'Now, now!' Pundit Lall said, pulling Sumati back by the shoulders. 'What kind of talk is this? You? You are more likely to come back as a dung fly, good-looking as you are.'

'She's my best friend!' Sumati screeched deliriously, batting his hand from her shoulder. 'The doctor – she needs a doctor!'

Amina's mother collapsed on the floor amongst the sobs and screams that had filled the room. Etwar, Amina's brother, stood staring at his older sister. Far, far away, Amina felt his presence and heat built up inside her as if she was already being engulfed by flames on a pyre. Sumati's face was squeezed through the bars of her iron bed-frame, as she pleaded with her friend not to leave her. Grief-stricken voices stirred the stuffy air in the wood-panelled room like mud in a churn. And then as if it was night, darkness fell.

Gradually people left, and, some remained and talked, moaning and wailing. But Sumati remained at Amina's bedside, barely taking her eyes off her friend. She chatted nonstop as if the girls were strolling around the school playground on a normal day. Devinia sat grieving at the bottom of her daughter's bed, and Etwar stood over his mother, soaking her shoulders with his tears. But not long before Sankar Banderjee returned home from work, like a miracle, the girl's eyes flickered.

TWO

Amina appeared to have no memory of her birthday drama. She spent the day drifting in and out of sleep or consciousness. Dimly, she heard her father's voice.

'Pa, is that you?' she mumbled. 'Everything is so bright. Why am I lying outside in the sun?'

'You are in your bedroom,' he said.

'I can't see you, but I can hear you.'

'Why can't you see me?' he asked, still struggling to understand what had happened to his daughter. 'Open your eyes and look at me.' He put his hand on her forehead.

'Your hand is cold. Stay with me.'

'I'm going nowhere.' Tears filled his eyes.

Amina's father, Sankar Banderjee, was so shocked when he heard what had taken place at the house the day before that he did something he had never ever done. He left his jewellery shop in Point Fortin closed up and stayed at home. Amina found his presence around her bed both reassuring and comforting, between the tumbling in her brain and the rumblings in her insides. It brought some peace – that is, until she heard the doctor's voice booming through the floorboards. It was Friday – the day a doctor visited the village.

The stamping of feet up the wooden steps outside her window caused Amina to jerk out of her sleepy state. The door flew open and three adults poured in. Doctor Douglas Boyle appeared remarkably calm as he peered over the iron bars of her bed, half-smiling behind the red hair around his face. 'So what has been occurring here, wee lass?' His smile turned into a frown. 'You don't look at all well.'

'Like I told you, doctor—' Devinia began, but was interrupted.

'Yes, I know what you *told* me,' he said. 'But I couldn't believe the stupidity!'

Devinia shuddered a little, but remained silent.

'I don't know what gets into her sometimes,' Sankar said.

Both of Amina's parents stared guiltily at their feet, while Dr Boyle strode heavily across the wooden floor of her bedroom and dumped his leather bag on the wooden blanket chest below the window. Amina's eyes opened wide, and her heart began racing.

'I trusted you to follow my instructions,' Dr Boyle said, looking at both parents accusingly. 'God have mercy on the child.' She opened her eyes as wide as she could, thinking it would stop him, but he just turned and wiped his sweating face on the long sleeves of his white shirt, and continued. 'Didn't I say, not to give the lass anything solid? Nothing!' Amina opened her mouth but could utter nothing. 'The gut is possibly ulcerated and so thin now that any food could well perforate it! But what did ye do?

And now you are going to lie to me about where you got the water you gave her. So I'll not even ask. I hope you can at least understand that?' Amina began to feel guilty for asking for food.

'Yes, doctor,' Devinia whispered. 'But we are not lying.'

'I thought this poor wee lass might be the one to pull through this. You don't realise what you've done,' he said.

Devinia's eyes filled with tears.

'Do you know how many people are dying from this disease – caused by dirty water? The government's put standpipes with clean running water in this village. Why don't you use them? When will you ever learn?'

'We don't go down the spring no more for water, doctor,' Sankar said, attempting to appease him. 'It's the truth.' Amina felt slight relief that her father had spoken up. But Dr Boyle wasn't done.

'My job is to save lives,' he ranted on, not appearing to hear. 'What's the point if you don't do what I tell you? Wasting my time having to trek out in this bush! Do you understand what I'm saying?'

Sankar nodded. 'Yes, doctor, we understand. We Indian, but we understand many English words. We call she Amina, but you call she wee-Lass.'

'Now listen – I will say this slow-ly. The child's gut is too thin . . . to withstand . . . any . . . kind of pressure that food puts on it. Especially your kind of heavy roti-bread and spicy-hot food. I know all about it – I have seen it. I'm not sure what will happen now.' He passed a forearm over his sweating brow.

Devinia moved forward, wringing her hands. 'I should never have given her that food. But it wasn't spicy-hot. Just boiled and fried a little – just how she like it.' Amina wanted to jump in and say what was in her head, but the doctor spoke again.

'*Fried*?' he asked. 'You're lucky you're not preparing to bury her today.'

Amina heard both her parents gasp together. Then her father straightened himself to his full height, and spoke in a low, clear tone.

'By the hairs on the chin of the Maharaja of India and King George the Fifth, King of England,' he began, 'things will change from today. You hear about King George at war with Germany? Who knows what will become of your people. Nothing lasts forever. I have connections in Port of Spain. I know what is happening.' He looked Dr Boyle in the eye. 'Man to man,' he said, 'I swear this will not happen again.' He wagged his finger. 'I will stay home and make sure myself.' He cast a cold stare at his wife. Amina did not miss it. She lifted her head to speak but it fell back on the pillow. Again, nothing came out.

'Good,' the doctor said. 'All I can do now is give her something to make her sleep. The rest is up to you.' He opened his bag and pulled out a glass syringe. Devinia brought in a bowl of water, a cloth, and a bar of soap for him. After the injection she took the bowl out.

Sankar pulled some cash from his pocket and handed it to the doctor. 'Listen, she is my only daughter. I will do anything to keep her safe. It was her mother. You know what these women are like, disobedient. You must know, you have a wife yourself. I will beat her tonight, I promise you that.'

Amina looked at her father with her mouth open, but nothing came out.

'Just make sure she doesn't do it again,' Dr Boyle said gruffly. 'The child could die, just like that.'

'I'm a jeweller, you know. I will pay you well. Also, I will make a gold chain too for you. A heavy one. And a *bera* for your wife. An Indian bracelet.'

The lines on Dr Boyle's face began disappearing and his skin was turning pink and dry again. 'I have a daughter too,' he said.

'Well then, I'll make two *beras*, and the chain.'

'Another thing,' the doctor said. 'You must get your son away from here. I told you before, he is also at risk from this typhoid.'

'Yes, doctor.' Sankar threw a glance at Devinia as she returned. 'I told you to send the boy away! And if I catch you giving her food again, I will . . . !' Devinia looked at him pointedly and he stopped short.

Amina's eyes opened wide and she looked at her father and Dr Boyle. With all her strength she whispered in a hoarse voice. 'It was *my* fault. It was *me* who begged Ma for food. And it was *me* who ate it. Don't blame Ma. And you're beating no one, Pa. I have things to tell you. I swam up there with the stars. A million of them. And I got to see heaven.'

ꟼ

The air in the house the following week was heavy. Those two days took their toll on Amina. Her parents did everything they could, but it didn't seem enough. Amina overheard some of their conversations even though her eyes were closed.

'We sent Etwar to your sister,' her father told her mother. 'Now we have to do something for the girl. I don't know what yet, but I have realised that the answer is not in just giving her jewels. That was too easy for me, although not cheap. We have done something wrong. This must be karma. I am sure of it. Our daughter is looking like a dried-up fig tree.'

'I want to clean her up,' Devinia said tiredly. 'We need more water from the standpipe. Please will you fetch some.'

When he left, Devinia brought up a bowl of warm water and washed her beloved child, who lay coma-like and barely alive. Taking a deep breath to hold back the tears, Devinia washed the girl and massaged her limbs with coconut oil. Amina flinched a few times and groaned as her mother dressed her and sang Indian songs. When she told her a story from the *Ramayana*, her eyes flickered and then closed.

'Don't be sad, Ma,' Amina breathed. 'I'm tired, but I'm not going anywhere.' Devinia sat up and listened to the girl speak. Amina opened her eyes again. 'Did you hear me?' she said. 'I'm going nowhere.'

'You are like a ruby, set amongst a thousand sparkling jewels,' Devinia said. 'Who else would swim among the stars and come back down here?' She looked into the girl's pale face, wondering if it was at all possible for her daughter to survive this terrible disease. 'But I think there's something up there. There's a reason you came back to us. I don't know what it is, but I just know, *beti*. Hush now. Sleep and get strong again.'

THREE

One afternoon, a few weeks later, Sumati called by when Devinia was in the kitchen outside.

'You know you are not allowed to see Amina yet,' Devinia reminded her. 'She's still too weak for visitors.'

'I know. I just have something for her. Will you give it to her?'

Devinia took the folded piece of paper. 'I'll see she gets it when she wakes up.'

When Sumati left, Devinia opened the missive and wished it was written in Sanskrit so she could understand it. If Sankar saw it, he would think there was something secretive going on. Devinia folded the piece of paper and put it in her pocket.

When she took it to Amina, she asked her daughter to read the contents out loud.

Amina did. 'You see, Ma? No need to be suspicious. Sumati wrote it because she knew you wouldn't let her come up and talk to me.'

'So that is all she said – that Moonia is getting married? I knew that already. The boy is from Couva.'

'Well, I didn't know that,' Amina said. 'Why didn't Moonia tell me herself? Maybe she just found out.' When her mother left, Amina read the letter properly.

My dear best friend, Amina,

How are you doing? They wouldn't let me see you, and I know why. It is for my own good, but not yours. So I thought you should know that our friend Moonia, who said she wanted to stay on at school forever, is getting married on Sunday. Poor Moonia. She is always crying when I see her and they have taken her out of school now. Like you, she wanted to do what Mr Clifford said and try to be a teacher. But as you know, none of our parents believe that it can ever happen. They think it is a BIG LIE that we Indian girls could ever become teachers. And they think it is a trick so Mr Clifford can have a big Standard 5 class and he can give evening lessons to pass his lonely time. If we all got married, he would have empty desks in Standard 5 and 6. I hope you will be well enough to come to the wedding. Tell me you will come. I will miss you if you are not there.

Yours truly
Sumati Balgobin

ꕤ

Amina sighed loudly. She put the letter under her pillow, closed her eyes and instantly fell asleep. A few hours later, she took a page out of her exercise book and started to write a reply.

ꝏ

Dear Sumati,

When did Moonia know about this marriage? She never told me they found her a match. I can't believe she didn't tell me. She and I were best friends before you and me. Do you think she is annoyed at me? Or maybe she knew I would have tried to talk her out of it. She's not like me, or you. She doesn't say what she thinks. She should talk honestly to her parents about it. Some parents are starting to understand why we don't want all the old Indian traditions. They hold us back. I'm so annoyed, I can't tell you how much.

When I come back to school, I won't have a friend at the evening class at all now. I am hoping you will change your mind so we can do the Pupil Teacher course together. It will be so much fun. You will enjoy it. Why would you want to go and work in the cane field in the hot sun, and get bitten by ants and scorpions, when you can just sit in class in the cool, and read and write, and talk about Wordsworth and Emily Brontë? Why would you choose to get burnt like coals in the hot sun? How will that make you happy? Education is so important. Look at Mr Clifford. He is so clever only because he did his education. Don't forget where he came from.

Girl, I miss school but I am so tired all the time. They think I might die. I am going to fight it though. I miss you, and I wish I could see you. I would not be allowed to go to Moonia's wedding even if I was able to walk that far. I can't even walk down the steps. She has to beg her parents to stop this wedding. Ask Mr Clifford if he would go to her house and talk to them. Seriously. It worked for me. Do something. Keep trying.

Your best friend,
Amina

ဢ

Amina asked her mother to give Sumati the letter at the standpipe.

'As soon as Doctor says, Sumati will come and see you herself,' Devinia said.

'We can ask him when he comes next time, Ma. Can't we?'

'You can ask him,' Devinia said, quivering a little.

'I will,' Amina replied boldly. 'I'm not scared of him, even though he's white. You shouldn't be either. He's just human like us.'

Devinia looked at her daughter in admiration and awe at her brave words.

ဢ

When Sunday came, wedding drums pounded through the early morning air. The gravel road clicked and clacked with foot traffic, the rumble of donkey carts and pony traps. Amina's window was open, and her heart was heavy for Moonia, knowing that Sumati must have been unsuccessful. She wondered if Mr Clifford had tried to talk to Moonia's parents after learning that one of his best pupils had left school.

'Ma, aren't you leaving it late to get ready for the wedding?'

Devinia shrugged. 'It's like any other wedding. I'm not leaving you.'

'I want to know what the bridegroom looks like.'

'Sounds like you're getting better,' Devinia said fondly. 'Sumati will tell you. In a letter maybe.'

'But I can't wait! I want you to go.'

'Why? The girl is marrying a man. And a man is a man.'

Amina was speechless. If a man was a man, why bother with them at all? If they were all the same, why did women in books fall in love with one man and not the other? Did anyone in the village know what love was? Or falling in love? They were children when they married. Her mother was five when it happened to her. She couldn't know – not first-hand. Or was 'love' something created by writers to entice readers? Her mother might be right. She said falling in love made people lose their mind and do stupid things. However, it would help to know that Moonia's bridegroom was at least kind-looking, young-looking, strong-looking and good-looking.

Then she spoke aloud. 'That's why I'm never getting married.'

She propped herself up on her pillows and opened her book. George Eliot again. *Silas Marner* again, the only book in the house that was written in English. Silas Marner was a man who didn't seem to have found a woman to marry, so instead he cared for a strange child called Ellie. If Ellie was to choose to marry, it would be to someone like Silas Marner. Someone with a heart as kind as he had. Much like the way Amina felt deep down about her own father. Sankar had agreed to her wish to stay on at school to become a teacher, even though he didn't think it would work out. The many pieces of jewellery he made for her, made her the envy of the village. But she realised that jewels did not make her who she was. Mr Clifford, the headmaster, had taught her that genuine sparkle came from inside, like a lighthouse from the heart.

FOUR

On his way to fetch drinking water from the standpipe, Sankar Banderjee spotted Pundit Lall walking up the gravel road, and felt uncomfortable. Fetching water was not a grown man's chore, but his son, Etwar, was not around to do it. And Pundit Lall was not his favourite person, due to the number of pujas Devinia had asked him to do at their home since Amina's illness. Each one cost money but Devinia felt they were worth it, even though Sankar didn't feel that any god could help his daughter recover. If that made him an unbeliever, he was not willing to argue about it, so he turned back.

Unfortunately for Sankar, Lall had already spotted him and was hurrying up the hill straight towards him. Sankar began to think of questions to ask him if he mentioned doing another puja. How could Hanuman, Shiva, or Lakshmi be so powerful if they were made of stone? And if they saved his daughter, why didn't they save the other three children who died from typhoid? Or the baby who got caught under the wheels of a pony trap a few weeks ago?

'I've been meaning to come and see you,' Pundit Lall said breathlessly.

'Me?' Sankar asked.

'Yes. How is your daughter? I was there when she almost died.'

'Yes, yes. I heard. I owe you.'

'Nah!' Pundit Lall said. 'I might have saved her life, but you owe me nothing. I was probably meant to be there right at that time. It was fate.'

'I've been wondering if the lovely goddess Lakshmi ever gives massages with those four pretty hands of hers,' Sankar said out of the blue.

'What are you asking, man?' Lall said. 'Disgraceful. Are you out of your mind?'

'No, no. Just wondering, thinking why she seems to be so well endowed with hands. Unless she is making rotis up in heaven twice as fast.'

'Listen, you are not thinking straight, but that is not surprising since you recently nearly lost your child. You will have to achieve Nirvana yourself to find out what the good goddess does with her four hands. But you can do me a favour for what I have done for you. If you come across a heavy gold ring. . .'

'And if I don't come across one,' Sankar said resignedly. 'I will make one for you.'

'Oh, all right then. So let me do you yet another favour, seeing as you are so much a busy and important businessman. And it is good karma.' Sankar listened, his chest swelling. Pundit Lall's eyes gleamed as he jabbered in Hindi. 'Might I tell you first, that you are doing a grand service for we Indians in your gold jewellery business. Goldliness is next to godliness. So me and you is alike. But might I be brutishly honest with you?'

'Please – don't spare me,' Sankar said, humbly. 'I deserve it!'

'Well, it's like this. Could it be that it was you yourself who brought this bad luck upon your family?'

Sankar looked shocked. His eyes opened so wide, three concentric circles stared. 'What makes you think that?'

'You may look surprised if you like, but I know full well you have plenty of money to throw at a white-man doctor's fees while you give me just a few cents for pujas. It's about karma, you see. Because you haven't done what you should have done, you are being paid back for your stinginess. Also, trying to be westernised will be your downfall. Mark me. It will bring down *all* our people. Take my advice and find a match for your daughter. It is a parent's first responsibility to the world, as you know. True, she is sickly and thin. She may get better, or she mightn't. So many have already died. . . But people don't listen! Ask yourself this: what can one white doctor do more than an army of Indian gods and goddesses? You see? It's in the numbers. You cannot put your trust in these white men. Because what do they know about us? We have survived thousands of years without them. And they have disrupted us with this Empire of theirs.'

Sankar scratched his head. 'That is all good, *Baba*, but I have things to do.'

The pundit grabbed him by the arm. 'Yes, but listen. Take the tea plantations back in India. Did we get rich? No. Yet we let them trick us to come thousands of miles over the *kala pani* – to sift sugar! And believing this trickery, we spent three, four months struggling over the black waters to get here. This place is not our world,' he snorted. 'Our people are strong – we survived – some of us. But we are not as strong as the black workers who toiled like slaves.'

'They *were* slaves from what I hear. They received no pay at all. At least our people get a pittance. You call me stingy?' Sankar gave the pundit a hard stare. 'But do you do pujas for free?'

'I am saying that we are weak in comparison. As black as some of us Indians are, our people cannot cope with that strenuous work. And what about those still living in slave barracks? When will they get out? They are trampling barefoot through each other's excrement to get to the latrines, catching hookworm, and cholera. There's not enough food to even half-fill their bellies to keep them going the whole day in the hot sun, cutting cane or chopping copra. It is killing our people. We will not survive.'

'I know this.'

'But you – *you* are sitting in the shade, high and dry all day in your business, making prrity-prrity-shining-gold-jewels, then coming home to your nice-big-board-house you build there – elaborate carvings of trelliswork all round. Mind you, I have seen bigger and better in Port of Spain. But you understand my meaning? In my line of work, I see all kinds of people. But mostly they are outside the whole day in the hot sun scratching a living. You understand me? Listen, Banderjee, think about *dharma* and do the right thing. We each have to do our own part to keep what we value, otherwise we all suffer. So, you must do your duty before your daughter gets worse. Then she will do hers. That is how *dharma* works. She is a jewel of a girl too. Very pretty face. Yes, I remember when she was not so thin and bony. Always drawing in the sand in the yard, or else had her head in some book.'

'But what can I do?' Sankar shrugged. 'I'm helpless. The child's mother wants her to stay in school and do that English-kind of education.'

'And you? What do you want?'

'The child has taken after the mother,' Sankar said, moodily. 'Sometimes when the mother looks at me, I quake. She has fire in her eyes. But my daughter was desperate for school every day – rain or shine. Sadly, no more.'

'Listen to yourself! You are frightened of a woman? You are the man of the house! So show them you are the boss – or your daughter will never learn to obey a man when she is married. Besides, marry her while she can still sit on your lap at the wedding, and you will have your reward in heaven.'

Sankar opened his eyes wide. He began nodding, caressing his chest with both arms. 'You are now making sense.'

'Good! Let me do you a favour and find a match for the girl. Leave it to me. It will cost you only. . . next to nothing.'

Sankar forgot his suspicions about Pundit Lall, and the two men walked back to the house together, talking and laughing. They sat under the coconut tree about twenty feet from the kitchen, drinking coconut water and jabbering away in Hindi. Pundit Lall told Sankar everything he needed to know about the boy he had in mind, and promised to arrange a meeting – without Devinia.

Sankar suddenly realised what was missing from his life: reaching heaven after death was an otherwise unachievable goal. He had no desire to return to earth after he died as some stray dog or starving rat – and who knew where it would end? He had to act fast if he was to skip the stages of reincarnation. And then there was the goddess Lakshmi with her four hands. . . It had to be done before Amina reached puberty.

'Do it,' he decided, staring at Pundit Lall. 'Make the arrangement. Fast.'

'It won't take long. The boy's father is a businessman like you, even richer. The girl will do well. So it will cost you.'

Sankar hesitated. Alarm bells began to ring in his head, but he couldn't retract. 'Yes, yes, yes! Do it quick. It will be worth it for a place in heaven.'

ഌ

It wasn't long before Devinia got another letter for her daughter. She took it up to Amina. 'From Sumati again,' she said. When her mother left the girl opened it.

My dear friend, Amina,

I am sorry to say that the good news I have has been taken over by bad news.

You might have heard that Moonia went ahead and married the boy last Sunday. She ignored everything I said to her. But the boy looked nice, as far as we could see all dressed up in a nice bridegroom costume and everything. The wedding went well, and she was crying like all brides do about leaving home. We didn't think anything of it. But this morning her father came to my house and gave us the most distressing news.

I don't know how else to tell you this, but Moonia is dead.

Our poor friend drank poison and yesterday her brother-in-law found her in their shed. She smelt bad, they said. They think Moonia drank weed-killer. Her father is going up to their house today in Couva. Her aunt is remaining here with her mother. As you can imagine, she is very distraught, and Moonia's father is worried about her.

I feel I should have done something more, but I don't know what. She was not too good before the wedding, always crying, and hardly speaking. Still, I don't understand why she took her life. I wonder if her husband did something to her? Or her in-laws? You know how some mothers-in-law can be wicked. Maybe they overworked her or lashed her with leather belts and sticks. Or the dreaded rolling pin. Or even threw hot iron pots at her.

I have to go now. But I wanted you to know. Longing to see you, my friend. I miss you so much. This has made me think. We must stick together, you and I. We cannot let this happen to all us girls. We need a plan. You are good at planning, what do you think? I am depending on you, Amina. You are the one with the brains. We might all have the same fate, but your brains can change that, I am sure. The trouble is with our religion. Some of it. They want to marry us off before we even pass our blood and are still a child. I escaped that with my trickery, remember? I crossed my eyes the whole time and put that suitor right off me. I think you might be close to your bloods, if it wasn't for the typhoid.

My mother says these things are not as bad as they used to be. She married when she was 9 years old. I told Ma, I will not marry a boy who I do not know. She will not speak to my father about it though. Maybe what happened to Moonia will make them reconsider. Do you think her husband raped her? Nobody talks about these things. Not mothers, not anyone. But I am sure he must have forced her to do it, and that is why she drank poison.

You are the luckiest of us. Your parents seem to be the best. They promised they will let you do what you want. Why can't all parents be like yours?

So long, my friend.

Yours truly,
Sumati Balgobin

ꕥ

When Devinia went up to Amina later, she was sitting upright, as pale as the letter lying on the bed, staring at the open window as if some wild animal was coming to get her.

'Look how my skin is wrinkled,' the girl said. 'I'm disappearing from inside.'

'Drink this,' Devinia said, touching her daughter's forehead. 'You're cold.' She looked at the letter on the bed. Another one she couldn't read. She pulled Amina and hugged her tight, hoping to squeeze away any evil spirit from taking hold of her child.

'A sandstorm is blowing,' Amina began murmuring, making no sense. 'Sand's pitching high in the air – in my eyes. I can't see.' She pulled away from her mother and curled up on the bed like a new-born, rubbing her eyes. 'The breeze is cool. Feathers floating down.'

'What did the letter say?' Devinia asked, when Amina stirred.

'Up there.' Amina pointed to the ceiling, her eyes flickering. 'Those people. Falling down. Struggling to stand up. The ship – it's rolling around. The water is deep and black. The people – their faces are sore and red. Pink pus is pouring, all over their bodies. The children are alone, crying, coughing. Their bowls are empty. A man – on the side of the ship! No! I think. . . He's going to jump. He's fallen in the water! The boat is going – leaving him behind.' Amina's breathing grew fast and distressed.

Devinia held her tight, crying, 'It's not real, just in your imagination. How do you know all this? My mother used to say these things about their journey from India.'

Devinia began to dread the worst. She had never witnessed a reincarnation before and hoped it wasn't that. Where would it end? Which was better – to be damaged by the fever, or to undergo reincarnation? She pressed Amina's forehead until the girl cried out in pain.

'Maybe the doctor will give you something,' Devinia said. 'If only my mother was alive, she might know what to do. I hope it is just her spirit that is watching over you.'

But Amina had fallen into a deep sleep and didn't wake till the next morning.

ꟹ

'Ma, I want to go back to school,' Amina announced. 'I keep thinking of Mr Clifford in front of the school doors after lunchtime, perspiration running down his face. I want to go today.'

'You are not well enough.' Devinia held Amina's hand. 'You talk as if you are seeing him.'

The girl stared at her mother's face intently. 'I do see him. I pray school prayers to Mr Clifford's God. And I think He is hearing me and will make me well. Headmaster says his God hears everything if you have faith. I think I am finding out what is faith.'

'All of us have a fate.'

'Not that kind of fate. Mr Clifford has fai-th in a different God – like a great spirit. Not hundreds of small gods. And his life got a whole lot better than his father's and grandfather's. Do you know they were born slaves? His grandmother was made pregnant in Jamaica by the plantation master. Then he sold her. Mr Clifford says he doesn't look like his mother or his brothers and sisters. He says he's more like coffee mix-up with plenty of condensed milk, that's why he's not so black.'

'What matters more is that your headmaster is a good man. He cares about the children in school, no matter what colour he is.'

'That's true, Ma. A lot of really bad things happened when they were slaves. They were raped, Ma.'

'What do you know about rape, child?'

'I want to talk about it. You see, I think Moonia was raped.'

'Moonia? Who by?'

'Who do you think?'

'Is that why they got her married?'

'Ma, Moonia is dead because she *didn't* want to get married. Did you hear she committed suicide? She was raped by her husband. Why don't you want to say the word? Rape, rape, rape!'

'Hush! You don't know what you're saying. I heard the girl died, but how could her husband do that? It's her husband. It's not possible.' But by the time the words left her lips, Devinia was already thinking again. 'I know what you're saying,' she told her daughter, 'but you mustn't talk like that. No one will believe you.'

'Then they are liars. They must know this is happening, and yet they still send their children to be raped by a strange man they call a husband?'

'Is it Mr Clifford who put this in your head?'

'I can think for myself. Mr Clifford said I could do anything if I put my mind to it, but not in a world where children are being married and sent away. He's not married. And he's a really good teacher and headmaster. I want to be like him.' She gritted her teeth hard. 'I'm never getting married. Because it'll stop me doing what is really important to me.' Amina looked at her mother questioningly and said, 'He says he told you I could be a doctor if I wanted. That Pa must have enough money to send me to England to study. Is that true?'

Devinia frowned. 'England is too far. But yes, Mr Clifford did come to the house and say that.' She remembered well when the headmaster told her and Sankar, *The girl is a star pupil, if only both of you could realise it.* Tears welled up in her eyes and Amina guessed why.

'Don't worry, Ma. I will survive and I will have a future. But you and Pa have to let me follow it.'

Devinia's green eyes lit up like jewels, just hearing her daughter speak of her future, whatever it was. Hope filled her until teardrops glistened her cheeks.

'Oh, Ma, I can see it.' Amina held her mother's arm and stared skywards in a trance. 'Look at all those books! How many they are! And all colours of people, reading and singing and praying. And wheels turning round and round, taking me. And, Ma, my hair is flying in the wind. I'm on a big new ship – we're sailing into the sky. . .'

'Where are you seeing this, child?' Devinia held her tight again, worried about her crossing over to the other side.

'It's a new world! I have to go back to school and learn how to teach. It's the only way to make things better. Too many of our people are poor. You can see that, can't you? It was the same for Mr Clifford's people. His family worked as slaves in the same cane fields where Indians work now. Did you know that, Ma? It changed for them, and he got a chance. He went to Port of Spain and studied a lot of books for a lot of years. If Indians at least knew how to read and write English, they wouldn't be working in the cane fields, getting stung by scorpions and dying, beaten up every day, and toiling for pennies to buy a pound of rice. People are still living in barracks. Everybody should learn, Ma. Everybody! I don't want to waste my chance. Promise me you'll let me. I want to help people somehow.'

'You're still so thin,' her mother chided gently. 'How can *you* help anybody? The doctor says you can't go back to school for several months. You're not even strong enough to use the latrine by yourself. And whatever happens, don't let your father know you talk like this. Wherever did you hear about Indian teachers in this place? And women Indian teachers? Just ridiculous!'

The girl heard the bitterness in her mother's voice and a fire rose inside her chest. 'I thought you understood. Ma, how could you say that? I trusted you! I hate, hate Indians. And you're no better. Why are you all like that? I believe Mr Clifford. And I will do it!'

Amina's big eyes stared at her mother, her face swollen with anger, and her eyes sank in disbelief. Trembling, she swung her wasted legs with all her strength to the edge of the bed. 'I'm going outside to the latrine,' she said. 'By myself.' But as she put her feet to the floor, her knees buckled under her and she collapsed. She burst into tears as her mother helped her back to bed.

'You don't understand,' the girl repeated. 'You all came and brought India with you – but this is not India. We have to change and get an education. No one can take that away. It will make us like them. Mr Clifford became like the white people. Can't you see?'

Devinia sat on the edge of the bed, holding her daughter's hand. 'I don't have education. It's true. But I am not stupid either. I know we got tricked. And yes, many people died. My father left India not knowing where he was going. Maybe that was fate.' Neither said anything for a while, then Devinia sighed heavily. 'You could be right. There may be Indian lady teachers one day. But first you must get well. Then stay at school as long as you want. I promise. Besides, your father and I don't want you labouring in the hot sun. His business is doing well, so you won't have to break your back like other girls. And when the time comes, you will get married.'

But Amina was almost asleep and failed to hear what her mother had said.

'Hate Indians, and you hate yourself,' Devinia continued softly. 'India too. It was not good to us, but I hear it is a beautiful country. Don't ever forget who you are.'

ꙮ

The next day, Amina sent a note to Sumati.

Dear Sumati,

I got your letter, and I am too angry to know what to say. I am definitely getting better. I did my own prayers to Mr Clifford's God. I don't care what anybody thinks. They treat me as if they wanted me dead. And I am following all the advice from Dr Boyle, and will definitely be in school before you know it. I am not just going to be sad about Moonia – that doesn't help anyone. Instead, I have a plan, but you and I must stick to it.

Do you remember what we saw by the well that evening after school? And we promised each other we wouldn't talk about it? Well, if our parents will not listen to us, we will have to use that against them. They will be devastated, but it's them or us. We have no choice.

Remain strong, Sumati. I cannot go to Moonia's funeral. Say goodbye to her for me.

Your loving friend,
Amina

FIVE

Amina knew her mother worried more about Etwar now, and less about her. He was a capable ten-year-old, but she knew that look in her mother's face, and wondered if her brother was alright. They had obeyed Dr Boyle's orders to the letter and more. Every day her mother still boiled all the drinking water, scrubbed the floors, swept the yard, changed the bedclothes, kept all visitors downstairs, and continued to turn away Sumati and other friends for their own good. But she heard her mother speaking to her father saying that she was afraid to even enter her room at times, because she feared the girl had crossed over to the spirit world and returned as some other person – as if she was like the demented young man who roamed the village and at whom the local children threw stones, calling him a *jumbie*. Amina wished she could get inside her mother's head, because there were things she couldn't understand.

ຍ

Devinia spent all her days thinking about this while working in the yard, or cooking, or milking the cow. If she was wrong, and Amina was not affected by the spirit world, she was surely affected by something – and it could be her own ideas which were getting out of hand. How could Indians ever become so English that they could work alongside important African and white people in government offices in Port of Spain? Or be teachers in the few schools she knew of, which were Catholic or Anglican schools anyway. Sankar had his own business so he wasn't dependent on anyone for work. But she wished she could read more than just the *Bhagavad Gita* and the *Ramayana*. She longed to read English books, or even the newspaper squares that hung on the hook in the latrine. But she was grateful that Amina's health was improving. It didn't matter who or what was responsible – the doctor, Lakshmi, Ganesh, or Mr Clifford's own God. It made no difference. She'd never understand. She had been married off at five, and had never gone to school. How could she?

In the last few weeks, Sankar had spent a lot of time at home. He locked up his shop early most afternoons, and the couple spent time together, reading their holy books and praying at the altar in their bedroom. They spoke to each other in Bhojpuri, a Hindi dialect, and got on well. But suddenly their differences got to her.

'Why are you putting that rice in her water?' he would say when she was taking Amina something from the kitchen.

'Why are you interfering?' she snapped back.

'I'm here to keep an eye on you. It was you that caused her to nearly die.'

'I am doing my best,' she said. His words stung.

'Our daughter is only reading English storybooks and not listening to a word I say,' her husband ranted on. 'These books have no value, no moral lessons. Teaching young girls about love. Huh! Follow love and you follow trouble!'

'Headmaster sent those books for her,' Devinia replied. 'It's what she wants. I think they're helping her to feel better.'

'There is something else,' Sankar said, grinding his teeth. 'I think a spirit is bothering her. We're doing wrong by ignoring *dharma* and we will all be sorry! Things will not work out. If I don't do my part, we will have no money, no house, no food. Do you spend your time reading storybooks? No! You stay at home and do your chores. It's how life works. We each must do our part. So must children. Amina must do as she is told but she barely listens!'

'What happened to you?' his wife asked, aghast at this outburst. 'Has a spirit taken you over? I will do puja this Friday.'

'No more puja! Are all the gods deaf, woman? Just listen to the doctor's orders.'

Devinia fixed him eye to eye. 'Why did you tell the doctor you will beat me?' she spat. 'I should learn to read English too. Then you would have more respect for me.'

'What kind of respect?' he questioned. 'Have I ever beaten you? You ask for respect. Do you know that white men beat their wives to keep them in order? I've seen it myself. That nice Mr Hart from Port of Spain who gives us the rose plants? He beats his wife: she had a damn good black-eye last time I was up there. When she saw me, she hurried inside the house so fast that her dress caught in the door and pulled her back. Dr Boyle was threatening not to return, so I had to say something. You are lucky I am not one of those kind of husbands.'

Devinia looked at him defiantly. 'Even so, I am glad our daughter likes school.'

'Yes, but not for long. We must do our duty and teach her the ways of our ancestors.'

'What happened was like a sign,' she said.

'Exactly my thoughts!' Sankar said, brightening. 'You see, we are both of one mind. We must return to our thousand-year-old traditions. We mustn't give them up for flimsy white-man ways. Amina will soon be a woman.'

'I didn't mean that,' Devinia said, alarmed.

'Well, I intend to do what is right for our daughter,' her husband replied firmly.

'She wants to remain at school. Become a teacher.'

'She's picked up that fancy talk from the headmaster.' Sankar's face was reddening.

'Maybe, but it's what she really wants. We brought her up different.'

'That is your fault,' he said. 'She is Indian! *You* are Indian! But you want to be like the white man *and* the black man. Your skin might be light, but you are forgetting yourself!'

Devinia answered hotly, '*You* might have come from Uttar Pradesh, *but she* was born here. *I* was born here. I want her to learn. Please, Sankar . . .'

But her husband was shaking his head, looking despondent. 'Your mother left India behind, as I did. We had to leave. But we didn't leave our hearts behind.'

'My mother didn't want to come here! She was stolen as a child from her back yard.'

'True. And I left in two minds. But there wasn't much of a choice . . . It looked like an opportunity, except it wasn't.

Not when we got here. Not even when we set foot on that boat in Kolkata. The rocking and rolling on that boat! Four months of sickness and death. You know what hell these eyes of mine have witnessed?'

Devinia's eyes filled with tears as she remembered her mother's stories, but she worried about where this conversation was leading. She had to protect her daughter. Sankar was much older than she was, already owning his jewellery business when her parents married her to him. It was the custom to send a young bride to her husband's home before puberty, to stop them bringing dishonour to the family. But Sankar lived in his house all alone. So in the absence of a mother-in-law to take charge of Devinia's upbringing, she was kept at home and sent to him after puberty, missing out on an education.

'If we make the promise now, the gods will look on us favourably,' Sankar said.

'But I already promised *her*! I thought you wanted the best for our child.'

'Which is why I work so hard. We have a responsibility. Reading English stories and singing Mr Worthward's poetry about daffodils is not who we are. You must teach her to read Sanskrit.'

'Shh! She will hear you. And it is Mr Wordsworth who writes the poems.'

'How do you know about Mr Werdwert?' He looked at Amina lying on the bed under the brown blanket, asleep, clutching the book to her chest. 'Let her hear me!' he yelled. 'Mark my words, she *will* be married inside a year. I will take her out of school. She will not get her own way on this.'

SIX

Devinia waited some weeks before asking Pundit Lall to conduct another puja, so as not to annoy her husband. Almost every god had already had their turn. The top right-hand corner of the yard looked like Commonwealth Headquarters with the colourful array of *jhandi* flags flying in the wind – pink, red, white, yellow, blue – each representing a different god.

Amina spent the whole puja wondering what she was missing or what was wrong, because Pundit Lall winked at her more than once and the girl didn't know why. Once she winked back at him just to be polite, but he frowned and looked at her sternly.

'Do you think there is a god at all?' she asked her mother after the puja.

Devinia raised an eyebrow.

'These pictures on the Almanac, are they real? Has anyone seen one move, or talk?'

Amina continued.

'You and your father have me confused.'

'I was only thinking,' Amina said.

'Too much thinking! Your father is already saying . . .'

'I heard him shouting. I wasn't asleep. You cannot do this to me, Ma. You will be sorry.' The girl's voice was passionate. 'You will make me do something you will regret.'

Devinia turned away, torn between her daughter and husband. But also between their own Hindu culture and the new confused mix of English, African, Spanish, Muslim, Hindu, Irish, Portuguese-all-in-one-curry-Creole-stew-and-rice around them.

'What am I supposed to do?' she appealed. 'If you heard him, you should know it's not easy for me.'

'And what about Etwar? Are you going to force him to marry too? When, exactly?'

Devinia picked up a piece of coconut husk and busied herself scrubbing the pots with ash, her head in turmoil, and her heart wracked with guilt. She had burdened the boy with worries and chores before sending him away. He never complained, but she worried it would weaken him and cause illness. She longed to see him and check his face, the lines round his mouth, the dimple on his chin, and the look in his eyes. It would tell her all she needed to know.

'I miss him,' she murmured, as she stared at the black, greasy ash on her hands.

༺

The quarrelling downstairs was probably the worst thing for Amina, apart from the typhoid she had suffered. She closed her eyes tight and called on Mr Clifford's God to make her parents stop. Suddenly it did stop, which shocked her. But then she heard different, unfamiliar voices calling in the yard.

Amina jumped. She climbed out of bed and pushed the window open. It was Etwar and her aunt. She'd brought him back. Her mother was pulling Etwar to her and hugging him tight. Etwar struggled free and she could hear him running up the wooden steps. He appeared at her door and Amina put her arms out to him.

'I wished it,' she said, happily.

'I couldn't stay away any longer,' he said. His voice was half husky. He was growing up.

'They've started quarrelling a lot,' she said. 'When you go back to school, will you ask Mr Clifford to send me a new book? I want something different.'

'I missed you,' he said.

'You got taller. And your voice – sounds froggy.' She laughed at him. Etwar jumped on the bed and pretended to fight her, but when Devinia came upstairs, her children were side by side, sitting on the bed chatting.

ℵ

Amina was in bed reading when Dr Boyle visited.

'Where's that blue book you couldn't let go of?' he asked.

Amina pulled it out from under her pillow.

'You carry that around like a doll.' He scrutinised her face. 'I think you're well enough to have friends come to visit. I'll tell your mother.'

ℵ

As soon as the doctor left, Amina sent Etwar to tell Sumati, who arrived the same afternoon.

'Looking good, girl,' her friend said breezily. 'Last time I saw you, your face was so white it was nearly blue!'

Amina looked into Sumati's eyes. 'Something's wrong, Sumati. What is it?'

'Oh, it's just I'm thinking about that lunchtime when you left school and never came back. I didn't realise you were so ill.'

'Well I'm better now, so tell me what's really on your mind.'

Sumati bit her lip. 'It's Chandrawatti. She's expecting.'

'Expecting what?'

'A child of course! She got married a few months ago.'

'I forgot. She should have stayed on at school. But what about you?'

'I always got you in trouble,' Sumati reminisced. 'Do you remember that time I pinned a tail on Mr Maggotty's trousers? And you told him that a jackass was following him. He looked round but never saw the tail. That still makes me giggle.'

They both burst out laughing.

'Should we be laughing?' Amina said eventually.

'Maybe not. But if you want to cry, go ahead. Me – I've no tears left. The funeral was horrible. The box was shut because she stank. We could smell it from . . .'

Tears welled up in Amina's eyes. 'I woke up this morning feeling angry. I can't cry when I'm angry. It eats me inside. But I'm so grateful for everything and everyone who helped me. I feel guilty, being angry. I'm back from the dead, and I have to be thankful for that.'

'You look different. Your eyes – they're like lights.'

Amina turned serious. 'We have to do something about our parents marrying us off before we even have a say. It's not right. Our life is finished before it has even started.'

'You're all right, Amina. Your parents are not like the rest.'

'Sumati, I remember you saying your Pa was ruining your life. How? Talk to me.'

The other girl sighed. 'Did I say that? Well, they're forcing me to get married to some old man with two children. I put off the last one, who wasn't that bad-looking. I wasn't going to let them marry me off without a fight. But now it's even worse. How can they do this to me? It's as if they're desperate to get rid of me.'

'Money is short, that's why. They think you need someone else to look after you. It's what they all think. My parents are better off, which is why they promised I could stay on at school. But now, my father has changed his mind.'

'What? You're joking.' Sumati began to laugh, but when Amina looked at Sumati, she was actually crying. 'There's no hope for me if your parents are forcing you to marry.'

'Listen, Sumati, I'm not doing it. I meant what I said in my letter. Every word.'

'But what can we do? And how?'

'I don't know. I'm not God.'

'God?' Sumati looked at Amina, confused. 'Which one?'

'School God. Mr Clifford's God. It's the one that got them out of slavery, and it got him to be a teacher and a headmaster. He said there's a big story about him and God. And I must ask him about that.'

'Mr Clifford doesn't think we have a god,' Sumati said. 'He told us in school assembly. Although he admitted he likes the puja food.' Sumati looked sad. 'I don't know what to do. But I can't live with this hanging over me. I wish I could run away.'

'That won't help anyone. We need a plan. And we must support each other for any chance of it working.'

Both girls sat quietly for a while, thinking. Sumati began to giggle.

'What is it?'

'I'm remembering the boy they brought,' Sumati said. 'The first one. Every time he looked at me, I looked back at him like this.' She crossed both eyeballs towards her nose. 'And I was right! He didn't care about me or who *I* was. I want somebody who will care about me. Like Elizabeth Bennet. And I want my Mr Darcy.'

'Who?'

'Oh don't worry, Amina. When you get back to school Mr Clifford's bound to make you read *Pride and Prejudice*. It's a book about a white English family arranging marriages for their daughters. If you think it's only Indians who do that, you're wrong.'

'I suspect that they weren't marrying off their ten-year-old daughters though.'

'Well, no,' Sumati conceded. 'But the daughters wanted to fall in love – like I do. Choose someone when I am ready.'

'That's the important thing. When *you* are ready. Everybody cannot be ready at the same time – like cows that are ready for milking. Seriously, Sumati. They don't have feelings, nor do they fall in love with a bull, do they? I want to read this *Pride and Prejudice*. Will you ask Mr Clifford to lend it to me?'

'I'll tell him tomorrow. He'll know you're getting better if you want to read about Mr Darcy.' They both burst out in hysterics, bringing Devinia running upstairs. She peeked inside the bedroom, was reassured, then left again.

'It's the first time I've enjoyed myself so much in months.' Sumati sighed. 'And by the look on your mother's face just now, you haven't laughed for a long time either.'

'They're arguing a lot,' Amina whispered. 'I can't wait to go back to school. 'Something's changed, I know it has. I heard my father threatening to marry me off but my mother argued back. It looks like you and me are in the same boat. But our parents are not going to succeed. We mustn't let them. We must make a pact.'

'I'll go and get a blade and we'll join our blood.'

'Until we do, let's join fingers.' Amina picked up Sumati's hand.

The two friends linked their little fingers together and swore. 'Sisters forever,' they said in unison.

SEVEN

The boys from the village were bathing and talking at the standpipe one evening. Etwar, now as tall as his mother, and with the same green eyes, high cheekbones and strong jaw, glared at them. He was anxious about his sister, and they were talking about her.

'Some Standard Six boys were discussing you at the standpipe,' he said to Amina when he returned home. 'Rajnath Kamalsingh, Farouk Ali, and some others.'

'I don't know any Standard Six boys,' Amina snapped.

'Yes, you do. Some of them play cricket for the school team. And it's not the first time they asked about you either.'

Amina frowned. 'How would I know who plays cricket? I only knew there's a team because Mr Clifford mentions it in morning assembly when they've won.'

'What's wrong?' he asked. 'You're falling asleep.'

'Etwar, will you ask Ma if I could have some cocoa tea?'

'You're allowed that?'

'Dr Boyle said I could start having some sweeter drinks, so long as they're boiled and watery. And ask her if she could rub my head? I have a headache.'

'All right. By the way, your friend Sumati seems to know those boys well. Too well if you ask me, by the way she was strutting up to them by the standpipe.'

'Why are you saying that?'

'Ramona's mother was there. Meena. She called Sumati a bad name for swinging her hips so much that the water was falling out of the bucket on her head.'

'She doesn't like Sumati. But Sumati doesn't care what anybody thinks.'

'She's not like you at all then.'

'Just get Ma!' Annoyed, Amina yelled so loudly it made Etwar jump.

ஐ

The following day, Sumati called on Amina on her way to the standpipe.

'She's perkier today,' Devinia said. 'That laughing yesterday must have done her good. Go up and see her.'

Sumati pushed open the door and found Amina sitting bolt upright in bed.

'Mr Clifford sent this book for you,' Sumati told her. 'He said he'll come over.'

'William Wordsworth!' Amina exclaimed. 'I like poems.'

'You look better.' Sumati sat on the edge of the bed. 'Have you thought of a plan yet? I don't know what to do. I can't even think about having children of my own, let alone looking after somebody else's.'

'I can't get that out of my mind either,' Amina said. 'Where did they find this man?'

'Somewhere up near Port of Spain. It sounds good, but it's not.'

'Is he rich or something? Or is it that nobody round here knows him?'

'Both.'

'What about the grandparents? And the wife?'

'She died. Don't know about any grandparents.' Sumati looked round furtively at the doorway. 'I've something to tell you.' She breathed in deeply. 'I'm in love.'

'In love?' Amina gulped. 'How d'you know?'

'I just do.'

'So do you think you love this old man? Or his money? Strange, but that's your problem solved. What happened to our pact? That didn't last long, did it?'

'It's more complicated than that. That's not what I meant. I'm in love with a boy.'

'What boy?'

'Farouk Ali.'

'A Muslim?' Amina looked horrified. 'You are in so much trouble now. Does your father know this?'

'No! And my parents are not going to find out either.'

'Don't tell them then. It'll pass.'

'You mean like a cold?'

'Yes! Like a really bad cold. But I hope it doesn't turn into consumption!'

Sumati began to snigger nervously, which started them both laughing, so loudly that Devinia stopped sweeping the sand in the yard outside and looked up at her daughter's window, smiling properly for the first time in months.

'How do you know you're in love?' Amina asked curiously.

'My stomach starts to churn when I see him. Or even think about him – like now.

He's on the cricket team. He's got nice big hands and is good looking. Square-jawed. Straight white teeth. Remember him?'

Amina shrugged. 'You could be talking about any of the big boys in school. I never notice them.'

'Well, that's the difference between us. We're like *dahi* and sugar – sour and sweet.'

'I expect you're saying I am the sour one.'

'Or cocoa tea and condensed milk then.'

'And I'm the bitter one? Don't forget that *dahi* must have sugar to taste good, and cocoa tea is nothing without condensed milk.'

Devinia heard them talking and rushed upstairs with two bowlfuls of *dahi*. 'The cow's giving too much milk these days,' she said. 'It's good for your stomach.' She laid the bowls and spoons down on the chest and left the room again.

'You're allowed to eat *dahi*?' Sumati asked.

'No. The doctor said *boiled* milk, and the *dahi* milk is made with raw milk.'

'I'll eat both then,' Sumati said, already spooning the thick curds into her mouth.

'You're still keeping something from me,' Amina said. 'What is it?'

Sumati looked ready to explode. She shuffled close to Amina under the blanket, leg to leg, arm to arm, cheek to cheek.

'Promise me on your mother's life that you won't tell anybody,' she hissed.

'I promise.'

'Farouk wants me to meet him somewhere!'

'Sumati,' Amina said solemnly, 'promise me you won't do that. If somebody sees you, you will look like a bad girl. That is all it takes for people to call you a bad name.'

'I don't even have to do anything for Meena to call me that.'

'I heard. But if you meet Farouk, who knows where it will end? Please. I thought we made a pact to put a stop to this child marriage thing?'

'I'm not getting married. I only said he asked me to meet him.'

'Don't make our parents right about marrying us off so young. They're afraid we will bring shame on the family.'

'I'll never do that,' Sumati wheedled. 'Nobody will see us. I only want a bit of fun, that's all.'

'You have to think beyond a little bit of fun.'

'Gosh, listen to you!' Sumati said.

'What about fulfilment in your life?' Amina went on.

'Now you're sounding like old Clifford.'

'I don't care, Sumati. All our parents marry off their girl children, without thinking that the world has changed. We want the change. They can't see that even when it leads to tragedies such as Moonia's suicide, rape, beatings, and girls being crippled for life.'

'Amina, you are right. I said you had a good brain. That will be wasted if they marry you off. Your mother has a good brain too, but she didn't get a chance to use it.'

'My mother married my father when she was only five years old. He was twenty! She never even had the chance to go to school.'

'I don't want to end up like my mother,' Sumati said. 'Although she's not stupid either. But she does everything for us. Never herself. Pa comes home drunk and calls her the nastiest names. Says he will slash her face so no man will ever want her. Threatens to strangle her if a man even looks at her. It's so unfair. My mother is the kindest person

I know. I want to be like her – but not married to a man like my father.'

'You see? If we marry as children, we're following in our mothers' steps of disappointment rather than fulfilment.'

'I think, my friend, that you have a point. We will talk to the others at school.'

'But it has to start with you and me, Sumati. Why don't you tell Mr Clifford you're coming to evening classes? Show your parents what you really want instead of going home and cooking roti. It's only a few times a week. Show them you're serious about your future. And stick to it. Fulfilment, not disappointment. That has to be our plan. Mr Clifford will support us, and anybody else who wants to join evening classes.'

'So our plan is to stay at school?'

'More than that. We can start the Pupil Teachers Certificate. That *is* the plan, Sumati. Now where is that blade? We have to mix our blood together on this.'

'Next time,' Sumati said. 'I'll bring a blade next time.'

'Don't forget it. It's important.'

EIGHT

Mr Clifford arrived at Amina's some days later, with a book in his hand.

'Good afternoon, Mrs Banderjee,' he called out in his headmaster's voice. 'And how are you all doing? I mean, all of you, not just the sick one. I gather she is recovering, but it must have been quite an ordeal. That child is lucky – the good Lord must surely be looking down on her. Typhoid is no mosquito bite. Now I'm not stopping long. Just a quick lunchtime stroll.'

Devinia jumped up from the hammock where she was sitting picking stones out of the rice before cooking, flustered and unsure which question or statement to answer. She pulled her *ohrini* over her head and tucked it behind her ears.

'Good morning, sir,' she said. 'Please sit down. Let me bring you something to drink.'

'I wouldn't say no,' he said, planting himself on the bench across from the hammock. He pulled out a grey, crumpled handkerchief from his pocket and wiped the beads of perspiration from his face. 'Just a cup of cool water. The midday sun is so hot!'

Devinia returned with a cup of coconut water and a piece of pawpaw.

'This is a treat. I haven't had a coconut water in weeks.' He looked up. 'I see your pawpaw tree is laden. Mrs Banderjee, I came to bring Amina a book. I'm hoping she will be back in school soon. Tell her she mustn't worry. She'll catch up quickly. She has a fine future ahead of her if she puts her mind to it. The good thing is, she likes learning. I'm pleased you care enough to send her to school. Some just keep their daughters home to plant rice and mind children. Education is a great opportunity these days. I have faith in Amina. She's a joy to teach.'

'Something has changed in her though,' Devinia blurted.

'I know.' He chuckled. 'She sent me a letter asking me about the universe.'

Devinia looked alarmed. 'I didn't know she was writing letters to you too.'

'Also, *How far are we from the moon?* I have read a lot but I am not sure if anybody knows. She even asked me if the Christian God lives in the sun, and whether I've seen Him!'

'Christian God?' Devinia grew pale. 'Something happened to her on that day. . . inside her head. It was as if she lost her senses.'

Mr Clifford continued talking and Devinia's anxiety turned into admiration. She marvelled at his passion. For things he said he didn't know about, he certainly knew a lot. Things so remote to her.

'Mr Clifford?' Amina said, appearing on the steps outside the house.

'There she is,' he beamed. 'Best pupil in the school. We miss you.'

Devinia smiled for the first time since he had arrived, her face having been stuck solid in concentration.

'Good afternoon, sir,' the girl said. 'I thought I was dreaming, but you're really here.'

'I brought the Austen book you asked for – *Pride and Prejudice*. Sumati told me. But she's not been at school all week, otherwise I'd have sent it with her.'

Devinia left them talking, until he left. Then she questioned Amina about the letters she had sent to Mr Clifford, now even more worried about her daughter's state of mind.

ඍ

Just before the August holidays, Dr Boyle visited and pronounced Amina's boredom to be a sign that she had almost recovered, and could return to school. But she should still take care with her eating for a few months yet and not handle other people's food, or be tempted to go down to the spring for water, or even to bathe there, he decreed. The family was overjoyed, but it reminded Devinia that she needed to teach Amina to cook like other girls of marriageable age.

When Mr Clifford heard the good news, he suggested she return to school at least for the last week of the term, but Devinia preferred to be cautious. So instead he brought books and writing exercises for Amina to do during the holidays. Devinia sat and listened to him talk about the importance of an education and the new opportunity for girls getting free schooling till sixteen. He also talked about his own difficult start in life, and how his mother suffered, which intrigued Devinia.

'Your daughter has a good brain,' he told her. 'It would be wrong to waste it. The trouble with an idle brain is that when it is given too much time without occupation, it thinks up nonsense. Amina needs to read, to feed the beast inside her head that is hungry to learn.'

'I worry something's already happened inside her head.' Amina had gone, and Devinia spoke very quietly. 'Maybe you know something about this, sir? You know a lot. People don't normally come back from the dead. Sometimes she talks so strangely, as if. . . We Hindus say that when you come back, it is as something else, depending on how you lived your life. I don't know how far over she went to the other side before she came back.'

'Don't cry, my dear. She is a real gift to you. What matters is that she is on this side now.'

Devinia looked at him, hesitating. 'But what does your Christian religion say? That you go to heaven? She's praying to your God now.'

'Well! We follow Jesus. And he raised Jairus's daughter from the dead. And Lazarus too. He brought them back to this life. Those were miracles. If the dead were going to heaven, I am not sure why Jesus brought them back here. Maybe God has a purpose with your daughter.'

Devinia was mesmerised. The way he spoke, it sounded as if he knew this Jesus man well. She stared at him in awe. Mr Clifford was possibly the wisest man she had ever spoken to, and knew things she'd never even heard of.

'You have children?' she asked.

'I have a school full of children. I consider them as I would my own.'

'Most people are too poor to scrape a daily living. That's why they take their children out of school and send them to work in the cane fields as soon as they are old enough – from eight years old.'

'I know,' he said. 'Many cannot afford shoes and clothes. But that doesn't stop me teaching them.'

'We Indians sometimes survive on our dreams. People dream of having their own plot of land to build a house. We save up penny by penny.'

'Some are lucky enough to inherit land from their parents who bought it cheaply from the government in exchange for their free passage back to India after their five years of working here. My mother and I didn't have that opportunity. My dream was different.'

'You're right. I was lucky. My husband built up his business from nothing. But many have nothing but their dreams. That is why it's impossible for Indians to become like you. Except . . . Amina wants to be like you. It will break her heart but it will never come true. She will be disappointed, but she will realise that some things are just dreams.'

'You don't know that, Mrs Banderjee. Your daughter has more than a dream. She has the potential, and the opportunity. I need to get back to work. Thank you for the refreshment, Mrs Banderjee. Now, I expect to see Amina in school in September, so that she may fulfil that dream. Make sure she is there.'

When Mr Clifford left, Devinia sat back in her hammock and wondered what made him so sure. She wanted to believe him, even though Sankar could never take these things seriously. But she wanted her daughter to shine in the world, and the only person who seemed to have that confidence in Amina, was Mr Clifford.

NINE

Monday 3rd September 1917. The first day of the new school year was a stark reminder to Amina that everything was not as rosy as she had remembered. She had lost so much time. Unable to contemplate waiting another two years to start the Pupil Teaching Programme, she planned to talk to Mr Clifford during the morning break about it. Still frail, she almost fell over in the stampede when the bell rang, as children ran into the lines in front of the school. When Mr Clifford's smiling face appeared in the double doors, her eyes welled up. Soon she was sitting in a familiar four-seater desk, with Mr Mortimer mispronouncing the children's names as usual during roll-call.

History was the first subject of the day, with the topic of the discovery of the West Indies by Christopher Columbus. This was followed by spelling, then arithmetic. Amina went home for lunch and was almost too tired to return, but she did. She enjoyed reading, penmanship, and English grammar, but when the bell went at three o'clock at the end of the school day, she was exhausted. She walked home with friends, and Etwar caught up with them halfway home. When they got to the top of their yard, brother and sister looked at each other in surprise.

'Can you smell that?' Etwar said. 'Smells like Christmas.'

'You think we have family visiting? Maybe Ma's relations from Dutch Guiana have come at last! Ma was telling me about them last week.'

'But they're in South America.'

'It's not impossible,' Amina said. 'People come over through British Guiana, then to Venezuela, then take a boat and sail across to Icacos.'

'How is that possible?'

'It's only about seven miles from Venezuela to Icacos. Then they could get a horse and cart, or a donkey cart to Granville.'

'Ma says you keep making up things in your head. Are you?'

'No, I'm not. It's true. People do come over on fishing boats.'

'Race you!' he said, and he was off down the yard.

She took off after him and they both ran down the path, sniffing the air like wolves. Etwar got to the kitchen two inches short of his mother's back, almost knocking her over. Devinia was busily rolling out flat rounds of dough and filling them with the seasoned, ground dhal. The aroma of dhalpuri toasting on the iron *tawa*, smeared with fresh coconut oil, hit the hunger nerve. A pile of hot dhalpuris wrapped in a cloth smelt good. They watched mesmerized as Devinia's long, nimble fingers flitted from *tawa* to pot, and pot to the floured board. When she removed the lid, the iron pot belched out a pungent haze of mouth-watering vapours, making the youngsters ravenous. Toasted cumin and garlic, mixed with the parched dhal, filled the air. It could only mean one thing.

'What are you cooking, Ma?' Etwar said, his eyes popping out on stalks like a crab's.

'Chicken curry and dhalpuri.'

'Why?'

She stirred the pot with a gravity that didn't escape them. 'Change into your home clothes and go and bring the cow from the pasture,' she requested. 'Quick as you can. Your father's coming home early. There's something we have to tell you.'

'I'm starving, Ma,' Amina said, as she turned to go upstairs to change into home clothes.

'Your father said he'll bring those rose earrings you wanted him to make.'

'I forgot about them,' Amina said. 'School was good, Ma. Aren't you interested? I don't ever want to miss another day.'

'You need to learn to cook,' was all Devinia said. 'You are a girl, and you still cannot cook. I want you to help me.'

'But the doctor says I must not touch anybody's food.'

'You're better now. Scrub your hands first.'

ဃ

By five-thirty that afternoon the family had finished eating.

'Did you cook this because Amina is better now?' Etwar asked, licking his fingers. 'Will you do it again tomorrow?'

'You can have too much of a good thing,' Sankar said. He took a deep breath. 'Your mother is an excellent cook.'

He wriggled uncomfortably, his normally flat belly a round bulge. He got to his feet, his body straight and Gandhi-thin, and gripped the back of his waist with both his hands.

'It was really nice chicken,' Amina said. 'But I ate too much.'

'Time to put on some weight,' Devinia said. 'The doctor says you can eat as normal.'

'What is it, Pa?' Etwar said. 'Is something wrong?'

'Ma said you were bringing me the rose earrings you promised,' Amina put in.

'Yes,' Sankar said. He sat down again. 'They're in my trouser pocket upstairs.'

'Have you bought another house, Pa?' Etwar asked.

'We can only live in one,' Amina replied, looking sickened. 'Some don't have a roof over their heads.'

'People live in Pa's houses and pay rent,' Etwar interrupted. 'That gives them somewhere to live.'

Sankar nodded. 'At least you have a business head on you, son. But you, my sweet, we have to look after you, what with your illness and what it has done to you. I have some good news. Your mother and I have found you a match.'

Amina's face fell. She stared at her mother, unable to breathe. Then Sankar began to explain what he had been doing that day, and the decisions he and Devinia took that morning.

'They live in San Fernando. It is a good family. They have a big business and the boy is extremely well-schooled. He's a very nice-looking boy too. Healthy and strong. They want to come and meet you as soon as possible. You can marry whenever you want inside this year but make it quick. That will be good for both them and us. The father was here this morning. We gave our word before he left. He is a busy man like I am. Both of us in business.' Sankar looked very pleased with himself.

'That is how it all happened,' Devinia joined in. 'It gave me enough time to catch a chicken from the yard. But the chicken kept flying away . . .'

Amina sat still, looking at her mother's mouth moving and at the words falling out of her lips. While she had been at school learning about Christopher Columbus setting sail on the *Santa Maria*, accompanied by two sister ships, the *Pinta* and the *Nina*, in search of gold and discovering the Caribbean islands, her parents had not just promised her to some strange man without her knowledge, but her mother had also managed to catch a flying chicken from the yard, wring its neck, pluck it, gut it, chop it up into small pieces, grind the masala, season it, and cook it by the time they returned home from school. That was a job that normally took the best part of two days. Making dhalpuri was no small task either.

'Well, say something, girl,' her father prompted. 'At least show some gratitude for your mother's hard work.'

'What can I say, Pa?' Amina said. 'You want me to show gratitude for you ruining my life? First you break your promise to me, and then you promise me to some stranger for the rest of my life, as if I am a bag of rice. Well I can't be grateful for that.'

Sankar's mouth fell open. 'Did you want to have a husband who works like a black slave in the cane field, with no prospects but to get beaten by the overseer? Have you any idea what that life is like? Look around you. You live like a queen in comparison.' He appealed to Devinia. 'Tell your daughter, woman. She is most ungrateful!'

'How would you know about those hardships, Pa?'

'I know because I too came on one of those blasted ships from Kolkata as human cargo. They lied and told us we would have a good life, making plenty of money sifting sugar. It was a trick. I tried it, and it was hard. Good thing I had a trade already from India and eventually I found a way to set up my jewellery business. Lucky for all of us, eh!' He stabbed a finger at his daughter. 'Very lucky you can live like a princess and now you think you can make your own choice. At your age – a girl-child.'

'I *can* make my own choice, Pa. You promised me. What will the gods say about you breaking your promise?'

'It has nothing to do with gods,' Sankar said. 'What can they say? They spoke to you so far?'

Amina looked at her mother and half-smiled. 'They don't speak, they don't hear, don't smell, don't feel. They do nothing. They have no life.'

'Don't say that, child,' Devinia said.

'Listen,' Sankar said. 'We made a promise to these people, and we are keeping it.'

Amina shot forward and slapped a mosquito that had taken a mouthful of blood from her ankle. 'Explain why this is good for me,' she said. 'Because I have a plan. I do not want an arranged marriage. I am twelve years old. I don't want to end up so unhappy that I drink weed-killer like Moonia or have a baby like Chandrawatti. And as you say, Pa, a promise is a promise. You cannot break your promise to me.'

Sankar stared at her. 'You think you are smart?'

'Maybe you should meet him, Amina,' Etwar said, trying to calm the atmosphere.

'Etwar, don't you take their side. He sounds like a half-brained idiot to agree to this. You say he's well-schooled?

I don't believe it. My parents are no different from all the other stupid Granville *coolie* parents. All in a hurry to get their daughters married off, no matter what the consequences or the disappointment. They will do it again and again, mastering the art of disappointment. No! Mr Clifford told Ma and Pa that I could have a good future, but they don't care. You see, I have a brain in my head and they cannot take that from me!'

Etwar whistled in awe – in awe of the lioness who was seated next to him. But Sankar was fuming. He jumped up, grabbed Amina by her arm and dragged her to her feet.

'That is all the gratitude you have?' he accused. 'After all we have done for you? You know you nearly died? And your mother was the one who cried blood to keep you alive. Running up and down doing everything for you? Doing pujas. Getting the doctor three times a week. Cleaning your backside when you couldn't even move. And now you show such disrespect. Where did you learn this evil thing?'

'Let me go.' Amina yanked her arm away. 'Evil thing? I was leaving this world. It was angels who brought me back. Not you, or Ma, or Hannuman, or Ram.'

Three pairs of eyes full of horror landed on her. Devinia touched Amina's neck.

'She's feeling a little bit hot,' Devinia said.

'A little bit hot?' Sankar repeated, furious. 'I will give her plenty of hot! Etwar, go and cut some sticks.'

Devinia looked at Sankar, shocked. 'No! You will not beat her.'

'There's always a first time!' Sankar snarled. 'Her insolence has gone too far.'

'No!' Devinia yelled. 'Over my dead body will you touch my child.'

Etwar didn't move. None of this was normal. Amina was the peaceful one, quiet and obedient. And this upheaval had started with just a few words. 'Wait,' he said. 'What did you promise her?'

'You think I care if you beat me?' Amina shouted, interrupting him. 'You want me to get married to some fool in San Fernando? And you want to beat me too? Well I'm not moving. Go on – beat me.'

Devinia pleaded, 'You have upset your father, beti. The boy is a good match.'

'You broke your promise, Ma,' Amina said, bitterly. 'I don't know how you can even look me in the eye.'

'You made your mother promise without talking to me?' Sankar shouted. 'You're spoilt rotten – but no more! The next piece of jewellery you have will be for your wedding. The one I made and brought for you today, you will only have it when you start behaving like a daughter. And start learning how to do things in the house.' He looked at his wife reproachfully. 'The girl is useless! Teach her to cook and wash, and mind house. Unless you want me to take her out of school tomorrow.'

'No!' Devinia said. 'I will teach her after school. Let her stay.'

'Mind you do it now,' Sankar threatened. 'She will be married this side of the year.'

'I am not getting married to anybody, good-looking or looking like a dog!' Amina screeched. At this, Fluffy, her dog, jumped up and started to bark.

'She's mad,' Sankar said to his wife. 'She must be coming up for her monthly bleeding to start – and you know what that means. We have to do it, whether she likes it or not.'

'Your father is right. If you start your bleeding in this house, we'll have more bad luck, and I wouldn't be able to bear it. I shouldn't have promised you.'

Devinia sat crumpled up in the hammock in tears, babbling on about the bad luck they'd already had that year, and how she'd been wrong to promise Amina she could continue at school. And she was to blame for Amina believing she could become a teacher, when she knew it was impossible for a woman to get a teaching job, let alone an Indian woman.

'Didn't I say you are a fool to put your trust in any headmaster!' Sankar was livid.

'But it's the headmaster who knows everything,' Amina replied equally angrily. 'He's the one teaching things about the world that you yourself know nothing about.'

'And he's teaching you this kind of disrespect for your parents? Is that because we are *coolies*?' Sankar's teeth were clenched so tight, that the words were barely escaping. 'And you expect me to keep sending you there?'

'It's no good talking back to your father like that,' Devinia whimpered. 'He cares for you. You have gone this far because I didn't teach you about our traditions.'

'There is no hope for us Indians in this place,' Sankar said. 'The white man has tricked us, bringing us to this slave country where the black workers would slave no more. We are the new slaves. Nothing to do with what kind of hair we have – straight or curly. It's about working for the white man in the cane fields for a pittance, living worse than dogs, and not even a sick man has the right to take to his bed for a few hours without getting thrown in jail for malingering. Whether you can see that or not,' he glared at Amina, 'I am not letting my own daughter fall into that trap. It has to be the Indian way!'

'You're not seeing that education is the only way out of that trap?' Amina said, looking directly into her father's eyes. 'Let me show you, Pa. Let me do it my way.'

'No!' Sankar yelled. 'It must be the Indian way for *dharma* to protect you. Thousands of years of tradition are not to be sneezed at and wiped away on your sleeve. We all have a part to play in this world. Parents have a duty, and children have theirs. Give us the room to do our duty and not disrupt the whole of the universe. Then *karma* will pay you good rewards. Let that be the end of it. But let me ask you this. Do you see your mother sitting down and reading storybooks instead of cooking, or sweeping the yard, or planting the rice and milking the cow? Eh? You take it all for granted! All we ask is that you obey us, and keep the traditions. That way, dharma will keep working for us. How is it that with all these books you're reading you cannot understand such a simple thing? We have a wedding to prepare for within the next twelve months, and we have a lot to do.'

'You had better go and bathe and get ready for bed,' Devinia said. 'I'll light a lamp and bring it up.'

Exhausted, Amina turned and left them, defaulting to obedience, a habit learnt since her illness, and a necessity if she was to ever recover. She went to the bathroom at the back of the house and had a cold bath that night. There was no pot of boiling water waiting for her, no special treatment. As she bathed, something strange began to happen inside her, like a bird fluttering, battering itself against the walls to escape.

༄

That night when she was almost asleep, she relived a memory of wading in the breaking waves at four years old, with her father and mother, who stood in their rolled-up trousers and hitched-up skirt. She had felt safe standing between them, before a stronger wave rose and broke, tearing her from their grip and throwing her face down in the salty foam, and dragging her completely under the sandy, soapy wash. She had felt her body rise and fall with the power of the sea, stones settling under her chest, forcing out the air; a sensation distancing her from reality, like the day that drew her into the tunnel of light. But she had survived then, and she would survive now. Her inner strength would see her through.

TEN

Amina woke at dawn the next day gasping for air. Her bedroom felt like a jail, dark and hostile. She went outside and washed in water from the barrel, cooled by the darkness of the moon, then flew upstairs to dress. Her mother appeared at the door, her eyes red and swollen.

'Wait for food. And your brother,' she said.

'I'm meeting Sumati for breakfast today. She invited me to her house.'

Amina hated to lie, but she hated the confinement of the home even more, and the dependence that had bonded her to her mother since her illness. She was determined to change all that. The girl hurried off shivering, through the haze of pink light strewn across the sandy path up the side of the house. A cat crossed her path. The gravel road was quiet apart from dogs barking at each other between yards. The dappled sunlight lit her face when she spotted Meena, Ramona's mother, walking up to the standpipe with a bundle of washing. She smiled at Amina.

'You have a face full of sunlight jewels,' Meena said.

Amina gasped in surprise. Meena was usually as bitter as a mouthful of seawater. She no doubt was being kind because of the typhoid, the girl told herself as she hurried down to Sumati's house to ask for a blade. There was something they had to do.

༄

Sumati spotted Amina from the open window through the leaves of the hog-plum tree at the front of the house.

'Come down to the beach with me,' Amina called up to her in a low voice. 'And bring a knife with you.'

'Girl, that sounds like my kind of day,' Sumati said, beaming. 'No school.'

'It's just for a walk. Not all day. And hurry.'

Sumati disappeared for a few minutes before returning outside, dressed and with her hair in one long thick plait.

The girls hastened out of the yard, treading cautiously to avoid snapping the dry twigs. As soon as they were on the road and out of earshot, the two friends spoke at the same time.

'How come you're up so early?' they asked each other, almost together.

Sumati answered first. 'I couldn't sleep for thinking about Farouk. If my father finds out, he'll kill me.'

'Oh, Sumati! What's going to happen to us? I want to run away from here.'

'Why? Are you in love too?'

'No, far from it! They've found me some stupid boy. Rich, they say. They don't know me at all.'

'At least they're thinking about your life. Being poor is not what anybody dreams of – except you,' Sumati teased her.

'Do you think that being a teacher will make me poor? I thought we had a pact.'

'We do. But that doesn't mean we have to do the same thing, Amina. We will always be friends.'

'Always. You are my sister. Almost. Where's the knife? I hope it's sharp.'

They sat down on the log of a fallen tree, cut the flesh of both their left thumbs and joined the blood that oozed out, looking at each other with pain in their eyes.

'Hold it tight,' Sumati said. 'Till it stops bleeding.'

Amina started to cry. 'It's horrible. My parents lied to me. How can I ever trust them again? My father doesn't care about me at all.'

'Mine only cares about himself – and how to get rid of me as fast as possible,' Sumati said, gloomily.

'He threatened to beat me last night.'

'What? I always thought he was different. Just goes to show how you never really know people.'

'I should've died. I wish I had now.' Amina wiped away her tears.

'Maybe you should ask to meet the boy. At least it will show them you're trying to see things from their side,' Sumati suggested tentatively.

'You think? I don't want to give them the wrong idea.'

'It will buy you some time.'

'I need to talk to Mr Clifford, and do the evening classes. But I can't tell them. What about you?'

'I told you. I'm in love.'

'Maybe you should talk to your mother about how you feel about Farouk. Your mother will most likely understand. Or you could just come to evening classes and we could go into teaching together.'

'Or we could just spend the day down by the beach.'

'As much as I want to, today is just my second day back at school.'

The girls turned around and walked, dragging their heels and kicking at the weeds that grew out of the white sand at the sides of the road. They reached up and picked a few Portugals from the low branches, then peeled and ate the small oranges as they strolled. Children overtook them, barefoot on the sharp gravel but in uniform. Others clip-clopped in wooden sappats, laughing as they went by.

'I think you should talk to your mother instead of your father,' Sumati said. 'She will understand. You're bright and you don't like boys. Not like me. I've liked boys since I was eleven.'

ꕥ

As they reached the school gates, the bell rang, and everyone ran in line.

'Amina!' Sumati whispered loudly. 'I'd marry him if he asked me!'

'QUIET IN THE LINES!' Mr Mortimer, their class teacher, bellowed behind them.

Sumati jumped. Both girls straightened themselves to attention.

'I don't know what some of you are doing in school,' he continued, scowling at Sumati before he strode off to the front of the assembly, waving his whip and lashing the fabric of his trouser leg.

'Who does he think he is?' Sumati muttered in Bhojpuri, their Hindi dialect.

Amina fixed her with a stare, willing her to stop.

'I am not afraid of him,' Sumati continued in English, and in a pitch loud enough for Mr Mortimer to turn and look at her.

The lines began moving, and Sumati hissed to her friend, 'Look! That's Farouk, in the Standard Six line. But he might be leaving soon. Like Rajnath, the one that Mr Clifford forced to leave last term, because he got into trouble with Mortimer a few times. Then *he* got put to teach our class. Yes, Mortimer got his match with Rajnath.' She grinned.

Amina had no idea who Rajnath was, and wasn't going to ask, because she noticed that Mr Mortimer had his eyes on both of them. As they reached the entrance of the class space, the teacher suddenly pulled Sumati from the line and shoved her against the wall, and Amina had a sudden flash of memory about school life at its worst.

'Get to your seats, the rest of you!' he yelled, his large hand still across the top of Sumati's chest.

The lines moved slowly, children hovering, watching while Mortimer switched his hand from Sumati's neck to the top of her arm and spun her round to face the wall. He pressed his hand between her shoulder-blades, at the same time pulling her skirt high and showing the hem of her pink drawers. He then began striking the girl across the tops of both legs with his fat whip.

Sumati bit her bottom lip hard and didn't utter a sound. It wasn't until the fourth slash against her skin in the exact same place that a grunt escaped her lips. After that she began squealing like a pig getting its throat slit before

Saturday-morning market. The line trickling inside the school building slowed to a halt, to watch. A beating was not uncommon, but it was unusual for one of the older girls to be punished this way.

'Somebody help!' Sumati cried. But no one interfered. The noise didn't stop. Amina unfroze and flew at Mortimer.

'Stop!' she yelled, tugging at his arm as it rose to deliver another blow. 'A big man like you? Shame on you!'

'Move out of my way, girl!' He pushed Amina so hard she went flying and knocked her head against the doorpost. Then he wrestled Sumati towards the classroom, shooing everyone else inside.

'Shame on you!' Amina repeated, almost in tears.

'Just don't *you* put a foot out of place,' Mortimer threatened, sneering down at her. 'Or you'll get a dose of the same medicine.'

Sumati limped to her desk, and lowered herself onto one of the wooden benches, her face twisted with pain. Amina was shaking so much that she could barely sit herself. When lessons started, Sumati shuffled uncomfortably, sitting on her hands most of the time. At one point, when Mr Mortimer had his back turned to the blackboard, she got up and left school well before morning break.

ꟸ

At break-time, Amina and her friends collected outside, subdued and incensed.

'Sumati's gone home,' Pryia began.

'I don't blame her,' Chandra said. 'Who does he think he is?'

'That's right!' Ramona exclaimed, nostrils flared. 'Although, some people say she looked for it, talking in line.'

'What people?' Amina demanded, furiously.

'Some people like Meena, your mother, Ramona,' Pryia said to Ramona. 'She doesn't like Sumati, does she?'

'Sumati didn't deserve that,' Amina said, hotly. 'Talking in line or not.'

'No, but that's what he did to Rajnath Kamalsingh,' Chandra said. 'That's why he left – because he wasn't going to take it.'

'I heard he had some kind of quarrel with Mortimer,' Pryia added.

'Who is this Rajnath?' Amina asked. 'Is that the big boy who was always getting in trouble? Always in the headmaster's office?'

'Yes,' Chandra replied, nodding. 'And he was the cricket captain too. He always seemed to be in trouble, but it's because he wouldn't stand for people hitting him up.'

'My mother says Sumati is the kind that will get everybody in trouble,' Ramona said, sombrely. 'Ma doesn't like me having much to do with her. But that's hard when she lives next door.'

'Do you think we should go and say something to Mr Clifford?' Pryia asked.

'What for?' Ramona asked. 'He won't care. He's a black man too, like Mortimer.'

'Mr Clifford's not like that,' Amina said, defending him. 'He's fair. He cares. And Mortimer pushed me so hard, I've a lump in the back of my head. Just when I'm getting better.'

The girls decided that somebody ought to tell Mr Clifford, and Amina volunteered. Just before the bell rang, Farouk went to ask Amina about the incident between Mortimer and Sumati. She told him what had happened, and asked him if he would go to see Mr Clifford with her.

'And what good will that do?' Farouk said. 'Rajnath was my friend, and felt he was man enough to take on Mortimer, but look where it got him! Clifford made him leave. He told Rajnath it was best he got a job, seeing as he didn't value education. He wouldn't believe Rajnath. Even though he was our main man for cricket.' He wiped his eyes, upset at hearing what had happened to Sumati earlier. He was angry. 'If I do something, it will get me in trouble – and everybody else around me,' he said bitterly. 'Believe me!'

'Well, I am going to see Mr Clifford at lunchtime,' Amina said obstinately. 'Somebody's got to have the guts to do something.'

ஜ

Mr Clifford was in his office eating his lunch and reading a book when Amina appeared.

'Glad to see you back at school,' he said. 'Any worries, come and see me.'

'Sir, I do have a worry. I'm not comfortable about what happened in class this morning.'

'That? My dear girl, I will not tolerate insolence towards teachers.'

'I was there, sir. There was no insolence.'

'Is that so? I'll have to talk to Mr Mortimer. Get his side.'

'Sir, I want you to know nothing happened to provoke him. He just flew at her.'

'Hmm. Still, I have to hear his side of the story. The girl in question . . . '

'Sumati Balgobin. She likes school, sir. It's her parents who are trying to get her married.'

'Maybe. But she was absent a number of days lately.'

'But I'm telling you why, sir,' Amina pleaded.

'All right. I'll look into it.'

The rest of the lunchtime, the girls talked but worried about Sumati, how much they hated boys in general, teachers, fathers, history, geography, and the advantages and disadvantages of learning Sanskrit and reading English novels. Early marriage had the edge when compared to the boredom some felt at school. But not for all.

While they were talking, Farouk turned up and handed Amina a piece of paper tied round with brown string, with Sumati's name written on it.

'Make sure you give this to Sumati as soon as you see her,' he said, and walked off.

Amina took it – a risky act if either were caught. She put it in her pocket before she could think, and hoped no one had seen her taking a note from a boy. Especially Etwar. If her parents found out, she was sure to be in even more trouble. She wondered whether to return to see Mr Clifford, but it had been a long day and she was worn out with a sore head. She decided the next day would be better.

ELEVEN

Roopchand, Sumati's father, arrived at the school around half past nine the following morning, smelling like a rum distillery. He stopped when he saw two of the older girls outside at the drinking taps.

'Where he? That modderarse teacher-man what touch up my daughter!' His voice grated as if he'd chewed gravel half the night. 'Sumati's teacher? Sumati Balgobin. My daughter.'

'That's Mr Mortimer,' one of the girls replied, pointing. 'His class is just down there.' Roopchand Balgobin stomped towards the classroom. His voice and presence drew the attention of those inside, and all eyes turned to him. Teachers were looking anxious. Mr Mortimer had already dropped his chalk and started briskly walking towards a quick exit from the back. But he headed straight into Roopchand, who had already spotted him and was powering ahead.

'You are Mortimer?' Roopchand demanded.

Mr Mortimer half-nodded.

'Who-who-who do you tink you is?' Roopchand couldn't stutter fast enough. 'Touching up my daughter. . . in the backside. Who tell you that you could do that?'

'I don't know what Sumati came home and told you, Mr, but . . .' Mr Mortimer began. He looked round at the class of pupils who were all gaping at them, open-mouthed.

'Ask the class,' he said.

'If you wanted my daughter, you should have had the manners to ask me first. You black people have no respect for the coolie man?'

'Mr Balgobin,' Mr Mortimer said, smiling in a superior manner. 'I don't know why you think I want your daughter in that way. And I didn't touch her anywhere private.'

'So tell me where you did touch her,' Roopchand asked, his voice a tad calmer.

'She was giving me a lot of lip, and I punished her. That's all.'

'Punished her – that's all?' the man mimicked. 'You lift up my daughter skirt to punish her? What make it right for a man-teacher to lift up a girl's dress in school? If my daughter needs to be whipped in the backside, that is my job. You understand?'

'You want to go and see the headmaster?' Mr Mortimer asked.

Amina stood up. 'Mr Clifford said he didn't agree with it. He said he would . . .'

'You went to the headmaster?' Mr Mortimer glared at Amina fiercely. 'I should have given you a good whipping too! You won't get away with it, I promise you.'

There was a sudden hush across the whole school. Mr Clifford was marching towards them through Standard Four class.

'What seems to be going on here?' the headmaster asked tersely, his eyes piercing.

'My daughter is going to get married and Teacherman here. . . he gave she a good whipping. Who will want she now? He really hurt her badly!'

'I don't think it happened quite like that,' Mr Clifford replied, with dignity.

'Putting my daughter's backside on show for the whole school to see, is all right with you? My daughter is a woman, by all rights. And besides, he damaged her body black and blue all over! Legs, back, arms . . . He beat my daughter like a jackass!'

'He lyin'! De man lyin'.' Mr Mortimer was screaming in colloquial language now, sucking his teeth loudly, his eyes fierce and wide. 'He come to make trouble. De man drunk. Smell the liquor on 'im!'

'Mr Mortimer?' Mr Clifford said. 'Please go and wait in my office. Now.'

The headmaster used a restrained tone, but his nostrils flared, and his expression was dark with suppressed rage. Mr Mortimer walked off, shrugging his shoulders and swinging his arms carelessly. Mr Clifford put his hand out to Mr Balgobin, but Roopchand did not respond. The headmaster kept his hand out, waiting till the other man stuck his hand out awkwardly and allowed Mr Clifford to take it, and to shake it vigorously.

'I am the headmaster here at Granville RC School, and I want you to know that I am aware that something occurred, but I have not yet gotten to the bottom of the matter,' Mr Clifford told him. I promise you, though, that I will. You say Sumati is getting married? When exactly? Please come.'

Mr Clifford led Roopchand away from the classroom and the two men disappeared outside. As soon as they left, the babble started and rose through the open-air school, so that no one could hear the teachers bellowing at the pupils to be quiet.

Mr Clifford reappeared ten minutes later. 'Standard Five!' he roared. 'Open your books and read. Amina, I want you to sit in front of the class until I come back. And if I hear a whisper from any of you . . .' He scanned the whole class with his steely eyes, 'I will thrash you myself and see which one of your parents will come for *me*!'

TWELVE

There was a noise in the back yard in the middle of the night. Sankar Banderjee got up and stumbled towards the bedroom window. He opened it and peered out.

'It's me, Daya,' a voice called up softly. 'Your neighbour. Is Sumati here?'

'Why would your daughter be here?' Sankar said, turning to Devinia. 'Is Sumati in the house? Her mother is looking for her.'

Devinia called out through the house, but Amina was already awake and came running across to her parents' bedroom.

'She was really upset yesterday in school,' Amina said.

'Yes, the teacher whipped her,' Etwar said. 'He really hurt her. And he did it in front of the whole school.'

'She must be with some other friend,' Sankar shouted out of the window. 'You want Devinia to go and help you look?'

'No,' Daya replied. 'We already went to everybody we could think of.'

'Leave it till light,' Sankar advised. 'She's probably staying with a friend.'

Daya Balgobin returned home. She sat in the hammock watching, waiting and listening. Dawn came. She stared through the branches at the birds noisily breakfasting, her eyes wet with worry. Then she pulled the blanket over her legs and closed her eyes until the wheels of the first donkey cart rolled past, taking chattering workmen to the cane fields. She got up and looked out just in case, then decided to start the day. As she returned from the bathroom to the kitchen to cook, she felt drained. Amongst the thoughts spinning in her head, not one brought a glimmer of hope. She would never wish ill on her child, but it could be the one time when a dead child would be a blessing compared to the fate that could befall them both. Roopchand, her husband, had vowed to kill her if Sumati ever brought shame on them. But Daya buried those thoughts.

The sun rose and shone through the kitchen onto her glowing face, freshly scrubbed almost raw with the loofah. She kneaded the flour with tears for her fate in life. In a way, her daughter was an extension of herself. A projection of who she might have been. Sumati was pretty, and had inherited her own good looks. But Daya was a modest woman, who never saw beauty in herself. Never saw the smile that lit her face, or the gleam on her lime-washed hair. It grieved her that Sumati's looks brought abuse from the neighbours, especially Meena, who never spared her a single one of her mean thoughts. Meena should know better, with a daughter of her own. A growing girl who was losing her pimples and developing breasts that showed through layers of a chemise and a cotton dress. But it wasn't just her neighbour Daya would have to endure.

Unless he was true to his word and killed her, Roopchand would torment her forever with threats and misery till she could take no more. Daya held her head high. She was a respectful woman and wife, who would never respond with argument. She balled the dough and covered it with a cloth. With her skin burning and hair still dripping, Daya prepared herself to pray. She poured some oil in a tiny clay pot around the wick, lit it, and took it to the corner of the room where she sat in front of the picture of Lakshmi Mata. And it wasn't long before she heard footsteps she recognised, coming down the side of the house.

'Ma!' A sudden whisper behind her. 'You cook yet?'

Daya's eyes remained closed, focused on her prayer. Her heart calmed on hearing the familiar voice. When she was finished, she returned to the kitchen and back to her daily routine, to cook for the day, but wondering how to talk to Sumati. She needed to explain to the girl about the kind of trouble she had brought upon herself, her mother, and the whole family. Daya wondered why she had never before felt the need to be explicit about the curse that would be upon them if Sumati ever spent the night out without them knowing where she was. Now she tried to imagine any innocent cause – but realised that the scenario facing her could only mean the worst. So Daya didn't want to know. She said nothing.

'I was over at Amina's house,' Sumati said. Her voice rang out the lie as clear as a bell.

'What were you talking about?' Daya asked.

'You know – about Mortimer and what he did.' Her hands went involuntarily to her bruises, and Daya's face dropped. 'Then it got late and everybody was sleeping, and Amina said to stay with her in her bed. I slept with my friend, Ma. We're like sisters. I didn't think you'd mind.'

Daya felt her heart begin to flutter and fall like a bird shot from the sky. How, she asked herself, had she managed to bring a daughter into this world who could lie so easily? If only she could turn the years back to Sumati's childhood so that she could see when the lies began, so that she could catch them and teach her differently. If Roopchand ever found out, life wouldn't be worth living. She wondered whether to tell Sumati outright that she knew she was lying – but this would cause an argument that was bound to wake her husband. A sure way to end the family as they knew it.

Daya was a quick thinker, and had already worked out a plan that would ensure everyone involved was protected.

'You say you're like sisters? I wish you were more like her. I hope she talked some sense into you. You're too much like a butterfly. A pretty one, but here one minute, and gone the next.' She looked deep into Sumati's eyes, hoping the message would reach her silently.

'I didn't mean to cause you to worry,' Sumati said. 'It's just that time passed so fast. Everybody was already sleeping, and no one could have walked home with me.'

'Go and bathe,' was all Daya said, knowing that Sumati was like a cane field on fire when she was opposed or exposed. In that, she resembled her husband. She had his wrong and strong behaviour. 'And when you've finished, come and help me make the roti.'

Roopchand was getting ready for work. Sumati was sitting in the lotus position in front of the altar in the corner of the room. Her eyes were closed.

'She home?' Roopchand asked. 'And praying? Did she explain where she was?'

'Didn't I tell you she was with her friend, Amina?' Daya lied.

'You went there last night but you didn't tell me she was there.'

'You were sleeping,' Daya said sweetly. 'I didn't see the point in waking you up.' The less fuss she made the better.

'Well tell her never to do that again! Staying out like that! Otherwise I will cut her arse worse than what Mortimer did. And another thing, if she ever gets herself in any kind of trouble to bring shame on me, I will hold you responsible. *You!* You may as well be dead. I hope you understand that.'

'You told me that already,' Daya said quietly. 'I know how you think.'

His eyes pierced into hers, and Daya felt a stabbing pain. Her heart could no longer bear this burden she had carried for so long. She knew what had to be done, and she was ready to do it.

ꟷ

Roopchand and Kesh, their son, left together. Daya served breakfast while Sumati hung her washing on the clothes wire between the coconut trees. Daya brought the plates and the two of them sat in the bamboo lean-to at the side of the house, she on the bench and Sumati in the hammock. The girl was ravenous. While she chomped and chewed, Daya waited for the right moment.

'You are eating like an animal,' she said. 'I am thinking that you are just sitting at home doing nothing. You are not in school or working. Your father wants to bring the wedding plans to the end of this month.'

'So soon? I haven't had a chance to swallow my food and . . .'

'It has nothing to do with a *chance to swallow food.*' Daya's voice was calm, but her heart was heavy.

'I wanted to stay at school, but I can't do that now. Amina wants me to do the evening classes.'

'We cannot go back and undo what happens in this life, *beti.*' Daya stared at clothes hanging in the yard and swallowed. She didn't want to be told why Sumati was so anxious to do her washing that early. 'We have to go forward, and make sacrifices for what is best for the future.'

'And what do you want, Ma? You want me to get married to an old man who already has children with another woman?'

'You have no choice, *beti. We* have no choice. The whole village is gossiping about you. You have to change what you do to show that you can be a respectable wife and mother now.'

'You mean that it will make *you* a respectable wife and mother!' Sumati was spitting bits of food with her loud, angry words.

'You see why I can't deal with you?' Daya said. 'I can't even talk to you. You need a strong man to keep you quiet.'

'I need *what*? You crazy bitch!'

'Sumati, don't talk to your mother like that.' Daya's voice was breaking. Her heart was already broken, or her hand would have at that moment raised a weal on her daughter's face. Wringing her hands, she continued. 'Tell me what I have left in my life, when my own child has no respect for me? But you will have to have respect for Baljit, because he is an older man. If you want your father to deal with you, you know what he'll do. He will beat you till you can't move. He has already threatened me.' Daya looked at Sumati to read her expression. The girl was gazing down at her plate, not moving. 'Don't think I don't know what is going on,' Daya burst out. 'You are my daughter, and I know when you are telling the truth. And when you're lying.'

Sumati put her plate down on the floor still half full of food and began pushing it around with her foot, whilst rocking herself on the hammock. Daya looked at Sumati's foot kicking the food she had cooked, and felt alienated and rejected. She longed to put her arm around her, but feared sending the wrong signal. She hadn't approved of her daughter staying out all night, or lying, and a stone wall was rising between them.

'You will marry this man!' Daya exploded. 'Soon! Because I care what happens to you. And I can see that *you* don't care about anybody.'

'Ma, I feel that you and Pa have never trusted me. Ma, I have to tell you something. The truth is, that I want to get married.'

Daya's mouth fell open and her eyes brightened hopefully.

'But to someone else,' Sumati said.

Daya's body wavered backwards as if a rock had hit her, and she almost lost her balance, but she never took her eyes off Sumati. She let out a scream. 'Who? There is no one else! And how can we go back on our word? We said *yes*. Turning on our word will bring bad luck. And disrespect. How many more pujas must I do for you? You will be the end of me. We have no more money to give the pundit.'

'I'm tired.' Sumati's eyelids were drooping.

'Well, go and lie down. And when you get up, you will think differently.'

Sumati went off and rolled herself up in a blanket as if she was ill, and Daya eventually struggled up in despair, to get on with her day.

ഋ

Amina returned home from school that afternoon, surprised to see Daya sitting with her mother on the bench at the far end downstairs. She was pleased to see the two women becoming good friends, and although they were chatting very quietly, she could hear the Bhojpuri tone of conversation in the breeze. Something occurred to her, so she hastened over.

'You know, Ma, if you talked more English, you'd learn more words.'

Devinia looked up sharply, her cheeks reddening. 'We are talking,' she snapped.

'In Bhojpuri. But I can teach you to read English. Both of you.'

Devinia looked at Amina sharply again, the green in her eyes glinting angrily.

'Where did you learn to be rude? In school?' she asked. 'You think we have nothing to do all day but read storybooks? You live in a different world.'

'I wish Sumati was in your world,' Daya said regretfully.

'I didn't mean to be rude,' Amina said apologetically. 'But perhaps you could manage half an hour, after school? I could start next week!' She turned around to go, but Devinia called her back.

'I found this in your pocket when I was washing your skirt.' She handed Amina a folded piece of paper. 'Good thing I checked the pockets,' Devinia said. 'What's it say on the paper?'

Amina was suddenly grateful that neither her mother nor Daya could read English.

'Oh, it's something Mr Clifford wants me to do. Some wall charts for the school's inspection. It will help him get permission for me to start Part One of the Pupil Teacher Training early. Next September.'

Devinia looked taken aback.

'It'll take two years,' Amina warned her. 'Then Part Two.' Aware that it would conflict with their wedding plans for her, she swiftly changed the subject.

'Did Sumati come home?' she asked.

'Yes,' Daya replied. 'But she could do with somebody like you to talk some sense into her. You have a good daughter there,' she said to Devinia.

Amina smiled at them both, then left to get changed and do her chores.

༄

Amina was ready to leave the house when Sankar called after her.

'What is your hurry?' he said, holding a red cloth in his hand. 'I brought this for you.'

'I have to go – sorry, Pa.'

'What is it with you these days? You've changed so much. Before you were sick, you couldn't wait to see what I brought for you.'

'The sickness has changed her,' Devinia agreed sadly. 'She is only interested in one thing.'

'Yes, my sister's really changing,' Etwar put in. 'She's getting some big plums on her chest.'

Sankar looked at his son and smiled 'I see there's nothing wrong with you or your eyesight.'

Amina threw a feeble slap in Etwar's direction.

Sankar opened the red cloth showing them the deep orangey-gold pieces inside.

'That is lovely!' Devinia said. 'Your father is a master craftsman. He used to make pieces for me too. All put away for special.'

'I just want you to choose which pattern you prefer. The flowers, or the ones with all the flat diamond-shaped gold splices.'

'I don't want them,' Amina said.

Sankar looked surprised. 'Why don't you come with your mother to market in Point Fortin tomorrow. Come to the shop and see what you like. I have some pieces ready for a woman whose daughter's getting married soon. Take a look at them.'

'I don't have time,' Devinia said. 'Just bring them here.'

'You want me to get beaten up on the way home?' Sankar huffed. 'Don't worry. The shop will most likely be full as it's a Friday. People appreciate my craft, even if you don't.'

'You sure it's the craft they appreciate?' Devinia said, holding herself back from telling him about the village gossip about his shop being full of women, and how it made her feel. But she didn't want to upset him or herself, so she went off to carry on with her chores.

THIRTEEN

On her way to the standpipe, Amina called in to visit Sumati with the letter from Farouk hidden in her pocket. Daya was in the yard and saw her.

'That necklace is as pretty as you,' the woman said. 'Your father is a clever man.'

Amina smiled modestly. 'I've just come to see Sumati.'

'I hope you can talk some sense into her.'

Amina dropped her bucket and hurried up the steps and peeped through the gauzy curtains blowing in the doorway. Sumati was sitting inside against the wall, shelling peas.

'Guess what!' Amina said excitedly. 'Our mothers are going to learn English. My first pupils! Wait till I tell Mr Clifford!'

Sumati didn't even glance up.

'You look like you just sucked a lime,' Amina commented. 'What happened to you last night?' She sat next to her friend.

'It's a jail in here,' Sumati muttered. 'They won't let me go anywhere. They're trying to marry me off – in a fortnight! At least you have some months to work out what to do. They don't want me here. Not even Ma.'

'Your mother just told me to talk some sense into you. What does she mean?'

'I think she's found out about – you know who,' Sumati whispered.

'Oh, Farouk? He gave me this to give you.' Amina handed over the letter.

'Shh! I'm in enough trouble! Keep watch for me.' Sumati grabbed the letter and disappeared into the bedroom.

Amina stood at the window. The chickens were scratching in the dirt. A hen dug a hole deep enough to sit in, and wriggled her belly frantically in the dust. Her wings were everywhere, flipping dust all over herself, using her feet to spray it up.

Then Sumati returned, her face pinker and happier. She shoved a piece of paper into Amina's hand, and warned her not to tell anyone. Not even Etwar. Amina stiffened when she saw the purple bruise on Sumati's neck as her hair swung back.

'What is that on your neck? *Soucouyant* sucked you?'

'I think so,' Sumati lied. 'I saw the red ball of fire just as it flew out of the window.'

Amina shivered. 'Gosh, Sumati. I've never seen a real one.

Sumati blushed. 'Maybe if I turned Catholic they couldn't force me to marry a Hindu.'

'They will be really upset with you, but you could be right.' Amina looked thoughtful. 'Maybe that is what I will do too. Tomorrow I'm going to ask Mr Clifford about his God. It is different from our god. For a start, there's only one of his. Makes things a lot easier. And you can talk to Him anywhere. He prays while he is walking. It must mean his is everywhere even though it's only one God. Christians don't even have to do puja. Come to school tomorrow and we will go and see Mr Clifford about it. He will be pleased.'

ꕤ

But Sumati wasn't in school the next day or the next. A few evenings later, as the light was fading, Amina was making a last trip home from the standpipe when she heard someone call her from the bushes. She recognised the voice, but the suddenness of the sound coming from the darkened surroundings frightened her.

'Who is it?' Amina's body jerked, and water spilt all down her clothes.

'It's me!'

'Sumati?'

'Yes. I just came to tell you . . . I'm going.'

'Going?' Amina asked. 'Going where?'

'San Fernando. Me and Farouk. We're leaving.'

Amina put her bucket down and stared, stunned. But Sumati began to laugh. Cackling in her usual wicked way when she'd done something stupid but funny. Amina's wet clothes stuck to her back and legs, and she shivered. 'You're not running away,' she said. 'You can't be.'

Sumati laughed again. Amina could see the face just in front of the bushes, the moon highlighting Sumati's cheeks, her eyes sparkling with joy.

'What about our plan?' Amina implored. 'Us sticking together. Our pact. Our blood joined.'

'I'll send for you when we get settled. We'll always be friends.'

'But it'll just make everything worse, can't you see?'

'I have no choice. I have a better chance if I leave home now.'

'Where will you stay?'

'I don't know yet.' Sumati giggled. 'Farouk said in the letter that he can't bear to see me so unhappy. He wants to take me away, otherwise he might do something to Mortimer and end up in jail. He found somewhere we can stay till we decide what to do. San Fernando has everything. We can work and save up to get a piece of land to build a house. I don't care, Amina. I love Farouk.'

'But you said you'd turn Christian . . . so they wouldn't force you to marry. Mr Clifford will talk to your parents for you. He hates these child marriages.'

'But they don't see us as children, Amina. My *business* started already. That's why they're in a hurry to get rid of me. I'm so excited. I can't wait to be with him – you know.'

Sumati looked so happy that Amina began to doubt herself.

'I have thought about it, but I couldn't just leave.'

'That's because we're different, Amina. Opposites sometimes.'

'But I'll miss you. I need you to help me get out of this wedding they're planning.'

'I told you I'll send for you. I'm leaving my bag here, and I'll pick it up when they've gone to bed. Don't tell anyone. Promise me.'

'What if they question me?'

'I'm asking. You're my friend. Promise me!'

'I promise,' Amina said against her will.

༄

That evening, as the moon rose and partly hid behind the clouds, Sumati arrived at the spot where she had left her belongings. As she parted the bushes, Amina stepped out.

'You!' Sumati looked at her friend, completely shocked. 'You're not stopping me.'

'No,' Amina said. 'I'm coming with you.' Sumati caught sight of the brown bag under Amina's arm, and the worry disappeared.

Half-smiling, Sumati spoke. 'We have to meet Farouk at the Syphoo Junction. Hurry.'

It took half an hour of fast walking before they saw Farouk.

'Don't ask!' Sumati warned Farouk, seeing the shock in his eyes. 'Yes. She is coming. She too is facing marriage to some man who will rape her. Is that what you want?'

'It's a long walk to the coast,' Farouk said. 'And we will have to wait for the boat to San Fernando. It could be an all-night wait. I don't know if there is a boat from Cedros at this time of night. I don't have much money.'

'I have some,' Amina said.

'I suppose you'll be of use then,' Farouk said.

'And I brought some food,' Sumati said, cheerfully. But Farouk said nothing.

The three of them walked along in silence. Amina struggled to keep up. Soon she was way behind until she lost sight of the pair as they walked arm in arm. She eventually reached the coast and found them sitting on a log. It was there she discovered the plan. Farouk had arranged for them to stay a while in San Fernando with a relative of his friend, Rajnath Kamalsingh, until they got on their feet and found work. Amina saw the glint in Sumati's eyes and envied her joy. She too could be that happy if she ignored her doubts.

'See?' Sumati said to her. 'I knew you would make it. I told you, Farouk. Amina can do anything she puts her mind to. And not just end of term tests.'

FOURTEEN

Daya discovered that her daughter was again missing, and this time half of her clothes had gone. The woman spent the day searching every friend, but with no luck. The following day the *panch*, the village elders, arranged a search. She had no choice but to involve them, though this could be harsh. Amina was the first on their list, but when they questioned her, the girl was totally incoherent. They continued to visit and question every friend, every person, every house. They searched every shed, every yard, every track – for days. But Sumati was not found and no one knew where she might be. They returned to Amina, but she was still in such a blubbering mess, that they couldn't force answers from her.

Daya spent her days walking up and down the village, going from house to house, searching under every bush, any piece of deserted land, and questioning anyone she passed. Everyone was on edge for weeks. Amina felt worried and guilty, but was unable to break her promise. She was sure that Sumati and Farouk would return soon like she had, when they thought it through. Now she was sorry she had left her money with them. She tried to plunge herself into schoolwork, the evening classes, and studying English literature, but it was like trying to keep a mad dog tied up inside her. She was frantic with worry and guilt. One day she talked to Mr Clifford about what Christianity taught concerning dishonesty. Her lies about Sumati weighed on her mind.

'It was the start of the downfall of man,' he said. 'Disobedience, lies, blame and guilt. *Ye shall not eat of the tree, neither shall ye touch it, for thou shalt surely die. And the serpent beguiled Eve, and told her, "You shalt not surely die. You will be like gods, knowing good and evil." And when God walked in the Garden of Eden in the cool of the day, and asked Adam, "Hast thou eaten of the tree wherefore I commanded you not to eat?" And Adam said, "the woman gave me, and I did eat." And the woman said, "the serpent gave me and I did eat". And the Lord cursed them all, and said, "for dust thou art and unto dust shalt thou return".'*

'So the serpent lied, but it wasn't an outright lie?'

'Lied nevertheless. The serpent meant to deceive Eve. And he was cursed – to crawl on his belly for the rest of his life.'

'That's like my religion,' she smiled. 'A talking snake.'

'Listen to me, girl. Who knows? It could well be a snake. But on the other hand, you know what temptation is like for us human beings. There's no snake that tells me to pick a ripe mango off somebody else's tree and eat it. It's my own mind making me do it! It is not the important thing. It is the *lying* that is wrong. The scriptures are full of it.

'Lying lips are an abomination to the Lord. But they that deal with truth, are a delight.'

Amina stared at Mr Clifford.

'What's wrong?' he asked. 'You seem distracted these days.'

'Yes, sir. I'm worried – about Sumati – and me. Your religion and mine are kind of similar, but so different.'

'An honest witness does not deceive, but a false witness pours out lies.'

'Sir, how do you know these things?'

'Honestly? I think—' He looked at her for a moment as if he wanted to say something he ought not to. 'I had the opportunity to get hold of such a book as the Bible in my younger days, from the house of a rich man where my mother worked. In English. Not Latin. English, girl! A King James Version. Fascinating! More than any work of literature I have ever come across.'

'The last time I saw Sumati, she was thinking of converting to Christianity. Did she talk to you about it? Is it even possible?'

'Of course!' he assured. 'Anything is possible. But she never came to see me.'

&

Amina returned from school to find Daya in her house, crying to her mother. She hurried upstairs quietly, but Devinia called her back down and asked her if Sumati had said anything recently about going somewhere.

Frightened and guilty, Amina turned hostile.

'How could I know? I've been here all this time, worrying about her just like all of you! How do you think I feel? We were friends – like sisters. Now she's gone, and everyone is harassing me as if I caused her to leave.'

'No one said that. Everybody wants to know. How do you think her mother feels? What if it was you who just disappeared?'

'I'm sorry,' Amina said dully. 'I really don't know where she is. I'm tired.' She ran upstairs and threw herself on her bed in despair. A few minutes later, Devinia entered her room and sat down.

'I wasn't meaning to cause you more upset,' she said. 'Her mother is not too good – saying some strange things. Roopchand is very angry and blaming her.'

'They are both to blame,' Amina spat. 'Forcing her to marry an old man who she has never even met. *And* he has two children. She is only fourteen! Moonia killed herself. Is that what you all want us to do?'

'The teacher beat her very badly,' Devinia said. 'Maybe that's why she ran away?'

'Then all she had to do was leave school. Not home. If school isn't safe, and home is even worse, what are we expected to do?'

'Daya thinks that school is putting too much pressure on children to remain. They need to go out and work. The money is more important.'

'That is where you are all wrong.' Amina glared at her mother. 'Learning is always going to be more valuable. It is the difference between the clever and stupid people.'

'Just don't say that in front of your father. You hear me?' Devinia wagged her finger at Amina and left the room.

ꕥ

There were nights when Amina slept very little, guilty about the lies she had told to keep Sumati's secret. Mr Clifford had recently taken to talking about keeping God's commandments at morning assembly, and saying that lying was abhorrent in the eyes of God, that it was a sin that would surely bring damnation upon those who lied.

Amina tossed and turned one night after another, trying to work out which was the one to obey – the Bible or the *Bhagavad Gita*. Mr Clifford, or Pundit Lall. One God or a hundred? The Ten Commandments and Jesus, or karma? Jesus was forgiving of sins, but karma was about paying for past lives. Jesus was about the promise of eternal life, and their gods made fate the only hope for the future. A future that could never be changed. Karma was not even about disobedience to the gods. It was just a reflection of a person's past life, good or bad. There was no repentance. So, if she lost her leg in an accident, she was paying for something in her past life?

Amina was sick with worry. It was impossible to repay your debts. It could go on forever. There was no Jesus to forgive sins, only reincarnation. So how could she redeem this lie she had told? There was no control of her future, and she could reincarnate as anything. Night after night she struggled to sleep, worrying which to believe – a God, or the gods. Amina craved some peace. She needed to know what form her reincarnation would take. She was a human girl now. Did that mean she had been good in a past life? But that could not be true, because why did she suffer a horrific illness such as typhoid and almost die? What could she have done to suffer so?

Each day she reached school more and more bleary-eyed than the day before, and confused from lack of sleep.

She asked Mr Clifford more and more questions, and he answered them in school assembly every morning. When she asked her mother questions though, Devinia would feel her forehead for a fever, and ask if she was feeling ill.

Amina made a decision once and for all.

ঌ

One morning, Amina called by to see Daya before she went to school, to tell the grieving woman the truth: that Sumati had left because she was in love with the Muslim boy, Farouk, and that she had wanted to escape the arranged marriage to an old man with children.

When Amina had finished, Daya was in a state of shock, but thanked the girl from the bottom of her heart for putting an end to her misery. Amina left, believing she had done the right thing.

FIFTEEN

A week earlier

Sumati and Farouk took the sloop from Cedros to San Fernando. The journey was rough, but it was their journey, and the beginning of a life together. They walked through the market and found their way to the address they had been given – a big gated house, about ten minutes from the wharf. The place looked like a palace compared to Granville houses, and they thought at first it was the wrong house. But they were tired and feeling seasick, so they called. Dogs bounded towards the gate at the sound of the voices, barking ferociously. Then a woman in her twenties appeared.

'Mr Amrit lives here?' Farouk shouted.

A minute later, a tall, well-built man, in clean pressed clothes, appeared at the door.

'Who is it?' he asked.

'Farouk from Granville.'

The man squinted and then called back. 'Yes, I have been expecting you. Wait there.' Amrit was an upright man in stature, and he strolled out, calling the dogs back before arriving at the gate. He opened it and let them in, smiling. Farouk and Sumati looked at each other, pleased at the friendly reception. After offering them refreshments, Amrit showed them to the rooms.

'Farouk only,' Amrit said. 'No badness going on here. The girl – you come. You can stay with the other girls. My nephew said you're looking for work?' He stared at Farouk. 'You will pay me back when you find a job. When are you getting married?'

Sumati began to giggle.

'Are you laughing at me?' Amrit said. 'Then – does your mother know you are here?' His voice changed from friendly to hostile.

But just then Dillip, his son, arrived and answered the question.

'Who cares?' he said. 'You all must join me for drinks tonight. We will talk about work. I might have something for you.'

Dillip was tall, broad-shouldered like his father, but well groomed. His voice was friendly, and he sounded almost like an English gentleman – like a son of a plantation owner. Farouk and Sumati smiled, relieved that they had begun their new life in a good place.

'Anything,' Farouk said. 'We will do whatever it takes to get work and save up to find a place of our own.' He cast his eyes longingly around the vast newly built compound.

'Yes,' Dillip said. 'I can see you have big ambitions. My father started with nothing. There's no shame in starting at the bottom.'

ꕤ

Later that afternoon Farouk and Sumati sat on the bench in the shade of the almond tree, chatting blissfully.

'They have a big shop here,' Farouk said to her. 'San Fernando is *the* place!'

'We're lucky,' Sumati agreed. 'I knew it would turn out well. Amina was so frightened to come. That's where we are so different. She'll get nowhere back there in Granville. They'll marry her off and she'll never get what she wants. Teaching! That'll never happen. This town has everything. It even smells different.'

'We've only just come,' Farouk reminded her cautiously. 'Let's wait and see.'

'But I can feel it!' the girl insisted.

After a big dinner, Amrit left Sumati and Farouk to have drinks with Dillip and his friends. Farouk and Sumati enjoyed the interesting new company, and were both happily inebriated for the first time in their lives. In fact, Sumati had to be helped up to bed by the woman called Tonia. That was their first day.

SIXTEEN

Since Amina had told Daya the truth about Sumati's disappearance, she had not seen the woman so, on her way to school one morning, she walked past the house out of curiosity. The kiskadee birds were particularly noisy that morning, squawking in the hog-plum tree at the front of the house, flying from branch to branch arguing over the ripe yellow plums, as if they hadn't eaten for a month. It was the plum season. Two ground doves flapped around under the bushes, pecking at seeds and fallen fruit. The house itself looked lonely. No activity was evident – not even a *saphee* on the clothesline.

She wanted to call in, but worried about facing Roopchand or Daya so she hurried off to school. Everyone was still talking about Sumati's disappearance. It had led to all sort of rumours and speculation, some of which were embarrassingly close to the truth. Amina tried to use the situation to gather support for Mr Clifford's evening classes, but although some said they did not want an arranged marriage, they did not want to take extra classes either.

'Maybe one day our parents will understand,' Pryia said.

'How?' Amina asked, gloomily. 'What are you doing about it? Did Moonia die for nothing – has Sumati run away for nothing? I miss them both.'

'I wouldn't know who to get married to, if it was up to me,' Chandra said. 'My mother will find me a good boy from *upperside*.'

'My mother says Sumati was trouble, and she was right,' Ramona said. 'Look what she's done. My mother says Sumati will get herself burnt one day.'

'Your mother is Meena, right?' Pryia said, loud and annoyed. 'But she doesn't have to act meanly!'

'What do you mean?' Ramona asked.

'Well, how does your mother know Sumati deserves all she gets?' Pryia asked. 'If it was you who was forced to marry some wrinkled-up old man, how would you feel?'

'Everybody has to marry somebody,' Ramona said matter-of-factly. 'The difference is, *I* wouldn't run away and bring shame on my family.'

'Because you're too good, yeah?' Pryia snapped. 'Why are you always repeating what your mother says? Don't you have a mind of your own? Do you even listen to anything Mr Clifford says?'

'People are jealous of how good-looking Sumati is,' Chandra put in.

'I expect Ramona is jealous of Sumati's freedom,' Amina said. 'If I'm honest, I am too – in a way. But we need to do something. Gossiping about her isn't fair. If we don't make our parents stop what they are doing, we will do the same to our daughters, because we'll be caught in that trap with no education and no decent job. Sometimes I feel I'm in a jail.'

'Me too,' Pryia and Ramona agreed.

ꙮ

The month of March was in the middle of the dry season. It was hot, and three o'clock, the end of the school day, seemed the hottest part of the day. The girls were at the water taps at school, cooling down before walking home – laughing, drinking, washing their hands, splashing their faces, and rinsing the dust off their bare legs from knees to feet.

'I think it's time we joined together to stick up for Sumati and her family,' Amina said. 'We should go and see the *panch* leader. They've put the family in *cujart*, so no one is talking to Sumati's family.'

'I don't even know who the leader is,' Pryia said.

'Sumati's family need people to help them, not put them in isolation as if they've got typhoid. Did you hear what Mr Clifford said today in assembly? "*Love thy neighbour as thyself*".'

'Who is *thyself*?' Chandra asked.

'It's *you*, stupid!' Ramona laughed her gutsy laugh. 'Ma will surely bust my head if she finds out, but I'm coming with you. I don't care.'

'If we annoy the *panch*, maybe our families will also be put in *cujart*,' Pryia said.

'That could be true.' Ramona shivered. 'I'm scared. I already got shouted at once today. I can't take another telling-off. Come to my house instead.'

'Ramona, you weren't scared of gawping at those dogs outside today.'

Amina and Pryia began to giggle.

'What?' Chandra asked innocently.

'I was only looking,' Ramona said.

'Yeah! At two stray dogs doing *it,* with your mouth wide open,' Pryia chortled.

'Are you coming or not!' Ramona said.

As they walked, flies zoomed around and bees buzzed from flower to wild flower. The girls headed for the trees, dodging the hot sun, and walking on the grassy verge to avoid the sharp gravel. Suddenly everything went dark. Heavy clouds hid the sun, and the birds stopped singing.

As they approached the bend in the road before Ramona's house, they heard the sounds of cries and shouting. They stopped walking and looked at each other, alarmed, before hastening to the corner. The noises grew louder. Low moans sailed through the wind. Then a crowd. Women were crying. Men were calling out. A girl ran towards them.

Two men were standing on a table, reaching up into the tree above. One who looked like Kesh, Sumati's brother, was trying to pick hog-plums. But all the noise – it didn't make sense. Black birds flew around, squawking, and people were chasing them.

'That's my uncle,' Ramona said. 'With Sumati's brother.'

'Looks like somebody's thrown something in the tree, and they are trying to get it down,' Amina said. 'Ramona – is that your mother?'

'Can't be,' the girl replied. 'She's supposed to be helping my aunt plant rice today in Point Cocoa.'

As they got closer they saw Ramona's uncle was standing on the table with Kesh, and through the gap, the girls had a full view of what was happening.

'Oh God!' Amina shouted. 'I don't believe it.' She stood, confused. Held her throat as if she had swallowed a mouthful of sharp gravel. Grabbing Ramona's arm on one side, and Pryia's on the other side, she held on to them as if she was drowning. Then she let out the first scream.

A person was suspended from the tree. A woman. Her head was bent forward; pieces of her oiled black hair had come loose and hair coiled like snakes on both sides of her face, and her legs dangled loosely below her long skirt. Her eyes were open and bulging – dark, swollen circles around them. Her lips were fat and blue, half-open, and her purple tongue stuck out between her teeth.

Kesh was leaning over the side of the table, white as a ghost. He looked up as the girls approached. His eyes, red and haunted, stared at them with his mouth open. No words came out. Then he held his stomach and howled. 'Ma! Oh God, not my mother!'

ഌ

Untying the knots in the tree around the branch where Daya swung in the hot air proved impossible. People shivered as they watched her legs being supported to ease the weight from the ropes. Villagers returning from work stopped to watch or tried to help. Everyone was in a state of shock. The girls were all crying.

'Just cut the rope!' Kesh screamed. 'She'll die!'

'There's no point,' Ramona's uncle said, heavily. 'She is already dead, boy!'

'No! No! No! She's still moving,' Kesh wailed. 'Look at her legs. Do something somebody! Ma, why did you do this?'

Ramona's mother, Meena, came and stood close to the girls. Her eyes were bloodshot. 'Come, all of you. Come inside.'

Just at the moment, Daya's body dropped limply into the arms of the men underneath. The dead woman's ankles were red and swollen as they fell on the table. People rushed forward to help support her. They struggled to cut the rope from her neck before carrying her inside the house. Then Roopchand arrived home from work and saw the crowds gathered in front of his house.

'What happened?' he asked. 'Did Sumati come home?'

Spotting Amina, he directed a fierce, angry look at her, then headed down the side of the house with long, loping strides.

'I don't know!' Amina called after him, feeling distressed. 'I've not seen her since she disappeared.'

The chattering outside was interrupted by a sudden wailing coming from inside the house. It was Roopchand – and the howl of grief went on for at least a minute. Then he appeared on the veranda with his head in his hands.

'She's gone!' he shouted.

Meena shuffled closer to the girls, holding on to them. 'Come inside,' she said gently.

As they turned to go with her, Roopchand came striding out, fast and furious, to the front of the house, wiping his face with his palm. His cheeks were red and blotched with dirty tear stains. Roopchand's big hand clamped on Amina's shoulder, and he was shaking her until her teeth chattered.

'It's your fault,' he roared. 'If it wasn't for you, she would have never run away in the first place.'

Before Amina could pull free, he grabbed the other shoulder and began shaking again till her head looked like it was falling off.

Meena heaved Amina away from his grip. 'Leave the girl alone!' she shouted. 'It's nobody else's fault but yours and that daughter of yours.'

'You!' he said, looking at Meena. 'You never liked my Sumati. Why? What did she ever do to you?'

'I really don't know how Daya lived with the both of you,' Meena went on. 'That is why she did this.'

Everyone gasped.

Kesh came rushing out. 'Pa! Leave the girl alone. You are just making everything worse.'

'Your mother trusted that Banderjee girl!' Roopchand wept, looking like a wild man.

Other people noticed and came forward to speak in Amina's defence, but the girl spoke up to Roopchand herself.

'I am sorry I was never able to stop Sumati doing what she wanted to do,' she said, and they could all hear the sincerity in her voice. 'Maybe that was my fault. But it was *you* who drove her away. This is what happens when parents like you arrange husbands for little girls before they're even old enough to go to the latrine by themselves.'

Roopchand reached out and grabbed Amina by the neck, but Kesh pulled him off, and dragged him back to the house, staggering as if he was drunk.

Devinia arrived soon after, running breathlessly after hearing the gossip. She squeezed her way through the crowd to find her daughter choking and coughing from Roopchand's stranglehold.

'What happened?' the woman asked.

'Ma,' Amina gulped and collapsed into the safety of her mother's arms.

'I heard what happened to Daya, but where do you come into it?'

'He blamed me – and he could be right, Ma,' the girl said, sobbing. 'Roopchand could well be right. It's all my fault.'

SEVENTEEN

When they got back home, Devinia sat down with Amina and tried to talk to her. 'Don't listen to that man. He has just lost his wife, and his daughter left home without telling them a thing. And they are in *cujart*. But I don't think people will take notice of that anymore. Everybody will be so sorry for him and Kesh.'

'You don't understand, Ma.'

'I know that you want to fix everything for everyone, but you cannot blame yourself for this. You will make yourself crazy if you do so. And you've been through enough.'

'But. . . '

'No. No more.' Devinia was tearful as well as angry with Amina. 'You're tired and upset. I will go and boil some cocoa tea for you. Drink it and go to sleep. Read your book.'

'I don't have one. I gave it back to Mr Clifford.'

'Then think about how to write one.'

Amina looked at her mother, both puzzled and shocked.

'You can read, you can write. You're always writing letters to people, so write a story.'

Her mother had a point. The startling suggestion worked: it brought down the girl's anxiety and made her realise she could only do things that were within her power to do. The ability to change the mind of every Hindu parent was not within her power. She was unsure if she could change the mind of her own parents. But she realised that she could change her own mind, and be truthful to herself.

ॐ

When Amina finally fell asleep, it was in her parents' bed. Her dreams were vivid and fitful, making her flail around all night. Devinia shook her more than once to bring her out of her nightmare. It wasn't until dawn forced beams of light through the invisible gaps in the windows, that Amina's sleep became more peaceful.

Devinia got up earlier than usual, giving up on any hope of her own rest. It wasn't just Amina's restlessness that had kept her awake, but her own conscience. If anyone was to blame for Daya's suicide, it would be her.

She got ready for the day and sat at the altar in her bedroom in front of the goddess, Lakshmi. She chanted many prayers so that her family would be safe, and so that it would be overlooked that she had not stopped Daya from taking her life. Daya had told her of her intention just the day before. Devinia thought she had dissuaded her, by telling the other woman that drowning was not an easy death. And that starting the afterlife in water would hinder, not hasten her crossing to the other side. And what would happen to her children? Sumati needed her calming influence and wise guidance. Devinia realised she had failed her friend. Now she felt guilty.

Sankar came to talk to her as she was making breakfast.

'Our daughter thinks it's her fault,' Devinia said. 'Roopchand blamed her yesterday, and he lashed out. If anything, it's my fault.'

'How, your fault? And why is he blaming *my* daughter? It's madness. I have a good mind to go and fix him up.'

'He didn't mean it,' Devinia said quietly. 'He is not in his right mind.'

But Sankar wasn't listening. 'I'm not having it! He has no business accusing *my* child like that. And what exactly you mean by – *he lashed out*? I hope he didn't touch Amina! Wake her – let me find out.'

'No. She needs to rest.'

'If he touched her, I am going to chop his hands off!'

'That family has been through too much,' Davina told him firmly. 'Daya was here the day before yesterday, not knowing what to do. Now she's gone. You can't bring her back.'

'I noticed Amina had a rash on her neck last night. What is wrong with her? I hope she's not ill again.'

'Maybe a fever,' Devinia lied, dreading him finding out about Roopchand's assault on their child.

'I'll go and talk to the man,' Sankar insisted. 'It was not our Amina's fault.'

'Leave it,' Devinia commanded. 'That poor man will have to bury his wife, and his only daughter has gone missing. He has enough to cope with.'

'Well, keep Amina home today,' Sankar said. 'She'll be in no fit state to go to school.' He looked closely at his wife. 'I hope you are telling me everything. Has anybody called the police? I hear Daya might have been strangled.'

ꕥ

The next day, Etwar returned home from school early. 'There's a half day school tomorrow, for the funeral,' he announced.

Amina broke down in fresh tears. 'I can't go to the funeral when Sumati's not here.'

'She might come back,' Etwar said gravely. 'I hope so. Mr Clifford made us spend five minutes in silence today as a mark of respect. I'm going to the funeral.'

'He closed the school?' Devinia asked, surprised.

'It was out of respect,' Etwar repeated. 'He's going himself tomorrow to show support for Sumati's family. And it doesn't matter what creed or race any of us are. He said we're all comrades.'

Pryia and Ramona called at the house not long after Etwar had come home.

'I can't stay long,' Pryia told Amina. 'Ma warned me to come straight home.'

'I keep dreaming,' Amina said. 'All kinds of bad things. That all of us went down by the sea, and one giant wave just came and lashed against us, tumbling us around so hard. And the water was full of sharks. And I couldn't find any of you. Then I got dragged into the sea . . . the tide pulled me in.'

'We were talking at school – we couldn't sleep either,' Pryia said. 'People are saying that somebody poisoned Daya. That is why her lips and face went black.'

'My mother said Daya was a good woman,' Ramona said. 'Too good for the rest of them.'

'People say that Sumati ran away with a boy,' Pryia said, in a low voice. 'If she did, it must be because of the beating from Mortimer. She couldn't face school anymore.'

ꕥ

Amina lay in her bed that night with all the windows closed up tight, but the knocking and banging from the house of the dead down in the village travelled up to her room, haunting her. Her parents had gone there. She pulled the blanket over her head, but each bang shook the house like a small earthquake. Hundreds of voices in the distance competed with the hammering of wood, and thoughts flew through her head like a tornado blowing the pages of an open book. She lay wide awake, frightened to close her eyes, wondering if the doctor had been, and what he had said. Had he called the police? Had Sumati returned yet? She needed to know. She couldn't be that selfish.

Amina sat up and swung her legs from under the hot sheets. She put her feet flat on the cool floorboards, wishing it wasn't night, because she wanted to go down to Sumati's house despite being scared of the dark. She got out of bed and eased open the wooden window. Moonlight lit through the clouds like gauze. A flutter of heavy wings suddenly cut the air and Amina ducked. A dark shadow passed over the house, and she shuddered.

She wondered if that was Daya's spirit, and she worried for Sumati. Her friend had spoken about wanting to turn Catholic. Was this her punishment? But by which god? Catholic or Hindu? She twisted her wrists till they hurt. She couldn't bear the loneliness.

Her father went to help them make the coffin, and she worried for him when he found out what Roopchand had really done to her the previous afternoon. Why did he go? His hands were not made for knocking and hammering. He had soft hands, that easily attracted splinters. Not like her mother's, which were used to outdoor work.

She shut the window quietly and crept back under her sheets, shivering, scared of roaming spirits, afraid even to go and wake up Etwar. She lay still, sinking like lead into the mattress, trying to imagine the sensible advice Etwar would have given her. She must have fallen asleep because she realised it was morning when she heard the cockerel in their yard responding to the one in the distance.

Her head throbbed and her mouth was dry. Her first thought was Sumati. And Amina swore then that whatever Sumati had or had not done, she would do just the opposite.

EIGHTEEN

The funeral procession left Sumati's house in the one o'clock heat of the following afternoon. The coffin bearers included Sumati's father, brother and uncle and Ramona's father. Most of the village turned out. Children walked in line behind the immediate family, in school uniform, together with Mr Clifford and some of the teachers. No one had expected this, but Mr Clifford had talked the previous day about showing united support for a pupil of the school. He didn't care what anyone said or thought. But he knew that he had to set a good example.

Amina wasn't in uniform. She wore an English-style navy dress with white flowers and a white sash around the waist. It had been a gift from her father, passed on to him by a customer, a seamstress who had made it for the child of a white family in Port of Spain. The child, however, had refused it because she had wanted a white dress with blue flowers, not a navy one with white flowers. Amina was pleased to have the dress, but had never had the opportunity to wear it before. She joined the procession, walking next to her mother. Etwar had gone ahead with the schoolchildren. It was about one and a half miles to Granville Cemetery. Sankar was at work that morning as he had pressing appointments.

Mr Clifford looked sombre in his black suit, white shirt and black tie. His face looked scrubbed and shaven to a blunt blueness, smooth and matt. He wore a black trilby hat as comfortably as a Victorian gentleman in English magazines. He had a white handkerchief crumpled up in his hand, occasionally wiping away the perspiration that ran down his face. Amina felt proud to look at him, neatly dressed, like a white man. Professional.

It was the first funeral Amina had ever attended. Of course she'd seen the processions pass the house. Some were full of singing, dancing and drumming, and when you looked more closely at the mourners' faces, they seemed weirdly happy. Her mother explained that those Indians belonged to a lower caste which embraced death because it was the only way their souls could finally find a better place to rest, to reincarnate.

Daya's funeral was not like that. Amina looked round, hoping to spot Sumati. Hoping that nothing evil had taken her away. At a time of death, anything was possible: every folklore tale, every fearsome religious story could materialise. Her mind raced.

'Ma? How do we know it's Daya in the coffin?'

'Who then? A *jumbie?*' Devinia replied crossly.

'I heard something fly across the house last night.'

'Her spirit.'

'But if you are Catholic, can you turn into a *jumbie*?'

'I don't know. Her face was badly discoloured.'

'What did the police say?' Amina whispered.

'It isn't the police you want to worry about,' Devinia said quietly.

'Why?'

'When you take your own life, it's as bad as killing someone else, so your spirit cannot rest. She will always be with them.'

'Well that will be good for Sumati then. And Kesh, and her father.'

'No, not at all!' Devinia sighed. 'It's best that people don't shed tears now. Too many tears create too much water, which will make it more difficult for her spirit to cross the river to the other side.'

'You're frightening me,' Amina said. 'Anyway, there *is* no water on the other side. I still want to know what the police said.'

'What for? To put her in jail for hanging herself? That's the least of their worries. Hush now, child.'

The procession stopped.

'Why are they stopping?' Amina asked.

'It was her parents' house. They will stop anywhere that was important to Daya when she was alive.'

The pundit began chanting, and threw a handful of rice towards the house.

'I know it's hard,' Devinia continued, tearfully, 'but at least it isn't Sumati that's dead. I'm sure she's high and dry somewhere.'

'I hope you are right.'

Despite the dilemma about the arranged marriage, Amina ached for those few months to return – when things were normal, and when Sumati was still around, and her friend's mother was still in the house doing the things that mothers did, cooking the roti and *talkarie*, and throwing handfuls of dry corn for the chickens in the yard on an evening. Sumati had tried to change her fate and her future, but all she did had ended up bringing woe on herself and everyone around her. Both of them, Sumati and Amina, had wanted to change their fate. But Amina could now see that one wrong action, however small, could change someone's life and those of the people around them, forever.

Was this a sign that she should accept the way things were?

ထ

The low-pitched beats of the *tassa* drums made things at least sound normal. Everything was done as it should be. Rice balls were placed over the coffin so that Daya's spirit could eat when it was hungry. Roopchand let out groans deep from his belly when the coffin was lowered into the ground, but tears were mostly subdued to allow the quick passage of Daya's spirit across the wide river into the next life. A few couldn't help themselves. Kesh bawled for his mother, and his aunt and a few others held him back from the edge of the grave. There was a lot of sniffing from Sumati's friends. Even Mr Clifford was wiping the corner of his eyes. People stood over the open grave for quite some time. Roopchand had his arm around Kesh, their heads bowed.

After the pundit finished, people scattered around the cemetery, walking, talking, laughing, leaving. Some were just arriving from work and went to throw a handful of dirt onto the coffin. While Devinia went to greet the other mourners, Etwar stood talking to one of the older boys who had left school.

Moments later, that same boy walked towards Amina and addressed her. 'I'm sorry about your friend's mother,' he said. Amina nodded. She wasn't allowed to speak to boys unless someone was there. He should know that. Who was he, with his shiny shoes, talking to her as bold as brass? She began to walk away. But then he spoke again. 'Your friend. Do you know where she is? She's not here at the funeral.' Amina was surprised he knew about Sumati, but then again, everyone knew everyone else's business in the village. 'When you see her, tell her I'm so sorry. For everything.'

Then Amina looked up at him, straight in the eye. Her lips were stuck. He looked genuinely upset as if he knew Sumati well, but she had never said anything about him. He walked off, leaving her staring in his direction wondering what it was about.

Etwar came up to her, and Amina asked who he was.

'He was the school cricket captain,' Etwar said. 'Don't you remember? His name is Kamalsingh. Rajnath Kamalsingh.'

'Oh.' Then she remembered Rajnath was the rogue who put Mortimer in his place before leaving the school. Now she couldn't forget his shiny shoes and the curl over his forehead. Before she could ask another question, her brother was gone again.

She looked around for Etwar, and froze in terror. Roopchand was standing so close to her that she couldn't see his face. Just his legs astride. She stepped back and looked around for help, but everyone else was busy talking to someone.

'Does your mother know you are chatting with boys?' he said. 'I was watching you! The *panch* will be interested.'

Amina stared at his wild, red eyes, his watery lips twisted with an anger so bitter, she could barely understand him.

'Don't play the innocent with me,' he hissed. 'Where has Sumati gone? Tell me and I won't tell the *panch* about you.'

'I don't know.'

'I say, tell me! You and your father think you're better than we?' Roopchand's hand shot out and clamped down hard on Amina's shoulder and he started to shake her.

'Hey!' a voice shouted. 'What's going on here?' It was Rajnath again.

'I-I don't know,' Amina stuttered.

'She well know!' Roopchand yelled in Bhojpuri, as he pushed Amina, causing her to stumble. '*Jagabat*.'

'Take that back!' Rajnath said to him. 'Who are you calling filthy names?'

Roopchand laughed at him. 'Boy! Who do you think you are talking to? I have known you since you were two foot high, running around naked. You think this *jagabat* makes you a man?' He looked sneeringly at Amina.

Amina could feel her blood boiling. 'It's no wonder Sumati ran away! She hated you!' Tears were rolling down her face.

'Look what you've done!' Rajnath said to Roopchand. 'Take it back.'

As Roopchand opened his mouth to laugh, Rajnath threw a punch straight at the man's last front tooth, making him roar out with pain.

'Don't you ever talk to this girl like that again,' the boy told him. 'Watch your mouth. *You* – you caused everything! You tried to foist somebody else's old husband

and children on Sumati. What kind of man does that to his own daughter? You know how many boys – men – would kill for that girl? But you! You treated her like a piece of old rag that washed up on the beach. And shame on you for bullying this other young girl here. I say take it back or I'll knock you head-first inside that open grave.'

'Why don't you mind your own business and leave the *jagabat* to me?' Roopchand said.

'I see it looks like there's only one way to shut your ugly mouth,' Rajnath said as he delivered another blow to the same side of Roopchand's face, knocking his tooth clean out of his mouth and sending it flying into the air.

'What is happening here?' Devinia came running.

Amina was shaking like a leaf.

'Ask him,' Rajnath answered instead. 'Ask that man what he's calling your daughter.'

'But why did you hit him, boy?' Devinia asked. 'You can't go around hitting people. This is a funeral. Show some respect.'

'Ma, Sumati's father said everything is my fault.' Amina burst into tears.

'How is anything your fault?' Devinia put her arm around Amina and looked at Roopchand. 'It is time you left my daughter out of your family mess. I'm warning you.'

Roopchand spat out a mouthful of blood on the grass. 'And what are you going to do?'

'Mister?' Rajnath said. 'Are you talking to me? You want me to show you what I will do to you?'

'This is not your business,' Roopchand mumbled.

'As from today, it *is* my business.' Rajnath stood firm, staring unrelentingly at Roopchand.

'Daya might be cold in the ground,' Devinia said, 'but

her spirit is watching you. She told me about your threats to kill her.'

'She was my wife!' Roopchand yelled.

Devinia took Amina's hand and led her away. Together, they walked out of the cemetery.

'Who is the boy?' Devinia asked her daughter.

'Etwar says he was cricket captain at school. But I never knew him.'

NINETEEN

Amina slumped in the hammock downstairs when they returned from the funeral.

'Where's your poem book?' Devinia asked. 'Read *Lucy Gray* for me. There's a nice one about . . . a butterfly. *Stay near me, do not take thy flight! A little longer stay in sight . . .'*

Amina stared, surprised, at her mother. 'How do you know about that poem?'

'From hearing you say the words out loud. I like them.'

'I'll teach you to read it yourself.'

'I don't know anymore. Daya is not here.' Devinia's eyes filled up. 'Everything's going wrong.'

'We can't undo what has already happened, Ma. But I promise you, if you keep learning English, things will become better. You will understand more things, and be able to use your brains.'

'Something happened to you since that typhoid. I know.'

'Yes, that's how I know you must learn to read,' Amina

said, her eyes sparkling. 'Don't let Pa hold you back, or that *panch*. They're afraid you'll know more than them. And you are a woman – with no brains.'

'No brains?' Devinia frowned at her daughter. 'Don't think I am stupid.'

'I don't, Ma. *They* think so. Use your brain to learn something and you will be happy.'

'You heard what Roopchand said about you? That makes me so angry, because mud will stick.' She shuddered. 'I'm glad what the boy did. I hope Roopchand leaves you alone now. It's not your fault.'

'That boy causes trouble,' Amina commented. 'He just lashes out.'

'Yes, but Roopchand deserved it.'

Amina needed to get away for a while. 'I'm going to get water.'

ᢀ

Amina picked up the bucket and went down to the standpipe only to find that Rajnath was there. Placing her bucket under the tap, she tried to fill it quickly.

'Hey,' he said. 'It's you again. Remember me?'

'I can't talk to you,' she reminded him.

'But I can talk. Your bucket's overflowing.'

She picked it up and turned to leave.

'Did you ever wonder where your friend went to when she ran away?'

'No.'

But that was a lie.

Amina walked off, angry. Of course she wanted to know, but she was trapped between loyalty to Sumati, and being truthful. And because she chose to be truthful, she now had to live with the guilt of Daya's death.

She balanced the bucket on her head, and kept walking. When she turned around, Rajnath was still in the distance, watching her. As much as she wanted to return to talk to him, she kept walking so fast and furious that when she got home the water from the bucket had sloshed all over her clothes, and she was soaking.

ꝏ

The evening light was dim, and the two gravediggers were the only ones left at the cemetery, packing up ready to leave, when a young woman appeared.

'Where is the grave?' she asked.

The man looked up. 'Daya Balgobin?' He pointed to the far right. 'Over there.'

The girl set off in that direction on the other side of the cemetery.

'You'd better hurry up,' he called after her. 'The police are looking for you.'

She turned, a plea in her eyes. 'Me?'

'Yes, you, God help you. Hope it was worth it.'

Stumbling on, she hastened towards the fresh grave strewn with flowers.

'You going to be alright?'

She watched as the two men left the graveyard and disappeared around the corner in the twilight. Alone, she dropped to her knees in the mud.

'Who did this to you?' she cried. 'What happened, Ma? Talk to me! I had to go – you know why I couldn't stay. I don't know what to do. I need help. Who can I talk to?

You're not going to be there anymore for me. Give me a sign, Ma. Say something. Talk to me!'

Frantic, she banged at the mound with both fists.

'How could you do this? What about me? You can't just go! You know I can't live how you and Pa want me to – I'm not like you. I'm not like anybody else! I'm me. There are things I need to tell you, Ma. Ma? *Ma!* Help me!' The darkness dropped silently from the evening sky like a black silk curtain, separating her even further from her mother. An owl fluttered and hooted nearby. Sumati held still for a moment. Then she began pulling at the neck of her dress, tearing the front, sobbing, 'I'll kill myself, and then I can be with you. There's no other way.'

'There is always another way out,' a voice came from behind her.

She looked up, trying to focus through the tears. 'Is that you, Ma? Are you really there?'

'No, is not your Ma. It's me.'

Then she realised. The voice was deep – a man's voice. She spun round on her knees, scared. Someone was standing behind her. She saw shiny shoes, caked with dirt round the edges. It was one of the boys from the village. Farouk's friend – the boy whom Farouk had trusted. The one who had given them an address in San Fernando where he said they could stay safely until they worked out how to find a place of their own.

'Where is Farouk?' he said.

'You!' she exclaimed. 'What are you doing here? This is my mother's grave! Get out!'

'The cemetery is a public place, girl,' Rajnath said. 'I was walking home, and I saw somebody in the half-dark. Then I realised it was you. How could I have just gone home?

What has happened to you? You look like you haven't seen water or a comb in days. Do you know people are worried about you?' His voice was a mixture of concern and condemnation.

'Don't pretend you don't know,' she said indignantly.

Rajnath looked at her questioningly. She was distressed as well as looking a mess, but his head was throbbing after the kind of day it had been.

'Where is Farouk?' he asked again.

'Don't ask me about Farouk!' Sumati screamed. She began striking out at Rajnath like a madwoman. 'It's all your fault! If it wasn't for you, this would not have happened. My mother would still be here.'

With both hands Rajnath wrenched her off the ground by her shoulders, and brought her up to eye-level. He wanted to tell her it was *her* fault that her mother had had no choice but to hang herself. But he didn't.

'Some people just cannot take responsibility for what they do,' he said, sternly. 'You chose to go. You ran away from what, I don't know. But what I *do* know is that you, miss, have no right to behave like the victim when you are the one who is alive. Now, where is Farouk?'

'Is that all you can think about?' she shot at him. 'What happened to my mother is also his fault.'

Rajnath frowned, confused. She wasn't making any sense. 'You still don't understand what I just said. Where did you go? And Farouk?'

'You well know where we went. It was you who gave Farouk the address of that accursed place. What do you want with me?'

'For the last time, where is Farouk? What did you do to him? He cared about you.'

'I don't want to talk about it!' she shouted. 'Leave me alone.'

'I can't leave you alone,' Rajnath said. 'It is getting dark, and you are a girl in a cemetery. What d'you think I am? I'll walk home with you.'

'Home? This is my home. Here, where my mother is sleeping. I'm staying here.'

'She wouldn't want you out here in the dark all alone all night,' he said, his tone more gentle now.

'Why are the police looking for me?' she asked.

'I don't know,' he said. 'Who told you that? Come.' He took her up by the arm. 'I'll walk with you.'

ഇ

It was completely dark now. The moon had disappeared behind the clouds. Rajnath and Sumati walked two feet apart along the piece of asphalt road, which was still warm and soft from the heat of the sun. Sumati's sniffing was the only sound, apart from the hooting of owls and the chirping of a bird settling down for the night. Candle flies lit the darkness in front of them. Then Rajnath decided he had to say something.

'What are you going to say if someone sees us together?'

'In the dark too,' Sumati said, dully. 'Things couldn't get worse. I'm an outcast, anyway.'

'Actually, it could get worse if they found out who you went with, and where.'

'You know, after everything that has happened to me over the last few months, I no longer fear anything. Except for my father. I don't know if I could ever go back to living under the same roof as him.'

'I can understand that. He seems to be in the habit of bullying other people's daughters too. Maybe you shouldn't go back home tonight. Why don't you go and stay with a friend?'

'I can't face anyone yet. And my father's bound to find me by tomorrow if I stay at someone's house. Besides, who can I stay with, without causing them problems?'

'Well, girl, I can't leave you out here in the dark. What kind of person would that make me? There might be *jumbies*,' Rajnath said, smiling. 'If you believe in that kind of thing.'

'You don't believe?' she asked, surprised.

'Well I have never met a *jumbie*,' Rajnath said. 'And I don't think that one ever met me. Because if they did, they would know about it when I was finished with them.'

'Look, is that not your house?' Sumati said, as they went past the rose mango tree.

'I know where I live. And I know where you could stay, but just for the night. Come.'

TWENTY

Mr Clifford listened patiently while Amina poured out ten minutes of anxiety. Then he spoke.

'Worrying is a lazy man's way of avoiding getting off his backside and doing something to solve his problem. Or using his brain to figure out a solution. That's not you. Remember that fruit is not born in a basket full of worries, but from direct connection, action, and nurturing, right up to the completion of the task.' He laughed. 'You may well look bemused! Here, come, I have a job for you. Engage with it, and take your mind off your concerns. Believe me, a solution will appear when the mind is at rest. And you'll be doing something useful for me.'

'Sir, I was only interested in what your God had to say about these things.'

'I don't know if you have noticed,' he said patiently, 'but the whole school is trying to get ready for School Inspection. What would be beneficial, is if you could help the teachers fix up their class areas with their charts and things on the walls.'

She smiled. 'Yes, sir. I understand.'

'Excellent! It will be good experience for you – and it will help me out too. Mr Franklin, the Standard Three teacher, is sick. I don't know how long for, but I need that class area prepared for inspection. I want this place to look like a first-class school by Monday morning, and for the inspector to go back to the Catholic Board and tell them. We need more books and supplies. We also need the latrines fixing. I think they have forgotten about us, so let's remind them. I want every wall covered with teaching charts.'

'Yes, sir. If you show me, I can do it.'

'You can do it, no problem,' he said, confidently. 'Pull down some of those old charts. Make new ones. Times-table charts. A map of Trinidad. Use your imagination.'

Amina's face lit up. She felt important.

'And about what you asked me,' he added. 'The man Jesus said, *Let the dead bury their dead.* Of course the dead cannot literally bury the dead. But you must not concern yourself with those who worship idols. It is all very nice, the rituals, but they are stone dead. Yesterday was most interesting, I must say. And some of it seemed to make sense. Of course, it will. But I can't say I understood that much about the balls of rice and such.'

'I think it is for Daya's spirit to eat when she gets hungry.'

'Well, what can I say to that! Why would a spirit need to eat?'

'I too don't understand a lot of what my parents believe and do. That's why I ask you what your God says.'

'You seem to ask a lot of questions about my God. I don't mind. It's good to ask questions about anything. When you stop asking, you stop learning. But each person must come to their own conclusion about what path to take in life – like anything else. You seem to be at loggerheads with your culture and religion in more ways than one. But you are an intelligent girl, so choose wisely. It is better to be like Mary instead of Martha in that respect. Both followed Jesus, but Mary chose to be close to him. To learn. *Seek ye first the Kingdom of God, and all things will be added.*'

'What is Kingdom, sir?'

'An end to the misery of this life. Paradise, girl, a new world where Jesus will rule.'

'You know such a lot, sir. I want to read it myself. Where can I get a Bible?'

The headmaster held up a hand. 'First I want you to concentrate on this task,' he said. 'It will mean a lot to the whole school if we get more supplies as a result of pleasing the inspector.'

ﻉ

Amina was late home that afternoon, and arrived with roles of paper.

'This is called the alphabet, Ma.' She unrolled one of the sheets of the old charts. 'It will help you learn English words. Makes it easy with the pictures.' Devinia stared in amazement. 'And this one – a map of Trinidad,' Amina continued.

'How do they know how to do that?' Devinia asked.

'Somebody went all round the island a long time ago and drew out the shape on a piece of paper, and that is how we know what it looks like. These are the mountains – see?' Amina pointed. 'These are north of the island, these are in the middle, and some south, near here. Look – oceans and seas around us. This says Columbus Channel.'

'Big words.' Devinia stared in admiration. 'It's pretty.'

'I did that one today.' Amina had used shades of green chalk to show where the cane plantations were, and yellow and brown for higher ground.

'Put it carefully upstairs,' her mother said, 'so the dog can't eat it.'

That night, Amina burned three candles and the oil lamp, working on the geography charts. The next day she started on the times-tables charts. There were six of them, two on each chart, with all the tables up to twelve times, differentiated by colour.

When she took them all in two days later, Mr Clifford gasped. He nailed them around the walls, then offered her services to other teachers. Gradually that week, the school walls grew colourful, with Amina's pictures of Columbus's ships, the *Santa Maria*, *Pinta*, and *Nina*, floating on dark green waves; parts of an insect; and various geographical and arithmetical charts, ready for the Schools' Inspector on the Monday morning.

ꕥ

Monday morning, School Inspection day. Mr Franklin returned to his Standard Three class and his eyes popped. Every inch of wall was covered with colourful charts, the attendance register was up to date with neat entries, and every book in the cupboard was in straight, tidy piles, and spotless. He was surprised.

Amina returned to her Standard Five class where she belonged as a pupil and sat in her usual place in Mr Mortimer's class. The whole school was warned that morning, and the noise level was low in anticipation of the inspector's visit. The day was tense.

At morning assembly on Tuesday, when all pupils were lined up in front of the double doors, Mr Clifford announced that the inspector had been most impressed. Mr Clifford praised everyone for being well behaved, and every teacher for the work they'd put in. At lunchtime, Mr Clifford saw Amina.

'You're looking pale,' he noted.

'Just a bit tired, sir.'

'The inspector was impressed, so it was all worth it. You did very, very well. You know the best thing? Those charts were so good, the inspector thought I'd done them myself when I said Mr Franklin was off sick last week.' Mr Clifford chuckled. 'Funny how it happened, because all I said was that I was up till late the night before, and he assumed it was me, and I . . . well, I found it hard to contradict him. I didn't have the heart to say a twelve-year-old pupil did it.'

'I'm twelve and a half, sir.

'I know, I know. You have the mind of a twenty-one-year-old sometimes. The strange thing is, the inspector wants me to go and show some of those schools up in San Fernando how to create colourful and informative charts like those. How did you do them so well?'

'I don't know, sir. I just looked in some of the map books in your office.'

'Could you do some more?' he asked. 'The practice will be good for you. And I'll put in a good word for you to start your teaching course a year early. Maybe you could begin when you're thirteen. Because you're so good at these charts, you made me have to tell a lie.' He laughed.

Amina smiled at the compliment, but her heart was pounding. 'Did I do something wrong, sir? Except . . . I don't want to cause you to go to hell, sir.'

'Hell? Why?'

'You didn't say the truth to the inspector, sir.'

'The truth? Oh, that. A white lie or two won't send me to hell. Not if I go to confession and say a few Hail Marys. After all, I am Catholic.'

'I didn't realise,' she said, feeling disappointed in him. 'But I can start the teacher training next year?'

'Oh of course.'

Amina decided that it was not worth telling him about her plan to teach the women at home, in case he advised her against her better judgement.

TWENTY-ONE

Amina and her mother got three other women from the village interested in learning English for half an hour at a time. The girl forgot her worries, and was delighted to be making a start on her project. She seated them all under her house at the far end, and began by showing them some familiar packaging such as a tin of condensed milk, Wright's Coal Tar Soap, and Vicks VapoRub, teaching them to recognise words by looking at their shape. Then she introduced her alphabet chart.

Sankar arrived home early one day and interrupted her class.

'Look what I brought for you,' he said, eager to show Amina something.

'Later, Pa,' was all she said, glancing at the red cloth in his hand.

'Just take a look,' he insisted.

'She say later,' Meena spoke up, giving Sankar one of her evil looks.

Sankar retreated looking dejected, and stroked Fluffy, who followed him halfway up the stairs. After the women had all gone, he rebuked Devinia in the bedroom for not warning him about what was going on and making him feel like a stranger in his own house.

'You have to get used to it,' she asserted. 'I am trying to support our daughter. She wants to help people her way. Have you forgotten how dangerously ill she was? It is the least you can allow her. Otherwise she will put her trust in other people.'

'Like who?' Sankar said.

'Like the headmaster.'

'She is Indian – our flesh and blood,' the man scoffed. 'He will never be able to convince her completely.'

'Don't be so sure. Sumati was her mother's flesh and blood too – and look what happened. And remember their friend Moonia? And the others? We cannot ignore it.'

'Well I cannot guarantee it, but I will try to go easy on her,' Sankar relented, then rebuked his wife again. 'But you must tell me everything. You made me look like a fool in front of all those women and my daughter.'

Hearing her father's angry voice, Amina went into the room. Seeing her, his face changed, and as promised his voice became calm and controlled.

'Listen, *beti,*' he said. 'I wanted to show you what I made for you. I finished it and polished it up today.'

He opened the cloth to show her the sparkling necklace he had made.

'Jewellery is important to us Indians,' he went on. 'You will be married soon. And a woman who wears a lot of jewellery shows she's well taken care of. It makes me swell with pride to see you walk down the road with gold around your neck, and hanging from your ears. Pride is important. Without it, what are you?'

Amina stared at her father. '*Before destruction, the heart of a man is proud*. Pride didn't keep me alive when I nearly died, Pa.'

'What is she talking about? You are her mother – do you know?' Sankar looked at his wife in bemusement.

'Don't ask me,' Devinia said. 'That is between both of you.'

'Between both of us?' he echoed. 'You were right before – it is that headmaster. What is he teaching you in that school that you are becoming so insolent and disobedient? Telling me about my destruction! You were a good child – but now? I don't know who you are.' Her father's voice cracked. 'You are killing me.'

'Amina,' Devinia said, 'just look at it. It is the most pretty, shining necklace your father has ever made. These things take a lot of time and gold.'

Amina glanced at it then looked away.

'Are you feeling well?' Sankar touched Amina's brow. 'Listen, it's also a practical matter. Jewellery is an investment. You can pawn it if you hit hard times, so it's as good as hard cash. But let's hope it will never come to that.'

'At least listen, Amina,' Devinia begged. 'Your dowry shows your value. The bride must have worth.'

Sankar nodded. 'Your mother is right. You see? She's come around to the correct decision,' he snorted. 'Endless education is for people who don't know the value of work.'

'My education will be my worth,' Amina said. 'And it is you, Pa, who is forcing Ma to say things.'

'Why don't you stop resisting, and choose at least the rhinestones for the big pieces? I've just got a new shipment.

Come with your Ma to the shop. You and she could look for the sari and *champals* too.'

Amina was seething, but aware that this argument could go on half the night, she relented.

'You see?' her father said. 'That wasn't so hard, now, was it?'

Devinia put her arms around Amina. She realised that education was a better option, but was not convinced that marriage was all bad. She had done it and it had worked well. The truth was that Devinia had a foot in both camps, which was now becoming painful as the camps were drifting further apart, causing conflict between her culture and her heart. Sankar made sense, and his reasoning was sound. The gods were on their side again – her prayers answered. Amina was alive, and Sankar's business was prospering. They wanted for nothing. They had land and properties, and their main dwelling was set in six acres filled with fruit trees and coconut palms. It wasn't a mud house with dirt walls and floor, or a shack sitting on the bare ground. It was wooden and well-built, and safe on high stilts. And Sankar was a well-respected man.

Amina listened to her parents and managed to slip back into the child she had loved being a year ago. It was safe and comfortable, and a relief from the turmoil in her mind.

ꙮ

After their evening meal, Devinia lit the kerosene lamps and sent the children to bathe.

'Your father wants to talk to you,' she told them.

After his wife's evening prayer at the altar, Sankar got them all together, and Amina and Etwar sat on the goatskin rug with their mother. The children looked at each other in the candlelight wondering what all this was about. It was usually their mother who would tell them tales from the *Bhagavad Gita*, or read from the *Ramayana*, not their father. He then sat cross-legged in front of them.

'The two of you are old enough to know what is what,' he began. 'And it's time I talked to you. This place is Trinidad, but it's not where I was born. But I chose to come here.'

'Yes, Pa,' Etwar answered first. 'I know.'

'I'm telling you this because they are not going to teach you this in school – that's for sure. To them it's not important. But to you, it should be. It's how you came to be here too. Maybe hundreds of years from now, they'll tell your great-great-grandchildren. But they will tell them a different story, I have no doubt. And not really how it happened.' He gazed up at the ceiling with a pensive look in his eyes. 'I'd like to be around if and when they do, though.'

He then cleared his throat, straightened his back and addressed them directly.

'I, your father, Sankar Banderjee, came from India.

I was a young man, accompanied by my older brother, and we had travelled a long way, from Uttar Pradesh in the northern part of India to Kolkata on the coast. But I had decided it was the best thing for me, and also for my brother, Narine. His situation was bad. He had to escape.'

'Escape? Why?' Etwar echoed, wide-eyed.

'We had heard of these ships,' Sankar continued. 'Coolie ships, they called them. Coolies. That's what they called Indians – all of us. But we are not coolie caste. Not labourers. I just want to make that clear to both of you. My caste was Thakuri. We were landowners. Anyhow, when my brother and I got to the docks in Kolkata, we found there were thousands of people – all kinds of people – waiting there. Every caste. It was a terrible ordeal. We managed to get through all the checks however, and filled out the forms. They told us there was money to be made if we came over here. A lot of it – in a land of plenty. England couldn't get enough of the sugar they were producing, they said. It was much encouragement.'

'What kind of encouragement?' Amina asked.

'I will tell you,' Sankar replied, smiling at her interest, then he murmured, almost to himself, 'Did I ever tell you that you look like my mother?'

'Yes, Pa.'

'Well, at the docks, they said all we had to do was sift sugar. Sift sugar? They were total tricksters! Needless to say, that was a lie. But Indians were so poor that we would have been taken in by anything. We had no idea where we were going. But I liked the sound of an adventure. We got on board a ship and took their word for granted. *Ram-ram-sita-ram*, it took us a good four months to get to this island. Four whole months!' he groaned.

'What did you eat?' Etwar asked. 'Did you catch plenty of fish in the sea?'

'That would have been a good idea,' his father replied, 'but nobody seemed to have thought of it. There were no nets, not even a broomstick to hit a fish if we did see one. Son, the food was terrible. Dried food – and half-boiled rice most of the time, with a spoonful of tasteless dhal. I mean, how is it possible to make dhal tasteless? There was no salt. Except sometimes we got an inch of dry salt-fish. Me and my brother, we were strong and healthy, but many others fell ill. Cholera and dysentery spread through the ship. Some couldn't take it, and jumped overboard to their deaths. When the rest of us finally got here, we were weak. They sent us to a place called Nelson Island – put us in quarantine.'

'What happened to your brother?' Amina asked fearfully.

'My brother . . . highly intelligent, but he did a stupid thing – he decided to . . .'

'It's time for the children to go and get some sleep now,' Devinia interrupted.

'No, Ma, I want to know what his brother did,' Etwar argued. 'That's our uncle.'

'I was adventurous,' Sankar sighed. 'I brought money – I had been working in India.'

'Were you making jewels there too?' Amina asked.

'Yes. I had just finished my apprenticeship, but people were handing down their jewellery more and more early, instead of buying new. So, my trade was not going that well. Everyone was hard up. Anyway, when we finally got here, we were put into those filthy barracks.' Sankar pulled a face. 'I decided then, I was not going to live like that.'

'What was wrong with it, Pa?' Etwar breathed.

'You mean what was right with it! Twelve people living in a small box. All strangers. Nothing private. You had to tread human filth, to get to the latrines, boy. And one small coal-pot to cook for the lot of us. Food rations were small.'

Amina curled her toes and shuddered.

'As for my brother . . .' Sankar continued, 'well, what I didn't tell you was that instead of listening to me and leaving quietly, he ran away with his sweetheart.'

Both children's eyes practically jumped out of their heads.

'You never told us that before,' Etwar said.

'Your mother never wanted me to tell you. You see, this is

what happens when you break the rules. In India anyhow. My brother fell in love with the daughter of a Brahmin.'

'Like you and Ma?'

'We are in Trinidad, not India.'

'But you are Hindu,' Amina said.

'It is hard enough to find a suitable other Indian for your children, let alone worrying about which caste they are from. Look at your mother and me. She is Brahmin, I am Thakuri. Since on the ship, no one bothered about caste. We were all brothers and sisters on those journeys.' He sighed. 'All that sickness and death just brought us closer.'

'So, we are all the same caste then!' Etwar exclaimed.

'Quite right, son.' Sankar nodded approvingly. 'If we consider ourselves brothers and sisters, how can there be any caste difference between us?'

'But many are still looking for caste matches for their children,' Devinia said.

'People will always want what they don't have instead of making most of what they *do* have. And working for it! They always harp back to India. They can't embrace change.'

'I'm glad you said that, Pa,' Amina told him. 'Because that is what I think too.'

'What happened to the girl?' Etwar asked. 'Did she run away from home as well?'

'She did, unfortunately,' Sankar said. 'I told my brother to leave her behind.

"You'll forget her about her soon enough," I said. "You'll have a new life." But no! He didn't listen. He had to be with her. He was struck down with love. . . But they couldn't stand the barrack conditions when they arrived.'

'So where is our Uncle Narine now?' Etwar wanted to know. 'Did he go back to India?'

'Enough. No more of this,' Devinia interjected.

'Are you mad?' Sankar continued, ignoring her as he replied to his son. 'If they went back to India, they would be made to suffer. They would be outcasts, and nobody would speak to them. That is why some people ran away to the ships in the first place. It was a chance to escape all of that.'

'So where are they now?'

'Sadly, my son, I have lost touch with him. My only brother.'

Devinia ushered the children off to bed, leaving her husband quietly brooding, reliving the past. She knew he needed to be alone to think about those he had lost. Sankar remained there deep in thought about what he had lost, and how to smooth the path for his own children.

TWENTY-TWO

One day, the gossip at the standpipe changed again. Someone said that Sumati was back home. Apparently, the missing girl had been found wandering near the Cedros docks, battered and bruised, and asking her way back to Granville. Amina gulped for air. Cedros was a long way off San Fernando, where she and Farouk had headed.

'Was anyone with her?' Amina asked.

No one seemed to know. Some had guessed that she was with Farouk as he also had disappeared – which was why both their families were *cujart*, being shunned.

When Amina asked around, Ramona said that Sumati had definitely not been at home because she would have seen her. But Pryia said that someone had told her that the Kamalsingh boy who lived near the big rose mango tree, had been spotted with her.

'I can't believe that,' Amina said stoutly. 'He was at the funeral and he was on his own. Besides he said . . . No – nothing. I'll go past her house. There's bound to be washing at least on the line.'

ꝏ

The day after Daya's funeral, Rajnath's father, Kamal Singh, was up early as usual. He worked at the Coromandel sugarcane plantation as an overseer, and was never late. As he made his ablutions, he noticed that two of the wooden slats on the bathroom walls were broken, leaving an immodest gap facing the house. There had been a wind in the night, but he hadn't thought it was that strong. He went to the woodshed to get some wood to mend it but as he entered, he jumped back in shock.

Two chickens flew out of the shed as if they were possessed by some spirit, and ran off into the yard, squawking madly. He couldn't understand why they would be there at all, unless they had got locked in by mistake. They normally roosted in the trees with the others, huddled close together on a branch. He wondered if they had become too fat to fly because Parbatee, his wife, was over-feeding them hoping they would lay more often. He rummaged through the different lengths of logs and bags of charcoal, looking for something suitable, when he had the strangest sensation on finding a big bundle of something soft in the corner.

Kamal Singh backed out of the shed immediately, his heart pounding. He closed the door behind him quietly and hurried across into the house to find Parbatee. He sat on the chair at the side of the bed, breathless and barely able to speak. His wife had just woken up.

'What happened?' she yawned. 'You look like you've seen a *jumbie*?'

'You had better come outside and see for yourself. Come on.'

'What? Are the chickens dead? Mongoose got them?'

Parbatee kept guessing as she hobbled out in her chemise, but all she could see was her son, Rajnath, in the yard in his vest and shorts, a knife in his hand, cutting a *datwan* from the hibiscus bush to clean his teeth.

'Morning, Pa!' the boy called.

'I thought you were still asleep,' Kamal Singh said to his son.

'You want me to get a thrashing?' Rajnath replied, a sly grin on his face. 'You know what overseers are like if you're late.

Rajnath worked as a cane cutter on the Galapados sugarcane estate, a different one to his father, and since their altercation some months back, he now spoke to him as little as possible. The quarrel had ended with his mother and brother Annan having to separate the two men physically.

Ignoring his son's rudeness, Kamal Singh was surprised to see the shed door open. He was certain he had closed it behind him. He quickened his pace to the doorway, beckoning Parbatee to come with him.

'What are you looking for?' Rajnath said.

'It's gone.' Kamal stood at the doorway with one hand on his hip, scratching his head. 'I must be going mad.'

'Yeah, Pa! There's no *must be* about that. Old *and* mad.'

Parbatee was waddling as fast as she could, dragging her feet, inside the wooden slippers. She stood next to her husband, who was staring inside the shed full of chopped pieces of firewood and logs.

'Well I never!' he uttered, and pulled the towel tight around his waist.

Just then a big bird fluttered past them, out of the shed, leaving them shivering.

Parbatee began to shake. 'It's a sign,' she whispered. 'And it's suddenly gone cold.'

'You felt that too?' Kamal asked.

'What is it you called me outside to see?' she asked grumpily.

'There was something inside here,' Kamal said.

'Kamal Singh has gone mad.' Rajnath laughed out loud. 'An owl just flew out of there. What did you think it was – a ghost? It was nothing.'

'Boy,' Parbatee said in a pacifying tone, 'watch your mouth. He is your father. Don't forget that.'

'Nothing?' Kamal said quietly. 'It was *not* nothing. I know I saw something.'

ꟽ

That afternoon, Rajnath wasted no time leaving the plantation after clocking out. He rushed past the men, women and children who were chatting and plodding towards the tool sheds and got home by five o'clock just as the sun was lowering in the sky. He stripped off his grass-stained work clothes and muddy rubber boots, and filled a bucket with some rainwater from the copper at the back of the house to bathe. It was warm from the sun but refreshing. He splashed a few calabash-fuls over himself and scrubbed the day's plantation dirt off with the block of blue marble washing soap. As he washed, he was mulling over what he was about to do. Half-dry, he hurried inside and took a clean, pressed shirt, hoping his mother wouldn't ask any questions. Then he laced up his shiny boots and slipped away down the road towards the standpipe.

He passed people walking home from work, or from their day's gardening with garden forks and machetes swinging, and jute bags full of fruit and vegetables over their shoulders. Dogs barked from yards, and branches rustled in the late-afternoon breeze scented with orange blossom. Rajnath smoothed his wet, oiled hair with his hands as he got to the standpipe. He looked for Amina at the standpipe but he had either missed her, or she hadn't yet been to fetch water. He continued walking and spotted Etwar on his way back home with a bundle of grass on his head.

'How are you?' Rajnath called out.

'All right, man!'

Moments later, Rajnath saw the glint of gold on a thin figure gliding across the road, her diamond-cut earrings slicing the sunlight, giving her away. His heart jumped and he turned around and hurried towards her.

'We have to talk,' he said abruptly. 'It's about your friend. Meet me by the spring.'

'No,' Amina said firmly. 'I'll be in trouble. Besides, no one goes there anymore.'

'That's good,' he said. 'I have to talk to you alone. It's important. Be there.'

He turned and disappeared through the gap in the bushes which led to the short cut, leaving Amina bemused. The pink Jump-up-and-Kiss-me flowers were still open, catching the last rays of the sun. Rajnath headed towards the old wooden barrack building about fifty yards from the main spring. It was empty. Passing a tangerine tree, he jumped and pulled down a low branch full of fruit.

Meanwhile, Amina returned home from the standpipe with a bounce in her step.

'Ma,' she called, 'I'm just going to see one of my friends. I'll get more water later.'

'Don't worry about the water,' Devinia replied. 'Go and see your friends.'

Amina hurried off, worried about getting caught. A clandestine meeting with Rajnath would give her as bad a reputation as Sumati, but she had to go – for Sumati's sake. As she walked she tried to turn back but her legs went faster, until she got to the spring, breathless.

There was nothing but a heap of clothes sitting next to the top pool, where the water gushed out through the rocks and pebbles, clear and blue from the sky's reflection. She hadn't been there for months. Memories of early childhood returned: her mother washing clothes under the shade of the green, overhanging trees; children running around the grassy banks between the white items spread stiff on the grass to bleach in the blazing sun; naked children splashing in the shallow end of the pool, while older people bathed in the deeper, downstream end, in skin-soaked pink petticoats, or long johns. She recalled the day she had slipped and felt the water cover her nose . . . Amina broke out in a cold sweat, and looked around to see if anyone had returned to claim their washing. But no one was there.

She leaned on the trunk of a tree and watched the water, remembering how the spring would swell when it rained, and the fun she and Etwar had splashing till it turned murky, drinking it as they bathed. The doctor said that although that water looked clean, it was more than likely where she might have picked up the typhoid. Her father refused to believe it. He said the water was given by the gods. It could never be dirty. The doctor said different, and Amina did not know who to believe. But the doctor was a learned man who must have read scores of books. Her father had the sort of learning that could not be read in books.

The spring looked inviting, and she longed to strip off and leap in, but not after having suffered typhoid.

Then something swirled in the water close to the huge rock, and a head appeared. It was a young woman with long hair. Her slim curves hugged the pale chemise, clinging, wet around her body, and the water ran down her skin as she rose to full height. Amina couldn't believe her eyes.

'Sumati? Is that you?'

The woman was wiping the water off her face and neck, and wringing out her hair. Then a man's voice shouted, crystal clear.

'I got some,' he said.

Rajnath was coming out of the old, disused barracks, walking towards the spring, calling out to Sumati. He didn't look around, and so didn't see Amina on the other side. He was naked to the waist. His shirt was hanging on a low branch of a tree. It looked like the one she had seen him wearing earlier.

Amina's legs went weak. It was Sumati, all right. Thinner, but still her friend. The girl got out of the pool, shaking herself and smoothing down the wet chemise even closer around her body, twisting her hair into a bun as Rajnath approached her. He handed her something pink – a pomerac. She bit into it ravenously. In no time it was gone, and she flung the stone into the bushes and took another.

Amina gripped her stomach. The two of them were laughing intimately. Why would he ask her to come to watch this? For reasons she couldn't understand, she felt foolish and also wretched. She knew Sumati liked boys, but where was Farouk? She stood rooted to the ground and watched them walk together. Rajnath reached up, took his shirt off the tree and threw it over his shoulder. She watched it fall around his bronzed, muscular arms, and felt confused.

As Sumati picked up the pile of her clothes from the grass and strolled towards the barracks, Rajnath turned and saw Amina.

'Hey! I didn't think you were coming.'

'Yes, I can see that,' Amina said. 'I can also see you have made friends with Sumati. How do you know her?'

'She's in a lot of trouble. She needs help. I came across her last night at the cemetery, near her mother's grave. She had nowhere to go. She hasn't eaten today.'

'So you brought her pomerac?'

'I forgot to bring her food. She spent the night in our shed – but don't tell anyone.'

He saw that Amina still looked upset and appealed to her.

'I couldn't leave her like that. She was desperate.'

'I understand that. But did you tell her that her father blames me? That she is the good girl, and I am the *jagabat?*'

'Stop! You don't know what you're saying. I don't think you even understand that word.'

'Well, I'm not stupid.' She looked Rajnath straight in the eye.

'Don't bother about Roopchand,' Rajnath said. 'The man is out of his mind with misery.'

Sumati eventually emerged from the barracks, dried and dressed, but without her usual bouncy gait. Something had changed. Sumati was definitely a woman, and Amina felt a child in comparison.

'It's so nice to see you,' Sumati said, smiling.

'Nothing's changed, then.' Amina stared at her.

Sumati's smile disappeared. Her eyes filled. 'Nothing will ever be the same again,' she said. Her voice saddened.

'You're right. I've spoilt everything – for myself, and for everyone else. I'm a bad person. You don't want anything to do with me. Nobody should.' She turned to walk back towards the barracks.

'Go after her,' Rajnath said. 'Talk to her. She is your friend, and she needs you. *You!* Go on.'

Amina followed Sumati and caught up with her.

'I'll walk home with you,' she said.

Sumati sighed. 'There is no place to call home anymore. Home is where my mother is.'

'Your mother wouldn't want you to just wander around outside. I know that.'

'Then why did she do what she did?' Sumati cried out.

'Who knows? She couldn't take the strain.'

'My fault then.' Sumati looked to the ground, grinding the earth under her heel.

'I don't know where you have been or what happened to you. But not going back home will not help you, or your father, or your brother. Especially you.'

'You don't have any idea what it is like out there in the world.'

'That is true. I don't. But I do know that you should go in and make it up with your father. Think about Kesh. He needs you. You all need each other.'

'My father might just kill me,' Sumati said tiredly. 'But I deserve it.'

'Do you want me to come in with you?' Amina offered. 'Your father doesn't like me but I don't care. Or you could come home with me instead. Till you're ready to go back.'

'No, you're right. I should go home.'

Without another word, Sumati turned and strode in the direction of home. Amina followed, and watched her disappear down the path at the side of her house. She waited, listening for any disturbing noises, before leaving. Twilight was falling, and she could see Rajnath's silhouette in the distance. Her pulse began to race, and by the time she got home her head was in turmoil. He had explained himself but it wasn't enough. And Sumati had said nothing about where she had been or how she'd become so thin. But why was Rajnath so bothered about Sumati's welfare? And why was she, Amina, bothered that he was?

TWENTY-THREE

It was Saturday morning, and Devinia came into Amina's bedroom and flung open the windows, letting in the sun.

'It's late,' she said. 'Breakfast is ready. And there's a pot of hot water for you to bathe.'

Etwar's voice came sailing fast through her doorway. 'Why didn't I get warm water?'

'Don't be a girl!' Sankar shouted from the bedroom. 'A good cold bath is what you need first thing in the morning. It'll make a man of you! Listen, I need a strong boy with me today. We are going to help your mother fetch a heifer from Bonasse.'

'Who's going to look after another cow?' Etwar asked, looking worried.

Amina burst out in fits of laughter. 'You, that's who.'

'No!' Etwar said. 'It's not fair!'

'*Dharma,* boy! That's your job,' Sankar grinned. 'Didn't I tell you?'

ꟸ

Amina was sitting in the hammock eating her breakfast when Sumati appeared, carrying a big brown-paper bag. Her cheeks were drawn and her eyes sunken. Devinia looked as if she had seen a ghost.

'I can't stay there,' Sumati blurted out.

'So it's true,' Devinia said. 'You have come back – to be the woman of the house.'

Amina looked at her mother, alarmed.

'But I don't want to,' Sumati pleaded. 'My mother made it bearable to be there. I can't be in the same house with my father. You don't know him.'

'Give him time,' Devinia counselled. 'He has a lot of worries, but you are his daughter.' Devinia's eyes glistened. 'He will change. You're no longer a child and you already left home, so you'll be able to manage the house till you're married. At least do it till then.'

'You're still getting married?' Amina gasped.

Sumati rolled her eyes and twisted her mouth.

'Ma,' Amina said. 'This has nothing to do with us.'

'I'm only giving my advice,' Devinia defended herself. 'Judging by how her life's going so far, not in school and not working, what's her choice?'

'Her mother's just died.'

'That's why she must think straight. Daya cannot think for her now. Go! Take her upstairs. She could stay one night, that's all.'

'Thanks, *Tantie*,' Sumati answered sheepishly, but relieved.

That night in bed, Amina did most of the talking. Sumati seemed to have little to say. The wind outside rustled the leaves, and a bird tweeted unexpectedly. Devinia shouted for them to blow out the candle. They did, but continued whispering.

'Amina,' Sumati said all of a sudden. 'I'm so worried. I think something's happened.'

ꙮ

The next morning, the girls were downstairs eating their breakfast, sitting in the hammock shoulder to shoulder, rocking gently, when Sumati suddenly stalled the rocking with her heel.

'Don't tell anybody what I told you last night.'

'Then don't talk so loud,' Amina said. 'Look, I've no idea what you could do, but I'll think about who to ask.'

'What y'all whispering 'bout?' Etwar said, appearing out of nowhere. 'Boys!'

'Boys?' Sumati snorted. 'That's the last thing on my mind.'

'You might think boys are important,' Amina added, 'but they're just the nastiest, wormiest creatures we could think of right now.'

'Alright,' Etwar said, twisting his face. 'But your brother's up the top of the road, looking at you.'

They all glanced towards the road. Etwar was right. Kesh was indeed there.

'Duck!' Amina said. 'Kesh must be looking for you, or me.'

But Kesh turned away and continued walking. Amina was now trembling with worry. She was out of her depth, even though Sumati seemed to expect her to come up with some wise plan. As they walked back towards Sumati's house, she did her best.

'If it was me, I would see the doctor when he comes to Granville next.'

'Sometimes you know nothing.' Sumati sounded exasperated.

'At least I know when I know nothing – like you right now. Which is why I am suggesting you see the doctor.'

'You know, there was a time when there were no doctors. But there was always somebody in the village who knew what to do.'

'But you wouldn't contemplate that!' Amina was indignant. 'You want to go to some Obeah woman?'

'Not exactly.'

'Then talk to somebody,' Amina implored. 'Somebody who you trust. Older. And just because you didn't have your bleeding doesn't mean what you're thinking. Sometimes that could just happen. I read in a book once, that it could be because of starvation or some kind of bad illness. And you have become very thin. Weren't you eating?'

'A book?' Sumati repeated. 'Starvation? What kind of book have you been reading?'

'A proper book I got from Mr Clifford's cupboard. I think you'll be all right.'

'You think so?' Sumati said nastily. 'Well, you're the one with the brains.'

'Just keep your head down. Do what you have to do to stop your father and brother from making your life miserable. Soon you'll have a life of your own.'

'My life will never be my own, Amina. I can't believe you're saying that I should marry that old man.'

'There might have been a better way if you hadn't run away in the first place. I hope you realise that, so please don't do that again. You would have had more choices. Like staying on at school, or showing your parents that

Farouk was as good a match as any. Especially when he got a job. They might have seen you would be happy. Instead you ran away with him, and he had no job.'

'And that is why my mother killed herself. I know.'

Amina didn't reply. Sumati could be right, especially that she had left with a Muslim boy.

When they reached Sumati's house, Amina ran to peer down the side to see if Roopchand was there. He wasn't, so Amina left. But as she walked back up the road, she spotted Rajnath heading straight towards her.

'Where have you been?' he asked, looking alarmed.

'Just down to the spring.'

'You have to be careful,' he warned. 'You shouldn't go there on your own.'

A mosquito bit her hard on her arm, and Amina realised that she had just done something she abhorred. She had just told a lie.

ꟿ

Sumati was bathing in the spring one afternoon when she heard someone whistling. Seeing no one, she hid behind the big rock to watch and listen as she could hear the whistler approaching. She almost jumped out of her skin to see Rajnath, swinging a cricket bat, spinning it around his fingers and circling his shoulders. As he looked towards the middle of the spring, Sumati dropped herself into the water up to her neck, and stared at him.

'How's it going with your father?' he shouted. He sat himself down cross-legged on a rock at the edge of the water, oblivious to the fact that she was bathing.

'Have you heard from Farouk?' he asked.

'I could ask you the same,' she called back. 'He's *your* friend.'

'But you persuaded him to run away. I know he was worried about leaving.'

Sumati squeezed her nose and ducked her head completely under the water, drowning out anything he was saying. Rajnath stood up fast. Girls couldn't swim. Thinking he'd upset her, he ripped his shirt off and jumped into the water. But she rose up as fast as she had gone down. When he surfaced, all he could do was stare as the water dripped off her curves.

'Why have you come here pretending to be interested in Farouk?' she said. 'If you were his friend, you'd know where he is.'

'If something has happened to him, I want to know.'

'Both you and me then,' she said.

'I have a right to know.'

'What right? What will people think if they see you in here with me? Get out of the water.'

'Let people think what they want,' he said, stepping up to the bank.

'It's lies and gossip that put my mother in her grave.'

'People see what you are showing them,' he said. 'You ran away with Farouk. You gave them something to gossip about. And then you came home without Farouk, with no explanation.'

'You want an explanation? Me too! He left me. He abandoned me without explanation.'

'Here – dry yourself and walk with me,' Rajnath said, holding her towel up. 'We need to do some serious talking.'

Sumati took the towel and stormed off towards the empty wooden barracks, where she would change into dry clothes.

Rajnath sat down on the bank, picking up pebbles and throwing them into the water, muttering to himself, 'The Farouk I knew would never have gone off and left you. He's not that kind.'

When Sumati reappeared, her damp clothes clinging to her hips, he had to force himself not to stare.

'Walk this way with me,' he said sternly. 'We'll take the bush path and you can tell me what happened to my friend.'

'So you don't care if somebody sees us then?' she said. 'Not even Amina?'

'What do you mean?'

She didn't reply. They walked through the bushes in silence. The grass underfoot rustled; the birds twittered, hopping from tree to tree, ravenous for ripe fruit; a dry coconut dropped, bouncing like a ball; overripe mangoes fell as a sudden hard wind shook them off their stalks. The air felt chilly.

'What kind of a person are you?' Rajnath cried, breaking the silence. 'Maybe I should give up trying to help you. What are you thinking? Do you in fact think at all? All I did was tried to help the two of you. I thought you were in love. I thought you had the real thing. If I didn't help, you would have had nowhere to stay. Did you really think you could run away to nowhere? For how long?'

But Sumati refused to listen; it was too painful to hear him say the words that made so much sense. Too painful and too late.

She took off and ran, and this time, Rajnath did nothing to stop her.

TWENTY-FOUR

Roopchand tried to ignore his daughter's presence in the house. She was a constant irritant, but at the same time she reminded him of her mother and he felt relieved to have her there. At times he wanted to tear every hair from her head, but at others, he wanted to hug her tight till he almost smothered her. But hugging was not his thing.

The girl was being helpful, doing things that Daya used to do, which in a way eased his burden. But her natural buoyancy got on his nerves. It wasn't always like that though, and he knew that her heart was heavy. She took to meeting Amina in private to talk, away from either of their houses. Roopchand knew this. He worried because her mother had taken her life, and he didn't want her to go the same way. So he let her go.

One evening, after she met with Amina, her mood seemed lighter.

'I've been to the doctor,' Sumati told her friend. 'I was right. I'm having a baby, but . . . I don't know who the father is.'

'What? How many fathers could it have?'

Sumati sighed. 'You don't know anything, do you?'

'You always try to make me feel bad for not knowing what *you* know. What is it I'm supposed to know this time? I know how people get a baby in their stomach, Sumati – that's not hard to find out. But you went with Farouk. So, you and Farouk did it – right? And now you're saying . . .'

'It's not him,' Sumati interrupted. And seeing her friend's incomprehension, she shrugged and muttered, 'San Fernando is not a good place.'

'What do you mean? What does that have to do with it? And that cannot be true about the whole of San Fernando. My mother goes there to buy all sorts of things from India – saris, champals, and so on. She would never go to a place that was bad.'

'I'm telling you – there are some places that you wouldn't want to go. Really, really bad, girl. Look, I want you to come with me to find wild yam.'

'You cannot eat that. It's bitter.' Amina looked at her friend curiously. 'I've heard it's poisonous.'

'I know.'

'You're not going to kill yourself, are you? I can't believe you can even think about doing that!'

'After my mother hanged herself, is that it?'

'Should I tell you a lie, Sumati? What happened to us being friends? Sisters.'

'That stopped when I left Granville.'

'Not for me. I was annoyed, but I hoped you were happy. You said you were in love. It looks like something happened to you and you don't trust me enough to tell me. Where is Farouk?'

'He caused all of this. I don't want to speak about him, and if you and me are still friends, like you say, you must help me get rid of this thing in my belly. Find some wild yam.'

'I am going to help you as much as I can,' Amina told her, 'but I am not going to help you kill a baby inside you, and yourself. That is murder, and I can't let you do it. *Thou shalt not kill.* Promise me you will stop thinking about it. We will find a way. Really, we will.' She embraced her friend tightly, wondering which one of Mr Clifford's books would have the answers.

ઇઌ

That Sunday morning, Devinia woke up Amina earlier than usual. She instructed her to bathe scrupulously clean from head to toe with the warm water she had left in the bathroom, and to dress with care in the outfit she would lay out on her bed. Devinia had been shopping in San Fernando and had bought her a number of pretty and expensive items imported from India.

'Where are we going, Ma?' the girl asked. 'Why have I got to wear . . . that? Is there a wedding today? I can't hear any drums.'

'Hurry up,' was all Devinia said. 'We are expecting visitors later.'

Etwar also had similar instructions before Devinia disappeared into the kitchen to finish making the Indian sweets she had started.

'I think we might be having special people visiting,' he said to his sister.

It was around eleven that morning that two men arrived while Amina was still upstairs putting on the new earrings her father had made. Devinia called her from the bottom of the steps.

'Come down slowly, child,' her mother said. 'You don't want to trip.'

She looked beautiful as she walked down the steps in the new green and gold sari, with matching champals on her feet which dragged a little as they were slightly too big. As she turned the corner down the steps, two men stood next to the bench, and sat down when she sat next to Etwar.

'Ma?' she began. But her mother looked at her very sternly, so she stopped.

Devinia brought out drinks and Indian sweets and offered them to the men as well as to the family. From the conversation, it was clear that they were business people, and from their outfits, a jacket and tie, they were pretty much anglicized and well to do. There was no Bhojpuri or Hindi being spoken, so it was a very easy environment for the children. Although her mother did struggle a little, Amina and Etwar listened, smiled when appropriate and even giggled on one occasion. The younger of the two men smiled a lot and spoke particularly good English, even better than Dr Boyle, who did speak a little oddly at times. They took the two men around the garden, and told them how much land was at the back of the house, and at one time both Etwar and Amina looked at each other, wondering the same thing. But they dared not interrupt to ask.

After a good long while, both men left and said that they were pleased with everything and would definitely be in touch.

When they had gone, the children couldn't wait to find out the news.

'Why are you selling the house?' Etwar asked his parents.

'What makes you think that?' Devinia asked. 'Don't

you know that is the boy we have in mind for your sister?' she went on. 'You heard them. They are well to do, and well-spoken in English. Educated to the best standard too. What do you think?'

At first Amina wasn't sure she had heard correctly. 'You are not talking about me.'

'Who else?' Sankar said.

'It cannot be me. You made me dress as if you're selling a piece of furniture? After all I've said? There is nothing you can do to get me to agree to that! Nothing.'

'You will do as I say,' her father said. 'You are my daughter and will do as I please. People have put ideas in your head that are very much against our customs. You are Indian. You cannot change that. It's time to stop playing at being English.'

'Ma?'

'Your father has chosen well,' Devinia said. 'The boy is good-looking, and he was educated in a top school in Port of Spain. Also, they have a good thriving business.'

'All you think about is money and business. Well I'm not interested. And his education is not mine.'

'I tried hard to find someone suitable,' Sankar said. 'Pundit Lall had good contacts.'

'Him?' she said. 'Now I understand. Do you want me to do something you will regret?' With that Amina stormed off up to her room, stripped herself of her new clothes, shoes and jewellery, flung it all out of the window and threw herself on her bed.

Devinia went outside and picked up Amina's things and slumped in the hammock.

'Leave her,' Sankar advised. 'Let her stew. She is bound to come to her senses. The girl is not stupid. She knows it is money that gives her a comfortable life so that she can pursue this education nonsense instead of a paid job.'

Amina overheard him. 'You are so wrong, Pa!' she screamed. 'You have just done something you will always regret.'

TWENTY-FIVE

Rajnath spent the whole day at work worried about why Sumati was being so secretive about Farouk. He had been so distracted that twice he was warned by the driver at work, who took the whip to him once. When he got home, Rajnath picked up his father's gun for the second time in two days, and headed out. The previous time he had returned with a good catch from their forest land, and that was his first time hunting alone. Parbatee was pleased he was at last a man – bringing home the food.

'Ma!' he called out. 'Do you know who owns the piece of land behind our Bonasse land? I want to buy it.'

'Buy it with what? We have already promised you the three acres of forest land – as soon as we fix a wedding date. But first, we need to find you a wife.'

'I will find my own,' he said abruptly.

'Do you know how we got that land?' she asked her son. 'When your father first arrived here from India, he worked as a labourer in the cane fields for five years, before the government offered him the chance to return to India, or remain. He stayed, and got the three acres kind of cheapish. They were encouraging people to stay, but only paying twenty-five cents a day for labouring. Your father was made overseer, because he was more educated than the others, and could speak the English like an Englishman, as you know. And we had been promised to each other to marry, so he chose to remain. He was lucky because he had good schooling in India. Of course he spoke Bhojpuri too – an asset on the plantation. So, he bought the maximum amount of land – three acres.'

'Ma, you know you have told me this already?'

'And I will tell you many more times,' Parbatee said severely. 'You think everything comes easy? That you were just born lucky? Look around you – mud huts and half-built board houses ready to blow down in a puff of wind.'

She looked at her son. 'Where are you going with your father's gun again?' she asked. 'I don't want any more squirrel. We don't eat it.'

'I'm going to fetch a machete, so I can clear out some of the land. There's cocoa growing there, and the squirrels are damaging every pod.'

Rajnath went to the shed and pulled open the door. As he stepped inside, something big fluttered under the roof. A shadow moved from the narrow beam of daylight coming through the gap in the top slat of wood. He stopped still and looked up, shivering as if a blanket of ice had dropped over him.

'Help her.'

Rajnath stood frozen to the spot. He turned to bolt, but before he could do so, the flutterer flew out in what seemed like a flash.

'There's owls in that shed,' his mother shouted. 'I don't know when they started living there, but one just came flying out. Your father thinks it's something else in there, though!'

She stopped and looked at her son. Rajnath was stumbling oddly, and leaning on the doorpost.

'What is it?' she said. 'You're as white as a sheet!'

Rajnath didn't respond.

'What is it, boy?' she said urgently. 'You're frightening me. Did a scorpion sting you? Tell me, quick! It could kill you.'

Rajnath closed the door, shuffling as he went in the house. His mother followed.

'It's not a scorpion,' he said. 'But there's something in that shed.'

'Well, your father said so too, the morning after the funeral. But I'm here all day and I only ever see birds sometimes. It's just owls, nothing more. They fly in, and they fly out if you go in. Otherwise, they don't come out till dark.'

'It's . . . something else.' Rajnath spat his words awkwardly. 'Birds don't talk.'

Parbatee gaped at him, looking puzzled.

'I'm making sweet tea for you now,' she said. 'I think you must have a fever. I was right the other day. You had better lie down. Come, son, rest yourself.'

Rajnath stumbled to his bed and closed his eyes, unable to even think about arguing back.

ஐ

Rajnath decided that the only way to find out what had happened to Farouk was to go and see his uncle in San Fernando. He took the sloop from Cedros harbour, instead of going by horse or donkey cart. It was cheaper and more straightforward. He left home at dawn with his breakfast and lunch wrapped up in brown paper, feeling daunted.

When he arrived at the wharf in San Fernando, he disembarked and walked up the back of the town. Everything seemed different to what he remembered. The new buildings were huge, and filled the spaces along the road, which made the trees seem smaller. He approached the house with memories returning of school holidays, kicking empty cans and dry coconuts around the yard with his cousin Dillip, and pelting stones at ripe mangoes on the trees at the rear of the house. For a while, nostalgia chased away his worries, and he almost expected to see Dillip running up, ready to jump on him, throwing him to the ground and them rolling around over each other. But instead, he heard another familiar voice.

'Look who it is!' His Uncle Amrit punched Rajnath gently on the arm. 'What are you doing here? You came to San Fernando for shopping? Come! Come inside. Sit down.'

'Thanks, uncle.'

'Look at you – the big man.' He held Rajnath by the shoulders and looked him up and down. 'So handsome!'

Rajnath smiled, embarrassed by the compliment.

'I can't believe my sister's son is so big. She must be so proud. Me too!' He slapped his nephew on the back.

'Where's Dillip?'

'Dillip has gone out on business. He'll be back later.'

The two of them sat on a bench under the almond tree

in the front yard and chatted, drinking rum and coconut water before lunch was brought out from the kitchen.

'Who is the woman in the kitchen?' Rajnath asked.

'Your mother didn't tell you that Kalouti just packed up and left me one day?'

'No, I didn't know.'

'Yes. I came home one day and caught her at it. She was planning to clean me out – furniture and all.'

'But why would she do that?'

'You surprised? Boy, I was surprised too. No explanation – not a damn thing worth listening to, anyhow. Left me high and dry. We didn't eat for two days after she left. Mangoes and coconut water, that's all. I had to get somebody in. That woman in the kitchen, that is Tonia. That's why she's here. Tonia will do anything for me. Anything.'

'Oh,' Rajnath said. He watched the large bachak ants walk in a perfect line, following each other with pieces of green leaves in their mouths. 'You built up a big place here. When did you put up all this extension?'

'Extension? That is a separate whole new building on that side. We did that last year.'

'So, business must be going well then,' Rajnath remarked, looking around.

'Which business?' Amrit sounded surprised. 'Oh, you mean the shop. Not too bad.'

Rajnath frowned, a little bewildered. 'Well, it's looking busy. You have a good few customers there, right now.'

'We have a good hotel business too. Many businessmen stay here. I told your mother, "When the boys get married, I will pay for everything".'

'Thanks, uncle. But first I have to find a wife.'

'I'm looking. I told your mother to leave it to me.'

'I didn't know about that either,' Rajnath said. 'When is Dillip coming home?'

'Don't bother about Dillip. He comes home when he's ready.'

'Hmm! Things really have changed around here!' Rajnath commented.

'Dillip is another story. We don't see eye to eye on a few things, starting with the company he keeps. Maybe you could talk some sense into him.'

'I don't know, uncle. But what about Farouk – when is *he* coming home?'

'Farouk?' Amrit laughed. 'He was no good. He disappeared a long time ago. Ran off not long after he arrived with the girl. She was very upset, but we managed to calm her down, gave her a place to stay. Then said she wanted to go and see her family. But she never returned.'

'Really?' Rajnath was surprised. 'She is back in Granville, but refuses to talk about Farouk.'

'If you ask me, she is another ungrateful one. We gave her everything. She just ran away one day and didn't even tell anyone. We searched for her, but we didn't find her.'

'I thought you said she wanted to go and see her family?' Rajnath asked, feeling uneasy.

'You told me she was in Granville,' Amrit reminded him.

'You said it first, uncle. Or maybe I am mistaken. Anyhow, have you any idea where Farouk is?'

'When you find out, let me know,' Amrit said, easily. 'I have no idea. Look, the lunch is here. Tonia is a master cook.'

Rajnath felt confused, but he said no more about it. Maybe Kalouti leaving the way he said she did, had addled his uncle's mind. The two men ate, and didn't wait for Dillip. And Amrit was right about Tonia's cooking.

TWENTY-SIX

Rajnath saw Amina again at the standpipe and told her he had news for her. She hurried back home to empty her bucket before darting down the road to meet him. She turned the corner after Sumati's house, melting into the shadows below the trees. By the time she got there, she was breathless. Rajnath was leaning on a coconut tree trunk with a blade of grass between his lips. Her heart thumped from guilt about breaking the rules on meeting boys.

'I see you are not bothered so long as nobody's looking,' he said, grinning.

'You well know that this will only bring trouble. But you said you wanted to see me because of Sumati. So?'

'I said that? I went to see my uncle in San Fernando on Saturday. But I didn't find out anything.'

'What does your uncle have to do with Sumati?'

'They went to his house to stay till they got on their feet,' Rajnath explained.

'So was it was you who sent them there?'

'I was trying to help out a friend.'

'Why?' Amina asked. 'Do you think running away is a good thing?'

'No,' he said. 'But forcing somebody to marry isn't right either. Especially if that person is in love with somebody else.'

Amina's eyes opened wide. 'In love? She told you this?'

'No. Farouk did.'

Amina folded her arms, unsure how to put her thoughts into words.

'Did Sumati say anything to you about what happened?' the young man demanded. 'Or why Farouk left the place?'

'She wouldn't say anything, except that San Fernando is a bad place.'

Rajnath stared into her eyes. 'Don't play games with me,' he warned her. 'Something surely happened, but nobody is saying. Nobody! Someone is lying, but who and why? I want to know. And that is not all. There are strange birds in the shed. And my uncle is saying that Sumati took advantage of them and left without telling anyone.'

He gripped Amina by the arm. 'Tell me the truth. Talk to me! You never talk!'

Amina felt scared. She hardly knew him and there he was making demands of her.

'You believe your uncle?' she said in a small voice. 'Sumati says nothing, but I believe there was something bad going on.'

'Did she say what they did – all the loving-up they were doing?'

'What?'

'Well, I know how you girls talk. I'm not stupid.'

'Why do you want to know that? Are you in love with Sumati?'

Rajnath glared at her. 'The girl needs help. Her mother's dead, and I am trying to find out what happened to Farouk. He is as good as her husband because I'm sure they . . . *did it* – and intended to live like husband and wife. But he's disappeared. And now she's an outcast. Who'll want her now?'

Amina couldn't stop the image in her head of Sumati and Farouk *doing it*. 'You could be wrong about a lot of things,' she said, and wondered if she could trust him with Sumati's secret. She looked at him, standing in front of her in some kind of pain, and wondered how he would react if she told him. She so badly needed to confide in someone.

'Look, I care about Sumati, but not the way you're thinking,' he said. 'And I care about Farouk, because he is my friend, and nobody seems to know or care what happened to him.'

'She thinks she is making a baby,' Amina heard her voice saying. But a weight immediately fell from her shoulders.

'I knew it!' Rajnath shouted. 'Damn and blast, I knew it!' He picked up a stick and strode off. Suddenly he threw the stick up in the tree so hard that it hit a bird, which came down with a light thump on the grass. Amina shuddered. The bird was fluttering its last, then it stopped still.

Amina watched him walk away, and felt guilt and fear of the consequences of betraying Sumati.

❧

School felt like a huge relief – calm, and predictable. It took her mind away from the turmoil in her life, with the advantage of gaining some new knowledge every day. Mr Clifford had started giving her more responsibilities and lending her out to various teachers to assist for a few hours at a time. She would listen to children read, or help struggling ones with arithmetic. But hovering in the back of her mind all the time was the fact that she had told Sumati's secret to Rajnath. If it came out, Sumati's father might beat her to death, after the village *panch* had cut them off completely once again. But what occupied her thoughts more than anything else, was the riddle of how it could be possible for Sumati not to know who the father of her child was, and there was no one she dared ask.

ꟃ

As evening drew in, Rajnath and his father sat under the bamboo canopy, talking about the birds in the shed.

'Is not birds, boy,' his father said.

Rajnath stared at his father. 'I saw birds in the shed,' he said. 'Ma sees them all the time.'

'I'm telling you, boy, it's not birds,' Kamal Singh insisted. 'You want to know the truth? Ask your mother.'

'Pundit Lall is coming to see us next week,' Parbatee said, from where she stood folding up a big white sheet from the washing line.

'Your mother thinks the same as me,' Kamal said, darkly. 'You can think what you like.'

'But just the same, it could be nothing,' Parbatee said quite matter-of-factly.

'You call that nothing?' Kamal looked at his wife as though she had lost her mind. He turned to his son. 'What did you think was going to happen when you brought that . . . girl here and put her in the shed? Her mother still warm in her grave and she, with that reputation she has.'

'Girl?' Rajnath's face grew blotchy red. 'What reputation?'

'Why is it,' Kamal said, clearly annoyed, 'that because you have some hair on your face, you think everybody round you is stupid?'

'And why is it that *you* think that it's me who is stupid?' Rajnath retorted.

'Raj, son, don't talk to your father like that,' Parbatee chided. 'Show some respect.'

'He talks to me as if I come out of my mother's belly just yesterday!' Kamal complained, staring angrily at his wife. 'It's all your fault.'

'When the pundit comes, he will tell us exactly what is what,' she replied calmly.

'And how much money and provisions are you going to give him for that?' Rajnath demanded insolently.

'What do you have against the pundit?' Kamal wanted to know.

'He's keeping us Indians together,' Parbatee told her son. 'You young people better watch your step. And don't think I haven't heard that you're getting close to that Banderjee girl too,' Kamal put in. 'You trying to upset her family? And are you doing things to cause gossip about you and that whore, Sumati?'

'There's a lot you don't know about her, Pa!' Rajnath said hotly. 'Sumati's good looks aren't her fault. As for the Banderjee girl, she is Sumati's friend – that's all. Sumati needs help. But people in the village are more interested in criticising and punishing those who need guidance and understanding. As for me, I'll never get thanks for helping anyone, but when did I care what people think of me? It's not a wonder they ran away from this place. Who could blame them. It could have been me.'

Rajnath stalked away, leaving his parents staring at him stunned and puzzled by his insinuation about running away.

TWENTY-SEVEN

Amina stormed out of the house. She was adamant to uncover whatever secrets were being withheld from her. She was no child. It was time she had a frank conversation with Sumati.

When she marched into Sumati's yard, Roopchand was standing at the window. Her blood ran cold. She strode forward, willing the man to do his worst. His eyes followed her as she continued boldly down the path till she got to the back door.

'Come!' he called. 'Sumati is inside.'

She hesitated, surprised at his friendliness that seemed like a trick to get her inside.

'Come,' he repeated. His voice was strangely gentle.

'I wanted to tell you,' Amina began, 'that Sumati is my friend, and I would never do anything to hurt her.'

Roopchand's breathing was laboured, his eyes red and staring. Amina gazed back up at him from the step below. He looked lost, and confused. She began to feel pity. Not even his own daughter liked him. She wondered if he was finally breaking – ashamed of his behaviour at last. What kind of a man would threaten to kill a vulnerable and loving woman? She saw a glimpse of a grown man, so afraid of his daughter's behaviour that he resorted to threats that would hang over his wife all her life, until she took it herself.

As he looked at Amina, a spark of light shone from his dull eyes. 'You remind me of her,' he said. 'Daya.' Tears began rolling down his cheeks. 'You are the only one that will save her now. I failed.'

'Save Daya? How?'

'Come in. Don't mind me. Don't be afraid of me. I'm just an old fool who can't tell gold from a piece of coal.' He gestured to her. 'Come inside. I am talking about Sumati. Talk with Sumati. Young people need other young people to talk to. She and you are friends. She has nobody else now. Come. Stay as long as you want.'

Amina nodded. She slipped through the gauzy curtains that were blowing in and out of the doorway, and took off her shoes. Inside, Sumati was sitting on a bench, picking out stones from the rice in a calabash bowl. She looked up and smiled one of her special smiles, and her face lit up like a ray of sun.

'What's going on?' Amina asked Sumati. 'Still not bleeding?'

'No, but trying everything I can to throw away the thing.'

'What?' Amina's eyes were bulging. 'But why are you so happy?'

'Because I don't care,' Sumati said. 'I've done everything I can. I ate a whole big hot pepper in my food, lifting the heaviest things I can find. You know how many buckets of water I carry every day?'

'Wouldn't that just make your arms hurt?'

'I was hoping it strains my belly enough to get rid of the thing.'

'You've got to talk to somebody,' Amina said gravely. 'You don't even know who the father is. You really need a real grown up to help.'

'That will just get me in trouble.'

'But you are already in trouble,' Amina said. 'Ignoring the problem will not solve it.'

'The truth is, there's nothing I can do. So, my father went to see the man I'm going to marry and everything's going ahead.'

'What! And you're happy with that?'

'Yes.' Sumati smiled as if a heavy shower of rain had just washed her troubles away.

'So, you don't want to find Farouk?'

'Why do you think I'm here all alone? Farouk left me.'

'Does your father know you're having a child?' Amina whispered.

'Yes. He guessed.'

TWENTY-EIGHT

Rajnath decided to talk to his mother about the problem on his mind.

'Ma,' he began quietly, 'did you know that Kalouti left Uncle Amrit?'

'My brother told me that she went back to her mother's house. Shame on that woman. If they still lived in Granville, the whole village would be talking. Good thing they live in town.'

'He has some other woman there, helping him with the jobs. But there seems to be a lot of people coming and going.'

'That's because your uncle is running a big business there. He needs plenty of help in that shop. He is a good man – he gives people work. And keeping a big hotel too, with big-shot white-mans all the way from England, coming and going to the cane field. Engineer men from America and England too. They are testing the ground for oil. Didn't he tell you?'

'He said about the hotel. The rest I didn't know. He seemed more concerned about Dillip misbehaving.'

'Misbehaving? How?' Parbatee sounded doubtful. 'Like you, Dillip is a good boy. He might have a little mouth on him, but what boy don't have a mouth at that age? Don't get mixed up in that. Nobody will thank you for interfering between father and son.'

'He wanted me to talk to Dillip, but Dillip never came home while I was there. I don't know if he's keeping bad company.'

'Let me tell you something. My brother is my brother – I care about him. But all I want is for you and Annan to be happy. Get married and give me grandchildren one day. Soon.'

'And what about Pa? All *he* wants is to get rid of me. Uncle Amrit said he will look for a girl for me. I laughed.'

'That is not a bad idea,' his mother said thoughtfully. 'He must know many good families in San Fernando.

Maybe Amrit will also find Dillip a wife soon. A wife and children will give him responsibility. Keep his feet on the ground.'

'Is that why you are trying to look for a bride for me?'

'I think I might be lucky. There is a girl up in Chaguanas who . . . '

'Ma, I was joking. I will find my own girl when I am ready. How do you know that I haven't already found one?'

'By yourself? You? Ha!'

'Why are you looking at me like that? You think I can't find someone myself?'

'You are my son,' she said sternly. 'I can look at you however I please. And I also know when you are hiding secrets. I was the one who made you – don't forget that.

You didn't make *me*.'

'Ha! But you're not as clever as you think,' Rajnath chuckled.

Parbatee pulled a white sheet off the clothes wire extra hard and it rewound back onto itself. She stood frantically trying to unravel the sheet, while Rajnath stood laughing.

'I'm so glad you find everything a matter of amusement and a good excuse to laugh at me,' she said stiffly. 'But don't think I know nothing. Gossip will travel like dysentery spread on the *Fatel Razack* – and smell like it too! But don't forget that the *Fatel Razak* was a ship on the seas and they could leave the stink behind. Here, it will remain.'

'Oh, Ma! That's disgusting. I'm not stopping to listen to this. I'm going for a walk.'

TWENTY-NINE

Devinia worried herself frantic about Amina's behaviour. Balancing on the rope between her husband and her daughter in trying to please them both, was looking more like a noose. If Amina's bleeding came too soon, that would bring more bad luck and she couldn't bear that. Dealing with Amina's typhoid had been more than enough. She longed for her mother to talk to, but had to resort to Sankar.

'I think I'll try to get something from somebody to stop her bleeding from coming,' she told him.

Sankar looked at her. A deep frown crinkled the smooth skin over his eyes.

'Somebody like an Obeah-woman?' he asked, startled. 'That is foolish.'

'I don't know what else to do.'

'You shouldn't even consider going to Obeah,' he said. 'It is not Indian. You don't know what kind of poisons they will concoct for you.'

'There is something else – but I don't know where to get it from. *Wild pepper*.'

'*Wild pepper*? Is that what they call *monk's pepper*? Have you lost your mind, woman? That will stop the child from growing altogether.'

'But not for long,' Devinia replied, already regretting talking to him. 'I shouldn't have even asked you. You just don't understand like a woman. Carrying the shame.'

'I understand that it's stupid to give the child something that will stunt her growth! I might want to get to heaven, but I am not that foolish or selfish. You must let life take its course. Remember *dharma*? And *karma*? Don't go against nature. You have no business stopping what is natural.'

'Nothing is making sense these days. Our daughter doesn't want to get married, but that is in the way of *you* going to heaven. And what will happen to the rest of us? I don't even know if I believe in that. I agree with her! I agreed with her in the first place. It's your *dharma and karma* causing the confusion.'

'You are like a ship on stormy seas, my sweet rose,' Sankar said, folding his work trousers carefully, and looking at her with pity.

'And you keep rocking the boat.'

'But we have found her a good boy. I don't believe we can do better. Karma is good to us. We must take what we get. He is bright and educated. But you are right – our daughter is not herself. She is not the child we used to know. It seems she is going to cause us worries.'

'It's as if she doesn't want to be Indian.'

'Well, she is Indian,' he said firmly. 'And she will live like an Indian if it kills me.'

'I think we are making it difficult for her,' Devinia said.

'It's like taking her hungry to a dinner, and then telling her she is not allowed to eat, because the food is not Indian enough. Do you see? She's bound to eat it in secret if it looks good.'

'Why would she want to eat something that wasn't Indian food?'

'Because she spends every day in a place where they teach everything that is not Indian. Not a single thing is Indian at school.'

ꟹ

The following evening, Sankar brought home earrings he had made for Amina's dowry. He also wanted to talk to her quietly while everyone else was out of the house.

'Amina, my little rose petal, my sugar-flower,' he began in his sweet voice reserved just for her. A big, broad smile covered his face. 'I hear you're not going to school these days, my little gold-piece.'

'Why is everybody lying?' Amina flung the question at him like a sharp knife.

Sankar stepped back. 'What is wrong with you? Your mother's right.'

'About what?'

'Your mother is concerned for you, and now I can see why. You are behaving unreasonably. Like an overfed cat that has nothing to do but lie around and wait for the unsuspecting bird.'

Amina gasped. 'So now you're calling me idle and lazy? What have I done? You are ruining my life.' A tear fell from her eye.

'All I did was ask you a simple question and you jump at me like a tiger in the Bengali Forest.'

'Getting married is not a simple question,' his daughter replied passionately. 'You will ruin my life.'

ജ

Amina visited Sumati that same afternoon. 'You're showing,' she remarked.

Sumati pulled at the tight material stuck to her hips and jerked the skirt down hard. 'I'm just eating too much,' she replied in a huff.

'Well, you should slow down on all that dasheen and yam then, because you are going to have to explain to people when they ask how all that food in your stomach got there and *stayed* there.'

'Nobody comes to see me anymore. It's as if I have consumption or something.'

'You had better decide what's wrong with you, because Mr Clifford has been asking.'

'What can he do to me that is worse than this?'

'He's concerned about your education.'

'Well, I am not. I have more to worry about. Did you find the wild yam?'

'I'm not doing anything that mad, Sumati. Nothing is worth you taking poison.'

'You're so ignorant! You know nothing.'

'Yes, that is what you always say. At least my ignorance didn't get me in this mess.'

'I was wondering when you were going to throw that at me. Thanks! It takes a real friend to tell you the truth.'

'If I was any kind of a friend, I would have stopped you from running away with Farouk in the first place.'

'How? Oh don't bother to answer that. You're a little girl who knows nothing. Nothing at all about feelings. I am fourteen and a half, and you come here with your twelve and a half self, and tell me Clifford is concerned about my education? Look where school got me!'

'I was good enough for you last year when you didn't have any friends left in school,' Amina reminded her.

'That was when I could trust you to keep your mouth shut.'

'And I have. I told no one.' Amina blinked fast, realising too late that she was telling another lie. She'd already told Rajnath because she had to tell someone. 'Well I...'

'My plan is this,' Sumati interrupted. 'Listen hard.' She pointed to her stomach, poking it hard. 'It's to get rid of it. This thing.'

'And how do you do that once it's already there?' Amina asked.

'You really are stupid!'

'You know what? I don't know why I bother about you. I have enough worries of my own. Go on – do what you want. Kill yourself. You call *that* a plan?'

THIRTY

Rajnath opened his eyes, startled to find himself on the cold ground flat on his back. It was pitch black and the air was cool against his face and bare chest. It had to be the middle of the night, but he wasn't in his bed. He tried to think why. As he reached up to rub his painful ankle, a mound of earth glowed in front of him in the moonlight. The hairs on his body stood upright and a shiver shot through him. The hoot of an owl made him jump to his feet.

'You don't listen.' A voice swished in the wind.

Rajnath spun around. He realised where he was. The air turned thin and cold. 'Who is it?' Rajnath asked shakily.

A rustle of leaves on the trees around the cemetery blew in another owl-voice.

'*You are the only one*,' the voice said.

'Who is it?' Rajnath asked. 'What do you want? And why are you following me?' A worrying thought crossed his mind. 'Is that my grandmother? Nanny? Is that you?'

'Your nanny left with disappointment in your mother.'

'I know,' he said. 'But who are you? And why're you here?'

'I want to help you to help her. Help my daughter.'

'Who is *your daughter*?' His teeth were chattering.

'And him. Find him.'

'Find him? Who?'

'Find your friend. You are no friend if you don't find Farouk. Go to Bonasse. Before the edge of the water, you will see a house . . . three coconut trees . . . fishing boat under a sea grapes tree.'

The air became hot and stuffy. Rajnath began sweating.

'I think I must be coming down with something,' he said to himself.

The air had thickened again and grown clammy, making it difficult to breathe. The voice had vanished, and Rajnath found himself alone once more. Had it all been a dream?

ꕤ

Parbatee was up early as usual the next morning and couldn't believe her eyes.

'Boy!' she shouted up to the house, but no one replied. She marched up the steps and into the bedroom, but Rajnath wasn't there. Only his brother.

'Annan?' Parbatee called. 'Where is your brother?'

Annan grunted, still half asleep.

'Where's that fool of a boy gone again?' she repeated.

'I don't know, Ma. He must have gone to work,' Annan mumbled.

'Two foolish boys!' she shouted. 'One gone to work on a Saturday, and the other one too lazy to even get a job.'

Annan opened his eyes. 'What's the problem, Ma?'

'Your brother put on his new shoes last night and now they are thick with mud. And he left them out in the dew to get wet. Now he has disappeared.'

Annan sat up and rubbed his eyes. 'I think I heard him making some strange noises last night, but I didn't hear him get up this morning.'

'Well, he can't have gone to work,' his mother said. 'It's Saturday.'

Just then Rajnath himself appeared. Parbatee stood shocked, staring at him, while Annan's mouth dropped open an inch.

'What's happened to you?' Parbatee asked, her eyes filled with horror. 'Did you get in a fight?' She clutched her chest. 'So early in the morning you fighting?'

'I have to find him!' was all Rajnath said. His expression was set with determination. He picked up some clean clothes and took them out to the bathroom, together with his boots.

'Go with your brother,' Parbatee instructed Annan. 'I'm frightened for him. Something has happened.'

'Go where?' Annan yawned and stretched.

'Anywhere!' Parbatee shouted at him. 'Don't ask silly questions.'

'Right,' Annan grumbled. 'Doesn't matter that I'm still half asleep then.'

Parbatee flung her arm sideways and landed her younger son a heavy backslap across his cheeks. He let out a scream.

'You want me to bust the other side of your face?' she warned him. 'Don't give me no lip! Just go with your brother. Keep an eye on him. I have a bad feeling he's in trouble.'

'Well, that is his business?' Annan retorted, rubbing his stinging cheek.

'His business is your business! There's no way your brother would've worn those new-expensive-catalogue-shoes in mud if something wasn't wrong. I know him. He is particular about his things. And always fighting for other people. He doesn't think of himself. You watch out for him – I'm relying on you.'

Annan was still sulking. 'One day, Ma. One day, he will go too far.'

Rajnath, meanwhile, didn't say a word. He bathed, ate a small breakfast and went out.

'Go!' Parbatee urged her younger son. 'Go with him, boy! Put on your shoes fast.'

Annan threw his arms up in the air. 'He doesn't want me with him. I'm just wasting my time.'

'What time?' Parbatee said. 'You have time to do anything but waste? Get your backside after him!' She picked up a stick and raised it at Annan, which sent him running.

'Wait up!' Annan shouted to Rajnath. 'Since you are insisting on being a complete idiot, I am coming with you!' When he caught up with his brother, he was breathless. 'Are you going to tell me what this is about? Ma's not here now, so you can tell me the truth. Why are you behaving as if you've see a ghost?'

Rajnath did not answer. He walked as fast as he could, with Annan hot on his heels.

'Slow down please!' Annan said. 'I think I know what this is about. It's that Banderjee girl, Amina. Isn't it? I have a feeling about you and her.'

'Who told you that?' Rajnath turned and stared at him.

'I am right then,' Annan said gleefully. 'So, what's the problem with the little ...'

'Careful what you say,' Rajnath warned. 'She's done nothing to you.'

'But she's done something to you,' his brother quipped. 'You are not yourself since you've been hurrying down the road to the standpipe for no water. Of late.'

Rajnath quickened his pace, leaving Annan struggling to keep up.

'I definitely know what's making you behave from mad to madder,' Annan continued, breathlessly.

'Really? What are you talking about now? You, who can't be bothered to get a proper job. The fact is, something's badly wrong and I can sense it. Farouk and the girl from the village went to stay with Uncle, and *she* has come back, as you know, but in one hell of a state. But Farouk is still missing. I have to find him. No one is talking but somebody knows something, and I mean to find out.'

'Oh!' Annan said. 'Well I better get back home, see what Ma wants me to help with.'

'Ma told you to help me. Or have you suddenly got disobedient and helpful at the same time?'

Rajnath grabbed Annan by the collar and shook him. 'You will tell me what you know. I am not playing with you now. It's somebody's life! But I know you don't care!' He pushed him away in disgust.

'I care,' Annan said, straightening his clothes. 'Of course I do. Why do you think I made Dillip send Farouk somewhere else? Because I care. Listen, Rajnath, who in their right mind would keep those two lovey-dovies like husband and *not-married-at-all-wifey,* under Uncle Amrit's roof? And my own brother sent them there. You caused me shame, I'm tellin' you. Raj, big shame.'

'So that is where you used to disappear to for days,' Rajnath said. Things began to make sense.

'So what? You expected me to cut cane in the hot sun and mud, like you? For twenty- five cents a day? Snake bite and scorpion sting might be nice for you but not me. No sirree. Some days you come home so black with cane-fire ash all over you, that not even Ma recognises you.'

Rajnath ignored him, saying, 'What were you doing there, Annan? You went to play with Dillip? Is that it?'

'At least Dillip knows how to play,' Annan sniggered.

'So, what can he play? Latin verbs?' Rajnath asked indignantly.

'Jealous-jealous.'

'If it was me who spent nearly two hundred dollars a year on education for my son,' Rajnath said, 'I wouldn't want to be as disappointed in him as Uncle Amrit is in Dillip.'

'Two hundred dollars?' Annan looked shocked.

The brothers walked, heads down in silence, for a while.

'So, when we were small, and we went over there, where did you think Dillip was?' Rajnath asked. 'He was never there on a weekday. Remember when Ma used to take us to Friday market on Mohammed's horse and cart?'

'Yes, but where did Uncle get that kind of money for school fees in those days?' Annan asked.

'He was running the shop, probably making a good profit, even then. According to Pa, Uncle Amrit's life was never straightforward. I think he never really got over Tanti Rani dying. You remember his first wife?'

'A bit. Fair-skinned and pretty, with a heart-shaped face. Deep brown eyes and long wavy hair. Tall and shapely. It was sad she died. I liked her.'

The sea was in open view now, the air smelling of surf and seaweed. Sea gulls swooped down against the bright blue sky and pecked at the white sands of Bonasse beach. Three coconut trees stood high and lean, and curved towards the road and away from the house that snuggled in the triangle between the sea, sky and the road. He'd never noticed it before, and Rajnath felt a cold wind swirl surround him.

Annan began to shiver. 'I need to go and see somebody,' he said hastily.

'Hey! Where are you going?'

But Annan was already far down the road, not even looking back. Left with no choice, Rajnath continued towards the house at the edge of the sea. The clump of coconut trees swayed, and dropped three coconuts on the sand in front of him. Wide stone steps snaked from the ground around the side of the house to the upper floor. The green shutters were closed, but the door looked open.

'Good morning!' Rajnath stood on the bottom step and shouted up. But his words came out in a whisper as the wind blew them away. Then someone appeared.'

ᛟ

Rajnath was quiet for most of the walk back home. Annan didn't speak either.

'Tell me something about Dillip,' Rajnath eventually said. 'Anything at all.'

'What *exactly* did you want to know about our cousin? One question, then it stops.'

'Farouk went to that house on the beach,' Rajnath said. 'Did you know this?'

'Yes, Uncle sent him there.'

'Why would Uncle do that? And don't lie to me. Why send him to *that* place?'

'That is three questions, big brother.'

'I will finish when I'm finished,' Rajnath warned him.

'Uncle must have told you when you went there,' Annan said.

'No, he didn't tell me anything.'

'Maybe Uncle didn't know because it was Dillip's idea about that particular house.'

'Who lives there?' Rajnath asked. 'And what goes on there? Because Farouk's not there now. The old man said.'

'And you believed him. Poor you.'

'He looked honest. He said I could go inside and check for myself.'

'And did you?'

'Maybe I should have gone in,' Rajnath admitted sheepishly. 'But if you knew something, why didn't you tell me, instead of getting caught up in all this crookedness. And whose idea was it? We had better go back and check it out now.'

'Not me!' Annan said immediately.

'I'm not surprised. You can't take any sort of responsibility.'

'Very well. I'll do my best to find out,' Annan promised, relenting.'

ഇ

They had already gone to bed that night when something occurred to Rajnath. He jumped up and threw on his clothes.

'What now!' Annan rolled over, hearing the commotion in the room.

'I'm going out,' Rajnath whispered.

'Take care if you are meeting that girl,' his younger brother said insolently. But Rajnath ignored him.

ꟸ

The following morning Parbatee couldn't believe that once again, Rajnath had left his expensive shoes outside. 'This boy doesn't care at all,' she groaned, picking up the shoes carefully. 'He has it too easy. Some people are going barefoot without a single pair of shoes to their name. And this son of mine sends away for catalogue-shoes from England, like he is the plantation manager. And then mistreating them. Is not like him.'

Parbatee went to the kitchen, tore a strip of rag, and cleaned the shoes. She placed them near the open fire where she was boiling a pot of cocoa tea.

'It's your fault,' her husband said, meanly. 'You spoilt him by not making him pay his way. Everybody else does.'

'I know,' Parbatee replied. 'But at least he is the one out of both our sons who is working.' She looked worried. 'Something bad is happening, and I'm not sure what it is. But I can feel it drawing near.'

THIRTY-ONE

The next Saturday couldn't come quickly enough for Rajnath, who intended to make another trip to Amrit's. Early that morning he walked the same route that he'd walked so frequently of late: the road to Bonasse – the road to *that* house – the same road to catch the sloop from Cedros to San Fernando. The morning was cool and still dark when he set out. An owl hooted, and he flinched. He speeded up, slowing down every hundred steps or so to fill up his lungs.

As he approached Bonasse beach, the sky was dawning pink, with a semicircle of gold drawn sharply on the grey-white horizon. The Port of Spain ship from Cedros was being loaded.

'Is this one stopping in San Fernando?' Rajnath asked the man at the booth.

'Yah. Stoppin' by San'do wharf. After they done load up.'

Rajnath bought a ticket, sat down on a rock and reached in his canvas bag for his breakfast. He watched the boat rocking gently in the shallow waters as he ate the roti-wrap, savouring the salty sweetness of the pumpkin talkarie inside the floury dough – then almost choked. Someone appeared in his vision – someone he had never expected to see.

ഇ

Meanwhile, in San Fernando, Amrit was up early, sweeping the leaves off the concrete path next to the new building where guests were staying. It was shady and still cool, and the breeze rustled down the gap between high-sided wooden buildings from across the wharf. Amrit's properties stood in two acres of land, halfway between the town and the wharf, with a view of the Colonial Hospital that was fifteen minutes' walk up the hill. Dogs were barking furiously, competing with engine noises from the growing number of automobiles on the road. The tooting horns brought heads out of windows in houses high and low, but the dogs took it as provocation, and raced after the cars, never managing to catch up with them, unless they happened to get caught below the wheels – with a thump and a squeal, before the ensuing silence.

As he swept the yard, Amrit heard noises coming from an open window upstairs – a punter and one of Dillip's "girls". It reminded him of Kalouti, and the reason why she had left him. It plagued him not to be able to resolve his disagreements with his son. The more he tried, the worse Dillip responded, and Amrit felt ground down. Dillip was winning. That school in Port of Spain had been an expensive mistake. The boy had learnt little else that was useful. To make matters worse, Dillip had started drinking Scotch –

too much and too often. And now here was Rajnath asking questions about Farouk and Sumati. Amrit had liked Farouk, but Dillip seemed to prefer the girl. Amrit had argued that Rajnath was family, and Farouk was Rajnath's friend . . . but Dillip wasn't bothered. The couple needed to be split up, Dillip insisted, otherwise it looked as if they were encouraging shameful behaviour. How could Amrit disagree with that?

At that moment, Dillip himself appeared on the path right in front of Amrit. He spat on the stones. 'I said I will get rid of her, and I mean it,' Dillip told his father.

'I'm not starting another argument this morning,' the man answered tiredly. 'You said enough last night.'

'Don't you think you're a bit too old to be getting up to this kind of rudeness behind my mother's back?'

'*Your* mother's back?' Amrit stopped and looked shocked.

'You chased my mother away so that you could put another woman in her place.'

'You're saying *I* chased Kalouti away?'

'Kalouti was not my mother!'

'Your mother died. Kalouti was like a mother to you. The worst part is . . .' the man sighed.

'What?'

'That I paid good money to send you to that damn expensive college, in Port of Spain – a school that no Indian boy could normally get into. I turned Catholic to get you in there, just so you could talk to me like this now? So disrespectfully? How do you think I feel?'

'Feel? You sent me away to Port of Spain to get rid of me when Ma died. Did you care how I felt? And don't call my Ma a bitch again.'

'I never called your . . . oh, I see. You are talking crazy to make me annoyed.'

'Crazy? You called me a sonofabitch last night!'

'You really think you're smart!' Amrit exclaimed, red with anger. 'Trying to tie me up with your cross-talk you learned from that college! Boy, get right out of my sight.'

'So that's it?' Dillip said, in a choked voice.

Amrit was close to tears. He looked at Dillip. His face was red.

'Now you are telling me that I am stupid?' Dillip stormed. 'Insulting my intellect. If there is one thing I learnt from that expensive college, it's that I am not a fool.'

'Intellect? It was me who paid for them to teach you big words, and you pay me back with disrespect. Didn't they teach you any of the simple things in life?'

'Nothing I learnt in school was simple. They didn't charge you for *simple*. If you wanted *simple*, you should have sent me to cut cane like Rajnath. Instead I learnt how to cope with being beaten up by white boys and pestered by father priests. You know what things those priests wanted me to do?'

'Silence! You are just being ungrateful,' Amrit said. 'And selfish.'

'You're the selfish one, Pa. What payment do you want from me? My mother paid you with her life – my real mother, the one I barely remember. You sent me away because she died, and you didn't want me reminding you of her. That's what you paid for. But I paid too – in ways you don't want to know.' Dillip was wound up – spitting with anger.

'You really want to know why Kalouti left?' his father asked.

Dillip looked at Amrit through tear-filled eyes. 'I'm not interested in talking about Kalouti!' he screamed. Bringing his real mother into the conversation was not having the desired painful effect on his father.

Amrit could see that Dillip was in pain. 'Look, son,' he tried. 'I should not have said what I just did. Kalouti *was* like a mother to you in every way. She loved you like she would have loved a son of her own. That's why she couldn't put up with the way you were treating her. She told me, but I wouldn't listen. I put you first. And I shouldn't have. That is why she really left.'

Dillip's mouth dropped open.

'I should have stopped you from sending Farouk away,' Amrit said, bitterly. 'I was too weak.'

'They came like beggars looking for favours,' his son scoffed.

'No, they were like family, looking for a place to *stay* until they found work, and to build up a life for themselves. I promised my nephew! Rajnath – you remember him? You have had it too easy. You have no idea what it's like to have to start from nothing. From nothing! That is what *I* had to do!'

'And you did it. Nobody helped you.'

'How would you know? We Indians were like brothers on the ships. Yes, people helped me. You can't be too proud when you have nothing. But how would you know?'

'I know what it takes to build a business, Pa.'

'You think you did it on your own? It is my business I built that you are taking over. Now you're forcing me to lie to my own nephew! Making me look like a fool.'

'That's because you are one,' Dillip said carelessly. 'Rajnath and me just happen to be blood cousins. That's all. I owe him nothing, and neither do you.'

'Blood is everything,' Amrit said. 'The simple things in life, again. One day you will realise that when it is too late. You hear me? Too late.'

'Why's he working in the cane field?' Dillip sneered. 'Rajnath is nothing but a damn loser! Although Annan might be different. But neither of them have what it takes to do business. And while we are talking about business, Pa, I'm expanding. I've got some brand new ideas . . .'

ꕥ

Rajnath sat on the rock, looking at the boat. Two men were struggling to haul aboard what looked like heavy jute bags. Eventually they loaded the cargo, and a third man joined them. It was time to get on board. He could delay no longer.

The deck rocked as Rajnath walked along, which was comforting in a way as his mind rolled in turmoil wondering what would happen next. He sat between the tightly packed, sourish-smelling jute bags and a familiar figure walked past. The boat set sail, and the bags shifted and squeezed him tight. The man walked past again. This time he was sure it was Farouk. Rajnath hauled himself up hard, almost knocking himself out on the tea chests opposite.

He stood still, breathing in the sea air deeply, to push his breakfast back down in his stomach. The deep green water swirled and rippled around the swaying vessel. He was desperate to see the man's face and wondered if all was well with him. Another man appeared and asked to see his boarding paper. Rajnath handed him the ticket from his shirt pocket without a word, then picked up his brown canvas bag and headed down the boat. Farouk was sitting on top of a wooden chest.

Rajnath touched the man, but the man didn't appear to recognise him. He stepped back to get out of the man's space, feeling foolish to have assumed it was his friend. The wind was strong. He pushed his hair from out of his eyes and squinted to check the man's face again, before boldly reaching out and lifting the man's stubbly chin.

'Farouk?' he said. 'Is that you!'

The man turned his head into Rajnath's grip, and looked him up and down.

'It's me – Rajnath. What happened to you? Where have you been all these months? You are you looking so . . . I was worried. Do you have any idea what is going on at home? You remember Granville? Talk to me, Farouk. I just want to know.'

But the man sat like a stone, not a flicker of light from his eyes.

'You coward!' Rajnath burst out. 'You remember that pretty young girl you spoilt and then took away? You begged me to help you, and I was fool enough. I thought you were *in love* with her. But I should never have trusted you, sonofabitch!'

The man flinched and looked at Rajnath with a wild, mad dog stare.

'Say something!' Rajnath yelled, grabbing him by both shoulders. 'You bastard! You used to be my friend. I trusted you. I thought you had it right, running away from those blasted arranged marriages. I thought that whatever happened, at least you loved the girl enough to stay with her till the end.'

The thin man's Adam's apple moved up and down, but he made no sound. He looked weak and vulnerable. Rajnath seized his shirt and hauled him up.

'Farouk! Say something! Did a *jumbie* take you over?'

'I don't know you,' was all the reply he got.

Rajnath looked at him, shocked, and let him go. But some instinct made him ask this haggard-looking man to open his hand.

'Not that one,' Rajnath said. 'The left hand.' He forced open the fellow's hand, then cried, 'I knew it!'

'It was a good thing your hand split when you fell out of the mango tree that time. You could have fooled me otherwise.'

They sat quietly until Rajnath asked, 'What happened to you, boy?' He pushed Farouk's hair off his forehead and looked into his old friend's eyes. They were becoming agitated. The fellow started shifting his bony bottom uncomfortably on the wooden crate.

'I can see that something happened,' Rajnath said, 'and that you had a hard time. If somebody has mistreated you, you have to tell me. But you don't seem to know how much that girl wanted you.'

Farouk winced, staring into his lap, twisting his clasped fingers, cracking each joint.

'Say something!' Rajnath pleaded.

'You really want to know? Well I'll tell you.' Farouk finally spoke.

Rajnath moved closer until the two young men sat side by side, inches apart, facing the same expanse of deep-green ocean. Farouk didn't move. The boat turned smoothly west with its tall, triangular sails billowing outwards. It rocked along the western coastline of the island. Rajnath leaned back and said out loud, 'This day is a miracle.'

He realised he had been so consumed by worry lately, that he had been hearing and seeing things that weren't there. But this was real. Farouk was real.

Farouk started to talk. 'We got there all right,' he said. 'It wasn't too hard. Your uncle seemed pleased to see us.'

'I'm glad about that,' Rajnath said reassuringly. 'He's a good kind man.'

'But then he didn't want me there any longer. He and your cousin sent me away.'

Rajnath looked confused. 'And Sumati?'

'I don't ever want to see her again.' Farouk clenched his fist hard. 'And *your* uncle is not what you think.'

Rajnath couldn't believe what he was hearing. Sumati and her family were shattered, she had lost her mother, her lover, and her future. Rajnath felt disgusted, and his pulse began to race.

'Do you realise that you cannot show your face in Granville again?' he burst out. 'Because no one will even spit on you if you were on fire. Did you know Sumati's mother died?'

'People die,' the stranger replied without emotion. 'How is that my fault?'

Rajnath stamped his foot almost through the deck. 'What is wrong with you? What kind of man are you, to heap all the blame on your woman? You caused Daya to put a rope round her neck! You caused her father to blame Amina, her friend. Roopchand tried to strangle her, you know! Man, you deserve whatever you get now.'

'Maybe.' Farouk's tone was flat and resigned. 'You probably don't want to know, but your uncle is a crook. And your cousin is ten times the crook your uncle is.'

'Why are you saying lies? Accusing my uncle and cousin of being criminals? If they forced you to leave, what stopped you from taking Sumati with you or going back for her?'

'You think a lot of your family. But I see a different side.'

'You see the side of a small-minded little man. You see them with big business, and you're jealous.'

Farouk laughed. It sounded like a goat with a cough, which irritated Rajnath.

'My uncle works damn hard for what he has,' Rajnath said hotly. 'You had a chance. But instead of working hard yourself, you ran away.'

'Amrit and Dillip are doing business with white people only.'

'My uncle can do business with whoever he wants. Why is that bothering you?'

'Not just me,' Farouk said. 'You know where his wife went?'

'She died.'

'Kalouti died?' Farouk went pale. 'When?'

'No, no, no. Not Kalouti. His wife, Rani, died, and he never recovered for a long time. Rani was Dillip's mother. My uncle sent Dillip off to that expensive Catholic school in Port of Spain. Never saw him for weeks, if not months. I know Dillip ran away once . . . came home crying. Know what Uncle Amrit did? He put him in a car and sent him straight back.'

'That cousin of yours is a rotten egg. And that education has really paid off, because he's putting it to use – and I don't mean in a good way either. He's smart in a crooked way.'

Amrit had suggested something similar, Rajnath recalled. They both sat staring into the empty horizon. The seagulls squawked, following the boat, swooping down and cutting the water like arrows, emerging with flapping fish across their beaks.

'You are looking tired, Farouk,' Rajnath said. His voice was gentle, empathetic.

‘I should have fought for her.’

‘But it’s not too late.’ Rajnath looked at him hopefully. ‘She is having a child.’

&

The minutes passed. It was as if Farouk had not registered what Rajnath had said about Sumati’s condition. Farouk began to talk, and they both did, forgetting about the huge void that divided them. They talked about the wind, the sea, the cricket, the late afternoons spent standing around the standpipe or joining the older men on a Friday night drinking illegal *mountain dew*, smoking a tobacco roll-up or taking a sneaky puff of the ganja pipe. For a while they managed to forget the rest of the world. Farouk unwrapped a brown paper parcel, tore off a corner of dry roti, and munched, chewing about fifty times before swallowing.

‘My chances are all spoilt now,’ he said.

‘Every day is a new start,’ Rajnath said, trying to encourage him.

‘You don’t understand. Some people just fail.’

‘When you fail, you learn something new. That’s life. But there’s always a chance.’

Rajnath felt himself sitting neck-deep in guilt, lies and miscommunication, having sent Farouk and Sumati off to their destruction. He realised he had to face up to some truths. It was why he was on his way to San Fernando, and was worried about discovering more than he could deal with. Meeting Farouk had softened that blow. But having bad thoughts about his uncle made him feel wretched. Family was family. Why though, was his expensively educated Latin-scholar cousin be so mean to Farouk and Sumati?

'Where are you going today?' Rajnath asked.

'Up to Port of Spain.'

'That's a long way from here! I'm going to San Fernando. Come with me to see Uncle.' Rajnath caught a glint of fire in Farouk's eyes. 'I've a serious bone to pick with him. Dillip too. I'm going to give them a piece of my mind.'

Farouk was visibly agitated. 'Did you understand what I just said?'

Rajnath looked at Farouk. His friend truly had changed. He hadn't grown like a man. He looked starved – and there was something else. He had failure in his eyes and was broken. This made Rajnath even more upset with himself. He wanted Farouk's friendship. Needed it. But he feared it might never be the same. He wondered if Farouk was bad at making good decisions, or if it was all his fault. His head hurt, crushed under the worry that Farouk might never recover, and that Sumati was in a mess because of it.

The sloop eventually arrived at the docks in San Fernando. Rajnath tried to persuade Farouk to go with him to Amrit's, but the young man insisted he couldn't go there.

'You know, you've not told me anything. You can't stay away for ever. I miss you, Farouk.'

'My family don't want to know me.'

'By the way,' Rajnath said, as he jumped off the boat. 'I hear Sumati's getting married in a few weeks.' These were his final words. Rajnath hoped they would prompt his friend into action.

Farouk shouted something, but Rajnath had already turned his back and disappeared into the throng of bodies busily hurrying through the pandemonium of the wharf.

THIRTY-TWO

The rain had belted down earlier and the road was still wet and steaming when Amina and friends were walking home from school, still unsure about visiting Sumati. By the time they reached her house, the sun was blazing down again, and Chandra and Pryia decided to go home instead.

Amina looked at them in despair. 'She's trying harder than you realise. And she's still our friend.'

'I thought you and she had an argument,' Chandra said.

'You heard what Mr Clifford said this morning?' Amina asked. 'None of us are perfect. *Do unto others as you would have them do unto you.*'

'It makes sense,' Ramona said. 'If we did, no one would hurt other people. But they do. Which means that we don't think about how it would feel if we were the one being hurt.'

'Anyway, I'm going to see how Sumati is doing,' Amina said. 'It could be any one of us. I want to make sure she's all right there on her own.'

ꙮ

Amina and Sumati sat together, chatting. 'I just want to get married and end all this,' Sumati told her friend.

'To that old man with children?'

'Do I have another choice?' Sumati said in despair. 'It's all arranged. Only ten days to go.'

'If you need anything I'm sure my mother will help,' Amina said. 'She's going to Port of Spain soon. She could get you some things. Who's making your wedding outfit?'

'I have everything I need,' Sumati said indifferently. 'My mother's things – that will be enough. I have more important matters on my mind.' She moved closer to Amina. 'I'm not feeling right. It's my head . . . I don't feel like myself.'

'Go and see the doctor,' Amina advised. 'He comes on a Friday. I'll go with you, except Mr Clifford might want to know where I am. He dislikes absenteeism.'

'Clifford minds people's business too much,' Sumati said angrily.

'He cares. I care too.'

'Anyway, I know what's wrong with me. I don't need to go to the doctor again. Best if I just get married. It's what my father wants. He guessed. And I had to tell him. I'm glad I did. I didn't exactly make it easy for him to find me a nice boy. But that's the price I have to pay for playing the jackass with my life. I thought I was in love with *somebody*, and I made a fool of myself.'

'No, Sumati. *He* made a fool of you.'

Sumati's eyes were full. 'You wouldn't understand. A while after I started bleeding, I started to feel like a different person. I couldn't help myself.'

'Even though you knew how people gossip? And the trouble it would bring?'

'I know that now. I was stupid. Don't be like me. People take advantage of you when you're like me. I trusted everyone. That was a mistake.'

'Maybe you shouldn't have trusted the people where you stayed. But how were you to know? Maybe falling in love does that to you. Makes you think everything is like sunshine.'

'In a way, yes, it does. Something takes you over. And you have to be with the one you're in love with all the time.'

'But even sunshine can get too hot, or just disappear when rain comes pouring down.'

'Once the thought of running away came to my head, I stopped thinking straight. I just couldn't spend another day here. Farouk thought everything would turn out all right. Now I wish somebody had actually tied me down and made me stay home. Or locked me up. I actually miss school. Can you believe that?'

'School is easy compared to what you're going through,' Amina said. 'I'm staying there for as long as I can. There's always something to do, and our friends are still there.'

'I wish I had known this would happen. Nobody talks about these things.'

'Aren't you worried that your child does not belong to this man you are going to marry? I wish we could find Farouk.'

'I don't want to see Farouk ever again.' Sumati's voice went hard. 'It is a man's child. I don't care which man it was. I didn't put it there myself.'

'I could ask Rajnath if he's found out anything about Farouk.'

'No!' Sumati said. 'I don't want him or his family to know. Please don't tell them!'

There was a voice shouting from the yard.

'It's Ramona,' Amina said. 'She said she would come and see you.'

'Don't tell anyone what I told you,' Sumati warned her friend. 'Nobody must know, otherwise I will hang myself just like my mother, I swear!'

'Stop saying that,' Amina begged, tears in her eyes. 'I won't tell anybody. I promise.' But she had already broken that promise.

THIRTY-THREE

Amina worried about Sumati's careless manner towards the prospect of marrying this old man whom she had previously rejected. She was sure the marriage would backfire somehow, bringing more dramas.

Her own life also seemed complicated. She sat outside in the sun feeling like an overripe watermelon, ready to split and spill its red flesh and seeds on the ground. Both her parents had commented on her low moods, but she couldn't help it. Then one day, the depression flowed away, along with the show of her first menstrual blood.

'Now your business has started,' Devinia said, 'things will be different. Stay home from school and look after yourself. The bellyache will come. Just go lie down. I'll show you how to wash your cloths. Soak them in the half-a-drum behind the bathroom.'

'I can go to school tomorrow though,' Amina said, confidently.

'You are going nowhere for the next five days,' her mother stated firmly.

The next morning, Amina tried to get up early when she heard Etwar's voice, and her mother clattering in the kitchen outside, but she was too tired to move and fell back to sleep. When she woke, Devinia was in her room with breakfast – something she hadn't done since the typhoid. As she ate, Devinia talked to her daughter about womanhood, customs and hygiene – what she was allowed to do and what she was not. Not too much bathing, not touching food in the kitchen, soaking and laundering stained clothes, rubbing them with a lot of soap and bleaching them in the sun behind the shed, out of sight.

'You never told me this was going to be so hard,' Amina said, feeling dismayed.

'I'll help you. But this is normal now. And don't talk to boys. Don't go anywhere alone with a boy. Never, never, never.'

'What about boys at school?'

'Even in school, never be alone with a boy. If a boy respects you, he will never ask you to go somewhere with him alone. You don't want to be making a baby before you are married.'

'Really? Talking to a boy will cause that?'

'Talking can give a boy the idea.'

'I can see what you trying to say, Ma. But it's 1917. Things are different now.'

'Things like that are never different. A boy is a boy. They only want one thing! Don't give them the wrong idea about you.'

There was little point arguing with her mother. Sumati had talked to boys at the standpipe, and she must have given boys the wrong idea about her. In fact, she had given the whole village the wrong idea about her. But Amina was thinking about this *business*. Sumati described *the business* as some kind of new freedom. A different mind. A different body. But to Amina, this issue of blood every month looked more like a bad spell, and she dismissed what Sumati said about *wanting to be with a boy* as complete nonsense. She tried to read, but was unable to focus. Now she was beginning to understand why women were mostly confined to the home, and girls were unable to attend school. How on earth would she get to Port of Spain to Teacher Training College?

'How can I go Sumati's wedding?' she asked her mother.

'Depends. You have to rest, and wait and see.'

'There must be something to stop it.'

Devinia laughed. 'You have to stay close to home. You don't want to make a shame of yourself for everyone to see. It's the first time, so it might stop early. Drink plenty of milk and eat enough food. Bhajee is very good for making blood. Anything dark green.'

'I am eating properly. But I don't want to make more blood!'

'You'll make yourself weak and sick if you don't eat the right things. I will make you some *haldi* tea.'

But Amina couldn't stop thinking: how to support Sumati over the next few days; how unfair life could be. What if they had switched places? If Sumati had been born to the Banderjee family, and she had had Sumati's parents and home, how different would their lives be? That small difference would have made a big change for both their lives.

ꙮ

There was a lot of banging and nailing noises coming from down the road. Wedding preparations had started at Sumati's, erecting the main tent, the *mandap* where the bride and groom sat, and the kitchen tent.

'I need to be there to help Sumati with the wedding,' Amina said to her mother. 'Will you help too?'

'They haven't asked me.'

'You don't have to wait to be asked to help somebody, Ma.'

Devinia looked at her daughter, a little taller, a little paler, a little fuller. She smiled.

'Nobody's going to stop me,' Amina warned her.

'Nobody *is* stopping you,' Devinia said.

'Sometimes it feels as if everybody is against me doing what I want to do,' the girl said. Trying to make me do what they want me to do. Getting married isn't my idea. It's yours, and Pa's and everybody else's. You should never have tricked me like that. You made me feel like I don't matter. And I know I matter. You're looking for wedding saris for me even though I have said NO. I don't want to get married. My mind is made up.'

'I know that this wedding between Sumati and that man is not helping you. It's what's turning you anxious. But your marriage will be as good as ours. We made a good choice. The boy is rich, good-looking, and well-educated. Go and read a book. Read poetry about the daffodils flower.'

'I can't concentrate on any book now.'

Devinia looked at her daughter, a little dismayed. 'You are not yourself right now. And you think too much. This idea and that one. It's not like a girl your age to do so much thinking.'

'What is happening to you, Ma? It's you who are changing. Have you forgotten that it was you who wanted me to stay on at school and get an education?'

'Pundit Lall says we can't argue with dharma,' Devinia said. 'How can I disagree with that? Everyone playing their part for the good of everyone else. A woman's part can never change. Doing a man's job only makes it hard for a woman. And that is only if a man would allow a woman to do a man's work. Teaching in school?' She shook her head. 'How?'

'Why not? I can teach just like any man. See how I am teaching you all to read?'

'But you are doing it at home. That's different.'

'How is it different? Do you think the school building will object? Really, Ma!'

They both sat in silence, Devinia wringing her hands, wondering if she was wrong. It was she who had wanted her daughter to get out of the mould. She who had wanted Amina to make changes, but without the waves. Now she became afraid of her own voice, for fear of being overheard by the gods and being cursed for destroying their ancient traditions. She wanted Amina to fight for her survival in this new world, taking the opportunities such as education for girls. It was already bringing some equality between the white man and the black man. So why not between man and woman? Women could be at least equal to men if they had the chance. Devinia frightened herself with her thoughts. But wasn't there equality between gods and goddesses? Didn't they all have equal power? She was no fool, so why did she allow herself to be carried along by the opinions of others? Devinia felt hot blood rush to her head. Anger rose within her.

'Ma, I could help you cook?' Amina asked.

'No! You can't! Read. Read books. Read poems. Besides, you can't touch food in the kitchen yet.'

'How do you do it though?'

'Because there is no one to do it for me! I was never lucky like you. I was married at five years old and went to your father when I was eleven. I had no mother-in-law to help me. Sometimes it makes sense to break the rules. How else will we eat?'

'So, I was thinking,' her daughter said, 'now that my bleeding has started, I don't really have to get married. Because it must be bad luck for the family if I get married now.'

'You're right. Except you have to get married faster now. If you leave it till later, there'll be more bad luck. And what good is it if no man wants you all your life? That's worse. It's why it's better to get married young, and pretty, and before the bleeding. Then the man knows that you are good and clean. Because later, how will he know where you've been?'

'Where I've been? Now you are talking madness.' Amina quickly fell silent, not wanting an argument. She couldn't bear it when they fell out. So Amina decided to drop the subject, because her mother was not making sense.

THIRTY-FOUR

The hustle and bustle at Roopchand's house over the days before the wedding was more than Sumati had expected; she said she wanted a wedding smaller than small.

'I'm not doing all that Mehendi and Pedthi, Pa,' she argued. 'And you can't make me.'

'You always did everything your own way,' Roopchand said heavily.

'I'm going to marry the old man you got for me – isn't that enough?' she snapped. 'It doesn't seem right that Ma's not here.'

Roopchand's head sank into his neck. How could he help his girl? He couldn't bring back her mother. And his daughter had already escaped most of the pre-wedding traditions, which would have taken up days. The last remaining few were just for appearances' sake. He felt as confused as she did.

'Your mother would have wanted you to do things the right way,' he tried weakly. 'What does it matter about his age? He is a good man.'

'What do I care? I am having a child. I am having a child, Pa! You hear me? You never say anything.'

Roopchand fixed his eye on his daughter. 'What do you want me to say? I know what's going on under my own roof. How do you think I feel? I blamed your friend, instead of you.' He ran his hand over his face and muttered, 'sometimes I think that your mother did the best thing.'

'I thought you would throw that in my face one day! Well, I wish it was me instead of her,' Sumati wept. 'I miss her so much. Tomorrow is my wedding day, and I don't have a mother. Do you know how that makes me feel?'

'And do *you* know how it makes me feel to be here with a daughter like you?'

Sumati dropped her head in shame. 'I know, Pa. But it's my wedding tomorrow. Don't turn on me now. I'll be gone soon.'

'For how long? What will the man think when you drop that child in the next month?'

'It'll be a few months – enough for him to get to know me. I'll be good to him. Care for his children.'

'He will kill you, and you will deserve it. You know, there's a part of me that wants you to stay at home for good. Never get married.'

'Pa, I am sorry,' Sumati sobbed. She fell to the floor on her knees crying out for her mother to return. 'I would do anything for you to be here with me. Ma. I wouldn't ever do wrong again. Never. And I am willing to take any punishment. I don't want anything. I will wear rags for the rest of my life, and I will be happy with that.'

Outside, the wind was blowing up a storm. The weather had suddenly turned wild, yet it was the middle of the dry season. The hot air blew icy cold, and Sumati wrapped her arms round her shoulders. Kesh, her brother, rushed outside and brought in the tools that were scattered round the yard. Roopchand ran out to help him. Sumati sat inside, unable to move. Something fluttered around her ear. She heard whispers, and knew her beloved mother's voice.

"My daughter. Don't let my death be in vain. The rope is not a kind companion. Learn from my mistake. Make the most of your life. Care for those who care for you, and whom the gods thrust into your warm embrace. Watch your children with loving eyes, and a helpful heart. Love his children, and pray he will love yours. Take my blessing, for I will always be with you, my daughter. When the day is over, leave a plate of food behind the wedding tent. My soul will eat and find rest."

ၿ

Roopchand rushed inside the house, windswept and anxious. 'The wedding tent's nearly blown down!' he shouted. 'It will be destroyed! Come and help us. We have to secure the tarpaulin. It'll blow away if that wind comes back again.'

Sumati turned her head to the window. 'No, it won't,' she said quietly. 'It's gone. It was just a breeze off the sea.'

Roopchand looked at her, frowning. 'Are you cracked in the head?' he demanded. 'All the clothes on the line are scattered far and wide. Go and pick 'em up!'

'I'll come out and help you in a while,' she replied coolly. 'I have to check on my clothes for tomorrow. Where is the silk sari that Baljit sent for me to wear? And where is Ma's jewellery?'

'Baljit?' Roopchand asked angrily.

'What am I supposed to call him? He is going to be my husband tomorrow. I may as well call him by his name.'

'That is most disrespectful, and you know it! You will provoke him.'

'Just because you and Ma never called each other by name doesn't mean that other people don't do it. Amina's mother and father call each other by name.'

'Them?' he snorted. 'They don't know who they are. Can't be pure Indian!'

ꝏ

Sumati's Aunt Dulcie, her father's sister, arrived that same day, followed by all her baggage and entourage.

'I have come to do my duty,' she said, in a sort of high-class Bhojpuri accent.'

'We are not doing a big thing, sister,' Roopchand said. 'I didn't expect you till later, but it is good to see you.'

'Well, we'll do our best, nah?' Dulcie replied, bustling her body about.

'We have people who offered already to do all the cooking,' her brother informed her. 'They brought food, and they're in the back tent chopping up vegetables, kneading flour, grinding masala, and whatnot.'

'Very well. Leave it all to me,' Dulcie told him, authoritatively. 'Kissmiassi is here too. She knows how to do these things, and I trust her. *Chulloh*! Come, Kissmiassi.'

'Tantie, I'm pleased you've come to help,' Sumati said graciously, genuinely relieved that at least some of the burden was taken from them. From her in particular, as there were no other close female relatives living nearby. 'But the neighbours are doing a good job. They've been so helpful of late.'

'I thought you were *cujart!*' Dulcie exclaimed. 'Wedding come, food to eat, and they changed their mind?' She turned and stared at Sumati. 'And if it wasn't for you, your poor mother would be here to do her duty herself.'

Sumati bit her lip hard. Her aunt was right, and she felt she should have considered that, and kept her mouth shut. 'Yes, Tantie Dulcie,' she uttered, subdued.

Dulcie looked at Roopchand. 'You would have done well to keep your children in better order, rather than encouraging answering back.' She looked sideways at Sumati.

'We're pleased you could come,' Roopchand said, trying to placate her. 'Really. I can't manage on my own. I'm going out of my mind. You take over. Do it your way. I'm sure those women in the back will just do as you say. They're a good bunch, I can tell you that.'

'I'm sure they will.' Dulcie marched to the back of the house in all her travelling finery, saying, 'Take my trunk up to the bedroom, brother. You had best put us all in with Sumati. It'll be more convenient.'

'No, no,' Roopchand insisted. 'You take my room. I'll squeeze in with Kesh.'

'All right.' Dulcie looked at the companions she'd brought with her. 'Go and sort out the bedroom. Move what you have to and make space for us all. I have my own sheets.' She beckoned two of them. 'You, come with me. The rest of you, get out everything to start the *mehendi*. And you, Sumati, go and bathe and we will do the *mehendi*.

We'll have to let it dry for about three hours, and then we will do the *hardi.*'

'Oh, Tantie,' Sumati said. 'I didn't know we were going to do all that.'

'What did you think I came all this way for? Nothing? Go! Clean yourself up. Quick!'

Sumati left, half-smiling, suddenly happy to go along with the traditions that would make her look like a bride and help her feel like one. Her aunt was brusque in her manner with her, but Sumati took it for care, and felt grateful.

ꝏ

When they found Sumati half an hour later, her hair was still wet and she was crying.

'Come, let me dry that hair,' Dulcie said. 'Bring a dry towel, not these thin pieces of cloth. I don't know why my brother can't do something properly for once in his life. Go, Sumati. Find the good linens. Your mother must have had some put away for best.'

Sumati knew where they were – in her mother's trousseau amongst fifty camphor balls. 'I can't use those,' she objected. 'They are my mother's, and they're her best ones – for special.'

'Well, isn't this special?' Dulcie said. 'A most special time for a mother. Nearly as special as a son getting married. A son brings a wife to the home though. Someone to help around the house. A daughter goes to join somebody else's family to bring prosperity to *their* home. See? But still. We have to send you off well. Who knows what they will think of us otherwise?'

'Well, we had better leave it for when Kesh is getting married in that case,' Sumati said.

'No! You want a slap? Are you trying to be deliberately awkward?'

'No, Tantie,' Sumati said, surprised. 'I just thought to keep . . . '

'Shut up and go and get the damn towels, girl. You will catch a cold standing here in wet hair.'

Sumati went off instantly.

'Kissmiassi!' Dulcie shouted. 'Follow Sumati and bring her back here. I cannot wait for ever.'

ᘓ

The next morning, Dulcie woke Sumati up at dawn and sent her out to bathe while she got her something to eat. The cooking tent was already heaving with helpers. The aroma of frying masala in hot coconut oil filled the air as Sumati crossed the yard to the bathroom.

'You know that you have to eat early, and then fast until after *Saptapadi* – the seven steps of the ceremony,' Dulcie said.

'It shouldn't last long,' Sumati said. 'Pa said we're doing a quick thing.'

'What does your Pa know about anything? It will be done the correct way so long as I am here. We will do your mother proud, eh. She would want it for you. Her spirit might well be waiting to see this day.'

Sumati looked at Dulcie suspiciously. How did she know? Had she also seen, felt and heard what she had?

'Any mother would want it,' Dulcie said, as if reading her mind.

Sumati took her plate of food, hurried over to the hammock under the mango tree, and flopped into it. The sky was turning light and the birds were singing. The cockerel in the yard started again, crowing furiously. She began dreaming of what could have been. And then she heard a familiar voice that made her heart soar.

'Amina!' she shouted, nearly choking on her roti. 'What are you doing here this early?'

'I couldn't keep away anymore. Anyway, how could I sleep last night with all the noise coming from here? Besides, I knew you didn't have anybody to help you, apart from neighbours.'

'Tantie Dulcie came yesterday.' Sumati sounded relieved. 'You remember her?'

'Well, no matter. I'll do what you want. I'll do your hair and face and things.'

'I don't know, girl,' Sumati said. 'She brought a whole load of women with her – they're up here. There's Kissmiassi and . . .'

'*Who*?' Amina started to giggle. 'For real? Kiss-me what?'

They both burst into uncontrollable laughter, Sumati holding her stomach.

'I haven't laughed in such a long time,' she said, then suddenly went pale.

'Sumati? What's wrong?'

'Oh, my stomach. I think I just felt something – I think it was a kick. Oh! And again.'

'Oh, Sumati! What did it feel like?'

'I don't know. Like a kick from inside. Boom.'

'What is going on out here?' Dulcie shouted across the yard.

Neither of the girls realised that Dulcie had been watching them from the bedroom window. Shocked to hear her voice, they jumped to attention.

'You remember my friend Amina, Tantie Dulcie?' Sumati asked. 'Well, she's come to help me.'

'Oh, well that's nice. She is the one with that boy at your mother's funeral? The boy who knocked your father's teeth out? My brother? Eh?'

Neither of the girls answered. Amina was embarrassed.

'He never recovered from that! And on the day he buried his own wife too. Some people have no shame. And to turn up here on a day like today.'

'Tantie, she is my friend, and that was not her fault. You know well that Pa caused it.'

'That is a matter of opinion. But it was all to do with *her,* though.' She glared at Amina. 'If you have come to help, you had better go and see what they want in the kitchen. Or better yet, go and tie out the goats.'

'Sumati, do you want me to tie out Dulcie instead?' Amina whispered, giggling. 'I am going in the tent to help with the cooking.'

❧

There was a lot of laughing and merriment in the cooking tent, which was better than being around Dulcie. Amina didn't remain standing around for long although she wasn't used to cooking. Soon she was fetching clean water, washing vegetables, and helping to roll balls of flour for the roti. She watched and learnt how to make a piece of dough into a smooth floury *loyah*, the size of a cricket ball, ready to be rolled flat into roti. Two hours later, she left the tent and sneaked into the house.

'Today is my wedding day,' Sumati said to her. 'The first day of the rest of my life.' She placed her hand on her stomach and looked at Amina, beaming. Then she went pale.

'Sumati, you're alright?' her friend asked anxiously. 'You want me to get a cup of water for you?'

'No. I'm fasting till after the *Saptapadi*. It's just the kicking again. Amina, you won't tell anybody about this, especially Dulcie, will you?' she pleaded.

'No, of course not. You'll have to wrap your sari loosely. I'll go home and get dressed then come back to help you.'

'There are plenty here to help, but I rather they didn't, so come back soon. Hey, is Rajnath coming to the wedding?'

'I don't know.'

'I hope he does comes. I really like him. He has been a true friend when no one else wanted anything to do with me.'

'Yes, I know,' Amina said.

THIRTY-FIVE

Amina climbed on a stool and got the case down from the top of the wardrobe. She opened it and pulled out some of her wedding trousseau outfits. The blue silk sari and matching *choli* were beautiful. Really, she should keep them. But this day was important too. She decided to try on the choli and found it fitted surprisingly well, even though it was made with growing room. She pleated the sari into the waist of the petticoat and continued wrapping it round and round, before throwing the long piece over her right shoulder. The mirror reflected a better image than she had ever seen of herself: she looked taller, and more mature. She got out the brown paper bag containing the new pairs of champals and chose the turquoise and gold pair.

Amina decided on the nicest jewellery – a pair of three-layered earrings, spliced with scores of thin, diamond-shaped gold pieces that glinted in the light as they swung. With them, she wore the three-tiered gold necklace, a pair of bracelets and an orchid ring. Everyone wore their best clothes and finest gold jewellery for such a special occasion. She wasn't going to ask her mother's permission, the girl decided. Her father had spoilt her with his own creations, and the jewellery belonged to her. She sneaked out before Devinia could catch her to tell her she would surely bring bad luck upon herself if she wore those items before her own wedding. Amina had long since given up believing in luck, for the gods of good fortune seemed to be the bringer of more pain than joy.

ᐧ

Tassa drums were pounding the air for miles, and streams of people were arriving at the wedding house. Sumati had said she wanted a small do, but the whole village had become involved, ignoring the *cujart* placed on the family.

Amina went into the house half-expecting Dulcie to send her away. It would be the last day she would see Sumati as a single girl, and she was determined not to be put off by the woman. As she pushed her way through the tent towards the back of the house, she heard an imperious voice.

'Hey, you!' the voice called. 'Where do you think you're going?'

Amina turned and spotted Dulcie through the scores of school-friends, parents and neighbours, gathered at the back door chatting and laughing. Ignoring her, Amina headed into the house to Sumati's room and shut the door behind her, with a sense of relief.

The bride in the mirror was a beauty. Her face was already painted with kohl around her eyes, white powder over her eyelids, and blue and silver dots over her brows.

The red and gold sari lifted her complexion, which was pale of late. And her lips were luscious red.

Sumati was dressed more elaborately than Amina had expected. She sat in front of the mirror while two or three women helpers fussed about her hair, pinning it up off her face, and laughing. But Sumati's choli seemed tight, flattening her breasts.

She gasped with delight when Amina entered. 'You got in.' She rolled her eyes. 'I think my father tried talking some sense into Tantie Dulcie. But I'm surprised that stopped her.'

'I brought something for you,' Amina said, edging closer.

'You look so pretty,' Sumati said. 'Is that a new sari?'

'My mother bought it for my trousseau.' Amina opened the brown bag she had with her, and poured out the contents into Sumati's lap.

'What's this for?'

'It's for you. Take it. It's my present to you – for luck.'

Sumati's eyes welled up. 'I can't believe it. These are the ones you said your father made for your wedding.'

'Ssssh,' Amina said. 'Just take them. I'll not be needing them anyway.'

'Don't say that, Amina! You will need them soon enough. Your parents picked out a rich, educated businessman for you. You're lucky.'

'I disagree. It's unlucky for a girl who wants to remain in education. Sumati, I want you to have them. They won't fix anything, but I hope they make you feel special.'

Sumati picked up the elaborate necklace. It was exquisite. Tears rolled down her cheeks and dripped onto the jewellery in her hands. 'Look what I'm doing,' she said, wiping it.

Amina took the necklace, put it around Sumati's neck and fastened it at the back. She inserted the long droplet earrings into her ears, and took two of the bracelets from her own wrists and put them onto Sumati.

'These are yours,' Sumati objected. 'You're wearing them.'

'I love you as a sister,' her friend said tenderly. 'Remember the pact we made? We joined our blood. We are sisters. Take these, and always wear them, with my love.'

Sumati stood up and pulled Amina to her chest. 'No one has ever been this kind to me.'

Amina rearranged the sari, making it hang more loosely around her friend's waist. She got a pin to fix it in place over the tight choli that Sumati was almost bursting out of, and placed a gold *sirbandhi* around Sumati's head with the heart-shaped *bindi* directly in the centre of her forehead.

Pryia and Ramona stood behind them, sobbing.

'Oh gosh,' Sumati said shakily. 'You all will make me cry. I wasn't going to cry at all.'

'Ah yes, but you will be crying for all the right reasons,' Ramona said. 'Because you're happy, not because you're sad to leave home.'

'What is that?' Sumati asked.

There was a sudden hush in the bedroom and they all rushed to the window to see what was happening at the front of the house.

&

'There're loads of them!' a chorus of voices chattered. Everyone was peering out of the window.

'It's him!' Pryia cried. 'The bridegroom! He's here.'

Sumati's face went pale. 'What's he like?'

'Is he good-looking?' Amina asked, pushing to see.

'I don't know! I can't see!'

'He's up in that . . . urm . . . thing! They're carrying him up high.'

'Sumati, are you all right?' Amina asked.

'I don't know.' Sumati looked up at her friend as if pleading for something. 'I'm not sure. Hold my hand.'

Dulcie came rushing into the house, followed by a trail of her women helpers. They burst into the bedroom.

'Quick! The *doolaha* is here,' she said. 'Get yourself ready. Why didn't you put on the yellow sari like I told you?' she scolded. 'You don't do anything you're told. I should never have left you with this lot. The red one is for later! Come now, it's too late. They're here. I have to go and do my part.'

Everyone stared at Dulcie issuing orders and scolding all in the same breath. Sumati was panicking, but Dulcie just turned and hurried out of the door on the same breeze that blew her in. From the window, the girls could hear her striding through the crowds making her way to the front yard. Roopchand was already there, moving slowly towards the bridegroom and his entourage. The bridegroom had no father, but an uncle in his place. He took the brass cup of water from Roopchand. Pundit Lall took the coins from the bottom of the *lotah* – the brass cup, and divided them between the two older men from both sides. When this purification ceremony was done, Dulcie did the ritual blessing – the *Arti*, that Sumati's mother would have done, before the groom was helped down from his chariot, while Dulcie's married helpers showered flowers and scattered rice over him. He was to be treated as king of the day, and Dulcie was set to do her very best to keep the Indian traditions under the circumstances. She and the women escorted the groom to the *mandap*.

Both Roopchand and the groom's uncle now had to perform their part of the ceremony before the bride arrived. They put leaves, money, rice and flowers on the wooden bench and showered each other with flowers. Then they both rocked the bench containing the rest of the rice, flowers and money so that it all fell towards the decorated bench where the couple would be sitting for the ceremony.

Roopchand did the three-mango-leaf ritual, dripping water on the feet of Baljit, his son-in-law-to-be, as if to wash them. He then offered Baljit a small bite of the bitter mango leaf dipped in honey so that he could taste the bitter-sweet nature of marriage. Both men participated in more rituals, before the handover of the leaves to the pundit of the bride and that of the groom.

When Dulcie returned to the bedroom she noticed the jewellery Sumati was wearing. 'Where did you get this?' she demanded suspiciously.

Just then a rush of cold wind blew through the room, extinguishing the candles and creating havoc with saris and clothes flying around. Everyone froze. Sumati was the only one who remained calm. When the gust died down, she stood up smiling, towering over her aunt who was still reeling in fright.

'It's time to go,' Sumati said. '*Chulloh*,' and she burst into Indian song.

'Come with me to meet my groom,
To meet the one that waits for me
To enter this bitter-sweet union,

I hide my countenance till he binds the knot, . . . '

They all looked at her in surprise. A new song she'd made up, singing, standing tall in all her bridal glory, her womanly curves more pronounced below the layers of silk. '*Chulloh* my sisters. Come. Take me to my destiny.'

Dulcie picked up the edge of her own sari, as if she were the mother of the bride, and placed it on the head of her niece, covering her face, while offering Sumati five mango leaves dipped in honey, once again symbolising the bitter-sweet state of marriage. Sumati opened her hand and Dulcie placed the leaves in her cupped palms. One of the women gave a ball of dough to Dulcie.

'You won't leave this house empty-handed,' Dulcie said. A tear fell from Sumati's eye.

As they reached outside, the groom's family showered Sumati with gifts – five gold pieces, jewellery and clothes – but Baljit's family were not very well off. Sumati scanned the crowd to see who might be his children, but there were so many that she soon became distracted with the rest of the proceedings, and began concentrating on finding her way to the mandap where her future husband was already seated.

ఐ

Dulcie escorted Sumati to the canopy and sat her down on the bench opposite the groom, who was dressed in bright pink and maroon, with a cream and gold turban on his head, decorated with sequins and tiny mirrors. On top of the turban was a gold-coloured crown. Sumati couldn't help but raise her bowed head to look at the man she was about to marry and who she had never properly seen before. Although he had been to the house once, she had not really taken any notice as she was not interested. She remembered him as being just too old, and may as well be wrinkled and ugly as molten lava.

But he was not. And she was wrong. Surprised at what she saw, she raised her head even higher to be sure she was right, but Dulcie pushed it back down, and placed the ball of dough with silver coins and gold jewellery embedded into it, into Sumati's right hand. Then she put Sumati's left hand into the hand of the groom. Amina strained her neck to see his face, thinking he must have been a very young man when he first married. Then she spotted Rajnath standing not far from the ceremony, and wanted to speak to him. She scanned the surroundings to see if her parents were around before beckoning to him. While the pundits were conducting the ceremony, the two of them melted away, unseen.

'Well,' Rajnath said. 'It's happening. Farouk is missing out, that's for sure.'

'It's for the best . . . she wanted this.'

'Is that why she ran away with Farouk?'

'That was then,' Amina replied. 'She has no choice now.'

'She had a choice to just be happy, instead of chasing happiness. And what has she got? An old man. Now she will have to learn the truth about happiness.'

Amina blinked twice and looked up at Rajnath. 'Which is what?'

'Patience. Contentment. She could have had anybody,' he said roughly. 'Most men would give away their grandmother to be with somebody like her, just once.'

'Most men including you?' Amina looked at him, surprised.

Rajnath looked embarrassed. 'No! I meant men in general.'

'Now I understand.' Amina sighed. 'Well *you* missed *your* chance.'

'I didn't want one,' Rajnath said. And he stalked off looking angry, leaving Amina on her own outside.

The girl walked back into the wedding tent, listening to the pundits chanting various mantras. She saw Dulcie move her hand away from Sumati's, allowing it to fall into Baljit's hand. Noises and voices were building up from the edge of the wedding tent, sounding like a commotion. Then Amina heard another disturbance coming from the opposite direction. She didn't know which way to turn. But when she looked around to see what was going on inside the wedding canopy, she couldn't believe what she saw.

THIRTY-SIX

Sumati had collapsed to the ground. Roopchand was lurching forward to reach her, and the pundits were both hovering. Dulcie herself was striding towards Roopchand. People around the wedding bower were looking perturbed. Amina then spun towards the commotion at the other side of the tent to see Rajnath arguing with someone. By the time she reached him, Rajnath had the man backed up against a cashew tree about ten yards from the corner of the tent.

'What's going on?' Amina demanded.

'Talk, Farouk,' Rajnath hissed. 'Tell us why are you here, today of all days. Have you come to make sure you've got rid of her?'

'No,' Farouk said. 'I wanted to see her for the last time.'

'The last time? Like a good riddance kind of *last time*?'

'I loved that girl. But she left me.'

'You lie!' Rajnath snarled. 'It was you who left her!' He moved closer, his fist in the air. Amina got between them and tried to push them apart.

'If you loved her, why did you treat her so badly, then left her when she needed you?' Amina asked.

'You've got that wrong,' Farouk said. They both heard a ring of truth in his voice. 'I never saw her after the first day. Except once. It was on the third day, when I went up to her outside on the bench. She gave me one hard look and said she hated me, and never wanted to see me again. That it was best if I just left her. Then Amrit and Dillip told me that my being there was no good for Sumati. They said they had a job for me down at Bonasse. It seemed like the answer, so I took it.' He gave a long shuddering sigh.

'You weren't bothered enough to ask her why?' Amina asked.

'She had rejected me. I felt hurt. And stupid for taking her there. Then on the boat, Rajnath told me to come back. That she was having a child.'

'So you came back on her wedding day?' Rajnath exploded. 'The girl you loved and left with a child? What a man you turned out to be!'

'You want to blame me?' Farouk asked. 'Well, go ahead, if that will make you feel better about your family. I told you Dillip is no good!'

'Leave it, Rajnath,' Amina said, looking at him redden with anger again. 'There's no point.'

'Amina, why don't you go and see if your friend is all right,' Rajnath said in return. 'She's looking unwell, and needs you.'

Amina looked across at the mandap, and immediately ran off.

'If you really wanted her,' Rajnath said to Farouk, 'you'd have done something about it earlier. She's making your child. *Your* child . . . you son-of-a-bitch. And she's going to another unsuspecting man with that child. The fool might even think it is his if she succeeds.'

'My child?' Farouk asked. 'That's the other thing I don't understand.'

'This is no time for your games. This is your chance. It's now or never. If you want the girl, go and get her!'

'You want me to interfere with the wedding? Now? When she is making a child?'

'What? You don't care about your own child? You believe that she and your child will live a good life when that man finds out the truth?'

'My child?' Farouk asked. 'But it's not . . . '

Rajnath's fist came flying through the air and landed on Farouk's left cheek. 'What's wrong with you? You know that one and one makes two, right? Well, sometimes it makes three!'

Farouk cradled his cheek, looking puzzled.

Rajnath turned his eyes to the skies. 'What is the matter with him? Lord Krishna, come to my aid!'

'Oh, I see what you mean.' Farouk's eyes suddenly brightened as if Rajnath had struck a match up to his face.

&

Over in the mandap, Sumati lay flat on her back. She had fainted. Her eyes were only just rolling open. Roopchand sat her up, took a cup of water from someone and handed it to her.

'Drink this,' he said. 'Did you eat something this morning?'

'I gave her food early,' Dulcie said defensively. 'She must fast till after everything's finished – after tying of the knot, after the seven times round the fire and everything . . . '

'But that will not be for another two hours,' Roopchand objected, thinking of Sumati's condition. 'We are not doing all that,' he said firmly.

'You want a quick wedding now?' Pundit Lall asked with concern in his face.

'Well, it's up to him,' Dulcie replied sulkily. 'But he brought me here to do what I think is best. Now he wants a quickie-quickie wedding that mightn't last.'

'Is all right, Pa,' Sumati said weakly. 'I'll be fine now.'

'Well, if you're sure . . . ' Roopchand said worriedly. 'Go ahead then,' he prompted Pundit Lall.

'Just give me five more minutes,' Sumati requested.

'Take your time,' the pundit said.

Sumati bowed her head, wondering if it was really Farouk she had seen. But she dared not ask, nor speak his name. Amina stooped close to her, and put her arms round her. The groom, Baljit, said nothing. He looked stunned, staring silently at Sumati, then at Amina. Amina herself was keeping an eye on Rajnath. She could barely see him from where she was sitting, but he and Farouk still looked tense.

ꙮ

'It can't be my child,' Farouk was saying, looking at Rajnath. 'I just came to see her – to find out if it was true that she was getting married. If not, I was just going to see how she was.'

'Oh, just a little hello? Distant friends? Running away must be what you are good at.'

'Rajnath!' Farouk raised his voice for the first time. 'I care about her, but did you hear anything I said? Why did you send me and Sumati up there?'

'You know, I ask myself that nearly every day,' Rajnath replied exasperatedly. 'You caused more trouble than I expect to see in a lifetime. You told me you were in love with the girl, and you wanted to marry her. What will happen to her when that man finds out she's carrying a child that's not his?'

'He wouldn't know. She just looks a little bit fat.'

'He's not stupid. He already had a wife and children. He'll throw her out.'

'What can I do?'

'It's never too late to do the right thing, Farouk.'

'What – you want me to just tell the groom to move over?'

'Why not? They're not officially married yet. There's still a long way to go. They're not married until they've tied the knot and walked around the fire seven times. And the rest.'

'I cannot take on a child.'

'Take responsibility!'

'Do you know what they're doing? Your Uncle and Dillip are doing bad business. I knew you wouldn't believe me.'

'Stop talking about Dillip!'

'That is why I never told you. How do you think I am living where I am?'

'You mean that big house in Bonasse?' Rajnath asked.

'If you know about the house, you must know about the business.' Farouk lowered his voice. 'Contraband things. Illegal. Between Venezuela and Icacos. Slooping it up to Port of Spain.'

'Why would I know that? You're helping them? Shame on you, Farouk! What is it? Cigarettes? Mountain dew?'

'That too. Rum and emeralds, from what I have heard. What did you expect me to do? I had nowhere to go. I couldn't go back home. Dillip threatened to kill me. Don't let this get out, otherwise you are in trouble. Dillip has some really rich, really bad friends up in Port of Spain. If you so much as look at them they'll chop off your hand. I have seen it happen.'

Rajnath stepped back and scratched his head. 'I don't know what to say. You're serious?'

'I kept it to myself all this time. Before Kalouti left, she had a big row with them. I heard Dillip telling Kalouti that if she didn't like the new business, she could leave. He was really rude to her, and Amrit never said a word. She got really upset. She packed her bags and left straight away. I never thought your uncle would let Dillip talk to your Tantie in such a disrespectful way. But then again, Dillip is not like us. He is a law unto himself.'

'That is what you get when you pay a lot of money to educate your child in the white man's world. My cousin had to fit in somehow.'

'He's a crook,' Farouk said tersely. 'Keep away from him.'

'I still think you should have protected Sumati. Just because my cousin can talk like an Englishman it doesn't mean that he's smart. You should have come back and told me. You know how much support you would have got from everybody here?'

'Support? What world do you live in? Sumati's father would have given me a good beating. You know the temper on that man?'

'So you saved your own skin! That makes you a selfish coward. Sumati deserved better.'

'You're changing your tune.'

'Tune? If I was singing, you wouldn't even know the damn song. You said you loved the girl. Why do you think I helped you?'

'As it happened, Raj, you didn't really help me.'

'It's best that you leave here and never come back,' Rajnath told him. 'Nobody here will talk to you, not now. You were the one who killed Sumati's mother.'

'I am sorry.' Farouk dropped his head. 'You're right – I don't belong here. Will you explain to Sumati that I am sorry, and that I wish her a good life? Please?'

Rajnath was no longer angry but saddened. Farouk looked devastated. He looked like he'd lost everything.

'That's the price you pay,' Rajnath said. 'I'm sorry how things turned out but you have to find a life somewhere else. Maybe we can be friends again, but I don't know when. Right now, I have to think what to do. And believe me, I will do something. I just don't know what yet.'

'Whatever you do, do not tell Dillip what I told you. Otherwise we are both dead.'

Rajnath felt like a clay pot that had been smashed into a thousand pieces with no way of mending it. He knew Farouk would be feeling the same. He watched Farouk straining his eyes to see through the strings of flowers around the bridal tent, casting a last wistful look of regret. Then Rajnath turned and walked away.

As he strode along the road, he couldn't answer the question that was bothering him. How could one act of kindness turn out so wrong? His uncle and cousin were apparently engaged in some illegal trade? He was torn between his friend and his own flesh and blood. How could he give up on either of them? In the end, he felt as much to blame as Farouk.

THIRTY-SEVEN

By the time Rajnath got home, he had made a decision.

'Annan, tell Ma I'm going up to San Fernando.'

'If you say so,' his younger brother replied. 'I'm guessing you will be back in two hours, seeing that there is no boat today. That will give you just enough time to walk down to Bonasse, turn round, and come back home.'

'That's why I borrowed a bicycle.'

'Well, we will see you in two weeks then – if you survive all the snakes and *Diablesse* on the way. By the time you get up there it will be dark. So watch some *soucouyant* doesn't find you first, or some gang doesn't beat you up.' He clapped his big brother on the back. 'Anyway, don't worry. I will tell Ma when they come home. She might be having puja tonight.'

'Puja tonight? She didn't tell me.'

'That's because she didn't know. She didn't know you were sick in the head.'

'You think you're funny, Annan? You should put your mind to better use.'

'You wouldn't notice if I did. Look, I don't know what you're up to, but take care.'

'I'm going to see Uncle Amrit.'

'Like I said, I don't know what you're up to.'

'You can be so annoying. Just tell her, please.'

Annan raised his hands. 'I give up. Don't say I didn't try to stop you.'

Rajnath took a few pieces of food and wrapped them in a piece of brown paper and put it in his pocket. Then he left.

ꕤ

Rajnath was on the road half an hour before the sun began to lower behind the trees, and for the first time he took stock of what he was doing. He had never travelled to San Fernando by bicycle before. The temperature was falling, his back was getting cold, and his thoughts were being invaded by scary folk tales. He pedalled faster and faster while he cursed Annan for deliberately putting those things in his head. The bicycle lamp was flashing on and off, but he dared not stop to check it. The night grew colder, owls hooted and cicadas screeched. Fireflies led the way, but took him into bushes where he hit a rock and fell off the bike head first, and mosquitoes began to feast on his face and arms.

After hours of pedalling, the lights of San Fernando appeared in the distance, and his heart leapt. Two cars passed by and town noises started filtering through the air. He struggled on and when he reached the house three hours later, he was so tired, he could barely speak.

ꕥ

A young woman entered the room, bringing with her a waft of sweet orange blossom and fresh coffee. The sun streamed through as she unbolted the window and pushed it open. Rajnath saw the room plainly now. Newly painted white wooden walls, white gauze curtains draped across the window. Branches of a tree laden with green and yellow guavas touched the open window, and cockerels crowed and dogs barked at each other. The sounds were familiar but the smells were different.

'Mr Amrit sent me to see if you want something to eat,' she said. 'It is nearly eight o'clock.'

'Really? It's morning?' Rajnath replied.

'You didn't eat your food last night.' She stared down at the tray. 'You look better though.' She half-smiled.

Rajnath lifted his head and stared at the girl. Her skin was smooth, the colour of milky cocoa. She spoke softly as she touched her neat cane-rowed hair around her oval face, and he couldn't help but notice the slim, muscular arms as she smoothened her skirt around her slight hips. She walked across the room and picked up the blanket from the floor, and he could see she was grown, but not fully.

'Who are you?' he asked. 'I mean, are you from round here?'

'I live here most of the time. I go home sometimes.'

'How often?'

'Every three months,' she said. 'But it gets busy here this time of year.'

'How's that?'

'I don't know. It's what Mr Amrit says. But we are always busy.'

'How old are you? And what kind of work are you doing here?' Rajnath asked.

Just then, Amrit entered the open door.

'There you are!' his uncle said in a loud, cheerful voice. 'Did you sleep well?'

'Yes, thank you,' Rajnath replied.

'So, what brings you here at that hour of the night? Has something happened at home? Have you fallen out with your father? Is your mother well? You didn't make much sense last night. You collapsed and we had to carry you upstairs. I couldn't smell any rum on your breath though.'

'I wasn't drinking, Uncle Amrit.'

'The first thing I want to know is if everybody is all right at home.'

'Yes, yes. Everybody's all right,' Rajnath reassured him.

'Well, go and take a bath and we'll have breakfast under the almond tree. You can tell me then what's going on.'

ꟗ

The girl returned with a bundle of clothes.

'Mr Amrit say to bring these for you,' she said. 'Looked like you fell somewhere in the mud last night.' Her eyes were bright and clear, her cheeks dimpling as she spoke, her teeth glinting as if someone had brushed white paint over them.

'How old are you?' Rajnath asked.

'Thirteen next month.'

'What work do you do here?'

'Whatever they want me to do.'

'And where are you from? Your parents?'

'I am from Comuto village.'

'You are a long way from home.'

'What do you want me to do for you?' she said.

'Nothing,' he said. 'I just wanted to know.' But she was already removing her skirt. Rajnath sat up in shock.

'Where do you want me?' she was asking.

'What? Please – put your clothes back on.'

'I thought you were interested.' She looked crestfallen. 'Can I do anything for you?'

'Who taught you to do that? Is that what you do here?'

'I told you – I just do what people want me to do. Mr Dillip doesn't like the girls who disobey. He will beat them till they do it.'

'Has Dillip beaten you?'

'He never had cause to beat me,' she said proudly. 'There was a girl who ran away after he beat her a few times. But she used to give him lip every morning when she got sober. She was a good-looking Indian girl from down south.'

'What is your name girl?'

'Matilda.'

'And what was her name?'

'Sumati.'

Rajnath felt his hackles rise, but he tried not to show it. He needed more information.

'This Sumati, was she on her own, or with somebody else?'

'She was on her own. But when I came here, she was already here.'

'Oh. So why did you come here, Matilda?'

'Mr Dillip brought me and promised to teach me to read and write.'

'You didn't go to school?'

'There's no school in Comuto.'

'Very well, you may go now. I want to get dressed,' he said. 'And don't tell anybody what I asked you. And hey,

Matilda. You look like a nice girl. Make sure you learn to read and write. That is your ticket to a better life.'

ಐ

It took all Rajnath's efforts to suppress his fury as he bathed and dressed in the crisp white cotton shirt and baggy khaki trousers from the folded pile of clothes. He then went downstairs where he found Amrit shooing the birds from around the table.

'Come, come, son,' the man said, looking at Rajnath. 'Sit down.'

The smell of cooking reminded the young man he hadn't eaten a proper meal since breakfast the previous day. The food arrived from the kitchen nearby, and Rajnath ate hungrily, but thinking all the time of what might be the best way to broach the subject of Farouk and Sumati.

'They have taken your clothes away to wash them,' Amrit said. 'They will carry them to the Chinese laundry down the road. It won't take that long. The girl said you had a piece of roti in your pocket.'

'You mean Matilda?'

'She told you her name?'

'She told me that Sumati was here and was beaten up by my cousin, uncle. Is that true?'

'I don't know too much about that, boy.'

'So what do you know about? This is your place, right? What do you sell in the shop? It looking very big from here. I want to see it.'

'Listen, you were asking me about Farouk the last time. I gave him work but he was lazy. He was quiet too. Didn't say much, didn't do much.'

'Is that why you sent him away?'

'It's what he wanted to do. Your friend didn't want to work – and he didn't want to stay here. It seemed as if he couldn't wait to get away.'

'I know what my friend is like and how he behaves, and you are not talking about him at all, uncle. Tell me the truth, please, because I am having some trouble with my patience right now.'

'Are you threatening my father?' It was Dillip, who had suddenly appeared. 'Tell him, Pa. What kind of man brings a girl under somebody else's roof, spoils her, and doesn't want to take the consequences?'

'What are you talking about, boy?' Amrit looked at his son with surprise. 'What consequences?'

'Come on, Pa, don't pretend. You yourself said that it didn't look good, bringing her here under our roof. And I agreed with you. But it was me who was man enough to do something about it.'

'Dillip,' Amrit commanded him. 'Stop talking. Only rubbish will come out of your mouth.'

'Which one of you is lying?' Rajnath asked. 'You didn't have enough time to get your story straight?'

'Raj, we just separated them,' Amrit said. 'We put the girl with the women.'

'The women? How many women do you have here? And why? Are they selling sand?'

'Ha!' Dillip jeered.

'Just Tonia and the others,' Amrit mumbled.

'Pa, Tonia is your whore. Where is she every night? I live here, remember.' He turned to Rajnath. 'Pa chased my mother away from this house, by bringing in that woman.'

'Dillip?' Amrit said. 'You are not right in the head. Why are you lying, boy? So many lies in one fast five minutes?'

'Tell him the truth,' Dillip sneered.

'I will,' Amrit said. 'Kalouti left because of what *he* was doing. He was calling it business. I begged him to stop it, but I didn't want to fall out with him. He's my son. You could say I let him get away with it, but not Kalouti. She couldn't. She was a good person.' He looked at Rajnath before saying, 'Dillip brought Tonia here because he wanted somebody to run a whorehouse for him. I'm ashamed to tell you this, Raj, but your cousin here – yes, my son! – was the one who made that little girl into a whore.'

Rajnath jumped. 'Who – Matilda?'

Dillip laughed. 'No. Your little friend, Sumati. Face it, Raj, she was no good anyway. She was already whoring with Farouk, and he was willing to do a deal. I mean, business is business.'

'A fast dollar at an innocent girl's expense?' Rajnath spat.

'What's your problem? Everybody was happy.' Dillip laughed.

'Only you were happy, Dillip,' Amrit rebuked his son. 'I was never happy with you for what you were doing, and are still doing. Kalouti left me because of you. She thought it was my fault, because I sent you to that college. And all you managed to learn was how to take advantage of people. And you brought all these white people you met in those white clubs in Port of Spain.'

'You mean those paying customers?' Dillip sneered. 'Hotel customers?'

'I was ashamed of you then, and I'm disgusted with you now. To think what was going on in my premises.'

'But you allowed it, uncle,' Rajnath challenged him. 'I am ashamed of and disgusted with both of you.'

'I didn't even know at first,' Amrit defended himself. 'I thought he was doing good business.'

'It was good business. It's where the money to build came from.'

Amrit held his chest and sat down heavily. He put his hand on Rajnath. 'What can I say?' he said. 'My son let me down. And I let you down.'

'Between the two of you,' Rajnath said, 'you let yourselves down. And me.'

'And what are you doing for a living, cousin?' Dillip questioned, in his haughty Port of Spain half-English, half-Indian voice.

'Something more respectable. I'm not using people who come to me for help.'

'You call cutting cane and getting whipped for not weeding a line, something respectable? You know nothing about business, you half-wit *country-bookie* Indian. I'd have offered you a cut if you weren't so stupid.'

'A cut?' Rajnath stood, angry.

'Yeah, man. But you are too much of a country-*coolie*.'

'Dillip, stop it!' Amrit shouted.

'Did I ask you for work?' Rajnath said.

'Pa, we should give Rajnath a few dollars for his part in sending that girl. She brought us luck. She had one sweet arse. And those white men know how to treat a girl eh. At least they know what to say and how to pay.'

'He's lying,' Amrit shouted. 'He's trying to make you annoyed, Rajnath. You want me to give him a good beating?' The older man got up and grasped a piece of wood from the yard – but by the time he advanced, Rajnath had already whacked his cousin.

ꕥ

Dillip coughed and spluttered. Blood was pouring from his open mouth. His right eyebrow was split and the eyelid was swelling. Amrit ran over to him and tried to help.

'What did you do that for, boy?' Amrit turned to Rajnath with a reproachful look in his eyes. 'I was going to deal with him myself.'

'You had your chance, Uncle Amrit, but you never did anything. You let your son use innocent people. Young girls! Sumati, Matilda here right now. How many more?'

Tonia came running out of the kitchen looking frightened, and then she ran back and emerged again carrying a bowl of water.

Dillip tried to talk but his words made no sense through his two broken front teeth.

'I think it is time you left,' Amrit said to Rajnath.

'I am leaving, uncle. I am going to the police station.'

'Listen,' Amrit said, in a pacifying voice. 'Go and take a lie-down. We will give you one of the special rooms on the new side.

'What you mean by a *special room*?' Rajnath asked suspiciously.

'You know,' Amrit said, and lowered his voice. 'The full treatment.'

Rajnath looked at his uncle, stunned. 'You're telling me, you're offering me a woman? One of these girls – a child? For the night?'

'Take your pick.'

'How many do you have?'

Amrit looked at Dillip, who was gaping at his father open-mouthed, unable to close his mouth against the two protruding front teeth.

'This is crazy,' Rajnath snarled, turning to leave the yard.

'Where are you going?' Amrit asked in a panic. 'You wouldn't get a boat back home now. And you won't manage to ride back home on that bike.'

Rajnath walked to his bike.

'Don't involve the police, son,' Amrit pleaded, following Rajnath. 'We are family. We will talk and settle it between us. I'll give you anything.' He began to wheedle. 'Come and work for me. I'll pay you good money. You'll never want for anything.'

'How much are you making, uncle?'

'I don't know,' Amrit shrugged.

'How much a month?'

'A month? Just a few hundred a day.'

Rajnath's eyes opened wide.

'Pa!' Dillip shouted. 'Pa knows nothing.'

Rajnath began pacing the yard. 'So that is the amount you are aware of, uncle. You know something? I always thought a lot of you. You were my hero, ever since I was a little boy. But your riches never meant anything to me. I didn't know how you got rich, and I never asked. But my mother was always proud of you – her brother! Although my father never liked something about you.'

'Well, your father never kept that a secret. He thought he was more educated than me, but he didn't have the business head on him.'

'My father and I have our differences, but he is not a thief.'

'Who are you calling a thief, boy?' Amrit said, feeling stung.

'You rob young girls of their virginity and their life,' his nephew told him.

'You don't know what you're talking about.'

'You promise them something you don't give, then use them to line your own pocket. That is a thief. You betrayed Farouk and took his life away when you trapped Sumati here. That girl might have been bold as brass, but she was a virgin when she came here. Unspoilt, I am sure of that. And what about Matilda?'

'Ha! Ow u no ah! Upid oron!' Dillip began making loud jabbering noises again.

'And you.' Rajnath looked at Dillip. 'You sold her virginity and her body for the promise to teach her to read? Have you kept that promise? I have no choice but to get the police, uncle. You're a crook. I am sure they will find out what you are really doing here – about illicit activities between Icacos and Venezuela.'

'All I wanted was to survive after Dillip's mother died. My Rani.' Amrit's eyes filled with tears. 'I did my best, and this is what it's come to.'

'We all make mistakes, uncle. Mine was to trust you. Yours started by not taking responsibility for your son. We all have to pay. I have to take this to the police.'

'You! You are the cause!' Amrit screamed at Dillip. 'You deserve that beating! And more! I would have done it myself if Rajnath hadn't got there first.'

Dillip groaned and cursed while he watched Rajnath wobble away on his bicycle.

ஐ

It was late afternoon. Rajnath cycled towards the police station, but the door was shut. He called but no one came out. He rode up and down the streets for a few minutes and then had a thought. It was Sunday. He headed back to his uncle's house. Amrit met Rajnath at the gate.

'Tell them you made a mistake,' Amrit begged. 'Don't involve the police. We are family. Look, I'll give you anything. Just name it.'

'Ten thousand dollars,' Rajnath said. The words fell from his tongue before he even thought about it.

'What?' Amrit began, stuttering and spluttering through a sudden coughing fit. At the same time Dillip was having a painful-sounding laughing fit.

'You're joking!' Dillip babbled. 'Crazy fool!'

'Maybe you could bribe the police instead?' Rajnath offered.

'That might be better,' Amrit said. 'I never thought my own nephew would threaten me like this – for money.'

'Well maybe I really am a chip off the old block. Just like you, uncle. My mother probably inherited some other disgusting trait, but mine must be travelling down the male line of the family.'

'I can't give you that kind of money, boy. Not right now.'

Now Rajnath realised that his uncle *did* have that kind of money – somewhere. 'Stop calling me boy, uncle.'

'Call 'im woman,' Dillip mumbled cheekily.

'Want some more of this, cousin?' Rajnath said, raising his fist.

'Boy, you have changed!' Amrit said.

'Yes, suddenly I am a man! So, please, less of the "boy". If you can't get the money, I'm going back to the police station.'

'Wait here.' Amrit sucked his teeth and turned.

'Pa!' Dillip called his father in vain as the man disappeared around the back of the old building and up the steps. He then returned and walked towards the road.

'Where's he going?' Rajnath demanded.

'Wait. Don't go anywhere,' Amrit called. 'I'm coming back in a while.'

THIRTY-EIGHT

On his return home, Rajnath collapsed and was barely able to get out of bed. Parbatee sent a message for a doctor. Dr Boyle visited and after a thorough examination agreed that the young man was not at all well.

'Doctor, the boy has been overdoing it of late,' Parbatee said. 'He came home in the middle of the night and I heard ructions. I got up and woke my husband and my other son, and Raj was there, lying on the ground outside. It took all three of us to bring him inside. We had to drag him up the steps and into the bed. He's not right these days – odd like. You will write a certificate so that I can send it to the plantation so they know he is sick?'

She disappeared and returned with a bucket of water and towel.

'I'd like to keep an eye on him,' Dr Boyle said. 'If he was closer to Port of Spain I'd have him in hospital, where we could run tests. Port of Spain is far, but if you can, get him to the infirmary in San Fernando.'

'You mean that infirmary in the poorhouse in San Fernando?' Parbatee asked.

'That is the closest place.'

Parbatee shuddered. 'That is where sick people wait on the long waiting list, and when they manage to get a bed, they die. They die there, doctor! That place finishes them off. I'm not having my son go there. You just write out a sick-paper so when he goes to work, he will give them it.'

'He won't be needing any medical certificate if he doesn't get better, Mrs Singh. He is seriously ill.'

'Yes, he will, doctor. You see, the foreman and the overseers at the plantation are very, very wicked. Bully boys. And they will make sure to punish him in more ways than one for not coming to work. They will never believe he was ill without the sick-paper. They have a habit of not believing Indians. Regular they get thrown in the jail. And they get big fines they can't ever pay back, that they will work all their life to pay back.'

'Very well, I will write out a certificate. But that will cost you an extra thirty cents. And you will have to follow my instructions to the letter. I have a strong suspicion that your son has contracted tuberculosis.'

'TB?' Parbatee began to shake. 'My son have TB? Oh Lakshmi Mata, RamRamSita! How he get that? You will have to give him injections,' she jabbered. 'And we will look after him. We will do pujas.'

'I can't do miracles. He should be in isolation. Kept away from everyone else. You see, he is infectious.'

'You really mean my son is going to die?' Parbatee went pale.

'I will be honest: the possibility is high. Although if he is a strong young man he could recover. But that is usually with good care in hospital facilities. Not at home, in these poor conditions out here.' The big Scotsman opened his bag. 'I'll give him an injection today, and will come back in a few days to check on him.'

'Oh praise be to you, doctor. And Catholic God of Roman, I praise You too. I will get you some money,' Parbatee said, full of hope, and hurried away.

'I'm Presbyterian, not Catholic,' Dr Boyle called after her. 'I'll see you outside in a few minutes.'

Parbatee looked confused but went outside and waited. She had prepared a bag of food provisions from their garden, together with the visiting fee and extra for the medical certificate and for the medicines he left.

When Doctor Boyle had washed his hands and came outside, he gave her care instructions for Rajnath. 'No visitors,' the doctor said, as he took the things from her. 'And for your benefit and your own family here, you must take precautions and isolate him as best as possible. I'll take this sample to the hospital and see how quickly they can do the test.'

He looked at the woman before him with pity.

THIRTY-NINE

Amina's life turned eerily quiet after the wedding. Sumati left Granville with Baljit, her new husband, who had been remarkably calm in the midst of the wedding furore. Amina waited some days for Sumati to return in disgrace, but she didn't, so she wished her well and stopped worrying.

When she returned to school Mr Clifford suggested she read as many books from his cupboard as she could, which would stand her in good stead for the rest of her life. The girl intended to do just that, for her appetite for reading was voracious. But one day it occurred to her that she had not seen or heard from Rajnath for a good two weeks, and wondered if he had given up on Farouk since Sumati had left. But Amina's father kept reminding her that her own wedding was approaching. She had to do something since her plan to persuade them was failing. So she went to see Mr Clifford about a different plan.

'Unbelievable!' he exclaimed. 'This is what I live for. You will be a teacher *and* a Catholic. That is wonderful.

'Now, you will learn the Catechism and when you are able, you will attend Mass. Your parents will come with us to Port of Spain for baptism, initiation and sacrament. But that won't be for a little while. Believe me, it will be of great help when you qualify as a teacher, for making good progress in a Catholic school.'

'Port of Spain?' Amina echoed. 'My parents?'

'Of course. They will be pleased you are making such good decisions.'

'I can't tell them, sir.'

'How can you do this if they are not consenting?'

Amina thought frantically. 'No, I mean that I have already talked to my mother about it.' Her voice shook as she told Mr Clifford this bold lie.

'Very well, I knew she would understand.' The head teacher smiled reminiscently. 'I remember when you were very ill indeed, how your poor mother would bring me Indian sweets from their prayers and ask me to read you poems. I visited your bedside once or twice, and read to you from Byron, Keats and Wordsworth.'

Amina hazily remembered the figure at her bedside on the wooden bench, a glowing lamp in the darkened room, and a husky, undulating voice.

'I remember,' she said. 'It's probably why I know so many of those poems by heart.'

'You have no idea how useful that made me feel. Maybe it *was* part of your recovery? God only knows. You could have died. And look at you now – entering the teaching service. I'm proud of you – as proud as if you were my own daughter. Tonight I will make *tullom*, and bring some to celebrate. You know *tullom*? Our version of sugarcake. My mother used to make it. A round sweetie made with molasses and grated coconut.'

Amina twisted her face at the thought of the sticky bitter version of sugarcake.

'This news makes me rejoice like the angels in heaven when one child turns to God. Let's hope you start a trend amongst your culture. Why is it that more Indians are not like you and your family? Maybe one day.'

'Because, sir, they find it hard to make enough money to buy food even. I'm lucky. My father has his own business.'

'Education is another way out of the poverty too. You will be an example to them all.'

'But it doesn't train their children for the kind of jobs they are able to get right now.'

'These people are illiterate,' he said dismissively. 'They cannot appreciate the value of education. They think about the next meal, when education is offering them the stars.'

'Sorry, sir, but when your belly is empty it is hard to think about reaching the stars.'

But the headmaster failed to hear her. He was rummaging through the book cupboard. 'Take this book. *Wuthering Heights*, by Emily Brontë. It's the one we're doing for the Part One Pupil Teacher syllabus this year at evening classes.'

'Yes, sir.' Amina's smile lit up her whole face.

The man nodded, pleased. 'I haven't seen you smile like that for months,' he said. 'I'll tell you now, that Sumati was not good for your focus. You have chosen well. Tell your mother I said so.' He patted her on the shoulder.

FORTY

Two months after her wedding, Sumati returned to Granville and hobbled over to see Amina that same evening, cradling her abdomen. They were all pleased to see her but surprised at her size. Devinia cooked and they talked for hours.

'So, what is he like, your husband?' Amina asked.

'Good.' Sumati beamed her usual broad smile.

'And your in-laws?'

'To be truthful? His sister said she was worried about him since his wife died.'

Amina stared at Sumati's belly. 'You look ready to drop.'

'I can't understand it – it's not time yet. I must be content. Baljit is a very nice man.'

'More like a father?' Amina asked.

Sumati laughed. 'Well, he likes children and wouldn't want me to miss out on having my own.'

'And what're his children like?' Amina asked.

'The girl is all right. But the boy tells me I'm not his mother.'

'So, Baljit didn't say anything about you being so big so quickly?'

'Not really,' Sumati lied.

'And you're not worried?'

'You know me, I don't worry when there's nothing to worry about. Anyway, I have you to do all the worrying for me . . . still! Listen to yourself!'

'I am worried what will happen when he finds out he's not the father, and Farouk is.'

'Farouk?'

'What's wrong? You don't remember who Farouk is? You remember fainting on your wedding day when you saw him there?'

'I wasn't feeling good,' Sumati said. 'I hadn't eaten since six o'clock that morning, and then when I spotted Baljit's face, I couldn't believe my luck.'

'I know what you are doing, Sumati,' Amina said. 'You're trying to forget all about Farouk, but you can't rub him out like a wrong word you've written with chalk on a slate. He exists. You did *things* with him, and you ran away with him, and lived with him. And that child in your belly belongs to him – might have his nose, his mouth, his eyes.'

'What are you trying to do to me? I told you before, he is not the father.'

'You are my friend. And Baljit is your husband. You shouldn't lie to people who care about you. When he finds out, he will kill you! That is what I'm worried about.'

'Sometimes you talk as if you're my mother.'

'Well, somebody has to!'

'I know.' Sumati let out a sigh. 'And I'm the one who's got to force you to jump off a cliff once in a while. Otherwise everything will pass you by. You're frightened of your own shadow.'

'I'm not frightened. I'm just not as . . . '

'. . . stupid as me? Is that what you're thinking?'

'Well, jumping off a cliff isn't too clever. You don't worry – and *that* makes me worry.'

'Look at my face, girl. Do I look like somebody who will ever worry? That man fell for me immediately. I am the best thing that's happened to him in years.'

'But when you lie, things get worse,' Amina said. 'Why don't you understand?'

'So, tell me, Miss Perfect, what about Rajnath? When's the wedding? And are you going to invite me? And how much have you lied to your mother about not meeting up with him alone?'

'Shhh! Are you trying to get me in trouble? My mother will hear you. Nothing is going on with me and Rajnath. He's just a friend – not even that.'

'Meeting up in secret? I think he likes you. So, what's happening with the rich match?'

'I saw him once, and I can't even remember what he looked like. Anyway, I am doing the Pupil Teaching Course now. And I'm changing my religion. It's a secret.'

'You. Have. Gone. Mad. Wait. You took all I said about turning Catholic seriously? I was joking. It's not possible.'

'It *is* possible. Actually, it is essential if you want to teach in a Catholic school.'

'Who says that? Oh, that will be the all-knowing all-seeing Mr Clifford.'

'Well, he does know something about education and teaching, Sumati. And he's not bad at giving good advice either. Actually, I wouldn't mind some of that rubbing off on me.'

'So that's what this is about. You, turning Catholic – to give me advice!' Sumati clasped her belly and stared at Amina. 'Well, advise yourself, Miss Perfect. Stop pretending you're better than everybody else.'

'I didn't say I was,' Amina defended herself. 'I'm trying to better myself, that's all. Why is that a crime? Because I'm a girl?'

Sumati stood up and arched her back.

'I don't mean to make anything worse for you,' Amina went on, 'but I wouldn't be any kind of a friend if I didn't say that telling lies as big as the ones *you* tell will come back to haunt you. If you want Baljit to bring up some other man's child, you should tell him about it. In the Bible, it is called truth and honesty.'

'The Bible?' Sumati looked at her in amazement. 'Do I know you?'

'Lying lips are an abomination unto the Lord. But they that deal truly are His delight. Proverbs 12:22.'

'What?' Sumati stepped back. 'And where in the Bible does it say about turning against your own religion, and your own friends? Where, Amina?' Sumati's eyes shone like clear rainwater in the sun.

'Deceit is in the heart of them that imagine evil. But to the counsellors of peace is joy.'

'So *you* are peace and joy, and *I* am deceit and evil?' Sumati spat angrily. 'Well, I never knew it would come to this. It's strange how a little bit of Catholic religion could turn you into someone so perfect. I leave here for five minutes, and you change into a different person. We are sisters, remember? Your God turned you so cold.'

'My God is the God of Love. And I care about you, Sumati. More than you understand. You are the closest I will ever come to having a sister. I want the best for you. I don't want to see you hurt.'

'You don't know the meaning of hurt, Amina. Just because I don't show it doesn't mean I'm not hurting.'

'*My* God is the God of Abraham, Isaac and Jacob.'

'And you are who? The daughter of Abraham?'

'We all can be daughters of Abraham, if we turn to the one true God. Have faith in that God and He will not turn His back on us.'

'I have to say, old Clifford is doing a good job on you, girl.'

'Sumati, I just happen to think that there is something in this Christian religion, and I want to know more about it. I'm learning something new, and it's making sense.'

'I am Hindu, and I don't see what is wrong with it. You have your new life, and I have mine. I know which one I want.'

'But do you know *what* you want, Sumati?'

'I am sorry for you, Amina. You always have to do what everyone expects from you. And you never do what you want to do. That is the difference between us. If you could accept we are different, we could still be friends.'

'But you always do what you want, Sumati – and hurt everybody around you. And that includes me. I have no choice when you act like you do. Who else will tell you? But if you don't want to be friends, I'm sad about that.'

Sumati left Amina. She walked up the path. But instead of turning right to go home, she turned left.

FORTY-ONE

At evening class, Amina asked Mr Clifford a burning question. 'What advice would you give a friend who was lying to her husband?'

'It depends on what she is lying about and why,' he said. 'Everything is not black and white. Some things are quite grey.'

'What do you mean by grey, sir?'

'Grey is the whole spectrum between black and white, good and evil, truth and lies, even. When you asked me about becoming a Catholic, I remember your face. You so wanted to do the right thing. But you have to look deeper into someone's motives. Their reasons might be more virtuous than the truth itself. Would you lie if it would save your mother's life?'

Amina looked puzzled. 'Maybe, sir.'

'Maybe? Ask yourself if you would like someone to lie if it would save *your* life. Think about it. Don't answer straight away. Rome was not built in a day. And maturity does not happen overnight.'

'I understand, sir. Well, I don't really, but I'm beginning to. Except in the Bible, you told us it says, *Thou shall not lie.*'

'Yes, indeed. And the Bible appears to be full of contradictions. But so does any message if you only read one line and ignore the rest. How can you *love your neighbour as yourself*, if you cannot put yourself in their shoes? Think like them, imagine yourself with their dilemmas. When the good man Jesus said, *Do unto others as you would have them do unto you* – what does that mean? It means to put yourself in their shoes and understand their position, their pain and their sorrows. Now you are not ignoring the fact that God abhors a liar. But you are putting it into some context. Including the commands of Jesus, who was sent to save us from our sins by sacrificing himself, to love one another, forgive, and not judge.'

'It's complicated, sir.'

'It is. Because it is a whole lot of books put together and you need to read them a number of times in the context they were written, and understand. I cannot say I understand it all. Not at all. But the real message is simple. To love.'

'Is it that easy?'

'Simple enough, but not that easy. We are told to love God. Love one another. Love our neighbour – a stranger – as ourselves. Even love your enemies.'

'I don't know how to do that, sir.'

'Love must be the answer. It comes in all forms – not just between a man and a woman. But showing kindness in what we do and say, even in our thinking.'

'Sir, it all sounds so hard.'

'Life is hard. Being kind makes it more bearable for us all. Listen, girl, you are doing the right thing by asking these questions. And I hope I am giving you the right answers.'

'I don't like to ask stupid questions.'

'There is no such thing as a stupid question. Although there is such a thing as a stupid answer. I hope I am not confusing you. The Pharisees in the New Testament often followed Jesus and tried to trick him with their questions. You are not doing that.'

'No, sir, I'm not.'

'Once, when he was healing the sick, they asked him this. *Is it lawful to heal on the Sabbath day*? Now they were referring to resting on the Sabbath day in the Law of Moses, given to the Jews directly from God, which is what the Jews followed, even today. Can you guess how Jesus replied?'

'Not really, sir.'

'Jesus answered with a question. A question to make them think! Now in those days, people bought animals with their money. Livestock is valuable. It represents wealth even today. People look after them – feed and water them every day. So, how do you think Jesus replied? He said, *which of you would have a sheep that falls in a pit on the Sabbath day, and not lift it out? How much better is a man than a sheep? Therefore, it is lawful to do good on a Sabbath day*. Jesus continued to heal the man standing in front of him, and the Pharisees got up and left.'

'He was a very wise man.'

'He, Amina, is the Son of God. And the Good Lord wants us to listen to His Son.'

'Is this what I have to learn to get baptised?' Amina asked. 'Because it is a lot. It scares me. But I really want to learn.'

'Nothing good comes easily. *The heights of great men reached and kept were not attained by sudden flight. But they, while their companions slept, were toiling upwards in the night*. That is a quote from the poet Henry Wadsworth Longfellow. Well, getting baptised is not the end of learning. It is but the first day of the rest of your life. Show me a man who has finished learning, and I will show you a fool.'

'Thank you, sir. I will try really hard to put myself in her shoes. It's not easy though.'

'I told you. Nothing worthwhile comes easy! That is why I will tell you this little thing, but I don't want you to repeat it to anyone. I could get into great difficulty if the Catholic Board gets wind of it.'

Amina opened her eyes wide. 'I will not tell anyone, sir. What is it?'

'Look, we will talk later. Let's go and sit down, and get on with the evening class.'

ꝏ

Before she even thought it through, Sumati had already started walking. She had to find out why Rajnath was really seeing so much of Amina, because it was not like her friend to break rules. There had to be some good reason why she was turning into a person Sumati could hardly recognise. So much talk about the Christian God and Jesus, learning Bible quotations and throwing them at her? No one in their right mind would turn from the comfort of Hinduism and all the rituals passed down through the generations. It was like a second skin. You didn't need to think, it was that easy. It was done for you. To turn from that to learn something so foreign was inconceivable.

It was a long walk and Sumati felt heavier every minute. By the time she got to the Singh house, she was breathless and unable to speak. Parbatee was alarmed when she saw the girl struggling into her yard and got her to sit down immediately.

'You live in this village?' Parbatee asked kindly, holding out a cup of water. 'You look familiar.'

Sumati nodded, still trying to catch her breath. 'What are you doing here?' Parbatee asked.

'Rajnath,' she gasped. 'I'm looking for him.'

Parbatee stared, shocked at Sumati's circumference. 'You want *my* son?'

'Yes, your son, if his name is Rajnath Kamalsingh. I am looking for him.'

'He did this to you?' Parbatee's voice dropped through her lungs as she watched Sumati gulp the water.

'Yes. I want to talk to him.'

'But first you will talk to me,' Parbatee insisted, pulling up a *peerha* close and easing herself onto it, unable to keep her eyes off Sumati's belly. 'When did this happen? Your mother died knowing that my son put the child in your belly?'

'No. She didn't know anything about it.'

'My son is sick. This is not a good time. He nearly died. Now he is getting better, but nobody came to see if he was dead or alive. Not one.' Parbatee was in tears. 'If that child in your belly is his,' she went on, 'I will be so happy. And pleased that you at least have come. It will be my only grandchild.'

'Ma!' a voice bellowed from inside.

'That is his brother.' Parbatee pointed in the direction of Annan's voice. Then she shouted, 'Your brother has a child on the way.'

'I will tell him,' Annan called back, sounding surprised. 'That will make him happy.'

'Come.' Parbatee beckoned Sumati. 'Come inside.'

Sumati got up and hobbled into the house.

'This pretty girl has come to see you. You must know her?' Parbatee said. 'What have you done? This is karma. You are getting the punishment.'

Rajnath half-smiled at Sumati. 'She's Amina's friend who got married the other day.'

'She's married?' Parbatee looked very confused. 'Amina's friend? What curse do you bring on us, boy?'

'You went to the wedding, Ma.'

'Me?' Parbatee asked, squinting at Sumati. 'You are not looking the same.'

Rajnath was lying in bed, his face thin and drawn and his cheeks and chin bristled rough. Sumati barely recognised him.

'What happened to you?' she asked.

'Well, I'm getting better now, but I've been here in bed for the last few weeks. You're looking well though. Is your husband treating you good?'

'Better than I expected,' Sumati said.

'I'm pleased about that, and I hope he continues to look after you. I am so sorry about the way you were treated when you were in San Fernando with my uncle and cousin. I never knew they were involved with those things. When I'm strong again, I intend to do something about it.'

'Who told you? And what can you do?'

'Don't worry, I had already started – then this happened.'

'What happened?'

'At first the doctor thought that I had consumption...TB. He was expecting me to be dead by now. But after a few weeks he realised it was pneumonia instead.'

'Well, you could have died with that too.'

Rajnath smiled. 'It's so nice having somebody visit me.'

'Your mother said nobody came.'

'That is because the doctor said I wasn't to have visitors because if it was TB he didn't want the whole of Granville getting it.' He looked at her. 'How is Amina?' he asked.

'We've fallen out. I want to talk to you about her. I know you've been seeing her. Why? Because she is going to get into a lot of trouble if the *panch* hears about that.'

'Why are you talking about that?' Parbatee interjected. 'It's more important to decide what you going to do about the child in this girl's belly. When that man finds out it is *your* child he will kill her and the baby. Talk, boy! Talk to me about that! You have a way about you that makes me sorry I didn't beat you enough when you were small. Did you tell the girl you have bronchopneumonia?' She turned to Sumati. 'He doesn't do things by halves, you see. He has to get two lungs infected, not just one.'

'There was something I had to discuss with you,' Sumati said.

'I can't concentrate anymore,' he whispered. 'I'm really tired.' And he fell asleep before her eyes.

Sumati hobbled down the steps then doubled up in pain.

'Are you all right? I'll get the neighbour to take you home on his donkey cart,' Parbatee offered. 'Wait.'

'No thanks, Tantie,' Sumati replied, wincing. 'I'll be fine. You go and see to Rajnath.'

'It is a long way for you to walk in your condition,' Parbatee fretted, but Sumati paid her no heed. 'Take care,' she called.

The woman rushed back up the steps to her son. 'When that child is born, make her bring it here,' she told him.

'I cannot make her,' he said drowsily. 'You can ask her.'

'I will *tell* her, and she will *have* to do it,' Parbatee insisted.

ɛɔ

After evening class, Amina stayed back to talk to Mr Clifford again.

'The right answers are important to me, sir. What were you going to tell me – about yourself? I promise not to say to anyone.'

'It's getting late, and your parents will worry. But quickly then, I will tell you. To be baptised a Catholic, you have to learn by rote a whole load of Catechism – nothing to do with the Bible itself. Now, I was exposed to the Bible directly in my boyhood, not Catechism. I was not always a Catholic, you see. I'm only telling you because my conscience will not let me continue to allow you to think otherwise. In my heart, I am not really Catholic. There – that's the truth.'

'But I thought . . . '

'I'm Catholic in name only. How else could I get a job in teaching? I had to join in order to work in their schools. Imperative if you want promotion.'

'But that doesn't sound honest.' Amina was appalled.

'Girl, you're like a shower of rain on a hot, dusty day. But how else can I help children? Remember the common sense that Jesus applied?'

'But how did you learn all these things? You talk about the Bible a lot.'

'Not from the priest!' Mr Clifford snorted. 'I'm not even sure he himself understands the Latin he recites. When I was a boy, I spent time at a large house where my mother used to work. There were many books there, including an

English translation of the King James Bible. It fascinated me. Also, I often overheard discussions about the Bible coming from the library after dinner. One day I found the book they were discussing: *Christendom Astray*. Written by a man called Robert Roberts. Anyway, I became interested in this book – and . . . actually I stole it.'

Amina gasped in horror.

He quickly corrected himself, looking ashamed – 'Well, I borrowed it for a while. I read a lot, as you know, girl. Fascinating!' He sighed. 'My mother was a cook in that house. A very good cook too. I might have taken some liberties because of it. The master of the house – he liked her a lot.'

The headmaster sat down wearily and gestured to Amina to sit beside him before he took up his tale again.

'It's interesting, sir – your life.'

'Interesting indeed. There were times they had a lot of people there, eating, drinking and talking. I heard parts of conversations through the door opening and closing. Sometimes people talked very loud. Heated. Not drunk though. But as if. . . deep in conflict about the churches and how they diverted from the Bible itself. And that Jesus who died on the cross could not have been a god, or God Himself in any way. No. It seems that He was entirely separate as the Son who was sent for a special purpose, to save mankind. To die, for the forgiveness of our sins. And God raised Him back to life, because He was too perfect to remain dead. The grave would not hold Him. The Bible says these things, girl. This *God loved the world so much that he gave His only begotten son* as a sacrifice, in order to fulfil His purpose to redeem men from their sins. That made me interested.'

'Men only?'

'No, no! "Men" as in all mankind. All human beings. You and me. Only if we believe in Him and are baptised in the water – thoroughly washed from our sins in the water from head to toe. None of the sprinkling on the forehead. Yes, in the sea or a river.'

Amina stared, bemused.

Mr Clifford gave a long sigh. 'Yes, well you won't tell anybody about what I just told you, will you, girl? Especially no one from school. As for your friend who is lying to her husband, what can I say? Unless you know the circumstances, you cannot give advice. But we shouldn't lie, as a basic principle.' He scratched his head. 'Although a lie here and there does slip out now and again. But we mustn't hurt people with our lies. And we must pray for forgiveness. That is a divine command. *Lies are abhorrent to the Lord.* But how do you know that your friend is not just trying to save her own life? If her lie isn't hurting anyone else, maybe she might be excused. I can't judge unless I know the full background. One thing about you, Amina Banderjee – you surely do test my intellect!'

'So, are you baptised?' the girl asked, slightly confused.

'I said you surely test me! That's an example. Well that is the dilemma, isn't it. I am Catholic, but one day – soon, I hope – something or someone will be sent to me. Maybe a John the Baptist.' He laughed. 'Till then, I try to live the best I can. But be careful how you judge your friend, because *you will be judged with that same yardstick*, by the good Lord Himself when He returns to judge us all. Matthew 7:13. Remember that you might have a plank in your own eye whilst you are trying to remove a speck of dust from your friend's eye. You see? *First take the plank out of your own eye* so you can see the exact nature of the speck in your friend's eye.'

'I think I understand what you mean, sir.'

ꟸ

Amina left Mr Clifford with a lot to think about. Once again, she felt as if she had eaten a very large meal. She passed Sumati's father's house, but could see no one from the road. When she got home she offered to help with the evening meal, but was too late.

'I feel useless,' she said to her mother. 'I have to do things too – not just learn things and talk about them. It's better to do than to talk. I want to feel worthwhile.'

Devinia looked at her and smiled. 'My mother and me, we used to *do* things,' she reminisced, 'but we read the *Ramayana* and the *Bhagavad Gita* too. And talked – a lot. You see, the more you read – and listen too, the more you have in your head to talk about, so the more good things you can say. And the more you *do*, the more useful you can be. So, do all – read, listen, talk, and do things. Then you have a better understanding for yourself, and so you are better off to help others.'

'Ma, you're more clever than you think!'

'That so?' Devinia said. A tear built up in her eye. 'I'm proud of you.'

FORTY-TWO

Sumati began walking, but before long a sharp pain stabbed the side of her belly, forcing her to stop and sit down on a fallen tree. She wished she had said yes to the offer of a ride on the cart. She realised she had to get home fast, so she got up and continued doggedly.

At the house, she was greeted by her father shouting angrily. 'Look at the state of you!' he bellowed from the kitchen. 'When you going to stop making me worry about you? Where have you been?'

A cold wind blew right through the yard and the house.

'It's Ma,' Sumati said, sounding relieved. 'That cold wind – it's Ma.'

'You walked all the way to the cemetery in your condition?' Roopchand yelled, even more agitated. 'Are you out of your mind? You never had any sense!'

'It's time,' Sumati whispered. 'My time is come, Pa.'

Roopchand sprang into action. His anger forgotten, he moved fast, hurrying her to the bedroom. 'Lie down and stay there,' he said. 'Kesh is not home, so I will have to go and fetch Elsie myself. If I find your brother, I'll send him straight home.'

'Stay,' Sumati pleaded. Then: 'No, go! Get somebody!'

After he left, she hobbled down to the kitchen to get a bucket of water, but dropped the full enamel bucket against the tin barrel. Ramona came running from next door.

'What's happened?' the girl asked.

'Nothing, nothing,' Sumati said, almost in a whisper.

Ramona stood looking at Sumati, now bent double in pain, water dripping down her legs.

'You'd better go inside,' her friend said. 'I'll go and find Ma.'

'No, just help me, will you? Please, Ramona.'

Worriedly, Ramona held Sumati's hand, led her into the house and helped her onto the bed. A cold wind blew straight into the bedroom. The cupboard door flew open and the towels dropped out.

'What's happening?' Ramona asked, alarmed. She picked up the towels and shoved them back in the cupboard, but they fell out again and landed on the bed.

'Ramona, you are going to have to help me, or get somebody,' Sumati groaned through waves of pain. 'My baby is coming. Hand me a towel and go and fetch some water from outside.'

Sumati grabbed the towel and bit down on it hard between her teeth. Ramona, meanwhile, hurried out. 'I'm going to get someone,' the girl said.

Sumati's room grew colder, but her face poured perspiration. She lay on the bed, waiting, writhing as each contraction gripped her and twisted from the inside. Sumati called out but no one came. Then she heard something.

'Ma, is that you?' she implored. 'I'm in trouble, Ma. I miss you. Take me with you, please. I'm begging you.'

The wind died down but the air in the room grew cool. Sumati stopped overheating, and her heart rate slowed down. Her breathing became shallower and shallower until it could no longer be heard. Her eyes closed, and Sumati went silent.

ꕤ

That evening, Amina was in turmoil, unable to get her mind to rest. The disagreement with Sumati was upsetting. Sumati didn't seem to realise that her don't-care ways hurt others. Without her mother, Amina knew she herself would struggle, but Sumati always pretended to shrug off her pain and appear jolly. People reacted to her negatively, as if to bring her down to earth. Amina loved Sumati, and realised they needed each other. Besides, this was not time to abandon her best friend – her blood-bond sister.

She desperately wanted to share her discovery with Sumati: a discovery that was helping her to see life more clearly. It was wonderful to feel free of reincarnation and the burden of misspent past lives that were destined to punish her in the future, forever, over and over again. Never knowing whose wrongdoings she was paying for – because she could never remember who she had been in a past life. Sadly, her arranged marriage came from this place of unknown traditions. There was no shortage of stories of girls who had reacted by committing suicide. Sumati had run away before she got to that state, which had kept her alive.

Amina admired Mr Clifford because he knew how to explain these things; he was free to think and believe what made most sense to him. She respected him for always answering her with chapter and verse from the Bible, and wanted to share that with Sumati.

She snuggled in bed with *Wuthering Heights*, but was unable to concentrate on the long sentences. Besides, Heathcliff was becoming annoying. Suddenly a cold wind blew through the cracks in her window, just like it had the night of Sumati's mother's wake, and Amina sat bolt upright when she heard the flapping of wings. Bats? She leapt out of bed and was heading down the stairs when Etwar came running in.

'Something's going on at Sumati's house,' he gasped. 'I'm sure I heard somebody screaming. And Ramona is running up and down the road, panicking because she can't find her mother. Have you seen Meena?'

'Sumati?' Amina rushed past him. 'Tell Ma where I've gone!'

Amina pelted down the road, barefoot, as fast as she could, and raced into Sumati's yard. Her heart was thumping hard and she began to panic, and started to pray to the God she had never really prayed to before. '*The God of Abraham, Isaac and Jacob, and Mr Clifford. Father of Jesus, Mary and the Jewish people, please hear me! I will do anything – anything. I'll give up everything I want and follow You. Just don't take her. I can feel that she's going . . .*'

Amina got into the house and pushed through the bedroom door. She couldn't believe her eyes. Sumati lay on the bed, sweating, but over her hung a frosty haze. The dying girl's eyes were rolling around and her face was red and dripping.

'Tell me what to do!' Amina pleaded.

'Help.'

'I don't know how.' Amina was panicking.

But Sumati wasn't replying. Her eyes had closed, and her cries of agony ceased.

ഇ

The news spread and people had gathered in the yard, unable to get into the house since the door seemed to be locked from the inside. Some left when it got dark and the screaming from inside had stopped. The air around the house seemed Arctic. They talked about breaking down the door, but Meena said that somebody had gone inside. They heard Roopchand had left to fetch Elsie, the midwife. But it was a good two hours before he returned with her.

'I tried to get in,' Meena told them. 'But the door was jammed.'

'It's all right,' Roopchand said. 'Elsie is here now.'

'You could make yuhself useful,' Elsie said in her high-pitched childlike voice. 'Boil some water. Plenty hot water. And make sure de bucket clean, eh? Wash it out first.'

Elsie was the descendant of African slaves. She had learnt her trade from her mother and grandmother, who told her that she would always be in work and never starve if she delivered babies for a living. They were right. Elsie was the only midwife in the village.

Strangely, Roopchand was able to push open the door easily enough. Elsie followed him into the bedroom but neither of them had anticipated the shock awaiting them.

'Oh God!' Elsie cried. 'I think we too late.'

Roopchand collapsed and fell to the floor just where he stood.

Sumati was lying on the bed. Her eyes were closed and her lips pale. She was covered from neck to toe with a pink blanket, and her thick hair was spread around her head like rays of sun. Next to Sumati, on either side, lay two small babies. Amina was in there, with glistening cheeks, and bloodstained up her arms and over her clothes. Her eyes were red and watery. She stood over Sumati, wiping her face with a cloth, but the girl wasn't responding.

'I did everything I could,' Amina said, looking at Elsie. 'I managed to get the babies alive. The afterbirths are in the bucket. I didn't know what else to do.'

'Sometimes there's nothing else you can do,' Elsie said, matter-of-factly. 'I seen this happen before, when the mother very young and not able to push out two of them. It hard on the body. She must be given up.'

This startled Amina, while Roopchand began howling.

'No, Sumati!' Amina shouted. 'Come back! You cannot go, not now, not after all you've been through. And what about me? I need you to wake up!'

Something began moving. It was the babies, kicking the blanket. One began to whimper, and the other began to bawl. Then they were both bawling. Then something strange happened. Sumati's hand moved towards one, from under the blanket, then the other hand reached the head of the second baby. Amina gasped.

'Come, Roopchand,' she said. 'Look it's your daughter and your grandchildren.'

Roopchand rose from his slump and stood over the bed.

'I did think she was just sleeping,' Elsie said, stepping forward. 'I seen dis before, where de modder jest stop like if she dead. Is tiredness in the body.' The midwife beamed a huge smile, her crowded teeth sparkling white.

She felt Sumati's forehead. 'But she body's cold,' she said. 'Somebody bring a cup a water. Milk if you have it.'

ꟸ

Elsie held Sumati up in bed while Roopchand fed her the warm milk. Amina fussed around, clearing up the mess of bloody towels and sheets she'd used while helping Sumati during her ordeal of giving birth. Sumati squinted, staring at Amina, half-smiling. Amina thought of the story she had read in Mr Clifford's Christian Bible, of a young girl who had just risen from the dead. She smiled at Sumati. 'Jairus's daughter,' she said. 'I will tell you that story later.'

Sumati opened her mouth to speak, but did not have the strength. With her eyes, she beckoned Amina. 'You saved my life,' she whispered. 'I can never pay you back.'

'There are important things I want to share with you,' Amina said. 'Pay me back by listening to them when we have time together. But more than anything else, you've already given me what I wanted. I wanted you to live. I prayed to Mr Clifford's God. Really hard. I promised my life for yours. You won't understand.' Amina's tears flowed down her red cheeks. 'Look at these beautiful little babies.' Amina collapsed helplessly into a blubbering mess. 'I've been so selfish,' she wept. 'I've been a stupid child. I could never do what you just did.'

Sumati took Amina's hand. 'And do you think I could do what *you* just did? Could a "stupid child" save me and my babies? I owe you my life, girl. Look what you gave me. Now you have three of us to cope with. Double trouble. One for me, and one for you.'

'For me?' Amina breathed.

Elsie picked up the smaller baby, wrapped it in a pillowcase and placed it in the crook of Amina's arm. 'You feed this one.' The midwife then picked up the bigger child, wrapped it in another pillowcase and handed it to Sumati. 'Take this one,' she commanded. 'The boy. He will suck hard and pull down the milk.'

When Elsie turned around, Amina was still only cradling the baby. 'Start,' Elsie urged. 'She small but she will suck.' Amina wasn't sure she had heard right the first time. She stared, shocked. People were still in the room, chattering, but no one noticed. 'It will take longer,' Elsie continued, 'but your milk will come down in the end. And if it don't, de mother will feed she in any case.'

'I can't do that,' Amina protested. 'Sumati can do both together.'

'She giving one of them to you,' Elsie said, patiently. 'Don't think you can't do it. How you think I have milk myself and I never make a baby? Give me, I'll show you.' The midwife was already unbuttoning her bodice front.

Amina's eyes opened wide. 'I never knew that could happen. But both babies need her. She is their mother. She didn't mean for me to really take one home. They're her children, not puppies.' She stood up, walked over to Sumati, and handed her the tiny baby girl.

'She needs feeding after,' Amina said. 'She's sucking her fist already.'

Elsie tutted and busied herself with the cleaning and wiping down of the bed frame and the floor while Sumati fed both babies, lying one side, then the next. 'You girls nowadays,' she muttered, 'you don't know nothing.'

'I can't believe you came,' Sumati was telling Amina.

'I don't know what made me come. I felt like something

was pulling me. At first I felt like it was your mother's spirit. But then I prayed hard to the Christian God to save you. And how did I know to pull the cords that were attached to the babies? It's a miracle.'

'Nothing will separate us – I know that now,' Sumati said tenderly. 'We are like the two sides of the same coin. Same, but different.'

'Yes, the same coin. I realised that some time ago, but I'm stubborn, while you're not. You follow your heart and your soul. And I follow my head and those who advise me.'

'I'll just go out and cook something for Sumati,' Roopchand intervened. 'You girls need to talk.'

'Nah! Nah!' The women around began to argue with him about who was going to cook, and who was going to fetch what food from their own homes.

'Listen,' one of them whispered. 'Is she the Banderjee girl, the jeweller's daughter who brought those babies in the world? With the house locked from the inside?'

'There's a jewel inside the girl,' another nodded.

'It's looking so,' Roopchand said proudly. 'She saved my daughter *and* my grandchildren,' he said as he gazed, beaming at the group on the bed.

'But how old is she?'

'She is the one who caught typhoid and was the only child in the village to get better from it. And did you know she died and came back on the same day she turned twelve? The jeweller's daughter. Her mother is Devinia. That child is Amina Banderjee.'

'Like Lakshmi Mata herself. A goddess. Bless you, child. This house is blessed.' They looked at the girl in awe, almost afraid to speak to her directly.

Within half an hour, Roopchand's household had gone from being *cujart*, an outcast, to becoming the favourite

Granville family, all because of Amina's good deed that day. The place was no longer under a curse. The village women began kneading flour, cutting up vegetables and grinding masala. Within an hour, they had made roti and vegetable talkarie for at least twenty people, to be washed down by a large pot of cocoa tea. They presented a plate to Amina first, to honour her like the goddess they now believed she was. Or at least sent by one.

ഀ

That night, Amina remained in the room for a long time, keeping watch over Sumati as she slept, admiring the babies, and picking them up when they cried. Elsie, too, had remained: she was snoring, wrapped up in a blanket on the floor. Outside the open window, the sky was black and lit up with diamond pinpricks glinting down over the village. It occurred to Amina that someone should send a message to Baljit, Sumati's husband. She wondered what the arrangement was between Sumati and him about her return home, and whether he would be frantic with worry.

There was a call outside, and Amina went to the window. It was her mother. 'I hear she had the child, and you helped. Why didn't you call me?'

'Twins, Ma,' Amina whispered.

'And Sumati . . . is she all right?'

'It's a miracle. All of it. The babies are so perfect.'

'She is lucky,' Devinia said. 'Lucky you were there. Are you coming home now? Because it's dark. And late.'

'I'm staying. I can't leave them. Sumati's so tired. She's fast asleep. Elsie too.'

'Well, you take care. You want me to bring anything?'

'No, Ma. I'm fine. I'm so pleased she's come through this safely.'

'Maybe teaching is not the thing for you. Maybe it's something else,' her mother said. 'I can't believe what you did today. People are talking. I don't know what to say, I'm so proud of you. You wanted to be the first Indian woman in Granville to be a teacher – to teach Indian women to read English, and change their thousand-year-old traditions. But look what you've done instead. And still only twelve years old. But remember, you don't know enough about babies. Wake up Elsie if anything looks wrong. You hear me?'

Devinia left, and Amina remained alert for most of the night. When Elsie didn't wake, Amina put the crying child on one of Sumati's breasts to suck. Both babies sucked frantically, even though Elsie had said they weren't really getting any milk. But it looked to Amina like they were getting something.

When the moon crossed the window, it was partly overshadowed by a cloud, and the wind rose, only just, but fell again as quickly. Amina eventually lay down at the foot of the bed, listening to Sumati's breathing, and must have fallen asleep. When she woke, it was around six o'clock. The cock next door crowed loudly as it walked below the open window, making her jerk awake to see the orangey-pink sky behind the coconut trees. The girl rubbed her eyes, forgetting where she was for that split second.

ꕥ

Elsie remained to care for Sumati and the babies, but neighbours brought in cooked food, cleaned the house, swept the yard, even fetched water from the standpipe. The house rang with voices chirping and singing, nattering and gossiping, and cooing at the babies. Roopchand took on extra work as a water carrier on the road to pay for the clothes and blankets for the babies, and for Elsie. He began to feel lighter in spirit, even though his heart weighed heavy at times for the loss of Daya, and he regretted treating her how he did. She would have enjoyed seeing her grandchildren, despite the shame and guilt.

It was strange to think how different it was now, as if the black cloud had been eclipsed by the gift of babies, bringing hope. In her heart, Sumati knew that the reckoning would come, but she was not going to think about it.

FORTY-THREE

When Amina returned home, Sankar looked at her admiringly.

'You are worth a thousand jewels,' he said.

'What do you mean, Pa?' Amina asked, bemused.

'I have heard all about it! You – delivering babies – at twelve years old? Mr Clifford was right. I have to admit I am a very stupid man for not believing him and not seeing the priceless jewel that you are. My own daughter.'

'Pa?' Etwar said. 'Are you feeling well?'

'If I am not well, your sister will see to it that I am cured. Many months ago, Mr Clifford came here and said Amina could be a doctor. And I was too selfish to even think about it. What a fool I was. Well, no more.'

The family stood staring at Sankar.

'How did you do it?' her father continued. 'Delivering not just one baby but two? I am the proudest father that took breath on this earth. How did you know what to do?'

'Pa,' Amina said, 'I really don't know. I didn't. It was as if something or someone was there with me. I did not do it on my own.'

'Are you saying it was this God you have been talking about to your mother? That Christian God? I have never heard of such a thing before.'

'It was something, Pa . . . but I don't really know.'

'Give yourself some credit, child,' Devinia said briskly. 'You did well.'

'She will have the best,' Sankar said. 'You are not going to be the wife of any San Fernando businessman if you can perform such miracles at your age. You will have your wish and remain at school and I will put aside money for your doctor training. If it means sending you to England, that is what I will do.'

Amina, Devinia and Etwar stood like statues, staring at him.

'Don't look at me like that. I am not too proud to admit when I am wrong,' he said. 'I am a selfish man. And I do not care if I come back as a dog or cat. Or not go to heaven. For me, this is the right thing to do. My daughter does not deserve to wash pots all her life, even in the home of a rich man.'

'So what are you saying?' Devinia said. 'You are going to cancel the wedding? But you promised them . . .'

'And a bad promise can be broken,' her husband replied. 'I have come to realise that her future is not mine to promise to someone else. She has earned the right to choose her life. At least I have learnt that lesson. I am proud of you, my daughter, and I want you to make me even prouder. We don't want to have to rely on the white-man doctors all our lives. We stand in their shadow and we treat our own children like fools when all the time they are shining like stars under our noses. I can make many jewels for you, but you can only wear them on the outside. I want to put the money to that jewel that is inside of you.' He turned to his wife. 'So, yes! I will go up to San Fernando and cancel the wedding. I am sorry, my sweet flower, if that upsets you, but the girl has more in her than we can see. I thought you would be pleased.'

'But *they* will not be pleased,' Devinia said apprehensively.

'Do I care about what they say? What is better – to do what is best for them, or for our daughter? I am not doing anything else except the right thing to do. We have changed our mind. That is all.'

'I can't believe it, Pa,' Amina cried. 'I can't believe you are actually going to cancel the wedding, and everything else. You have just changed everything you believed in yesterday, in one day.'

'Maybe Rome *can* be built in one day,' he joked, and chuckled. But Amina cried most of the evening, unable in her joy and relief to say anything coherent.

ꕥ

On Saturday morning, Sankar took a trip to San Fernando to do what he had promised, and returned home pleased that he had succeeded.

'Well,' he told his family, 'the father understood in the end, but the boy . . . he was very disappointed. In fact, I saw a different side to him. He wasn't the same as when he came here, meek as a lamb. Put it this way, I wouldn't want him for a son-in-law anyhow.'

Devinia looked worried.

'The father will talk him round,' Sankar reassured her. 'He'll get over it. But I will tell you this – it may not be that easy. The boy seems to think he is more important than even the father. And the mother was no better. She didn't even try to tell her son to show respect.' Sankar sat down and took a sip of cocoa tea. 'All I can say, is that fate is working. That boy was never meant to be part of our family.'

FORTY-FOUR

The same evening that Sumati went into labour on her way home from talking to Parbatee Singh, Kamal Singh returned home from work bringing a letter addressed to Rajnath Kamalsingh.

'You opened my letter?' his son asked, annoyed.

'You will need me to more than open your letter by the looks of it,' Kamal said. 'I knew something like this would happen.' He stamped his foot hard on the wooden floor, shaking the whole house.

'I have lost my job at Galapados,' Rajnath said, his hand trembling as he read the letter.

'I didn't think they would lay you off because you were ill,' Parbatee said. 'I thought your father went and explained to the overseer at Galapados. Didn't you take the certificate Doctor wrote out?'

'I did,' Kamal said grimly. 'But you know what they're like. They would do anything to get back at me.'

'Creole nor white man like coolie when coolie is equal,'

Parbatee said. 'It's because you are an overseer just like them, but you don't do the crookedness they have learned from the white man since they were slaves. But even so, they should know what it feels like, and not do it to my son.'

'They did it because he is *my* son, not yours,' Kamal said.

'Pa? Ma?' Rajnath said, in a quiet, tearful voice. 'There's more.'

'What, son?' Parbatee asked fearfully.

'They filed a case in court saying that he was malingering,' Kamal said. 'That's what. They don't believe him even with the doctor's sick certificate. Expect the worse, boy. You will get a summons to go to court.'

'No,' Parbatee said. 'The doctor will tell the truth. Most definitely he will tell them what is what.'

'Don't be so sure,' her husband warned her. 'The doctors are the ones that send people back to work, still sick, too soon. They just do what the planters say. If you had gone into the Plantation Hospital you would have probably died or run away. It's so bad there. And that is the truth. But I think if the nicer one, Dr Crow, had visited earlier, this might not have happened.'

'Pa, there was no way I could have stood up, let alone be forced back to work.'

'But none of them saw you,' Kamal explained. 'See, son, they have no proof from their own eyes. Dr Boyle never offered for you to go to the Plantation Hospital – maybe because he knows what it's like there. I will see what I can do, but don't hold out hope.'

ꙮ

A few days later, Parbatee went up the village to see someone about buying a goat. She went past the post office, when she heard someone calling her name.

'Hello! Rajnath-mother! Hello!' Parbatee looked up to see Miss Lottie, the post-mistress, waving frantically and running down the post office steps towards her. She was carrying something in her hand. When she got close, Parbatee saw it was a brown envelope.

'Here,' Miss Lottie said, puffing out of breath and stretching out her hand. 'It looks like it is important. But I didn't open it.'

Parbatee snatched the envelope from Miss Lottie's hand, annoyed that the woman had admitted to even having thought about opening the letter.

'In whose name is it?' Parbatee asked, annoyed even more that she had no idea what it said. And triply annoyed that Miss Lottie knew how to read, and would be the person she would have to ask to read it if she wanted to know immediately.

'It is addressed to Mr Rajnath Kamalsingh,' Miss Lottie informed her.

Parbatee took the letter and left Miss Lottie looking frustrated, her curiosity unsatisfied.

ꟷ

Rajnath was recovering. He woke early, on a bright yellow morning, feeling refreshed and stronger. He got out of bed and walked onto the veranda, stretching and yawning, amused at two kiskadees fighting over a piece of stale roti in the yard. Neither would give in and fly off. It was the spot where he remembered dropping the bike that night when he had returned from the ordeal of a journey from San Fernando: he had then struggled towards the steps before blacking out completely. Now he remembered a bad feeling about Dillip, a lot of money and a fight. Then he remembered, and went frantic. He scrambled around the yard looking for the bike, but couldn't find it, so he went and shook Annan till he woke up.

'You don't have a bike,' his brother replied, without opening his eyes. 'Go away.'

'Wake up! Where's the bag from the bike?'

Annan sat up reluctantly. 'As I said, you don't have a bike. Now why you don't go and brew me a nice strong coffee.'

'You know something!' Rajnath narrowed his eyes. 'You and Dillip! Uncle too. I don't trust any of you. When was the last time you saw Dillip?'

Annan yawned, pushing his fingers through his hair. 'I don't know what you're talking about. I hardly know them. You're the one that goes up there – too often, if you ask me.'

'Who told you that?' Rajnath asked suspiciously.

'You need to be careful. The police are sniffing around that place.'

'Police?' Rajnath began to think. 'The bike,' he repeated. 'Tell me where it is?'

Just then Parbatee came in, breathless from her brisk walk home in the hot sun.

'I have a letter here for you,' she puffed, wiping the back of her neck.

Rajnath took the letter and went outside to read it.

'What is it saying?' Parbatee enquired. 'Who is it from? Miss Lottie said it looked important.'

'Miss Lottie should mind her own business,' Rajnath grumped, throwing the letter on the table outside under the canopy.

Annan picked up the letter. 'Ma, it's a summons. They say Rajnath Kamalsingh is required in court on charges of desertion from the Galapados Plantation.'

'That is a lot of nonsense,' Rajnath said impatiently. 'I was dangerously ill. Everybody knows that. Didn't the doctor write a sick letter? And Pa took it in for me?'

'Yes,' Parbatee said, 'but you know what these people are like when they have it in for you. They will get you somehow.'

'Look, I don't care about that right now,' her son said urgently. 'I am looking for that bike that I left right here that night I came back from San Fernando.'

'That bike you borrowed?' Parbatee asked. 'The boy came and took his bike back a few days after you fell ill. He was annoyed that you left it in that condition.'

'There was a bag hooked up on the tray in front,' Rajnath said.

'There was no bag.'

'Yes!' he said. 'There was a bag. Who took it?'

'You are going out of your mind with worry,' Parbatee said soothingly. 'I can see that.'

Rajnath went in search of the bag all over the house. Then he checked the sheds outside, where he knew he would never put it, but it was worth looking. There he found the striped cloth bag in which his uncle had put the money. But it was empty, and lying on the floor of the shed half buried in the dust and dirt. Devastated, he dropped to the ground with his head in his hands.

As he crouched there, in utter despair, he saw a tobacco tin shining between two pieces of wood. He reached out, and his heart skipped several beats as he stared at the familiar gleam of the pattern on the tin. He opened it to find the wad of money Amrit had given him before he had put it in the stripy bag. Getting up, he pulled the door shut, and sat inside, counting out the banknotes in the dim light. How the tin had got there, he still couldn't fathom. But then a sliver of memory returned – of him opening the shed door before a feeling of being drowned in the darkness that overcame him. The money was all there, and he felt relieved. Nothing mattered now. He didn't care about the court summons or what it could mean. When Annan looked outside and saw Rajnath emerge from the shed looking oddly pleased, he put two and two together and realised why the police were sniffing around Amrit's place.

ஐ

Parbatee talked to her husband that night. 'I'm worried about the boy,' she said. 'It's like he's going mad.'

'I've seen it before,' Kamal said. 'You know how many men I know that happened to? And not their fault either. I tell you, Parbatee, this place is no good for us. We should have gone back to India; taken our chance on those ships like others did. At least we wouldn't be treated like slaves.' Kamal's eyes watered. 'It's out of my hands.'

'Is there nothing you can do? I don't want my son to go to jail. It will finish him.'

Kamal looked at his wife's anxious face. 'Make some cocoa tea for him. Put plenty of sugar and condensed milk in it to build him up. I'll have a cup too. I need it. And put some rum in it too. It will help him sleep.'

ꢡ

Parbatee begged Rajnath to look for a job elsewhere, but her son was adamant. He returned to work after his illness, clocked in and did a normal day's work. Everyone seemed pleased to see him. On the second day, the driver came up on a donkey cart.

'So you came back?' he said.

'Yes,' Rajnath replied.

'Brave man!' the driver said, spitting on the ground.

Rajnath worked as normal that morning, stopping once or twice to catch his breath. By eleven, the driver returned.

'The overseer wants to see you down in the next field after work,' he told him.

The day was hot, and Rajnath worked well apart from twice when he paused for a few minutes to gather his strength. At the end of the day he went along to the next field to see the overseer after work at four o'clock, feeling pleased with himself and ready to face whatever awaited him.

FORTY-FIVE

Evening class. Mr Clifford perched on the edge of the front desk, unrolled his sleeves from his elbows and buttoned up the cuffs.

'Right,' he said. 'English literature. *Wuthering Heights*. Characters: Catherine. What do you think of her? She seems so polarised in her behaviour towards Heathcliff.'

'This bit,' Amina said. '*Grinning and spitting at the stupid little thing*. It bothered me why someone who was so much more fortunate than the others in the village, would be so cruel to someone else who was clearly less fortunate. And to a stranger in the household too. Catherine is unkind and impolite. Definitely.'

'Maybe something to do with him not being white?' someone suggested.

'Well, it's a likely reason,' Mr Clifford said thoughtfully. 'Non-whites will always be seen as a slave in the white man's household. And Emily Brontë knew it, eh. She wrote him in deliberately.'

'Do you think that might change some day?' Amina asked.

'Good question,' Mr Clifford said. 'But hundreds of years have compounded that attitude. It will take a lot more than time to change it, if it is ever possible. The best way is to rise above it in a different way. Which is why I am an advocate of education – as you might have noticed.' There were a few grunts and giggles. 'I see you know why you're all here. Laugh if you must, but it's a legitimate means of getting ahead of that kind of prejudice. Heathcliff did not have that opportunity. So what did he use his God-given brains to do? He became a manipulative man, driven by hatred to get revenge. But he went beyond those who had actually wronged him, to take revenge on their whole families. That hate took hold of him and drove him into *self*-hatred, to the point where he couldn't even love his own son. His own offspring.'

'But he couldn't help himself, sir.'

'All he was left with was his wealth,' Mr Clifford said. 'Property had value.'

'It's still like that now, sir.'

'Very much so,' the headmaster agreed. 'Most things that divide our society have some kind of value that people aspire to. The poor want riches. Black people would want to be white, if they could. If a slave had been asked if he wanted to swap places with the white man, you'd learn the truth if you could see right inside his heart. But that wouldn't be about colour. It would be about opportunity and position.'

'But that is not good, sir,' Amina objected. 'We shouldn't hate how we were made.'

'Try telling that to a deformed child left to die with no food.' The headmaster cleared his throat. 'So, what other factors might divide people?'

'Education, sir!' Amina shouted. 'Although it is free, it is rare. And it divides people into literate and illiterate. Education does that amongst Indians, sir. Right here in Granville.'

'Agreed,' Mr Clifford said. 'But when they finally see the value and I think they will, in time – they'll come to appreciate it, and will do anything for it. Look at you few here. You're a start. And what you told me this morning about your father, girl, I myself can hardly believe it. He has changed his mind completely? I must come and speak with him. If you can study medicine you will add such value to the world. What else divides people?'

'Language, sir!'

'Yes,' the headmaster nodded. 'That is a part of education too.'

'Lady teachers,' Amina said eagerly. 'Women *will* add value to teaching!'

When they broke off from evening class, Amina's brain was buzzing, engrossed in Emily Brontë's world of fiction and her own. Her mind was spinning with similarities, yet *Wuthering Heights* was so far from her reality. To bring herself back down to earth, she called in to see Sumati and the babies as she did most afternoons.

ꕤ

Elsie's two weeks had come to an end, and Roopchand paid her generously with a hundredweight flour-bag full of ground provisions – cassava, yams, dasheen. And another with breadfruit, mangoes, avocados, two large mammy apples, some star apples, and a few eggs each wrapped in small squares of newspaper and placed carefully on the top. And a third bag with a live chicken sent by Devinia, with its feet tied and wings folded to keep it from flying out. Roopchand gave them to the midwife before pressing some cash into her palm.

Neighbours were still coming and going. Devinia brought a full rum bottle of fresh milk from their cow each day, and always had Sumati's best interests at heart. But she was concerned.

'Has Baljit come to see you yet?' Devinia asked Sumati one day.

'He sent a message to say he will come later,' the girl lied.

'How much later?' Devinia asked. 'When they turn into man and woman?' She threw a glance at the babies at Sumati's breasts. They had visibly grown since the birth. 'He married you with two children of his own. Now you have two. You're in the same boat.'

'That will be up to him to decide, Tantie.'

'You want me to talk to him?' Devinia offered. 'Just because you don't have a mother, doesn't mean he should take advantage.'

Sumati didn't reply.

'The children are very pretty,' Devinia continued. 'Fair-skinned too. He'll like them.'

Sumati glanced up at Amina who had just arrived.

'I'm not stupid,' Devinia said quietly. 'People make mistakes. Imagine if nobody ever made any mistakes.'

When Devinia left, Amina remained for a while to chat alone with her friend.

'Your mother is almost right,' Sumati said to Amina, 'but there are things I haven't told anybody.'

Roopchand returned home and started making a fuss over the babies, Amina looked anxiously at Sumati. But the new mother's eyes were fixed on her babies, who seemed to be staring up at the face their grandfather was pulling, so she left.

ꝏ

One afternoon Amina visited and was shocked to find Sumati already surrounded by school-friends cooing and passing the sleeping babies around, kissing them and giggling.

'You're going to make them ill!' Amina shrieked. 'Why are you letting them throw the babies around like that? They'll hurt them.'

'They're enjoying it,' Sumati told her. 'Don't fuss so. My father does worse. He holds them upside down by their ankles, and they are still living. They're strong.'

'Well, that one's vomiting,' Amina pointed out crossly.

'I thought you had an evening class,' Sumati said.

'It's over.'

'Amina, why are you bothering to go to them? It didn't work for me. It's not normal. It separates you from everybody else.'

'Oh. I see what you are saying,' Amina said tartly. 'You're saying that staying on at school and attending evening classes to get a better education is the same as running away with a boy?'

'No! But changing your religion . . . Do your parents know about you turning Catholic?'

'No! And don't you even think of telling them.'

'I'm wasn't thinking of telling them,' Sumati said. 'I was only thinking about your soul, while you're lying to them. Like me lying to my husband, who by the way, beat me up and threw me out.'

'Baljit beat you up? I didn't know. You didn't tell me.' Both girls were silent for a while. 'Etwar said he saw Rajnath coming down here yesterday.'

Sumati looked up knowingly. 'That's true. He's not happy about something. He has been really ill.'

'So, you and he are still good friends now?'

'You are jealous!' Sumati giggled. 'We're just friends. But he's the best-looking boy in the whole of Granville and San Fernando. I should know!'

'What will Baljit say?'

'Baljit can say what he likes. I am not going back there.'

Amina picked up one of the babies from Sumati's lap.

'But what will happen to you now?' Amina asked.

'He will not be able to beat me up again, that's what!'

'I'm worried for you,' Amina said. 'Then, have you named the twins yet?'

'Saraswatti and Patrick.'

'Patrick?' Amina asked. 'How come?'

'I heard it somewhere, and I like it.'

'Sounds English,' Amina said. 'Or Negro. Or mixed.'

'Rajnath liked it. He's good with the babies too – picking them up and winding them across his knee. I wonder how he knows how to do that. Anyway, I told him what I just told you about what happened with me and Baljit.'

'What did he say?'

'Not much. I don't know why he came, really.'

'Probably guilt,' Amina sniffed. 'Don't worry. Men don't take the blame for anything. But after what happened to you, I've decided I'm not ever going to get married. I might become a nun.'

'You? Mr Clifford said so? Your parents will have a heart attack if they hear that.'

'You'll never guess. My father has changed his mind completely. He's cancelled the wedding and I'm free to do what I want.'

'What do you mean?'

'He says I can go to England to study to be a doctor.'

Sumati's eyes were popping out of her head. 'But what will happen to me if you go?'

'You have the children – and you have your looks. Could be that you might have the most good-looking boy in the village after you. But I'm not leaving yet.'

Sumati's eyes lit up. 'You're right. I have everything I want right here. Why would I want to go to England? I don't even know the place.'

As Amina voiced out loud the possibilities of her future, and the fact that she seemed to have dismissed the chance of becoming a teacher, she realised that it was her father once again who was dictating her path to her. But it wasn't a bad idea. It was helping people, which was all she wanted to do. But she felt confused by Sumati's attitude; her friend seemed to be living with no regrets, no concern about her future or her children. And that was what she envied about Sumati – her carefree attitude. It was also, however, the one thing she despised about her.

ꝏ

One night, Sankar did not return home. Devinia was up at dawn, not having slept a wink. It was not like him to stay out. She wondered if her husband had worked late on jewellery that someone needed urgently, possibly a big job for a wedding. She cooked breakfast early, covered it over, and swept the yard clean of all the fallen leaves. The children hadn't even got up yet when two men called at the house.

FORTY-SIX

Early one morning, they heard voices calling from the front of the house and Fluffy was barking madly. Devinia hurried out to see their dog tearing into the sock of one of the men.

'Is this where the jeweller from Point Fortin lives?' the other policeman asked.

'Yes,' Devinia replied, surprised.

'Hold your dog, madam. Is anybody at home with you?'

'The children are home. My husband's at work.'

'We are from the Point Fortin police station, madam, and we are here to talk to you.'

It was with some trepidation that Devinia invited the men to sit under her house to talk. They questioned her about Sankar; who they knew in Point Fortin, how much money Sankar made in a week, where they had family and friends, if they had had any disagreements with anyone of late, did she know where Sankar was last night? For most of the questions, Devinia, wracked with worry, felt unable to give a substantial answer.

'He didn't come home last night. That is all I know. I don't know why or where he was. I expect he had a lot of work. You see, he was . . .'

'I have some bad news, Mrs Banderjee,' the older policeman interrupted. 'We're looking for the owner of the jewellers in Point Fortin. A man was found with his throat slit, and the whole shop was ransacked. We think it might be him.'

Amina got up immediately, ran out into the yard, and began to throw up.

'There's not much left there now, apart from shelves lying around everywhere, and the counter upside down and a few small bits of gold jewellery scattered. We want a family member to come and identify the dead man's body. It was taken to the mortuary in San Fernando Colonial Hospital.'

Etwar's face was swimming in tears. Devinia just stared, stunned, as if she had been hit on the head with a boulder from a height. Her face began to twitch. 'But . . .' she said. 'I don't understand. What are you saying? Who are you talking about?' Etwar shifted closer to his mother, almost sitting on her lap. Then he broke down crying loudly.

'What are we going to do now?' Devinia said to the policeman. Her whole body began to shake.

'Have you got any family?'

'No. Everybody has died, or was left in India.'

'Good neighbours? Get someone to come over. We will need you to accompany us to identify the body.'

ഌ

The next few days were the worst the family had ever experienced, apart from Amina's typhoid. Without Sankar to support them as husband, father, and breadwinner, they had lost everything. All the jewellery from the shop had been stolen, meaning that they had nothing of monetary value apart from their home. Devinia sold milk from the cow and had to use the little savings she had in the house for essentials. One day, Amina returned home with a handful of money.

'I sold my rose earrings, a necklace and a pair of bracelets to a friend from school,' she said, handing her mother the money. 'She is getting married.'

'Your father made those.'

'My father isn't here, and we need the money, Ma.'

'You shouldn't do that. We will find it somehow. I will have to get a job on the road carrying water. Or something.'

'I can't bear to think of you doing that. Pa would be very upset if he's watching,' Etwar said.

'Well, he's not here,' Amina said, 'and we have to do something. I'm going to talk to Mr Clifford, see what he says.'

'You think Mr Clifford and his God can help us now?' Etwar said in a sarcastic tone.

'Not if Pa has already come back as a cow or goat,' Amina said, equally sarcastically. 'When you go to bring the goats home, look them in the eyes and ask the question. "Which one of you is Pa?" Better still, count them to see if there's an extra one.'

'What is wrong with you, girl? Why are you being like this?' her brother asked.

'We have to find a way to survive,' she said. 'Pa should have taught you his trade.'

'What about the houses we rent to people?' Etwar said. 'We will get money from them.'

'Yes, Ma, the houses.'

'Your father sold them,' Devinia said, flatly. 'To buy gold.'

Their luck had finally run out, with their father dead and nothing to fall back on. Etwar couldn't believe why his father, an astute businessman, would have sold the houses to buy gold. But Devinia assured them that it was what the lawyer told her. She hadn't realised that business was so poor, but even so, she was shocked that Sankar would do such a thing without her knowledge.

FORTY-SEVEN

Rajnath had been back to work for two weeks. It was mid-morning when he heard shouting. It wasn't that unusual, so he kept his head down and continued weeding. But the shouting got closer, and soon he heard the neigh of a horse.

'You!' It was the driver. 'The coolie wearing de white-man hat!'

A few looked around. The driver fired a gunshot, and everyone jumped up. The driver started to howl with laughter. Then the laughing stopped. Everyone stood straight as scarecrows with fear in their eyes. Anything could happen now. Anyone could be plucked out and whipped right there. Then the driver pointed his gun at Rajnath.

'You – yes, you! Overseer want to see you in de next field.'

'When I have finished this piece,' Rajnath said.

'What piece?' The man trotted up on his horse and poked Rajnath hard in the shoulder with his shotgun barrel. 'I don't see you doing anything here today.'

That was a lie. He'd worked hard since seven that morning. Rajnath dropped his tools and got up.

'Aye!' the driver shouted. 'Bring you tools wit yuh.'

Rajnath grabbed his hoe and cutlass and strode over to the next field. The overseer was sitting in the shed, and Rajnath was relieved to get into the shade. He dropped his tools, took off his hat and wiped his face with the back of his hand.

'You is *that* Kamalsingh?' the overseer asked.

'Yes, sir.'

'You have good manners, eh,' the overseer said. 'That nice. You fadda teach you that?'

Rajnath half-nodded, looking slightly concerned.

'I have orders to send you home.' The overseer's voice was calm. 'The planter says you should never have come back to work so quick. The doctor said you was too sick.'

'But I'm better. And I've been back a fortnight now,' Rajnath insisted.

'No, no! Sick is sick. We don't want no sick man in the field. That not right. Maybe we will send you to the hospital right here. See what they say.'

'No, no, it's all right,' Rajnath said hurriedly. 'I don't need a hospital.'

'I told them you wouldn't go in the hospital here,' the overseer said. 'And I was right.'

'You want me to go home till when?'

'Till we let you know.'

Rajnath left and gathered up his things, bemused at their decision to send him home after two weeks of returning.

He didn't look forward to the long walk home in the heat either.

He reached home hot and still confused about the day, and decided to head to the beach. He sat under a coconut tree for a while, looking at the surf breaking gently on the sand. No one was around, so he stripped off and ran straight through the tepid shallow water before plunging his overheated body into the cold sea. He swam a few long, strong strokes into the deep water, before surfacing, swimming hard, floating on his back and staring at puffy clouds changing shape. He drifted and rocked on the waves, still wondering why they had waited so long to send him home. Usually they kept very sick men working until they collapsed.

Thoughts of Sumati and her babies drifted through his mind as he floated. There was something about her. Sumati's twins were both so very different, but he had never heard anyone mention it.

ஐ

On his return home, Rajnath decided to consult with his mother.

'Ma,' he said, when he returned home. 'Aren't twins supposed to look the same?'

'Why do you ask?' Parbatee said.

'Sumati's babies.'

'Somebody said one is a boy, one is a girl,' Parbatee told him. 'You think they're yours?'

'No! Of course not. They don't look the same though.'

'If they are not yours, why are you so interested?'

'She is a friend. Her mother died.'

'I wouldn't mind, you know,' his mother said gently. 'If they're yours, they're mine too.'

'I said *no*. They are *not* mine. But they're so different.'

'But how could they look the same?' Parbatee said. 'One is a boy, one is a girl! Of course they are different.'

'But . . . Nobody said anything about them?'

'You mean foolish people thinking that a boy and a girl is the same?'

'No, but nothing else?' Rajnath persisted.

'I don't know what you mean,' she said, frowning. 'Is there something wrong with them? Do they have two heads each? Like a god and goddess?'

'Nothing like that.'

'I hear she named the boy a white-man name,' Parbatee said. 'Or Creole. Some white-man names don't make sense. Something like Phut-ha-rik. I never heard it before.'

'Now I understand,' Rajnath said, looking relieved.

'You understand? In that case you are doing better than me, son. I don't understand any of this. But what are you doing home so soon?'

'The overseer sent me home because I shouldn't be in work yet so soon after the TB. I said I didn't have the consumption in the end, but they still said to go home. He said nothing about the letter I got. I'm just going to change my clothes and go down the village. I think I might go to Granville beach and catch some fish.'

'That will be good,' Parbatee said, relieved. 'And we will cook it this evening.'

When Rajnath went to wash the salt off his skin, Parbatee called him from outside the bathroom. 'If you going to catch fish by the sea, you don't need to change your clothes,' she said. 'Wear the same thing, rather than make more washing for me.'

'My clothes are dirty, Ma,' he said, having been caught in a lie. 'I'm changing them because I have to go and see somebody first.'

ജ

Rajnath came out of the house clean and neat, smelling of Wrights Coal Tar soap. His hair was wet and combed straight back, completely off his forehead, a few stray clumps falling to the side in a half-moon curl. His white shirt was tucked into his newly pressed khaki trousers, and his brown leather shoes had been cleaned and polished by Parbatee herself, and left outside his bedroom door.

'You going by the sea?' Parbatee teased. 'You don't fool me. What kind of fish you going to catch? The kind that wears a sari?'

He smiled and went past her and out to the shed to get the bag of money and the fishing rod. He then left the house, whistling loudly and calling good evening to everyone he passed.

'Good to see you too, Mrs Banderjee. And I'm sorry for your loss.' Devinia turned around and looked again, almost not recognising him.

Before he got to the shop at the T-junction, Rajnath turned swiftly right into Sumati's yard, slowing down at first. Sumati was walking from the kitchen across the yard to the door of the house, clutching both babies to her chest. Rajnath's feet suddenly became leaden.

'Who is that?' Sumati called out, pulling the babies closer to her.

'It's only me. Rajnath,' he called as he walked slowly down the side.

'What are you doing here?' she shouted. 'It's only me at home.'

'Oh,' he gasped, as she stood there, one shoulder bare, pushing the babies together in front of her. She smiled, half-surprised, half-pleased.

'I wasn't expecting anyone,' she explained. 'I'm here alone, funnily enough. People have been coming and going as if it's San Fernando wharf, normally. But nobody has come today.'

'Well, I'm not staying long,' he said. 'Don't worry.'

'It's you who should be worried.'

Rajnath laughed. 'I'm not bothered who's gossiping about me either. But I would worry if it gets worse for you because of me.'

'You see these two?' She looked down her breast at her children. 'These are all I'm worried about. Were you looking for Amina?'

'No, I wasn't. Strange question. I just saw her mother.'

'You know, there's something I really like about you,' Sumati said. 'You talk a lot of sense.'

'Really?' His face flushed as he smiled.

'But you could get some things very wrong,' she continued.

'What do you mean?' he said, frowning.

'Well, tell me this,' she said. 'What reason would a young Hindu girl have for suddenly wanting to become a Roman Catholic nun?'

'I don't know. Sounds like a riddle.'

'See? You don't know. And she's too proud to tell you.'

Rajnath looked confused. 'You? You want to turn into a nun?'

'No! I am talking about Amina. I know the two of you have been meeting in secret by the spring.'

'She told you?'

'Tongues talk. Trees whisper. School's boring, but I'm not stupid.'

'I don't think you're stupid. I really don't. I think you're one brave woman. But you have got it all wrong. We talk about you and Farouk. And where he's disappeared to.' Rajnath smiled, his eyes fixed on the babies.

'Hold him,' she said, pushing the boy baby towards Rajnath.

He held the child close, as if afraid he would slip out of his arms. Sumati disappeared inside the house with the other child, while Rajnath sat on the bench holding the baby. It was ten minutes before she reappeared, patting the girl baby's back.

'Look at his face,' Rajnath marvelled. 'And these hands.'

'Say it!' Sumati said, suddenly aggressive. 'Say what everybody's thinking.'

'Have I done something wrong?' Rajnath was alarmed at her sudden anger.

'The colour of their skin,' she blurted out. 'I saw how you were looking at him.'

It had just dawned on Rajnath why the children looked different from other local babies.

'You see his eyes? They're blue.'

Rajnath stared closely at the little boy. 'Oh yes – they're really blue. Is that normal? His skin's more transparent too, and he's so small. These babies need to be protected, and I am worried that you don't have anybody to help you.'

'So have you come to help? Are you saying I'm not managing?'

'I didn't come here to accuse you. I came to give you . . .'

'Give me advice? To see if the gossip is true?' Her voice was raised and fierce.

'No! Just the opposite,' he pleaded.

'Well let me tell you – I really don't care who thinks what about me. My mother's dead so everybody comes here to watch me. They come and sit down, gossiping and spying on me, talking about me as if I'm deaf.'

'I'm sure they come to help,' he said.

'So why don't they? Instead they come and sit together, gossiping *hush-hush*, their eyes following me. I'm not stupid.'

'These children are so pretty,' he said. 'What could they be saying?'

'I just told you! It's their colour – their white skin. The yellow in Patrick's hair.'

Rajnath stared at the babies. She was right. He hadn't noticed the detail, and now felt stupid.

'Well, let me tell you, Rajnath Kamalsingh, it wasn't my fault that I ended up like this. Yes, I did go with Farouk. That was my fault. But not this.' Sumati suddenly stood up and said, 'I'm tired of everybody. Just go! Leave me alone.'

'I didn't come here to upset you. I came to help – but you don't want it.'

'Help how? Look, you've said your piece so just leave me now. Go and find your nun!'

Rajnath got up and left, feeling wronged and misunderstood. He had never meant to cause her any upset. He had come to make amends, distressed that the pain in her life was caused by him. Something he could never reverse. But he was trying. He hung his head and walked out of her yard, wondering what she had meant about a nun.

The day wasn't turning out too well. Rajnath headed down to the beach, hoping to calm himself. Fishing boats lay on their sides beneath coconut tree trunks under the magical spell of clusters of green, yard-long fingers, waiting for the tide to float them again. Rajnath got up, his feet sinking into the dry sand. A hermit crab hovered at the mouth of a shell, then disappeared into the blackness inside, escaping to safety. Everyone seemed to be looking to hide. It was time to return home in case a message had arrived from work.

A sudden uneasiness crept over him and made him panic. He stripped off to his shorts and ran into the cool waves, diving head first and scraping his belly muscles on the seabed, swimming like a flounder out to sea for as long as he could hold his breath. When he surfaced, the wildness and solitude of the sea brought peace to his mind.

FORTY-EIGHT

Amina went to see Sumati. She needed a friend, but when she got there she couldn't speak. Instead, she burst into tears and wept for a good ten minutes.

'Do you think it's karma?' Sumati asked. 'I know that's what Pundit Lall would say. Especially if he knew about you wanting to turn Catholic as well as not get married.'

'Somebody murdered my father,' Amina sobbed. 'How could it be about me? It doesn't make sense.'

'I know. It's hard to make sense of something like that. What can I say?'

'Nothing you can say will make him come back.'

'Rajnath came to see me yesterday and I told him to leave. I didn't want to talk. He left that bag here.' Sumati picked up her friend's hand. 'Amina, I'm ready to tell you . . . what happened to me in San Fernando. It was all my fault.' Sumati's face had turned to stone.

'What is it?'

'When we stayed there – I was never given any food or drink all day. By evening I was so hungry and thirsty, I used to drink whatever they gave me. It was bitter, but I got used to it. Rajnath's cousin, Dillip, used to send women to dress me up. It was strange, but it made me feel happy – like they cared. I used to smell the food and wait for him to shout for me to come down from the room, and drink with them after they had eaten their dinner.'

'They used to starve you?' Amina asked, shocked. 'I thought they were rich.'

'Yes, they starved me so I would get drunk fast. I got breakfast, but that was all. They made me smoke a pipe as well. They used to say – pull harder – and I used to laugh and laugh. It was ganja. Made me dizzy.'

'Some people smoke it – like on a Friday night.'

'The whisky and rum went straight to my head. They mixed it with red sorrel drink, or orange juice or water. I drank it fast to finish it, but then they just gave me more. By then I was laughing and drinking it all down. Two of the women would take me across to the new side of the house, upstairs, where people were staying. Men. By the time I hit the bed . . . they were taking my clothes off. It was as if I was dreaming.' Sumati's eyes were sad and glistening.

'*They*?'

'Yes, the women helped. It was my fault. I think I must have wanted it.'

'Don't say that!' Amina exclaimed. 'How could it be your fault? I'm so angry. I wish my father was here.'

'I didn't fight hard enough. I let them. Then I wanted it . . . because they wanted me. Those men treated me well. Farouk had gone.' She grit her teeth. 'I hated him for that.'

Amina wrapped her arms round Sumati and the babies and squeezed them, tears streaming down her face. 'Why didn't you run away?'

'I was ashamed the next day. Every time. When I woke up I would find myself lying half-dressed in my bed and feel worse than the day before. Where could I go? I couldn't come back home in disgrace. My parents wouldn't want me. The women said I was always too drunk to undress myself before going to bed. They said that I liked the drink.'

'What kind of people are these?' Amina was furious. 'Rajnath's uncle?'

'I don't know how much Amrit knew, but Dillip is not a good person. He and his father quarrelled a lot.'

'What about?'

'Money mainly. And business. And about the men who stayed there. And Tonia – they quarrelled a lot about her. She was a servant, but I think she was Amrit's mistress too.'

'And this Tonia woman knew what was going on and didn't put a stop to it?'

'Worse. She was one of those who used to carry me up to the rooms and put me on the bed for those men. Sometimes there was more than one man. She would take off my clothes, and she helped to hold my legs open when I tried to fight.'

'Really?' Amina shook with rage. 'You can't trust anybody! Rajnath needs to know this. I'm not sure how to tell him this, but he needs to know the truth. What happened to Farouk?'

'He left almost as soon as we got there.'

'Sumati, something has to be done about this. It can't be allowed to continue. I will have to talk to somebody. Oh God, I want my father back!' Amina began to howl. 'I miss him so much. I wish I hadn't thought bad things about him sometimes. He was in the shop late, making jewellery for me – and I was too much of a fool to appreciate him. Did I tell you he changed his mind about the wedding? He cancelled it. He wanted me to be a doctor. How can I do that now? Everything is ruined. And now this! Men are not worth it! I wish he was here. I want to tell him I'm sorry for being a bad daughter. I want to die. Why wasn't it me? I nearly died, and instead I got selfish.'

'No, Amina. No! You mustn't say these things. He was wrong and he changed his mind because he realised that. Some contemptable criminal murdered him. Have they found who did it?'

'I don't think so,' Amina said dully. They sat in silence for a while. 'What about the other girls, Sumati? You actually got away somehow, but the others?'

'They are still there, I suppose.' She brightened up. 'There was one man who was nice. A white man. He wanted to take me back to Ireland. His name was Patrick Cassidy.'

'Where is this Irishman now?'

'He went somewhere on business but said he would come back. I waited two weeks and then I left. I tried to find him, but I couldn't. I don't know what happened. Somehow I managed to get on a sloop, but that's all I remember.' Sumati looked down at her babies, tears streaming and falling on their soft hair. 'I can't help thinking that if it wasn't for all that happened to me, my babies wouldn't be here, so I'm happy about that.'

'I know, but that doesn't make it right either.'

'I can't be sure, but I think their father was Patrick Cassidy. This one looks like him.'

'So, you called him Patrick.'

'Patrick and Saraswatti. I want to think he was a nice enough man, and would have come back for me.'

'I don't know. But Patrick and Sara are both nice names,' Amina half-smiled. 'Sara is a good Christian name. She was Abraham's wife.'

'So long as Abraham was a good husband,' Sumati joked, relieved.

'Abraham? He was a *friend of God*. So yeah.'

'That's good enough for me. It gives me hope for them. Thank you, Amina.'

ꕤ

Amina was more disturbed when she left Sumati's house than she had been when she got there. Horrible images went through her head. Her father, with a slit throat lying bleeding to death, Daya dangling from the tree with her tongue blue and protruding, and now Sumati's ordeal of being raped and abused naked every day. She shuddered. She was desperate to talk to someone who would know what to do, and take some kind of action. So she headed up the road to Rajnath's house.

ꕤ

After Amina left Rajnath's house, the young man sat and wept for a long time. After he had dried his eyes and recovered from the details of Sumati's experiences at his uncle's house, at the hand of his cousin, he disappeared into the bedroom and began writing a letter to the police in San Fernando, regarding Amrit and Dillip's illegal business practices. He folded it and put it safely under a clean shirt till he managed to get an envelope to post it. When he returned outside, his mother gave him a different letter, one she had received from the post office that same day.

'Miss Lottie told me that is your name on the envelope,' she said.

ഊ

That evening, the Singhs were all outside sitting under the bamboo canopy before dinner. The mosquitoes had started buzzing around their earlobes, piercing skin and drawing blood. Rajnath slapped one and splattered blood across his bare arm.

'Annan,' Parbatee said. 'Go and get the Cockset and light it.'

Annan left, returning with the Cockset mosquito coil, and lit the end. Rajnath's face was wretched, and his brother noticed.

'What did the letter say?' Annan asked.

Rajnath didn't reply. He just threw the piece of paper down on the table in front of him. Annan picked it up and read it.

'Oh boy!' Annan said. 'You are in the proverbial shit.'

'Annan!' Parbatee chided him. 'Who taught you to talk like that?'

'You mean *proverbial*?' Annan asked cheekily. 'Oh, I learnt that in school. And *shit?* I learned that from Pa.'

Kamal Singh was bathed and dressed for a relaxing evening at home, when he overheard his younger son back-chatting his mother. 'You are not too big for me to scrub your mouth with carbolic soap, you know,' he shouted. But then he too spotted Rajnath's face. 'What's wrong, son? Something in the letter?' He hadn't heard anything at work even though there was always gossip travelling from one cane estate to the next.

'Read it for yourself,' Rajnath shrugged. 'I don't understand it.'

Kamal picked up the letter and read it. 'What!' he exclaimed.

'What is it?' Parbatee asked.

'The court case is on Friday in Port of Spain,' Kamal said.

'And that is not all,' Annan added.

'The summons says that the offence is *refusal to work, desertion, and insubordination to the management.*'

'That is not true!' Rajnath said hotly. 'The doctor's certificate! We sent it, didn't we, Ma?'

'Your father took it in,' Parbatee said.

'But who is going to believe you?' Annan said, looking at Rajnath. 'That is why I wouldn't work for those lying dogs.'

'But they never said yesterday. The overseer told me to go home and rest. I don't understand.'

'They're a load of cheating bully-liars managing the cane fields,' Annan spat.

Rajnath felt overwhelmed. His bad day had just got worse. The world was conspiring against him, but it brought the family closer that night.

'Don't worry,' Annan counselled him when they were alone. 'They can break your back, but they can't break your spirit. You are strong, you are able, and you are brainy, my brother. Besides, you don't have to go back to that donkey-head cane estate no more.'

'What do you mean by that?' Rajnath asked.

Annan winked one eye. 'Dillip told me what Uncle gave you.'

'Oh, he did, did he?' Rajnath said. 'And did he tell you why?'

'I see you haven't told Ma.' Annan winked again.

'And I am not going to, because it's not for me.'

'I know you must be feeling like shit today. It's written all over your ugly face. But stay calm. Here's an idea for you. You could get a job in oil. They're setting up oil-drilling in a few places. When you go on the boat, you can see the oil rigs inland.'

Parbatee brought the dinner, but Rajnath had no appetite.

'Just eat a small piece of the roti with the pumpkin talkarie,' she begged. 'You must keep up your strength. I don't want you to get ill again.' She pleaded with her husband: 'Can you see what you could do about this court case?'

'There is nothing I can do,' Kamal said, heavily. 'Once they get this far, it is up to the judge. And they've not given us any time to get advice. Two days. Just two days!'

ꟾ

That night, Rajnath left the house and went down the road to Sumati's house to collect the bag of money he had left behind.

'I know you are angry with me,' he said to her, 'but you couldn't make me feel worse than I already do. I didn't come for a fight, but you must understand that I can't change what happened. I will regret sending you there for the rest of my life. Please help me and try hard to forget it. Just be yourself. Your children deserve that.'

'At least I have them. Maybe it's more than I deserve. You left your bag here.' She pointed to it, untouched, in the corner.

'Don't take any notice of what other people say,' Rajnath continued. 'Everyone has faults. Yours are no bigger than anybody's. Work out who you are, and what you want. One day it will happen. But you have to think about how to get there.'

'Dreaming didn't help me,' she disagreed. 'It only brought me trouble. Being myself didn't work out either. I'm an Indian girl. I'm not supposed to fall in love. I'm supposed to be given away. Taken and owned by someone else for them to do with as they please. I'm supposed to do as I am told. You tell me to think. Why? Where will that get me?'

'You must never stop thinking. You have a brain like any boy or man. One day it will show you a way. Think smart. And take all the opportunities you can get. I have something for you.' He opened the bag and pulled out some cash and handed it to her. 'Take this – for food and clothes. And don't ask where it came from.'

She looked shocked. 'How much food and clothes do you expect me to buy?'

'Buy some land and build a house,' he said, turning to go. 'You deserve it. And one day you will fall in love again, but make sure it is with somebody who deserves you and will look after you.' He took one last look at her and the tiny twins then said, 'I have to go.'

FORTY-NINE

It was the day of the court hearing, and Kamal Singh and Annan were accompanying Rajnath to Port of Spain. Parbatee had invited a gathering of friends and neighbours to help pass the time. She would have to cook and feed them, so she prepared paratha roti with a vegetable curry, *biagan chokha* with garlic and hot pepper, and fried bitter *caraili,* which was a favourite. She was up at three that morning, cooking by lamplight, for her husband and boys to have breakfast, and food to take with them for the day. It was bound to be a long and harrowing day. She boiled some rice, cooked thick dhal seasoned with salt and roasted garlic. She roasted the aubergines over the open fire till soft, peeled and mashed them, added a few crushed hot bird peppers, salt and coconut oil for the *biagan chokha.* Then she portioned the meals and placed them in a triple-stacked, enamel food carrier.

She looked at her boys and picked up a hand from each of them, clasping their palms together. 'Talk nice to them,' she said, looking at Rajnath. 'If the judge sees you are a respectable boy, he will have mercy.'

Rajnath grunted. 'If I murdered somebody I'd most likely get away with it. All I did was fall ill. This world has no justice.'

'I've been talking to people,' Kamal said. 'And everybody is saying that the planters don't fool the judges with their tricks these days. The ordinances the workers have to obey are too harsh, and bad enough without these prosecutions and punishments for no good reason.'

'What are these ordinances?' Parbatee asked her husband.

'Ma, we don't have time for this,' Rajnath said, impatiently.

Seeing that Parbatee was pale with worry, her husband answered her. 'They are the plantation rules for the workers,' he said. 'You know some of them already. No one is allowed to drink liquor in the estate housing – that is, if they live in the barracks, nor allowed to use disrespectful language to anybody in authority. That includes the overseer, like me. It's illegal to congregate outside the plantation, to discuss grievances. You remember when some of them tried to gather outside, protesting for more pay? They're not allowed to do that. So that caused them to lose more pay instead. Nobody is allowed to disobey what is called *reasonable* orders. And that could be anything, to tell you the truth. If the owner isn't satisfied with the work a labourer has done, he can make him do it again in the labourer's own time, and again, till he's satisfied with the work. And of course, an indentured labourer is not allowed to leave the estate without a written pass from the owner or the overseer. So the upshot is that breaking any of these ordinances will lead to a fine, or a fine *and* a jail sentence.'

Parbatee was crying. 'My son, I don't want my son to have these troubles.'

'But we all know how dangerously ill he was,' Kamal said. 'The judge will see this. The boy nearly died and the doctor said that right here. In fact, he himself didn't want to give you a medical certificate. You remember?'

'Oh yes,' Parbatee recalled. 'I had to insist that he wrote one out. Then he did. So they can't hold that against my Raj.'

'That's because the doctor thought he would die of TB,' Annan said. 'So that's why he wouldn't take the trouble to write out a sick certificate when he didn't expect my brother to return to work.'

'And what if they put me in jail anyway?' Rajnath said. He was shaking. 'Like they do to so many people. I know somebody who got jail for calling the overseer a modder-arse because the driver said he would have to do the whole weeding job again, without pay. But he was giving him a whole *new* piece of weeding to do, in a different place!'

'I know it is unfair,' Kamal said. 'That kind of thing happens every day. But it's one of the ordinances. *No disrespectful language must be used to the planter, nor the overseers.* No matter what unfair things they do to you.'

'None of you seem to realise that it is the blasted British Governor-General who is perpetuating this unfair justice system,' Annan growled. 'But I heard recently that some judges are trying to make it fairer on the labourers.'

'And how do you know that?' Rajnath snapped. 'You don't even work.'

'My eyes and my ears work,' Annan said coolly. 'And they are pretty reliable too.'

'He's right,' Kamal said. 'It's about which judge or magistrate you get. That is what I hear too. Let us hope you're lucky. We might see a lawyer before the case gets called.'

'Let's go,' Annan prompted them. 'We don't want to miss the bus.'

'Oh yes. There's a bus now,' Rajnath said.

'Yes, there is a new Mail bus coming from Cedros, but we have to go quickly.'

'Now, son,' Parbatee said to Rajnath, 'don't lose your temper with people, no matter how much they provoke you. Even if you're in the right.'

The three men walked out before dawn with a torchlight. An owl hooted, and flew low across the sky in front of them, and Rajnath took it for a good sign. They reached the junction five minutes before double lights shone at them from a distance. Kamal Singh waved at it, and the Mail bus screeched to a halt.

ജ

As they sat down, the smell of leather filled the air. The novelty of riding high off the ground and on the Mail bus reminded Rajnath of the letter he wrote to the San Fernando police – still hidden and unposted. He promised himself that he'd rewrite and post it as soon as he returned home.

The view from the bus was very different to the one from the sloop. They whipped through sleepy villages, almost brushing past people walking to work, fetching water, or taking animals to be tied out to graze. As they drove on, he noticed the villages closer to San Fernando were more populated and with more shops dotting the roadside –

Ramnarine's Stores, Boodoo's Rum Shop, and Patsy's Parlour – a shack shop, all in one village.

San Fernando itself was a stark contrast to rural life, with its majestic charm. The bus stopped on a smooth asphalt road in front of a white stone building. Annan was asleep bolt upright and Kamal was wide awake staring through the window, feeling lost. An hour later, the Mail bus was bowling along through miles of sugarcane plantation in the county of Caroni.

Rajnath dozed off, only to be woken by a sharp turn in the road. Port of Spain greeted them with its sea of impressive buildings, painted different colours. The buildings dominated the streets, many fronted with wide, curved steps and with pillars framing the entrances. Rajnath had never seen anything quite like it even in San Fernando. The bus jerked to a stop inside the bus station. It took them by surprise when the driver shouted, *'Larse stop. Everbody off de bus.'* They unstuck themselves from the leather seats, stood up and stretched, before dragging themselves down the steps and onto the pavement. After three hours on the bus, Rajnath felt stiff and nauseous. He called up to the driver and asked how long it took for a letter to get up here from Granville.

'In all?' the driver replied. 'A few days.'

The three men stood at the side of the road and looked at each other with the same idea of where to go. In the end, they paced the streets until they finally spotted their destination.

'See that huge red building there? That must be the Red House,' Kamal said. 'The Court House will be there.'

To get inside was a relief. The air was cool and the floors were tiled. The desk clerk asked the name of the lawyer representing them, but they didn't know. At 10am, a white-reddish-skinned man in a grey pinstripe suit and bowler hat approached them. He pulled a watch from his pocket, and asked their names. They all replied together, 'Kamalsingh.'

'My name is Richard Guppy,' the man said. 'And I am a representative of His Majesty's Court,' he said. 'Now, which one of you is Rajnath? I will be representing you today. Follow me.'

They walked off towards one of the side rooms that lay behind big wooden doors.

ങ

'There's nothing to it,' Mr Guppy said. 'You will just answer truthfully when I ask you any questions. But that might not even happen.'

'What about when the other lawyer asks him questions?' Kamal enquired.

'I see you know something about proceedings,' Guppy replied, half-smiling.

'A little. I'm a plantation overseer, myself,' Kamal Singh explained.

'Really? An overseer?'

Kamal nodded, and Mr Guppy looked surprised.

'Unusual! At least you will understand. I will do the talking for your son. He doesn't have to say a word. In fact, it will be better if I did all the talking.'

'Good,' Kamal said. 'Because this is all a shock for him. He has recently been very ill. The doctor said he could have died of TB – the consumption, you know.'

'But it wasn't tuberculosis, was it?' Guppy asked, thumbing through his papers.

'Well, the doc made a mistake, and it turned out to be real bad double pneumonia,' Kamal said.

'I was very ill,' Rajnath added. 'To be honest, I don't remember much at all. I was barely conscious.'

'Good,' Guppy said, looking at Rajnath. 'And I will cross-examine you and ask you that same question. The lawyer for the prosecution will more than likely want to know that too. Right now, I will go through some of the questions they might ask. The judge may well want you to speak. But we will see how it goes. At this point, I will tell you that the judge is Judge Samuel. He's new, does not stand for this type of exploitation of plantation labourers. Changes are happening. There has to be an end to it. Last week, Judge Samuel made that quite clear at another hearing.' He replaced the papers in his briefcase and closed it. 'There is also a good chance the plantation will withdraw the case because of this. They must know they have very little chance of winning. However, you could end up with costs if they request that of the judge. It's a bit much if you ask me, because it was they who brought the case to court. But at least you will get off. Jail is no place for a nice-looking young man like yourself at the start of your life.'

'What is the chance of them withdrawing the case, Mr Guppy?' Kamal asked.

'I would say a very good chance. There is a letter from a doctor here – Dr Boyle. But I can't seem to find any medical certificate. I took the liberty of getting hold of the doctor to ask about your situation. So it was a foolish thing for the plantation manager, Mr MacDonald, to even think of bringing this case to court.'

'Why would he do that?' Kamal asked.

'Your guess is as good as mine, Mr Singh,' Guppy replied.

'Why indeed? Does he have some longstanding grudge against you? Mind you, it doesn't necessarily follow. Men like him do it out of spite. But you must know the real answer to that.'

'I do,' Kamal Singh replied. 'I am an overseer, and that would cause Rajnath's overseer a problem. It is a racial thing. My plantation manager is fine about it, or he wouldn't have given me the job. Sometimes the driver and the overseer are the ones causing the problems!'

'I realise that,' Mr Guppy tutted. 'It's the world we live in. The races will never be equal in everyone's eyes, and it isn't just white and black. It is any race and any other race. And it's worse in England. My mother is Irish. But I normally keep that to myself in England.'

'I didn't know that about white people,' Kamal said.

'There's a lot you probably don't know about England, Mr Singh.'

They were all silent for a while, looking at the floor and the walls; pondering about race, black, brown, white, position and power, riches, poverty, education, overseers, drivers, rivals, newcomers in a country, foreigners, judges and lawyers, Trinidad, England, and each other.

'Well, it might never happen,' Guppy said. 'They will have to withdraw. I really cannot see Judge Samuel upholding this case because it would be a clear miscarriage of justice. And not what anyone in England wants to hear right now. Indentureship ended this year. Officially anyhow. This would cause the plantations labour shortage. These cases came to court and men and women were prosecuted for being unfit for work because of illness, and no one lost a single grey hair in the process. But things are changing. So, I suggest you relax. You have an hour before the cases are heard.'

Rajnath and Kamal felt relieved. When Mr Guppy left, they ate some of their food and got a drink from the water fountain, which was a novelty.

'Well you could be lucky,' Annan said. 'Or then again, you might just go to jail. But that white man is saying that he's going to get you off.'

Rajnath looked hard at Annan. 'This is not the time or the place for your damn jokes. I thought for once in your life you might be some help, even if you just could keep your mouth shut.'

'Stop it!' Kamal said crossly. 'The two of you could put your differences aside just for one day. Shame on you, Annan. Family must stick together. Who else will help us if we don't help each other? In the end, blood is thicker than water – just remember that. And stop doing your best to water down the blood that's running through your veins. It's all we have.'

ꟹ

Parbatee returned to bed after Kamal and the boys had left. She wanted just to lie down and think, instead of busying herself as usual with chores. She'd hardly slept since the letter, fretting constantly. She fell asleep until the village dogs began barking, calling and answering each other. Birds were chirping, doves cooing, squirrels skittering and scraping over the galvanized roof. She woke abruptly, realising she had overslept. Later, as she returned from the bathroom to the house, she heard someone call.

All morning, neighbours came and went. They came to help, to cook and to eat, to serve others, sixty in all that day. By the time it was dusk, Parbatee was exhausted, but the women were still passing the time singing *Bhajans,* and banging on makeshift drums. At nightfall, she lit a Cockset to keep the mosquitoes away, and sitting in the hammock, surrounded by a few friends, at long last must have fallen asleep.

FIFTY

Devinia was surprised to have a visit from Amrit Dass from San Fernando, although with every visit she had from anyone, she hoped that someone would help her make sense of her husband's pointless death. She immediately began to apologise to Mr Dass about her husband's decision to cancel the wedding, expressing her regret, and saying that they were now suffering for their selfish decision. Karma was paying them back, she said. Her tone was apologetic and friendly.

The man listened to her pour out her heart before politely offering his condolences.

'I don't know how you are managing,' he said. 'It must be most difficult, with your husband *and* his business gone. He will have been making a good living, with all the jewellery there. I was quite shocked to hear it.'

Devinia looked at him surprised. How did he know about Sankar's death?

'News travels,' he said gently.

'My husband was very well known.' Her voice sounded relieved and unsuspicious.

'Let's say I took an interest,' Mr Dass said smoothly. 'I am in business myself, and you were soon to become family.' He cleared his throat. 'Let me come straight to the point about why I am here, Mrs Banderjee. As I said, your daughter would have been my daughter until your husband changed his mind. My son, poor boy, cried for days.'

Devinia began to tense up, dreading what he was going to say next. How could she persuade Amina to reverse her father's decision and accept the offer of marriage once again?

'But there's no point me holding a grudge.'

This concession made Devinia feel doubly guilty. 'My daughter is still at school. We haven't decided what to do yet.'

'My son and I run a very good business. We employ many people, and pay them fairly. As I said, the girl feels like the daughter I never had. And I wouldn't want to see you suffer financial hardship. We are like family.'

Devinia broke down in tears. 'What can I do? She has her mind set on education. Her father wanted her to go to England to study to be a doctor. Now, I don't know what will happen.'

'That is just it,' the man said. 'I am offering her work in our business. She will send you the money, or I will save it for her. When she has enough, I will add more and buy her a ticket to England myself.'

Devinia stared at him, not knowing what to say. She searched his face, looking for clues, and found his eyes, staring at hers with shimmering kindness. 'She will have to find a place to live in San Fernando,' she said.

'She will have a place to stay with us. Free. We have plenty of space in the house. The girls working there are from far away. They all live with us. She can join them.'

'You have a big business?'

'Very big. You must come up and see it.'

Devinia felt overwhelmed. 'Why would you do that? You owe us nothing.'

'Do I have to owe you something to offer your daughter work? Who knows when I might need *your* help? Besides, I don't like to see a poor woman in such a situation. I help many in need. A few of them are fatherless girls, looking for work.'

'But why did you travel all the way down here to me?' Devinia wanted to know.

'Didn't I just say I consider you as family? Besides, it was my son who suggested it.'

'Thank your son. A generous boy like his father. I am sorry for the distress we put you through, cancelling the wedding so suddenly. My husband thought he was doing the right thing for our daughter.'

'Bring Amina up to San Fernando this Saturday,' Mr Dass said, standing up to leave. 'If I don't see you, I will know you don't need our help, and we'll help someone else instead who needs it more than you.'

ஐ

The barrister, Mr Guppy, was pacing the corridors of the Red House in Port of Spain. Rajnath's case had been delayed. The judge was late, and the prosecution lawyer seemed to be dilly-dallying. Mr Guppy was waiting for the other lawyer to inform them that Galapados Plantation had withdrawn the charges against Rajnath Kamalsingh. They were leaving it dangerously late, which would cost them the vexation of the judge and a fine for sure. In which case, he would file for costs too, which would mean that they would also pick up his costs if this ludicrous case continued. Mr Guppy became all of a flurry over the situation, but assured Rajnath, Kamal, and Annan that it was a minor mishap.

'The prosecution lawyer is playing a dangerous game,' he said. 'The judge will be furious if they withdraw too late.'

When the judge finally arrived, he turned out to be a different one. Judge Williamson-Peel. As the hearing finally started, Rajnath sat sweating with worry and sick with fear. The airless courtroom, with windows close to the ceiling, did not help. He realised now that he had everything to lose if Mr Guppy was wrong. He listened intently for the case to be withdrawn, but it seemed to be continuing. Mr Guppy began questioning the plantation manager. That, at least, seemed to be going to plan.

'Mr MacDonald,' Mr Guppy asked the plantation manager. 'Did you receive the medical certificate from the doctor attending Mr Singh?'

'Well, we didn't get it till a long time after, sir,' Mr MacDonald replied. 'By that time, we had him down for refusing to obey orders.'

'How could that be construed as refusing to obey orders, Mr MacDonald, seeing as my client was not even on the premises?'

'Well, that is it, isn't it?' Mr MacDonald replied.

'I don't understand,' Mr Guppy said. 'What do you mean by *that is it isn't it*?'

'Well, he wasn't there on the premises. I can't pay someone who is not working.' Mr MacDonald's face was turning red. 'Besides, if he is not at work, he has to hand in a doctor's letter. And there wasn't one.'

'You mean there wasn't a medical certificate at that time. But there was one, later. At a later date, you *did* receive a medical certificate from the medical officer, Dr Douglas Boyle. I have a copy of it here, Your Honour.' Guppy raised the piece of paper in the air, and the court clerk took it across to the judge.

'I can't see what the problem is here,' Judge Williamson-Peel boomed. 'This medical certificate shows that the defendant was ill during the dates in question. Is there some point to this?' He scowled, and looked at the lawyer for the prosecution. 'I am hoping that you are not wasting court time here,' he said sternly. 'And I hope, Mr Llewellyn-Jones, that you realise the costs of continuation . . . It will increase costs awarded to the defendant.' The judge was looking across the room at the lawyer for the prosecution.

'No more questions,' Mr Guppy said, and sat down. He glanced at Rajnath with a quarter-smile and one raised eyebrow, but Rajnath was not totally convinced.

Then Mr Llewellyn-Jones rose to his feet. 'May I question the defendant?' he said. This surprised them all, and Guppy took a few minutes' leave from the judge to speak to Rajnath. A few moments later, Rajnath walked up to the stand. After the formalities, Mr Llewellyn-Jones started his questions.

'Where were you between the sixteenth of March and the twenty-fourth of March?'

'Objection, Your Honour,' Guppy jumped up and said. 'The twenty-fourth of March was yesterday.'

'I don't see what your objection is,' the judge said. 'Answer the question,' he boomed, looking at Rajnath.

'I was at home, sir,' Rajnath said.

'I didn't hear that,' Mr Llewellyn-Jones said. 'Will you repeat that?'

'I was at home, sir,' Rajnath repeated, louder.

'You *was* at home,' Mr Llewellyn-Jones repeated. 'And *was* you resting well?'

'Yes, sir,' Rajnath said. 'I was.'

'Why was that? Were you ill?'

'Yes, well, no, n-not really,' Rajnath stuttered. 'I went down to the beach . . . '

'Were you supposed to be resting?' Mr Llewellyn-Jones asked.

Rajnath glanced at Mr Guppy, but the man was looking down, leafing through his papers.

'Yes, sir,' Rajnath said. 'I was resting.'

'Were you ill yesterday?'

'No, sir,' Rajnath replied.

'So, you were resting but you were not ill,' Llewellyn-Jones repeated. 'And you went to the beach.'

'Objection,' Guppy said. 'Badgering my client.'

'Continue,' the judge boomed. 'I hope you have some good reason for this!'

Llewellyn-Jones turned to Rajnath to resume the questioning. 'Can you tell the court why you were at home when you should have been at work? Hadn't you taken enough time off while you were supposedly ill?'

Rajnath's face was beginning to redden. 'I was told to go home.'

'You were told to go home?' Llewellyn repeated. 'And, why, pray, was that? Who told you to go home? And what was the reason?'

'Objection!' Guppy stood up, red and perspiring in the face.

'One question at a time, Mr Llewellyn-Jones,' the judge said.

But Rajnath was replying to all of them. 'Yes, I was told to go home by the overseer. The driver called me to go and see him, and he said that I wasn't looking well, and that I should go home until they sent me a message.'

'If that is true, did they send a message?' Llewellyn-Jones looked at him hard. 'I presume not. How would they know to send you a message, if they didn't know that you were once again at home for months at a time without even having the courtesy of sending a message to the plantation manager about your supposed illness?'

Rajnath gasped. His mouth was fell open. 'But . . . '

'*But* indeed,' Llewellyn-Jones said.

'I was in work and they sent for me and . . . '

'And what? I put it to you, Mr Singh, that you are one of many. A malingerer. Hoping to gain where you have not worked. Sending fraudulent medical certificates, for all we know.'

'Objection!' Guppy was on his feet again.

'Get on with it!' the judge boomed again.

'If he was really ill, Your Honour,' Llewellyn-Jones said, 'Mr Singh would have been in the hospital. The Plantation Hospital is there for illness. The plantation manager would have sent him there. Furthermore, there is no record of this malingerer ever going there, despite claims of having tuberculosis, and miraculously recovering. Then pneumonia. This is too much, and stinks of lies, disobeying the ordinances, disrespect of the law of the land, and sheer laziness. What will it be next, if we allow this to continue amongst these Indians?'

'I don't remember any of it,' Rajnath blurted.

'You don't remember any of it! Because you were not at work. I rest my case, Your Honour,' Llewellyn-Jones boomed. 'No more questions.'

ཐ

Back in Granville, it was night-time, and Parbatee woke up shivering in the hammock where she had fallen asleep, when a blast of wind whistled through the yard. She got up and went inside, rolled herself up in the blanket and fell asleep again until the cocks began to crow. For a moment, she forgot all her worries, thinking her husband had already left for work. He had done that once before when she was very ill. But there were none of the usual sounds of the three men who lived in the house, and slowly reality dawned on her. She remembered she was there alone. She hurried to the boys' bedroom to make sure she wasn't dreaming. Empty. They were not yet back.

ཐ

Devinia spoke to her children about the visit she had had from Amrit Dass.

'He wants to help us,' she said. 'What do you say?'

'I'm not sure about it, Ma,' Etwar said, frowning. 'Strange. Why would they want to help us? Didn't Pa cancel the wedding? Surely they would be annoyed.'

'He had a kind sort of look,' his mother said. 'And it isn't a job in the cane fields or hard work. It's in his business – indoors. They have a big store in San Fernando.'

'I'll go,' Amina said. 'Pa was right in the first place. If I hadn't tried so hard to go against what he wanted, maybe he wouldn't have died. I made him agree with me, and now karma is punishing me back. I will go – and whatever I earn, I will send it home for you and Ma, Etwar.'

'Saturday,' Devinia said. 'Saturday is when he wants you there. We will come with you. Start packing up your things.'

'I don't think that is a good idea,' Etwar said worriedly. 'Talk to Mr Clifford first.'

'I know what he'll say. But I'm doing the right thing. I was being selfish, trying to change our traditions. I want to please Pa, if he can see me now.' Amina broke down and cried so loudly that Fluffy jumped up and ran off.

'Mr Dass even said that he will save your wages for you and send you to England to study to be a doctor,' her mother said proudly.

'You're not thinking straight,' Etwar argued. 'Neither of you. Pa was wrong. The best thing he did was realise that. Besides, why would this Mr Dass come and offer you a job when Pa cancelled the wedding – and send you to be a doctor? This doesn't ring true at all.'

'Sometimes you have to trust people,' Devinia said.

'And sometimes you have to think about who to trust,' Etwar responded.

FIFTY-ONE

The day dragged on for Parbatee, as she worried that her husband and sons had still not returned home from Port of Spain. Then late that afternoon she saw her husband and younger son enter the yard in silence. From the first glance at Kamal, Parbatee knew something was very wrong.

'There was nothing I could do,' her husband said bitterly, dropping his bag on the table. 'Nothing.'

'What do you mean?' she asked, staring intently into his eyes, trying to read his face. 'What happened?'

'The lawyer said that nobody told him that Rajnath couldn't remember he was ill.'

'What does that have to do with it? Where is my son?'

Annan looked at his mother. 'I'm here, Ma.'

'Not you!' she said. 'Where is my eldest son?' Parbatee repeated.

'He has gone to jail,' Annan said, in an unusually subdued tone.

Parbatee dropped to the ground and began to weep. 'He never deserved jail.'

'I told them to take me instead, but they wouldn't,' Annan said. 'It's always the good ones that get the bad things happen to them.'

'What are you saying? You stupid boy!' Parbatee yelled. 'You think that would help me?'

'If anyone deserves to be in jail,' the boy said, 'it's me. The things I get up to! Raj is the hardworking one – and he is the one gets punished. You know why? Because he told the truth. Me? I would've lied.'

'How is he?' Parbatee said.

'I don't know,' Kamal said. 'They just took him away.'

'How long for?' she asked.

'They give him the minimum fine for leaving the estate without a pass. Five dollars. That is more than a month's pay. And two months in jail.'

'Oh, Sita Ram, that will finish him,' she wailed.

'The lawyer says he will appeal,' Kamal told her. 'But that will cost money.'

'We must pay it, and try to get him out,' Parbatee said. 'How soon?'

'Ma, by the time they appeal, it will be time for him to come out,' Annan said.

ꙮ

When Devinia woke up the next morning, Amina had already left the house. She spent that day getting her daughter's clothes washed, ironed and packed for Saturday. She woke Etwar to do his chores, and gave him a brown paper bag with some lunch for his sister. When he returned home from school that afternoon, he assumed that Amina had come back home for lunch.

'No, Ma,' he said. 'I didn't see her all day.'

'Maybe she went to visit one of her friends.'

'Or all of them,' Etwar said. 'If she is going on Saturday, she won't see them for a long time.'

It was after dark when Amina returned home that day, and Devinia was worried, but no doubt the girl had been to see Sumati and the others to tell them she was going away on Saturday.

'I've decided,' Amina said. 'If I'm going, I want to leave tomorrow. You have everything packed, what's the point of waiting?'

No amount of discussion or argument could change Amina's mind. She was adamant, and in the end Devinia gave in.

ꕥ

Early the next morning, Devinia and Amina caught the Mail bus from Syphoo Junction. They both wandered around looking for the house, trying to remember Amrit's directions. Amina spotted the big white-stone building of the Carnegie Library in San Fernando, and marvelled about the interior being full of books. She longed to step inside just to take a peek but it was too early. The library did not open until 9am.

'Ma, can we just walk around?' she asked. 'The town is so different from Granville.'

'You like it?'

'I think I do,' Amina replied.

Devinia noticed the excited look in her daughter's eyes.

It was a look of freedom that she herself had been denied, having married so young, but she was content to enjoy what life she could through Amina's happiness.

'I think I'll really like being here,' the girl continued. 'Look at the size of the library. I wonder how many books are in there. I could spend all my spare time reading them. I even like the sounds and smells of this place.'

'The smells?'

'I smell roast corn, and curry, and fried channa, and the sea, and business hustle-bustle, all mixed in.'

'I smell a cow pen,' Devinia smiled. 'But I know what you're saying.'

'Even the trees are different. And there are flowers in everybody's front yards. We plant kitchen garden in our front yards. Some of these houses look like palaces. But some look abandoned.'

'What do you mean by that?' her mother asked.

'Desolate – as if no one lives there any longer. Wouldn't it be nice to have one of those?'

'You're dreaming again, child. How will we ever do that now?'

Devinia's heart was breaking as she watched Amina stare longingly around her – the high stone houses standing on large plots of land across the road from the marketplace where vendors were busy setting up their stalls. The girl looked as though she was in the middle of a dream come true, with everything she could ever imagine all around her – pretty saris, glittering sandals, colourfully painted enamelled pots and pans and fabrics, from men's suiting to cheap and cheerful pink knicker-cotton. The smell of food made her hungry. 'Can we buy something to eat?' Amina asked.

'I brought our own.' Devinia reached in her bag and pulled out a roti and pumpkin wrap.

While she walked, she spotted the police station and remembered that Rajnath had intended to report his uncle; she wondered if he had done so. Could there be anything more evil than taking advantage of a young girl such as Sumati?

'I'm glad I'm not pretty,' Amina said out of the blue.

Devinia was startled.

'Who told you that? You're my daughter, and very good-looking. Take care of yourself – and watch out for men here who try to take advantage. But I think you'll be safe with Mr Dass and his family. They care about people.'

'I'll come home and bring you the money I earn. In a way I'm glad I'm doing this,' Amina told her mother. 'It makes me feel useful. You never let me help at home. Maybe some time in the future I will get a chance to go back to school. But I have to do this first – for you and Etwar. For us.'

Devinia pulled her close. 'Look for the Colonial Hospital on the hill. The house is near there.'

ൿ

They got to the gates of the Dass property and stood speechless. Amrit Dass was cordial and most respectful. He offered them drinks and had a meal brought to them as if he had been expecting honoured guests. Later, he took them around the premises and showed them where Amina would be staying, and Devinia expressed her gratitude. That afternoon, she left her daughter in San Fernando at the house and business of Mr Amrit Dass, and his son Dillip, feeling greatly relieved. Whatever anxiety she might have had and concealed from everyone, had ebbed away during their visit.

When she returned home, she told Etwar that his father had made a big mistake in deciding to cancel the wedding. They had everything that would make the girl happy. Besides, Amina liked San Fernando. It suited her. If she could have married the son, he was just the kind of educated young man who would make her an excellent match. He was rich too, and more than they could have hoped for in a husband for Amina. But it was too late.

'I can't see why,' Etwar said. 'If you think so, you should have said.'

ℬ

Etwar was fetching water one day from the standpipe when Sumati spotted him and asked if Amina was all right.

'She must be very busy in school,' the girl said sadly, 'she has no time for me these days.'

'School? She didn't tell you?'

'Tell me what?'

'She took a job. She's working now.'

'Teaching?'

'No. But if she didn't tell you, she didn't tell Mr Clifford either. Strange that he hasn't asked me about her though.'

'He probably assumes she's got belly pains.'

'You mean woman pains?' Etwar asked. 'I'm not stupid.'

'Except he would be wrong,' Sumati said. 'He would have persuaded her against her decision to go to work. But I can understand why she must have changed her mind. Look, I have to get back to my babies now. Tell your sister not to forget where I live.'

'I won't be seeing her for a good while. She's living away now – where she is working,' Etwar tried to explain, but Sumati had already turned her back and was hurrying off down the road.

ꝏ

That evening, as she massaged her children after their bath, Sumati sat thinking about how life can change when you're least expecting it. Amina had had everything planned out, and had tried to persuade her father not to get her married. Now she had got her wish, but everything was turned upside down. Karma had stepped in. Sankar Banderjee got killed as soon as she got her way. And somehow, Amina wouldn't trust the Hindu religion anymore. And instead of being the luckiest girl in the village, reading poetry and teaching children how to read and write, she had to leave school and work like everyone else in some cane field.

'Pa,' Sumati said. 'Is Amina working in the cane field? Have you seen her?'

'No,' he said. 'I've not seen her or heard about her.'

'She must be so ashamed that she never even told me.' Sumati's voice was sad.

'They must have lost everything,' Roopchand said. 'I heard the jewellery store got cleaned out by thieves.'

'Have they caught who did it?'

'You think the police care?' her father scoffed. 'If they did find out who did it, they would be taking bribes to keep it quiet.'

'Sankar used to make very nice pieces of jewellery,' his daughter recalled. 'Very special. He made beautiful flowers

– roses and orchids. No one else makes those. Amina gave me some for my wedding. Those pieces will turn up somewhere.'

'She is a generous girl. I saw you wearing them but I couldn't remember if they were your mother's. Well, I hope they find who did it. Nobody deserves to die like that.'

'You didn't like him, Pa.'

'True – but I never wished him dead.' Roopchand scratched his head. 'I was jealous. He had everything – money, a business, a big house. He had it all. Girl, life is more important than riches. I see that now,' he admitted. 'I have you – and your brother. More than money can buy.'

'You're right. It was riches that got him murdered. He lost his life because of his jewellery business.'

'We have to be grateful for what we have been given,' Sumati's father said, cuddling one of the babies. 'Life is short. Much too short. I miss your mother every day, you know. I will never stop missing her.'

ꕥ

Sumati made a trip up to the Banderjee house to see Devinia. She arrived with both babies straddled across her hips. Devinia was delighted to see her and made a big fuss of the children.

'Stay and eat,' Devinia begged. 'I don't see you so much anymore.'

'You cook like my mother, Tantie,' Sumati said. 'Thank you – I would love to eat with you.'

'Your mother was a good cook,' Devinia said gently. 'You must be missing her too. I can't tell you how much I feel for you, losing her like that. Come and see me whenever you want. I will always have time for you. It's only Etwar and me now. I miss Amina already. Both of them.' Devinia wiped away the tears that filled her eyes.

'It's hard on you, Tantie,' Sumati said, 'now that Amina's gone away to work.'

Devinia began to cry. 'Yes, but it's for the best.'

'I wonder how she's managing? It must have been a hard decision for her. Even harder for somebody like her. She's not used to that kind of hard work. Or living with strangers.'

'They seem like good people. A lot of people are there, working. The house is big, and the business too.'

'Business?' Sumati was surprised. 'I thought she was working in the cane field?'

'No, it is a big business. It's a good place to work. A lot of other girls are there. And she likes San Fernando.'

'A lot of girls? San Fernando? Etwar didn't say. Who owns the business?'

'A man and his son. Mr Dass.'

'Dass?' Sumati repeated, a feeling of dread overcoming her.

'Amrit Dass,' Devinia said. And when Sumati looked horrified, she asked, 'Is something wrong?'

'Is the son called Dillip?' Sumati asked in a choked voice.

'You know them?' Devinia asked. 'They live in a big white house with a red roof. Down the hill from the Colonial Hospital in San Fernando. The son – he talks like a white man. As if he went to school in England.'

'He went to a white-boy school in Port of Spain,' Sumati informed her. 'And he is a no-good. He is the one who caused me all of this . . . You must get her out of there. I don't know how to explain.'

'No,' Devinia obstinately. 'You're mistaken. I went there myself. I saw it. Very nice people.'

'You don't believe me? They took advantage of me.'

'No, you are mistaken, I say,' Devinia insisted.

'I'm telling you, Tantie!' Sumati's face changed suddenly as if thunder was rumbling inside her.

There was a pause, then Devinia spoke again, her voice defiant.

'Even if it's true what you say, Amina is different.'

'How do you mean?'

'She is not like you. You mustn't mind me saying, Sumati. But you ran away from home and you went there with a boy. That is the difference. I heard all about it. And you are now blaming those good people for you getting in trouble. Where is the boy you ran away with? He left you with two children? You brought trouble on yourself when you ran away with him.'

'So you really think that I asked for this?' Sumati struggled with her rising anger.

'I am not saying you asked for it. But what you did, showed everybody what kind of girl you are. Why do you think your mother killed herself? Poor Daya.'

Sumati hurt badly from these cruel words, but she put her feelings aside.

'I know what you're saying, but I also know what I am saying. Amina is no different from me in their eyes. *You have to get her out of there.*'

'They gave her a job. Did they give you a job?'

'I cannot listen to this anymore, Tantie. I have to go. I know I'm a bad person, but I learnt a lot from my own badness. I don't want my best friend to experience what I went through. I am begging you to go and get her out of there. That place is a hundred times as bad as me. If I didn't have my children to look after, I would go and do it myself.'

Sumati left Devinia's house as if she was on fire, fuming with anger and smoking with guilt. She didn't know what to do. After she got home and had fed the children, she asked her father to look after them, so she could go and see someone.

FIFTY-TWO

Sumati went to see the only person she knew could help. But when she got to Rajnath's house, the discovery that he was in jail was yet another shock she could barely absorb. And then Parbatee began talking what seemed like gibberish about Sumati's babies being her grandchildren.

'He was a school-friend, that's all,' Sumati said exasperatedly. 'Nothing more, I swear. The reason why I came to see your son was because my friend Amina is in trouble. Serious trouble. She has gone to live with his Uncle Amrit and Cousin Dillip. *Your* family.'

'My nephew?' Parbatee asked worriedly. 'Live? They getting married first.'

Sumati explained as much as she could, as fast as she could. And as she spoke, she began to think of a way she could enlist their help.

'Maybe I will go up to San Fernando myself and get the police involved,' she told them. 'Maybe that is what I should do anyhow.' As she turned to go, Kamal spoke up.

'What is it you want us to do?' he asked. 'I will go to the police myself. Family or no, this is sounding wrong. Everybody is somebody's daughter. You yourself have been through enough. Now another innocent girl from right here in this village is at risk at the hands of these greedy goats. I always knew something was wrong with them.'

ꕥ

The next day, Kamal Singh set off to Port of Spain to visit his son in prison, accompanied by Annan. Rajnath was not looking good, and Kamal was nervous about giving him the news from Sumati.

'Your probably-not-wife sent a message,' Annan said to his brother.

'Why are you talking in riddles?' Rajnath asked.

'That girl with the twins,' Kamal explained. 'She came to see us yesterday.'

When they told Rajnath the news, Rajnath was more devastated than they had anticipated.

'You seem to be taking it badly, son,' his father said worriedly.

'I can't believe her father was murdered and now this,' Rajnath said. 'Have they caught who did it?'

'The police will take their time with real criminals,' Annan said contemptuously. 'They're too busy locking up innocent people who are too ill to go to work.'

'She must be in a very difficult position to have agreed to go there,' Rajnath said. He struck his brow. 'What will happen to her now? She is probably the nicest person I know, and they are devils who will dishonour her.'

Kamal and Annan looked at each other.

'It seems you are not the only one to feel that way about that girl,' his father said. 'Her friend Sumati sent us up here to see if we could pay your fine.'

'You can't pay my fine. And even if you could, I would still have to do my jail time.'

'We will see the prison governor. He is bound to be sympathetic. You are a good boy.' And Kamal left them and went to see the prison officer.

'There's no damn justice in this world,' Annan said soberly. 'Look at that young girl, Sumati. And now Amina. This world is full of bad people getting away with doing bad things to good people. Innocent people.'

'What happened to the Annan I know?' Rajnath asked, trying to joke.

'This happened! *You!* I knew what Uncle and Dillip were doing, but I didn't say or do anything. I'll tell you something though. I wouldn't mind going up there and sorting out the bastards myself. The police are just turning a blind eye to it. They know what goes on. Uncle drinks with the police in San Fernando, he bribes them and he invites them to the house too.'

'Why didn't you say something?' Rajnath grabbed Annan by the shirt collar and shook him hard.

'Control yourself, man,' his younger brother gasped, struggling free. 'Think about who is the real enemy? I am just the easy target.'

Rajnath punched the wall in frustration. 'I have to do something,' he cried. 'But my hands are tied while I am shut away in here.'

ꕤ

The next week, Kamal and Annan returned to the prison to visit Rajnath to find him with both his eyes black and blue, looking demoralised. Rajnath told them that the guard had pushed him about.

'You brought what I asked you to bring?' Rajnath asked.

'Yes, I found it, but you seem to have a lot of money, boy,' Kamal frowned. 'You rob a bank or something?'

'No. I got it from Ma's family. Give it to me – not the whole bag.'

A guard came up and stood behind him.

'You have my clothes?' Rajnath asked him quietly.

'By the door.' The guard moved his eyes at the door.

Rajnath went over and spotted a prison overall wrapped like a parcel. He opened it and saw his clothes. He returned and handed the guard the package his father had given him.

'If it's not all here, I will hunt you down like a dog,' the guard spat. 'Like the dog you are. And this black eye you gave me will show how you beat me up and escaped.'

ಬ

After Rajnath's escape from prison, they all hurried into Port of Spain town centre and sat in a rum shop and talked. Kamal ordered some food and drink, and smiled at his sons, pleased to see them united.

'How did you pull this off, boy?' He was eager to know.

'Your son is not as stupid as you think, Pa,' Annan said proudly. 'Rajnath, you actually beat up the guard?'

'Yes,' he replied bluntly.

'So how did you get him to agree to let you out?' his father asked again.

'Money, Pa. Money will buy the moon if it asked a price.'

'So, are you going to tell me how you got all that money?' Kamal asked his son.

'Best not,' Rajnath said. 'Put it this way. We have something to go and straighten out. We are looking to travel down to San Fernando, and mete out justice in the household of my uncle and his very expensively educated son.'

'I brought you a clean suit of clothes,' Kamal said. 'I had a strange feeling . . . that's all.'

'Strange?'

'You are my son after all. I have known you since you were born.'

ꙮ

It was early evening when the three of them arrived in San Fernando at the premises of Amrit and Dillip Dass. All was quiet. The smell of home-cooked food hit them hard. Resisting it was not easy.

Annan led Rajnath and their father up the back path to where he thought Amina might be staying, but she was not there. He thought of another tactic and suggested his plan, but Rajnath was angry and wanted to just barge in even though Annan pointed out that it would get them nowhere. Annan took the others outside and left them to wait, while he boldly entered by the front gate and marched down to the kitchen where Tonia was working. The woman seemed a little surprised to see him, gently reprimanding him for not visiting for so long. Annan joked that he had found himself another true love, and Tonia seemed to appreciate the joke quite well, while remarking flirtatiously that it was his look-out.

Meanwhile, Rajnath was growing impatient, and had decided to go off on his own.

'That is not a good idea, boy,' Kamal said. 'Wait. Annan will come back soon. He knows this place like the back of his hand – something I wasn't aware of until yesterday. And he is very angry with your cousin too. Don't spoil it.'

'Well, Pa,' Rajnath said tightly. 'I blame him for everything! Getting involved with these crooks that Ma calls her family is bad enough, but he didn't even have the good sense to find a way to stop them.'

'And you think you can? Keep quiet and wait here like he said,' his father ordered. 'You were always too impatient. Annan will bring back the girl and then we will leave. You'll see. If you go blundering in, how can we make a quick getaway?' Kamal gave Rajnath a warning squint. 'What interest do you have in this girl anyway? You know her from school – is that it?'

'Yes.'

'But she's so much younger than you. You can't know her that well. You just want to take it out on Dillip, don't you? Did you two get in a fight or something?'

'Yes, something like that. Right – I've waited long enough. I'm going over there to take a look inside that open window.' Rajnath pointed across the gravel yard.

Kamal Singh watched his son walk away from him and felt his gut twist inside his belly. He whispered to himself, 'Lakshmi Mata, bring the boys back so that I can take them home to their mother. Goodness knows what state she is in.'

He leaned against the wall outside the gate under the shade of the almond tree branches. Before long he thought he heard something like a crash coming from the inside.

Then loud voices coming from the window directly above him. His body tensed. The boys had got into a fight. Nothing had changed – he couldn't even trust them to act together for the same purpose!

Kamal rushed inside the gate and followed the noise. It sounded like a man fight. He pulled out his belt from his waistband, prepared to administer what he had never done before, but what he should have years ago. Parbatee had said, *'Beating our boys will never make them good'*, but she was wrong. And he was wrong to have listened. It worked for everyone else.

Kamal got inside the house, and hastened up the steps inside, then pushed open the door . . .

ဢ

Inside the room was a double bed, a dresser and two rocking chairs which were tumbled over, one on top of the bed. Rajnath was hanging off the back of the chair, while Dillip stood by, panting. His face showed he meant business. This was no roll-around in the dirt.

'What's going on here?' As the words left Kamal's mouth, he noticed drops of blood falling on the white sheet below Rajnath's face. He rushed to his son.

'Help me up,' Rajnath said, and spat blood.

'No,' Dillip snarled. 'Leave him there and let me finish what I started. This is becoming a bad habit. Every time this bully comes to my house, he starts a fight. He said he came here to take my wife, Uncle Kamal. This is what you all are now? Wife thieves?'

'Your wife?' Kamal asked. 'What are you talking about?'

'The girl is not your wife,' Rajnath said. 'She is my

friend. Her father died and you . . . you . . . you think you have found another country girl to take advantage of. Just like you did with Sumati.'

'The girl was always going to be my wife. Her father agreed.'

'Is that why you just tried to sell her to me?' Rajnath said furiously. 'You told me you're sure she is a virgin. Apart from that, you are a top-class liar!'

'Sell the girl to you? You are one fool. You stole my money. Do you think I would just give the girl to you? My wife?'

'She is not your wife, or even your wife-to-be. Mr Banderjee cancelled the wedding before he died.'

Dillip pulled Rajnath up to his feet and shouted in his face. 'Nobody does that to me! Nobody! You hear? And what is it to you anyway? Why are you here? You break out of jail? The girl is mine. Don't you come here and try to take her for yourself? You think she wants a loser like you?'

Rajnath pushed Dillip away from his face, causing a struggle which turned into an all-out fight. As they knocked each other around, the oil lamp fell off the bedside table onto the bed, but none of them realised.

ቇ

Amina ran into the room. Neither of the two men who were struggling with each other seemed aware that a fire was blazing on the bed.

'Stop it!' she screamed out.

She was surprised to see that one of the men was Rajnath. What was he doing here? Why had he come? She launched across to separate them, but she got in the way and was knocked over. As she rose from the bed, she noticed her dress was on fire, and panicked. Amina ran to the door of the room but had to struggle to open it. She ran down the long veranda in the open air, screaming. As she got to the top of the stairs someone pulled her back and spun her into a blanket from the banister to stifle the flames. It was Annan, who had heard the screams and commotion.

'What are you doing, Raj?' he yelled at his brother, who had staggered out of the bedroom. 'Who set the place on fire?'

Rajnath then realised that Dillip was still in the bedroom.

'Hold on to her,' he said to Annan, 'I need to get Dillip out of there.'

'Let him burn,' Annan said callously.

'*No*. He's not getting away that easy. To jail is better than to burn!'

Kamal and Tonia ran around with buckets of water to throw on the fire, but it had spread everywhere. Mayhem erupted. The rafters caught aflame, and girls and men were running half-dressed, down the stairs into the yard.

'We need more water!' Annan bellowed, rushing down the corridor.

Amrit arrived home at that moment, to find the whole building on fire. Everyone was frantically dashing around with buckets slopping water, and shouting.

'Take her out,' Kamal commanded Rajnath. 'Go on – run downstairs, out to the road. Get away from the premises. I shall be right behind you. This is not our concern.'

As Rajnath and Amina headed downstairs, they could see that the fire was consuming the downstairs rooms of the new building. Amrit was calling for Dillip, cursing and swearing. Amina and Rajnath pushed the doors and realised that people were trapped in the rooms downstairs. Seizing a hammer and a short axe that he found nearby, Rajnath forced open the doors, and they both pulled the dazed occupants out to safety.

'The whole place is on fire! Somebody go and call the fire service!' Rajnath shouted.

'Amrit has already gone to get the fire service,' Tonia said, wringing her hands. 'Who started it? And where's Dillip?'

'That little worm has probably gone to save his stash of money!' Rajnath snorted.

Barrels of rain water were being thrown onto the fire, but nothing seemed to be working. The wind had picked up as if Daya were wreaking revenge, and while everyone was panicking and shouting, 'Fire, fire! – it's all his fault the place is being destroyed,' Rajnath and Amina stole away. They ran until they could no longer feel the heat of the flames, just barely hear the cries. But just before he got Amina to safety, he heard a cry from one of the rooms – a voice he recognised. He ran back following the cries to find Dillip overpowering a young woman who was struggling to escape.

'For this,' Dillip screamed at the young woman, 'you will pay – with your life.'

'I have two children,' she said. 'You can't do this to me. Haven't you done enough? Where is my friend? Have you used her like you used me? You want to tie me up and leave me to die now? Karma will get you.'

'No, I will get him first!' Rajnath shouted, his face red with heat and anger. 'I never thought you were as bright as you tried to be. No kind of education could get this out of you. Leave that girl alone.'

'Rajnath,' Sumati said. 'I didn't know who else to ask to save her, so I came myself.'

Rajnath pulled Dillip and threw him out through the window of the burning building, before freeing Sumati from the ropes with which Dillip had tied her up. Her face was bruised and blackened with soot. Rajnath picked her up in his arms and ran until they were well away from the premises. Black smoke bellowed into the blue skies, then they heard a bang and everything shuddered around them.

Rajnath held Sumati tight until she struggled to stand free, but he didn't seem to want to let her go. Her fingers were still holding his. He looked into her face and whispered,

'You are something. I'm never going to let you go. Do you hear me?' Sumati stared at him, not able to reply, but she smiled as if she was relieved.

'What are you saying?' she said. 'I thought you liked Amina?'

'Amina? Yes, I like her. But you . . . I feel differently about you. Put it this way. I couldn't live with myself if anything had happened to you today.' He put his arm around her waist and pulled her closer. Just then Amina, Annan and his father came up to them.

'You all okay?' Kamal said. 'What is this girl doing here? Sumati? I thought you were in Granville.'

'Well we're all here now, and the important thing is Amina is safe,' Sumati said. 'Girl, you have no idea what trouble you put yourself in by coming here.'

'Believe me, I know,' Amina said. 'I didn't know then, but I do now. And I can't believe all of you came to get me. I've put you all in so much danger.'

Together, they all walked away, Rajnath and the girls behind, leaving the smoke-filled yard of Amrit Dass's business premises, as people went in to help extinguish the fire and watch the wreckage.

ေ

The middle of the morning of the next day, two policemen arrived at Rajnath's home.

'He is not here,' Parbatee told them. 'He is in prison, my poor son.'

'And your husband?'

'Nobody is here but me. What do you want with my son and husband, officer?'

'Somebody went to a property in San Fernando and burnt it to the ground. The property of a Mr Amrit Dass.'

'That is my brother!' Parbatee cried. 'That can't be true. Why would my son do that to his own uncle? You are making no sense. Is my brother safe?'

'Mr Dass and his son are both safe. All the girls are safe too. But their hotel business is burnt down.'

'Hotel business?' she echoed. 'Girls? What is that about? No, no. My brother has a shop. Selling rice, dhal, pots and cooking spoons and such. He knows nothing about any hotel business. My father was a shopkeeper in India. Jaipur. That is where he learnt to run a shop. Not a hotel.' She shook her head hard.

'We were told your son was there – that he got away with one of their girls. A young girl from this village.'

'Young girl?' Parbatee's eyes jumped out from their sockets. Annan had never shown any interest in girls except to tease his brother. 'This cannot be true, officer? You cannot be talking about my son at all. You have got wrong information. I have a lot of work to do, and now you give me worries about my brother?' Parbatee began to cry loudly. 'I must go and see him. Where will he live, if his house is burnt down? My husband will not have him here. I cannot bear it. Please – leave me.'

'All right, we are going. But the place is not completely ruined. The old part is still there.' With that, the policemen left Parbatee sobbing into the tea towel she had on her shoulder.

FIFTY-THREE

It was around midday when the same two policemen arrived at Devinia's home asking for a young woman called Amina. She and Etwar were outside, and came to see what the men wanted. When Amina heard, she was furious.

'Mr Dass tricked my mother into sending me there. He runs a prostitute house. I'm not afraid to say it – I saw it, I was there. He uses poor young girls promising them good money and an education. That is no hotel. He is a bad man and his son is worse. Do you want to see my friend living down the road? See what they did to her? They used her to make money. Now she has two white babies.'

'Miss, is that why you burnt down their property?' one policeman asked.

'I have never touched a match in my life. It was an accident.'

'So you were involved. You will have to come with us to the police station.'

Devinia began to shout like never before. 'No! You are not taking my daughter to jail. She has done nothing. I will go instead.'

'That is not how it works, madam,' one said. 'We are not taking her to jail, although she might stay in a cell if we find her a danger to the public.'

'No! No jail. Kill me first. Take me down in the cell.' Devinia's voice could be heard from the road.

Just then, they spotted a man walking down the path. A stranger. An Indian, wearing a three-piece suit and dressed like an Englishman. Devinia stared at him in horror.

'Have you come with them, to carry my daughter to jail?' she challenged. 'Somebody murdered my husband, and now you are taking my daughter? This land has no justice. My poor husband was right. But they killed him. Who killed him?'

'That's a very good question you ask,' the stranger said. 'Maybe these kind gentlemen can answer it. They are the police. They must be investigating it.' He turned to them. 'How far have you got with the investigation into the murder of this woman's husband? Are you with the Point Fortin police force?'

Devinia, Amina and Etwar stared at the Indian man standing in his brown suit, brown leather shoes, and brown leather briefcase, and by his voice, clearly well educated.

'Do you know this man?' the policeman asked Devinia. Before she could say no, she had no idea, the man introduced himself.

'My name is Narine Banderjee,' he said. And all three of them jumped visibly from the spot they were rooted to. 'I am the lawyer acting for this family.' He stuck out his hand to the police, shook their hands and nodded at Devinia.

'Unless you are going to arrest anyone here, I suggest you leave these people alone. I am suspecting you have no evidence but hearsay from the desperate man who lost his property to fire, which more than likely happened as an accident, as the girl says.'

'Don't believe this is the last of it,' one policeman said. 'There's bound to be evidence.'

'Then I suggest you have it if you are planning to return here.'

ꟙ

When the police left, Devinia, Amina and Etwar stared at the lawyer.

'Who did you say you were?' Devinia asked.

'I am family,' he said. 'Don't look so alarmed. I should have tried to find you long ago, but I was worried how my brother would take it. Yes, he, your husband, was my brother. I'm so sorry he died.' Tears filled his eyes. 'I never thought . . . I kept putting it off.'

'What happened to your wife you ran away with?' Etwar said. 'Pa told us about you. How you ran away on the ship.'

'With a Brahmin's daughter? He told you?' There was a faraway look in Narine Banderjee's eyes. 'She got bitten by a snake. She withstood the four terrible months on the ship, and then a snakebite and fever killed her. It took me a long time to get over her.'

Narine dried his eyes and sipped the water Amina brought him. 'Anyhow,' he said, 'I went to England, and I studied law. I was so angry at the life we lived. But England is a strange place. Full of smog. Cold and wet. The people are like that too.'

'The people are wet and full of smog?' Etwar asked, bemused.

'I see you are a bit of a joker, boy. You remind me of your father. I have done some research into his case, and I want to try to help you.'

Etwar was wide-eyed, still looking for an answer. 'No, uncle, I was serious.'

'How do you know about my father's case?' Amina asked.

'I heard his name called when I was in San Fernando police station. Of course immediately the name meant something to me.'

'Do you know who did it?' Etwar asked. 'Who killed our father?'

'I can't be altogether sure, but I have a suspicion. Forgive me, but I am not at liberty to say anything yet. Besides, I want to ensure it goes to trial.'

Devinia's hands began to shake. 'People in Point Fortin were jealous of my husband.'

'People here too,' Amina said.

'You must tell me anything you know,' Narine said. 'What about the people he worked with? Everyone is a suspect – anyone who could have been there, that is. Think.'

'We wouldn't tell anybody,' Devinia insisted. 'I have to know who killed him. They could be living right here.'

'My dear sister, it isn't in anyone's best interests for me to give you false hope. Let me see if I can get somewhere first. The police should be investigating this, but I'm not sure how far they've got. You will be the first to know if I find anything out. I want justice for my brother, just like you do.'

'Yes, Ma,' Amina said kindly. 'Just let Uncle do his job. He is a professional lawyer. We're lucky to have him on our side.'

'Yes, here is my identification, so you're sure I am who I say I am.' Narine opened his briefcase and showed them his travel papers from India, and other papers with his name. And a photograph.

'This is my wife, Myrtle. She is from a town in Berkshire, England. And these are my children, Edward and Elizabeth. But we live in Port of Spain now.'

'Your wife is a pretty woman,' Devinia said. 'How old are the children?'

'Edward is eleven, and Elizabeth is seven. We call her Betts. Mischievous little thing.'

'I'm glad you came when you did today,' Devinia said.

'That was a stroke of luck. I overheard them, talking about paying a visit to Granville, yesterday, and that is what forced my hand to get down here right away. I was hoping to be here before them, but I got lost. Do you know where I can get lodgings around here? Is there a hotel?'

They all laughed. 'There's nothing like that here,' Devinia said. 'You will stay here with us. Your family.'

ꙮ

Mr Clifford encouraged Amina to concentrate on her goal, and she tried. But at evening class she became argumentative, questioning everything. She queried the weakness of Mr Bennet in *Pride and Prejudice* obeying his wife, whose motivation was solely to marry off her daughters to wealthy men. And didn't the English people send their daughters to be educated? So why marry them when they were not employed and not earning? Her father had promised to send her to England to be educated and she intended to use it every day at work, not become anybody's wife.

'Studying for a profession costs money,' Mr Clifford said. 'Only the rich can afford it. And for most, it isn't worth spending that money on a daughter, who will end up married and at home minding children anyway. The education is wasted. The money is wasted.'

'I thought you said that education is never wasted, sir?' Amina contradicted.

'That is my personal opinion. But it is wasted in practice.'

'It's not fair on girls!' she burst out. 'That's why I'm not getting married. But what's the point? I can't go to England to study anymore.'

'My dear girl, you must take opportunity as it presents itself. What is available to you. You can still become a teacher right here in Trinidad, like I did. Port of Spain is the place. England is cold and unwelcoming. They don't take well to black people either. Indians too.'

'My Uncle Narine studied to be a lawyer in England. I'll ask him.'

'Believe me, the white rich in England don't even like their own white poor.'

&

Narine spent a few days in Granville, mixing with the villagers, talking to people to get a sense about how they felt about Sankar. Because he omitted to mention Sankar was his brother, people weren't afraid to say what they thought. It turned out that some were jealous, and that not everyone knew him that well, presumably because, unlike Devinia, Sankar didn't mix much with the locals. They knew him as the businessman who owned the big house in the middle of the village, who was considerably richer than they were. This gave cause for concern to Narine, who felt that it would be easier to harm someone you didn't know personally or identify with – which placed many villagers as suspects. Trying to find out where people were on the evening Sankar was killed was more difficult, and he particularly noted the few who had no alibis or seemed edgy, whilst he was chatting in a friendly way as a new neighbour would.

'The man still warm in his grave,' Roopchand said nastily to Narine, 'and you move into his bed?' He addressed his daughter, scowling. 'Sumati, did you know about this? If Devinia wanted anything, she could have come to me.'

Narine smiled. 'You like her – Devinia.'

'She's a pretty woman,' Roopchand said. 'My wife has gone, and I know Devinia. We are both alone now. It makes sense.'

'What happened to your wife? Did she leave you? If so, mightn't she come back?'

'My mother died,' Sumati answered for her father. 'Pa, what are you saying? You had your eye on Amina's mother?'

'All I'm saying is that she is a woman, and I am a man. And she cooks like your mother. Huh! That man didn't appreciate what he had.'

'What, are you saying that he was unfaithful to his wife?' This was a shock to Narine.

'I saw him with so many women, every time I went up to Point Fortin. How he looked at the women in his shop. Touching them and putting gold chains around their neck. Bracelets on their arms. And . . . '

'Pa, do you know what you are saying?' Sumati interrupted, alarmed.

'I'm not stupid,' Roopchand said to his daughter. 'Even though *he* thought I was.'

'He said that?' Narine asked.

'He didn't have to say it.'

Once on his own again, Narine wrote down all his findings and studied them when he returned to the room he shared with Etwar.

ഇ

Etwar spoke to his sister about what he had noticed in Narine's notebook about their father and the women.

'I couldn't help taking a look at what he had written,' Etwar defended himself. 'It was right there. Anyway, it doesn't matter how I found out. What are you going to do about it? You must have known this rumour was going around.'

Amina stared at him, speechless.

'Why aren't you saying anything?' he asked. 'You know what a spiteful man Roopchand is? He threatened to kill Daya, that's why she killed herself first.'

'Maybe you should tell Uncle Narine about that.'

'I will. And in the meantime, best you keep your mouth shut before you upset Ma and spread bad rumours about Pa.'

ഇ

Amina told Sumati what Roopchand had said regarding her father, and reminded her friend that Roopchand was likely to be unreliable and biased, based on how he had blamed and assaulted her when Sumati ran away from home. Sumati agreed, but wasn't convinced.

'You only believe him because he's your father,' Amina said hotly.

'It's not that, honestly. It's the way he said it,' Sumati tried to explain.

'So you think my father deserved to get his neck slashed because he was decent to his female customers? Surely you can't be that stupid.'

Touching women was Sumati's big point. They squabbled before Amina understood why her friend was so incensed. Later, Amina spoke to Narine, telling him everything she knew and remembered which could be of use.

'I must go home and see my family in Port of Spain,' he told her. 'It's been almost a week. They might think I'm dead somewhere.'

The family were sorry to see him go and hoped to see him again soon. But it was almost as if they were suffering another loss.

ᘏ

On his way back from Port of Spain, Narine spent some time in Point Fortin to see Sankar's shop, explore the location, and to generally find out what people knew in the area. He walked up and down, visiting places like the bank, the general stores next door, the small attorney at law office on the corner of the street. In effect, he was doing the job of the police, but he felt it was essential for the sake of his late brother, the family, and himself. It was clear that family were struggling not to fall apart, and despite what Roopchand had said about Sankar, he seemed a little too interested in Devinia to be reliable. By the time he returned to Granville, Narine had discovered something quite interesting.

ꕥ

The following day Narine headed straight down to Roopchand's house to speak to Sumati, but Roopchand was at home.

'Are you well?' he asked the man.

'No. I was laid off work some time ago,' Roopchand replied.

'That would explain it then,' Narine nodded. 'Can we talk frankly?'

'Everything is frankly. You think I lie?'

'No, but it explains why you might be in Point Fortin during the day.'

'I go there sometimes. What of it?'

'And you were there in Point Fortin, at the scene of the murder, Mr Balgobin . . . the day of the murder?'

'Are you conducting some kind of investigation?' Roopchand stood tall and menacing. 'What kind of neighbour are you?'

'Oh, I'm only visiting my sister-in-law and her family. I might have forgotten to tell you. You see, Sankar was my brother, and he was murdered. And I know you were there on the day, looking into the shop window.'

'How you know that?' Roopchand raised his voice.

'You must tell me the truth so that the police can eliminate you from their enquiries.'

'The police don't know a damn thing! You are trying to trick me with your big English-talk?'

'Look, I am a lawyer, and my intention is to find out the truth. Now you can tell me the truth, or you can go to jail for it if the police get hold of you.'

'A lawyer?' Roopchand began to perspire visibly and mumble as he pulled at a bench and sat down heavily.

'I was looking to buy a piece of jewellery for my daughter. She was getting married.'

Hearing the raised voices, Sumati came out of the bedroom. 'I was already married, Pa, so that can't be true. And why didn't you tell me about work?'

Roopchand dropped his head, embarrassed. 'Truth is, I got laid off. Sankar promised to help me out.'

'Why?' Sumati asked. 'You and he weren't friends.'

'He owed me,' Roopchand said. 'That's why.'

Sumati stood dumbfounded and Narine stood silent; both were waiting for him to continue. But just then, Amina arrived after school to visit Sumati.

'Shh!' Sumati told the men. 'Stop talking.'

'That's not going to work,' Narine said. 'The girl is entitled to hear whatever your father has to say.'

'I expect she is,' Roopchand said. 'She should know what kind of man she was calling Pa all these years.'

'Why are you talking about my father like that?' Amina asked. 'What has he ever done to you?'

'He owed me money!' Roopchand yelled at Amina.

'You're doing it again,' Amina said to Roopchand. 'You are the most unfair man I know. I feel sorry for Sumati.'

'You don't know your father,' the man shouted. 'I had to keep reminding him to pay me.'

'Pay you? Why? Were you blackmailing my father because you were jealous of his business? You never liked him! And now you're accusing him about touching the women in his shop. He sold to them. They bought from him. That is why he was polite to them.' Her eyes narrowed. 'Was it you who killed him?'

'Amina!' Sumati cried. 'Stop it! My father is not a murderer.'

'Really? He threatened to kill your mother. And he tried to kill my father only a few months ago. I saw him – you did too.'

'We said we would never talk about that,' Sumati whispered. 'We promised we wouldn't.'

'But my father was murdered, so that promise can be broken.'

'Speak, Mr Balgobin,' Narine said fiercely. 'Your case is not looking too good. Why were you blackmailing my brother, and what is my niece talking about?'

'She's lying,' Roopchand blurted out. 'What she doesn't know is that Sankar tried to kill me that day by the well. What was I to do?'

'I saw you holding my father's head below the water,' Amina said, outraged. 'You only stopped when we threw a mango at you.'

'That was you?' he said, looking surprised.

'You thought the mango flew so far from the tree by itself?' Amina was livid.

'So, Mr Balgobin, you admit it?' Narine said.

'Yes, but this was after he hit me across the back with a cricket bat first.'

'We never saw that, did we, Sumati?'

'I don't remember,' Sumati said.

'Why would my brother do that?' Narine asked. 'It doesn't make sense.'

'Because he didn't want me to tell anybody the truth.'

'The truth?' Amina asked.

Roopchand went quiet.

'Mr Balgobin?' Narine prompted him. 'Something is not adding up. Is it true that you might have been asking for more money which is why my brother hit you, as you say? When was the blackmail going to stop? And why was he helping you financially in the first place? Was it his kindness you couldn't understand? It seems to me that there is a lot about humanity that you don't understand.'

'Just shut your lawyer mouth and stop giving me the bigshot, Indian-white-man talk. You are even worse than your brother.' Roopchand's eyes were flashing. 'You can do nothing to me. You are not the police.'

'Very well, if you want them to take over from me,' Narine countered, 'I'm happy to let them. I'm trying to help you here, believe it or not. You will be looking at a good fourteen-year sentence for blackmail in addition to life imprisonment for murder.'

'You are forcing my hand,' Roopchand said wretchedly. 'I don't want to do this.'

'Whatever it is, you have already done worse, man!' Narine said, losing patience.

'Daya told me something. Something terrible.' His voice broke. 'It was my fault. I got angry with her and slapped her. I wish I hadn't.'

'Told you *what*?'

Roopchand began sobbing so loudly that Narine sent Amina to bring him a cup of water.'

'Whatever it is, man, it's not worth going to jail for more years than you have to,' Narine reasoned with him. 'Did you kill my brother?'

'*No.*' Amidst his tears, the man choked out, 'She's not mine. My little daughter. The baby. Sumati – she is not my flesh and blood. Her mother told me Sankar was the father.'

ജ

Later that evening, Narine returned to the house with Amina, after he had managed to calm her down and stop her from battering Roopchand across the head, first with a tea towel, and then with the enamel cup. All her thoughts were about how her mother would take this second terrible blow. As they walked home, Narine said Devinia should be told before she heard through rumour. And she would get to know through the legal process anyhow, as she would be called as a witness to ascertain the amount given and how the blackmail took place. Roopchand had already admitted it, with them as witnesses.

Devinia had finished cooking some roti and pumpkin talkarie, with a roast tomato chokha as a special treat. When they arrived home, she didn't fail to notice her daughter's tear-stained angry face, but Amina said nothing to her mother at that point. Only that Roopchand had done his worst now and would be going to jail for the murder of her father. This shocked the woman deeply. It was then that Narine took a deep breath and repeated what Roopchand had accused Sankar of.

Devinia was embarrassed but not devastated by this revelation, as they had feared. 'Yes, Sankar told me long ago,' she said.

'You knew, Ma?' Amina breathed.'

'After he told me about the child, he said he felt he could only do his best by helping them with money,' Devinia said. 'They had to keep it secret otherwise it would have destroyed both families. I agreed. Do you know how I suffered to be Daya's friend?'

'But how, Ma? How could you talk to Daya every day like you did?'

'It happened before I was sent to live with your father. I was married at five years old, but I came to live with him when I was eleven. He was twenty years old, and well . . . he had needs. He told me about her soon after I came to live here. He never touched me for a long time because I was too young. I was pleased. He promised he would have nothing to do with them – with Daya – again. By then, she had got married to Roopchand. She was a very pretty woman. I was only eleven, but I understood what had happened. I knew I was a child, not yet formed into a woman.'

'But did you know that Roopchand was blackmailing him?'

Devinia sighed. 'Roopchand always had problems with his job. Your father had more money than we needed, and he had a child with the man's wife. It was only fair. I don't know why it had to come to blackmail though. Your father should have given him enough to prevent that. It's not easy looking after another man's child, day in day out. Especially as Sumati was the way she was.'

'You mean because she was good-looking and every man that saw her wanted to get inside her knickers?'

'Amina! Wash your mouth out!' Devinia yelled.

'It's true. She has already paid the price of her good looks. Both of them – Daya *and* Sumati. It's not my mouth that needs washing out, it's everybody's mind. Nothing is fair in this world. Nobody talks about the bad things that happen to girls and women. Because talking about it is rude? And the bad things that men do – is right?'

'No. But it happened long ago. He's dead now, poor man, so why go over it now?'

'Not just dead. Pa was murdered.'

'You know something?' Narine intervened. 'Roopchand is not looking like a guilty man. The only reason he was reticent was because of the nature of what he had to divulge. He didn't want to hurt Sumati or you. He and your father had a pact. They sealed it with money.'

'Blackmail!' Amina said scornfully.

'Not according to your mother. Your father agreed.'

Etwar stood in the background silently listening. The first they realised he was there, was when he spoke up. 'She is one of us,' he declared. 'Sumati is our sister. Pa has gone, but we have Sumati now, and her babies. We have to think about how to support them in any way we can. I have a niece and a nephew. You too, Amina.'

Amina was too annoyed to suddenly be happy, but she had to admit that her brother made sense. Etwar was a master at being pragmatic, becoming more like his father than either her or her mother.

Later, brother and sister talked well into the night, until their mother shouted through the walls to blow out the lamp and go to sleep. That night Etwar slept in Amina's room at the bottom of her bed. In whispers, they carried on talking about how they missed their father. Etwar persuaded Amina to look at the positive things that had happened. Not only had they discovered their uncle, but also a sister who was already a good friend, and her children, their niece and nephew. But Amina had something on her mind and she was not about to let Roopchand off that easily.

The next day, after Narine left Granville, she went up to Rajnath's house to persuade him to help her. Together they left Granville that morning and caught the bus to San Fernando. There was one last thing to do, before this story was over.

FIFTY-FOUR

Rajnath and Amina got to San Fernando police station by midday that day. She had a plan, and he readily agreed, still furious at the ill treatment his Uncle Amrit and Dillip had meted out to Sumati and Farouk during their stay there. Between them, Amina and Rajnath wanted Amrit and Dillip to rot in jail, to get their just deserts.

'The last time, the police laughed at me,' Amina said.

'They're in on it,' Rajnath told her. 'I sent them a letter, but nothing's happened. Uncle Amrit must've bribed them.'

'Also, I've seen the police going inside rooms with the girls too, at your uncle's place. But maybe if we tell them what Uncle Narine found out, they will listen to us. He has photographs of Roopchand looking through my father's shop window.'

'Proves nothing.' Rajnath shrugged.

'It proves he was there,' she argued, 'a suspect. And he admitted to being there that same day.'

'I can't believe it. I know Roopchand has a temper, and that is how he behaves. He doesn't have the words to use, so he uses his fists.'

'Are you sticking up for Roopchand?' Amina asked disbelievingly.

'We need the truth,' Rajnath said, 'not a scapegoat.'

As they were waiting for an officer, Narine arrived unexpectedly. 'Well, well! What are you two doing here?' He didn't wait for a reply. 'I have some news. I have found evidence that keeps Roopchand out of the picture.' Amina's face dropped. 'As you know, I felt he was telling the truth, and that he didn't kill your father. Now I have photographic evidence from the same studio that is working on a picture book of the town, Point Fortin. The photograph has caught two other figures. One is carrying a machete.'

'A lot of people carry machetes,' Rajnath said dismissively.

'In the town? Would they walk along the shops with it, dressed in smart clothes?'

'Depends on where they were going,' Rajnath replied.

Rajnath and Amina accompanied Narine to the police interview where the pictures were produced. It was the first time they had seen them. But these were two photographs that had been taken separately on the two days before Sankar died. It was evident who the men were.

'Now, officer,' Narine said. 'You and these young people all recognise at least one person in both photographs. The question is, what was that person who such a long way from home, doing in Point Fortin town centre with a machete?'

'Your guess is as good as mine,' the officer said. 'But we are going to look into it.'

'Before you go looking into it,' Narine told him, 'remember these people are not farmers or market gardeners. They have a hotel business and a shop that sells mostly imported goods. And we have evidence of other criminal activities on the premises. I will not be taking this very lightly, nor will my partner. Mr Amrit Dass and his son Dillip Dass have been responsible for a huge number of criminal activities for a good few years now, and will feel the hand of the law very soon. Not forgetting that my father-in-law is a High Court judge who is respected within his profession.' He gave the policeman a warning glare.

ꕥ

Narine and Rajnath went to sign some papers, leaving Amina alone in the waiting room at the police station. When Rajnath returned, he was shocked to find her lying on the asphalt road outside with blood pouring from a head wound.

'What happened?' Rajnath cried, as he stooped over her. But before she could reply, he too suffered a blow to the head and tumbled over in front the building. Dillip stood nearby, hurling drunken abuse at them both. Amrit tried to lead his son away, but Dillip fought him off too. Narine arrived in time to hear what was being said.

'You country people think you could make a fool of me?' Dillip slurred. He sniggered. 'Your father was begging for mercy in the end, little girl. He gave over everything he had. To me, Dillip Dass.' He leered at Amina. 'You could come and live with me if you want the gold and jewels, but you will pay too – on your back.' He laughed drunkenly. 'Those properties will help make up for mine that you burnt down, but they're not enough. Oh, and bring your mother too. I will put her to work in the kitchen. I hear she makes a good goat curry and dhalpuri.' His mood changed and he snarled at Amina. 'Your father made a big mistake when he cancelled the wedding. Nobody makes a fool out of Dillip Dass. Now go and tell your mother how I slit your father's throat open. Blood everywhere. But I give you this – he was worried about you. And I promised I would look after his family as if they were mine. Because you *are* mine,' he growled, his eyes bloodshot. 'Till you burnt my place. Except, when you make a promise as a Hindu, it cannot be broken.'

'I am not a Hindu!' Amina screamed. 'God will be punishing you long after I forgive you for the donkey of a man you are.'

When they looked around, they were surrounded by police officers and onlookers.

'Officer, there can be no doubt,' Narine said.

'Take him,' the sergeant said. 'Him too,' pointing to Amrit.

As they took both men away, struggling, Dillip shouted, 'karma will get you in the end!'

'If there's anything like karma, you will come back as a pig on a Saturday morning and get your throat cut!' she yelled, tears pouring down her face as Dillip was handcuffed and dragged away.

ஐ

Narine made sure that the rental properties were eventually returned to Sankar's estate, and back in the possession of the family. It took some time to come to terms with what had happened to them as a family, both the good and the bad. But with the help of each other and the new family additions, they worked things through.

Rajnath found a large property in San Fernando that Amina could turn into a school. He felt she would succeed in beating the wedding drums and never marry, and he intended to use his money to help her. Amina persuaded her mother to sell three of the rental houses and purchase a large one in San Fernando, where they could make a new start. Devinia wanted her daughter to think about going to England to study medicine, but Amina couldn't find a way to justify leaving all of them. Not yet. She still wanted her father to be proud of her, and make sure he didn't die in vain. But she needed to start her education in Trinidad. Later she would decide upon his wish for her to study medicine. There was something else. Rajnath. He seemed to make a good friend, genuine and honest. And good-looking. She wondered if he would always remain just a friend. Time would tell.

Etwar said he would remain in Granville and look after the house, together with a school-friend who would move in with him, and the family could visit whenever they needed to escape from the town. When Mr Clifford heard their plans, he was saddened, but suggested a good school in San Fernando where Amina could finish her Part One Pupil Teacher Training. He promised to keep an eye on Etwar too. Indeed, the lad was a good candidate for next year's evening classes, and would make a fine teacher himself. Pundit Lall, meanwhile, assured them that Sankar was enjoying the delights of the goddesses up in heaven together, with Amina's God, of course. He was not of a mind to cross a girl of her calibre, but he could lose respect in the village if he was not careful to support his own beliefs.

'The delights of God are not of this world,' Amina retorted. Pundit Lall knew he had spoken out of place. 'My

God is concerned with the new world. He wants to fill it with those who believe in his only begotten Son.'

'Begotten son?' Pundit Lall couldn't help himself. 'A reincarnation. Your Jesus is just another sadhu – a holy man, but one of many who have given up the pleasures of this world.'

An almighty rage rose in the depths of Amina's belly, and the pundit should not have been surprised, but he was. 'One God, one faith, one baptism. And one Son of God, who never had any pleasures of this world. My father should have never listened to you in the first place. It was you who brought these wicked people into our lives, and it was you who brought his death. All the bad luck my mother is suffering now, is because of your tricks to get my father to pay you for making me a crooked match. I will forgive you for that, but we are giving you no more money. I will beat the wedding drums, you'll see. . . and marry only if and when I choose.'

Pundit Lall was shaking. 'After all the favours I have done for you? You have a lot to learn, girl.'

Rajnath laughed to see Amina standing up for herself finally. He admired her zeal for improving life for herself and others, and he vowed to help her succeed in any way he could. He looked up, searching for Sumati. She had moved to the edge of the asphalt pavement, her figure slicing the sunlight. Rajnath realised that his heart had gone to her long before he cared to admit. He moved towards her, no longer able keep it a secret.

BAIGAN CHOKHA

(Serves 2-3)

Ingredients

2 aubergines
1 tbsp coconut oil (if solid, melt gently)
2 cloves garlic – crushed
1 pinch salt
1-2 bird peppers – chopped finely
A squeeze of lime/lemon juice (optional)

Method

1. Turn on oven to 200C
2. Using a sharp pointed knife, prick the skins of the aubergine 3 -4 times lightly.
3. Place aubergines in a lightly greased roasting tin and put into heated oven.
4. Roast for about 30-40 min until soft and skins are deeply wrinkled and flaking.
5. Remove from oven and allow to cool for about 10 min.
6. Peel skins off very carefully (do not burn your fingers). Remove all flesh from skin and keep in a bowl.
7. Scoop out flesh from the heads
8. Mash flesh with a fork to remove lumps
9. Add oil, salt, (lime juice), crushed garlic and bird peppers to taste, and mix in evenly
10. Serve with warm roti/flatbread or as a side dish.

PUMPKIN TALKARIE

(Serves 2 -3)

Ingredients

Half of a medium pumpkin (depending on size)
(butternut squash is an alternative)
2 cloves of garlic
2 tsp coconut oil
salt to taste
1 bird pepper (optional) chopped finely
1 tbsp fresh chopped parsley

Method

1. Peel and chop pumpkin into half inch cubes
2. Using a heavy pan, heat the oil
3. Add pumpkin cubes
4. Stir for five minutes making sure it doesn't stick to pan
5. Cover pan and lower the heat enough so it doesn't stick
6. Stir occasionally until pumpkin is very soft and mushy
7. Crush garlic and add with salt and bird pepper
8. Stir over heat for another 3 min
9. Using a fork, mash the pumpkin lumps to make fairly smooth
10. Sprinkle with the chopped fresh parsley
11. Serve with roti/flatbread or as a side dish.

ACKNOWLEDGMENTS

Thank you to everyone who was part of my writing journey over the past years before this book was born. For all your encouragement, inspiration and motivation, which kept me writing through difficult times, and when all hope seemed lost. To those who have passed on, fallen asleep in Jesus, or alive and well.

Special gratitude to my aunts **Carmen Seerattan** and **Diana Mungal**, and my father **Mark Johnatty**, all no longer with us, but who were always at hand to answer my queries about life in early 20th Century Trinidad. I am so sorry these cannot be here to see the novel in print.

To the many other relatives and friends who helped with the historical research and own ancestral stories of Indentured Indian labour in Trinidad. To **Patsy Seerattan**, for your help and accommodation on my research visits. To my school friends **Shanti Narinesingh** and **Indra Latchu** for your faith and interest in my work. To my good friend **Alison Rayner** who was never tired of helping me in the early editing days, and **Anne Ankers** my RNA friend who read the final draft and gave me useful feedback.

A special thank you to all those from the **RNA** who have given me encouragement, NWS critiques, advice, and strongly believed in the content of this novel. **Margaret James**, author, journalist and friend, you are one such. Without you all, this book would never be here.

To my supporters on Facebook, individuals and groups - Writers Support Station, and others. Having you all to relate to during the lonely writing stage, was most valuable.

To **Joan Deitch**, copy editor, who turned my manuscript into one more commercially acceptable. Her loveliness and faith in *The Wedding Drums*, kept me motivated.

To **Sarah Houldcroft**, of Goldcrest Books, who brought my writing from manuscript to publication - massive thanks to you and all involved in the process.

Thank you to my dear children and step children who have supported me over the years. To **Charmaine Gaitskell**, one of my earliest supporters, reader and critic. To **James Gaitskell**, another early supporter who remarked once that I am always in another world – how observant and how tolerant. To **Peter Rodwell**, who set up my blog, www.outofthecocoa.blogspot.com. To **Rebecca Rodwell**, who lived all of her school life in the hope that everyone would soon see the book her mother was writing, and the embarrassment that it was not published – until her final year at university. Thank you, my sweet child, for your unending love and patience.

Finally, to my husband, **Chris Rodwell**, who supported me emotionally, spiritually, and financially, and kept me motivated. I could not have done it without the endless cups of teas, your patience and your faith in me.

To my readers, I hope you all enjoy reading *The Wedding Drums*. It's the first, but it is not the last.

ABOUT THE AUTHOR

Marilyn Rodwell was born in Trinidad and is fourth generation East Indian. Her first job was at age seventeen, teaching Maths, Health Science and Art at a private secondary school, followed by Government primary schools. She comes from a family of teachers and head teachers, and did Bible study every day. As a teenager, her hobbies included playing the violin and painting. She arrived in the UK at the age of nineteen, and after a family holiday, began student nurse training in Swansea, where there was much curiosity about her heritage and Trinidad.

After having a family, she returned to education at Coventry University studying Business Studies, after which, she launched a design, manufacturing and retail company. Later she lectured in Marketing and Business, and following the birth of her third child, she decided to start writing fiction.

She lives in the Warwickshire countryside with her husband and spends her time doing church related activities, cooking and writing. The Wedding Drums is her first novel, and the chapter illustrations are from oil paintings which she did at the age of thirteen. The cover is also based on one of those paintings.

www.outofthecocoa.blogspot.com

Facebook.com/Author Marilyn Rodwell

Twitter @outofthecocoa

DISCUSSION QUESTIONS FOR READING GROUPS

1. *In The Wedding Drums, Amina and Sumati are described as opposites. How do their opposite personality traits affect their friendship?*

2. *Mr Clifford is encouraging his pupils to go into teaching as a career, and at times against the will of the parents. Discuss.*

3. *Why does Amina want to change her religion? How would you advise her?*

4. *If you were living in that time, how would you deal with the plight of Amina and Sumati regarding their arranged marriages?*

5. *Discuss the character of Rajnath Kamalsingh.*

6. *Describe the working conditions of the indentured labourers in the sugar cane fields in Trinidad. Compare and contrast with the previous era of slavery.*

7. *Would you like to live in those times? If yes, why? If no, why not?*

8. *Does Sumati change from the beginning of the novel to the end? In what way?*

9. *What advice would you give each of the characters at any point of the novel?*

10. *When tragedy hit Amina's household, and she makes the drastic decision to accept the offer of a job, how did you feel about it?*

11. *Which minor characters appeal to you? Why?*

12. *Whose story would you be most interested in reading about in a later novel?*

13. *What other similar novels have you read that are set around the 1917 time period? Where were they set? Discuss the differences and similarities.*

14. *The world has changed a great deal since 1917, but human behaviour essentially remains the same. How is this demonstrated in The Wedding Drums?*

Printed in Poland
by Amazon Fulfillment
Poland Sp. z o.o., Wrocław

49940988R00251